Scarlet Plume

The Gregg Press Western Fiction Series
Priscilla Oaks, Editor

Scarlet Plume

Frederick Manfred

with a new introduction by
Ted N. Weissbuch

Volume 3 of The Buckskin Man Tales

Gregg Press

A division of G. K. Hall & Co., Boston, 1980

With the exception of the Introduction, this is a complete photographic
reprint of a work first published in New York by Trident Press in 1964. The
trim size of the original hardcover edition was 5 ½ by 8 ½ inches.

Text copyright © 1964 by Frederick Feikema Manfred.
Reprinted by arrangement with the author's agent.
Introduction copyright © 1980 by Ted N. Weissbuch.

Frontmatter design by Barbara Anderson.

Printed on permanent/durable acid-free paper and bound in the
United States of America.

Republished in 1980 by Gregg Press, A Division of G.K. Hall & Co.,
70 Lincoln St., Boston, Massachusetts 02111.

First Printing, November, 1980

Library of Congress Cataloging in Publication Data
Manfred, Frederick Feikema, 1912-
Scarlet plume.

(The Gregg Press Western fiction series)
Reprint of the ed. published by Trident Press, New York, which was issued as
no. 3 of the author's The Buckskin man tales.
I. Title.   II. Series: Gregg Press Western fiction series.
[PZ3.M313705Sc 1980]   [PS3525.A52233]   813'.54
ISBN 0-8398-2594-3   80-19048

Introduction

SCARLET PLUME IS THE THIRD NOVEL IF FREDERICK MANFRED'S Buckskin Man Tales[1] are to be read in their correct chronological sequence. The Tales cover the period from 1800 almost to the end of the 19th century. The five volumes in this series depict differing phases of the Old West, beginning with Indian life in the period before the white man and ending with the period of the cattleman. While *Lord Grizzly* (1954) has remained the most popular of the five novels, for thematic reasons, *Scarlet Plume* is, in many ways, a more impressive and dramatic literary performance. The other three novels in the series are: *Conquering Horse (1959)*; *King of Spades* (1966); and, *Riders of Judgment* (1957). For the sake of chronology and continuity, this is the order they should be read:

> *Conquering Horse*
> *Lord Grizzly*
> *Scarlet Plume*
> *King of Spades*
> *Riders of Judgment*

Two features stand out in *Scarlet Plume*. First, it is obvious to the average reader as well as the scholar that Frederick Manfred has done a more than creditable job of carefully researching his material. Second, the author has created a most dramatic and fascinating piece of fiction, rich in religious symbolism and combining realism, naturalism, and a mythic quality.

The genesis of the novel began, according to Frederick Manfred, when he decided he wanted to do something about the

Sioux uprising in Minnesota, a piece of our history that had
vanished because the Civil War was afoot at the time. The Civil
War was so huge that even this great Indian uprising, which was
the biggest in American history, has found little or no place in
our histories. I had that pretty well worked out. But one day I
came upon a letter General Sibley wrote to his wife in which he
refers in scathing tones to a young lady they both knew who
preferred to go with her Indian lover into the wilds rather than
go back to her husband and child who were waiting for her. This
caught my eye. I wanted to know about that and so I read some
more in the area.[2]

What resulted was a final product that Frederick Manfred
considered "in some ways...the most moving, the most probing
of the books I have written...In fact, it is kind of eviscerative.
When you are reading it you are going to be somewhat disem-
boweled." The general's letter led Manfred from what he called
the "historical-looking" to the "character-looking."[3] He did not,
however, lose sight of the fact that, as he put it, "I am not
interested in just recording history. I am a novelist to begin
with."[4] It is in this context that *Scarlet Plume* can be compared
to the late Elliott Arnold's novel, *Blood Brother* (1947).

When *Blood Brother* was made into the 1950 film *Broken
Arrow*, Arnold was credited by many critics with changing the
way Hollywood filmmakers looked at the American Indian. In
the same vein, *Scarlet Plume*, when it appeared in 1964, helped to
further humanize and change the characterizations of American
Indians. This tradition, from the cigar store variety to the real
Indian can be traced in American fiction by examining the
swinging pendulum from depiction of the Indian as a filthy
savage in the work of Robert Montgomery Bird, *Nick of the
Woods* (1837), to James Fenimore Cooper's idealized and roman-
ticized noble savages in the Leatherstocking Tales, to the more
humanized and believable Indian characterizations in Adolph
Bandelier's *The Delight Makers* (1890), Oliver LaFarge's *Laughing
Boy* (1929), Hal Borland's *When the Legends Die* (1963), most of

the novels of Frank Waters, and most recently, Leslie M. Silko's *Ceremony* (1977).

Arnold's *Blood Brother* deals with the relationship of two historical figures, Indian scout Thomas J. Jeffords, and Apache Chief Cochise; Manfred's novel, while filled with historical figures, depicts as its main characters two fictional figures, Judith Raveling and her lover, Sioux Indian Scarlet Plume. It is also interesting to note that there are additional similarities in the writings of Arnold and Manfred. The former studied the Sioux extensively for his second Western novel, *The Camp Grant Massacre* (1976); Manfred totally immersed himself in research for his historically accurate depictions of the dramatic, destructive events surrounding the action of *Scarlet Plume*.

But, as stated above, more important than the accurate historical portrayal is Frederick Manfred's key underlying theme, the fictional, yet real, problem of the conflict between the white and the Indian. This theme was perhaps best stated by literary historian Roy Harvey Pearce:

Americans who were setting out to make a new society could find a place in it for the Indian only if he would become what they were—settled, steady, civilized. Yet somehow he would not be anything but what he was—roaming, unreliable, savage. So they concluded that they were destined to try to civilize him, and, in trying, to destroy him, because he could not and would not be civilized. He was to be pitied for this, and also to be censured...Pity and censure would be, in the long run, the price of progress and civilization over savagism.[5]

Again, basing his creative inventions on historical research, Frederick Manfred has said that,

I decided that the way to get at the whole Indian problem, what the white man has done to the Indian. . .not only has the white man raped his land in many ways. . .but in many ways the white man has also raped the Indian. He stole the land from the Indian and he debauched the Indian women and children. I thought one of the best ways to get at this problem was from a white woman's point of view, which would be the most touching, most vibrant, and most dynamic problem.[6]

And rape is not the most shocking of the events in *Scarlet Plume*. In less than the first one hundred pages, the reader is confronted with cannabilism, torture, mutilation, murder and the most bestial and brutal kinds of cruelty; yet, the white Judith Raveling, as well as various of the Indian characters are able to justify a great deal of the crimes that transpired during the Sioux uprising near New Ulm, Minnesota during that fateful summer of 1862. In many cases, the justifications are based on returning in kind what the whites had done to the Indians.

The reader first meets the Yankton Dakota Scarlet Plume when he attempts to warn Judith, her family, and the other whites of the bloody uprising and impending dangers. The Indians were well aware that the Union cause was not going well in 1862. Most frontier forts were undermanned or were in the hands of green, young troops. But Scarlet Plume's warning is too late. He does not participate but is present in the bloody slaughter which is carried out on the white community by falsely Christianized Indians. Judith is captured and in a state of near hysteria as she watches an Indian, Animal Voice, devour the heart of Claude Codman, her murdered missionary brother-in-law. Her own daughter is ravished and slain in her presence. Later, Whitebone, Scarlet Plume's chief, defends the cannibalism she has witnessed. In a speech reminiscent of Melville's *Typee*, he explains, "... it was a great honor for the Good Book Man when Animal's Voice ate his heart. Animal's Voice found the heart of the Good Book Man red and sweet. The Good Book Man was a brave man and Animal's Voice wished to acquire that bravery" (p. 112). The cannibalism theme reemerges later, when Judith is able to escape; hungry, she senses she is being followed and in her mind fantasizes: "If he were fat, all the better. She would overtake him from the rear and bash his head in. She would have good hearty meal at last.... People were fools not to eat human flesh...it had to be the best meat, no? since the human being was the true end of creation. The best for the best...." (p. 244).

Prior to her escape and during her captivity, Judith slowly rejects her conventionally orthodox Christian religion as she sees the positive side of the primitive, meaning simple, Indian beliefs. She is fascinated by animism as she secretly witnesses Scarlet Plume's divination, the calling up of a buffalo effigy into an animated figure which plunges over a symbolic cliff (p. 138). Later, the Indians participate in a dance to call up the buffalo. It seems to her that in their costumes, they *become* buffalo. Judith realizes that the dance is "heathenish, pagan, savage, barbaric, all these things, and yet at the same time [she] couldn't help but admit it was more profoundly moving, soul-rousing, than any Christian rite or ceremony she had ever witnessed in her life" (p. 141). As she comes to sense God's presence in Nature in the *Indian Way*, she realizes that it is more important than merely reading the Gospels. She composes her own version of the Lord's Prayer: "The wind is my shepherd. I shall not want. Perfumes make me to lie down in green prairies. Butterflies shall lead me beside still water. Singing birds restore my soul. The bird of fidelity leads me in paths of righteousness for its name's sake. Yea, though I walk through the valley of the shadow of savages, I fear nothing but their kindness. The birds and the flowers comfort me" (p.164–165).

Witnessing the kindness and giving nature of the Indians, Judith cries out to them, "What fools you are...[giving] is the very thing that will surely destroy you....Jesus Christ himself must have been an Indian. Give, and it shall be given to you. Lay not up for yourself treasures upon the earth, where moth and rust doth corrupt, and where thieves break through and steal, but give to him who hath need." Her religious confusion leads her to the belief that "The white man and the red man will never, never get together. One or the other has got to go under" (p. 179).

As her captivity continues, the Yanktons come to look upon Judith as a sacred white goddess. Scarlet Plume, silently loving her, unsuccessfully tries to talk the council into returning her to her own people. It is at this point that Judith manages to escape. Scarlet Plume secretly follows her, looking out for her safety. Later, he joins her when she becomes too weak to continue her flight. It is during this period that their love for each other surfaces. After they have made love and Judith has finally found the fulfillment she never experienced with her white husband, she asks herself, "Why was the devil's work so enticing and God's work so forbidding? Why couldn't it be the other way around? Perhaps Scarlet Plume was right when he said the whites were upside down in their thinking. Truly. Maybe the white man had the wrong name for his gods" (p. 266). Whites have destroyed not only the ways of the Indians, Frederick Manfred tells us through Judith, but they have also destroyed Nature and their own society: "How stupid of the white man. When he came upon this Eden prairie, why did he take by force what he could have had by love?" (p. 267).

Using strong biblical allusions, Manfred has Judith plead with Scarlet Plume not to return her to her white cities. Although her white husband still lives, she looks upon her beloved Indian as her true mate: "... I want to live with your people. I want to go where you go. Your people are my people and your gods my God. When I die I want to be buried beside you in a little lost valley somewhere. Let The Great Master Of All Breath punish me, and more, if I let anything but death part us" (p. 300). But no matter how hard she pleads, Scarlet Plume insists on returning her to her own people, knowing the meanwhile that it could well cost him his life.

And indeed, it does mean his life. Waiting for them is General Henry H. Sibley, drawn by Manfred in his full stature from life. Sibley, known to the Indians as Long Trader, was, as Manfred uncovered, despised by them. The Indians believed that years before the uprising he had swindled them out of $145,000, part of the money promised the Sioux for their lands. Sibley, a former governor of Minnesota, claimed the money was due his American Fur Company because of overpayments to the Indians for furs. It is believed that Sibley and the Indian Agent, Alexander Ramsey, had plotted to take the money. Ramsey was later also governor of Minnesota; it was he who appointed Sibley to command the Minnesota troops in the war against the Sioux.

Scarlet Plume brings Judith to Sibley's camp. During this bloody campaign Sibley had not been anxious to engage the Sioux in large encounters. Instead, he had set up a camp and "rescued" 269 women and children captives after they had been taken under the protective custody of Wabasha, a peaceful Sioux chief. After Scarlet Plume is arrested and imprisoned, Judith goes to Sibley to plead for his life. The General cannot believe that she can be in sympathy with "these red vermin," and he is unable to make a distinction between the "good" Indian who has saved her and the "devils in human shape." Of her experiences, Judith tells him, "I have come to know this: the old-line Yankton never molested women, red or black or white. It is only the renegade Indian and the backslid Christian Indian who did this" (p. 334). The General does not accept her arguments and when Scarlet Plume is found guilty in a mock trial, Judith visits Sibley again and gives her final defense of not only her lover, but of the Indian: "General Sibley, we stole this land from the Indian. It was their homeland, not ours. And whatever they may have done in retaliation to regain it, even the worst, can be excused on that ground. We would have done the same" (p. 342).

At this point in the novel, Frederick Manfred again makes use of his extensive historical research. President Abraham Lincoln did indeed intercede after the condemnation of over three hundred Sioux for this disastrous Sioux uprising, Eventually, on December 26, 1862, 38 Indians were actually executed by hanging. Hours later, officials discovered two Indians had not been on the list of condemned men. This information was not made public until nine years later. As Dee Brown reports, "One of the innocent men hanged had saved a white woman's life during the raiding."[7] In a final statement of her changed views, Judith compares Scarlet Plume, in his last hours, with Jesus of Nazareth as he rode "impassively to his fate, enduring chains and humiliation because a higher god expected it of him. . . . Scarlet Plume's road to Mankato was similar to Christ's road to Calvary" (p. 349).

What happens to Judith is not clear; she mysteriously disappears in the direction of the Indians she has come to understand. And perhaps this ending is intentionally vague as Frederick Manfred intended. Wallace Stegner has written that Frederick Manfred's movement from both reality and history to myth is inevitable. Mere reality is too small for Manfred's writing genius.

Ted N. Weissbuch
California State Polytechnic University
Pomona, California

References

1. For a discussion of the Buckskin Man Tales see John R. Milton's *Conversations with Frederick Manfred* (Salt Lake City: The University of Utah Press, 1974), pp. 50, 105, and 119.

2. Manfred, in Milton, pp. 41–42.

3. Manfred, in Milton, pp. 67–68.

4. Manfred, in Milton, p. 130.

5. Roy Harvey Pearce, *The Savages of America: A Study of the Indians and the Idea of Civilization* (Baltimore: Johns Hopkins Press, 1953), p. 53.

6. Manfred, in Milton, p. 66.

7. For accounts of the aftermath of the Sioux uprising, see Dee Brown, *Bury My Heart at Wounded Knee* (New York: Bantam Books, 1972), p. 38; and, Angie Debo, *A History of the Indians of the United States* (Norman, Oklahoma: University of Oklahoma Press, 1974), p. 187.

DEAR DAVID MCDOWELL —

 The import of this book may seem shocking to some people—still it is a book written in love, since it has always been my belief that if one wishes to speak with truth in the brain one must speak with love in the heart.

 My friend, if I have achieved this, I offer it all to you.

FREDERICK

PROGRAM

O F

The BUCKSKIN MAN *Tales:*

ONE rather handsome woman among them had become so infatuated with the redskin who had taken her for a wife that, although her white husband was still living at some point below and had been in search of her, she declared that were it not for her children, she would not leave her red lover. . . .

The woman I wrote you of yesterday threatens that if her Indian, who is among those who have been seized, should be hung, she will shoot those of us who have been instrumental in bringing him to the scaffold, and then go back among the Indians. A pretty specimen of a white woman she is, truly. . . .

I learn that Mrs. ———, of whom I wrote you, is displeased because I did not call to see her more frequently and will not interpose my authority in behalf of her Indian friend, who stands a fair chance of swinging. . . .

—GENERAL HENRY R. SIBLEY
Letters to His Wife

Contents

SCARLET PLUME

PART ONE

Skywater

A family of wild swans skimmed across Skywater. Something had disturbed them. Father swan was swimming a zigzag course in the rear and trumpeting hoarse warnings, mother swan was breasting the water up front and dipping her long neck from side to side, and four baby swans, two to each side, were holding up the edges of a swiftly cutting arrowhead. Father and mother were pure white, with a wash of rust over the raised high head; the little ones were an ashen gray, also with rusty heads. Except for the spreading wakes of the hurrying swans, the glistening lake was as smooth as the pupil of an eye. The trumpeter swans headed straight for an island; after a moment vanished behind it.

Presently, after the wakes had also vanished, natural sounds returned. A woodpecker worked in the scrub oaks along the shore. Redwing blackbirds sang in a swale. Bluejays cracked the solitude with raucous scolding. A turtledove moaned pleasantly for his mate.

Judith sat in a black rocker just inside the open door of a log cabin. It was early morning. A breeze had risen in the· northeast quarter and a perfume of sweet peas drifted in through the door. The night had been sticky warm, and the breeze felt cool, delicious. The breeze touched the back of Judith's hand as if it were the passing of a sprinkling of rain. It cleansed the air of stale nighttime odors.

Judith loved the cool mornings of the wild frontier prairie. It was the one time of the day she had to herself. At the moment, her sister Theodosia was at the mission church, her brother-in-law Claude was making the rounds in a new Indian encampment across the swale, and the children, her own Angela and Theodosia's Ted and Johnnie, were out playing Indian in the tall grass.

The sound of the singing of many birds came softly to her. Under it, like a bumping bass on a church organ, came the distant beating of savage drums. The birds might quit singing at dusk, but the Indians never seemed to stop their drumming, dusk or dawn.

Judith was a slim woman, tall for her day. She had sun-whitened gold hair, high-blue eyes, and a complexion like the skin of a pale-gold pear. She had only one blemish: four thick black hairs grew in a bunch on the edge of her upper lip. She hated those four black hairs and periodically pulled them out.

Judith rocked slowly back and forth. The runners of the rocker creaked on the puncheon oak floor with a comfortable sound. Out of the corner of her eye she saw movement outside the only window in the cabin. It was Theodosia's purple hollyhocks swinging back and forth in the light breeze. The hollyhocks brushed against each other and appeared to be trying to look inside the cabin at her.

Judith had a letter in hand. It was from her husband, Vincent Raveling, at the moment a soldier fighting the Rebels in Tennessee. Judith turned the envelope over. It had been posted in St. Louis, June 20, 1862. She glanced at the calendar hanging on the log wall. Today was August 20, exactly two months later. Looking down at the envelope again, she noted the many finger marks along its edges. In her mind's eye she could see the letter shuttling its way north: by stage to St. Louis, then on a steamboat up the Mississippi River to St. Paul, then by two-horse buggy down the Minnesota River valley to Mankato and New Ulm, then by one-horse sulky to Skywater.

The letter had come the day before. She had read the letter eagerly, even though she and Vince had not got on well the last years. It had really been she who had got Vince into the war to help preserve the Union. Vince hadn't wanted to go. Vince considered all wars futile. Wars proved little or nothing, he said. And this war, why, it was ridiculous. "I wash my hands," he often said, "of an invading race which, before it has settled its account with a red aborigine, is already fighting brother against brother over a black aborigine. And a black aborigine, I might add, which it imported from another continent and then enslaved." Vince preferred keeping the peace. There were good books to read in the evening—Lucretius and his scandalous notions of how a man should make love to a wife, Dante and his daring descent into hell—as well as whiskey to drink in a tavern with a doctor friend. Besides, Vince rather liked his job as clerk in a waterfront warehouse. But Judith kept taunting Vince more and more, about his growing potbelly, his humped-over shoulders, his soft, slack hands, until one day in a drunken pet Vince enlisted.

Glancing through the letter again, Judith noted that Vince seemed to have adjusted fairly well to army discipline. He was in charge of a burial detail and ate with the officers. She smiled grimly to herself. She wasn't too sure that eating with officers would make more of a man of him, but burying the dead might. Perhaps army life would stiffen his backbone after all. Judith and Theodosia Woods had grown up together in a large family. The Woodses lived on a farm near Davenport and all four Woods brothers had been rugged men. Judith missed in Vince the hardness of her brothers. Vince was too bookish, too soft for her. She admired a civilized husband, but she still wanted him to be manly, to take the lead in emergencies. Otherwise the civilized husband might just as well be the wife. Part of her was contemptuous of Vince. He was not half the man that she herself was. Bloodletting had been a common thing to her as a farm girl, while Vince had been known to shy away from a drop of fly blood.

Judith stared through the open door. The land rolled away in slow, even swells all the way to the horizon. There were no habitations in that direction. The few pioneer homes around, along with a general store and a mission church, lay mostly to the north in and among the fringe of oaks bordering Skywater.

The smell of sweet peas came to her again. She could just see them where they vined over the wooden fence around the garden. The potato vines had long ago ripened and lay in neat brown crumbled rows. The carrots were ready to pull. The beans were in seed. The lilacs were silent.

Birds lifted and sank above the flowing prairie grasses. The plover were plentiful. Asters grew in islands of gold glory. A timber wolf sat on a low mound sunning itself. The wolf's red tongue lolled wetly as if it were laughing and laughing to itself. The sound of Sioux drums continued to jolt the morning air. The drumbeat seemed to pound into Judith's very belly.

A film formed over Judith's blue eyes. She brushed her forehead, then brushed her sun-whitened gold hair back and down. She really still hadn't got used to being out on the wild and lonesome prairie. She missed St. Paul and all the good times.

After Vince had left for the wars, Judith had suddenly on an impulse decided to get away from St. Paul for a while and visit her sister Theodosia. Theodosia and her missionary husband, Claude Codman, lived among the Sioux Indians in southwestern Minnesota. The next thing Judith knew, she had agreed to stay at Skywater and help Theodosia teach Sioux children. Judith had once had a Sioux maiden work for her and from her had picked up a working knowledge of the language. Judith was also a quick learner and soon was able to handle the four clicks and the two gutturals and the nasal of the Dakota language.

Judith's friend and neighbor in St. Paul, Mavis Harder, whose husband had been killed in the First Battle of Bull Run, had also decided to visit Skywater with her. Mavis in turn found herself running a store and a post office on the frontier.

Judith looked musingly around inside the log cabin: at the rough oak table, at the circular rag rug on the puncheon floor, the precious single glass window, the bunk beds along the far wall, the precious china and silverware on the shelving, the red pipe of peace hanging above the mud-brick fireplace, the gold lettering on the thick Bible on top of her brother-in-law's bookcase. Her eye in particular fell on an old copy of *Harper's Weekly*. Only the day before, she and Theodosia had read an article in it telling of the terrible massacre at Spirit Lake. The story of the rape and captivity of Abbie Gardner was especially haunting. What a monster that Inkpaduta must have been. Evil.

Judith said aloud, "Yes, what in the world am I doing way out here? The farm country around Davenport was brutal enough." Slowly she rocked back and forth. "This is all so wild here." She rocked some more. "It's still all like a dream to me!"

She heard yelling outdoors. Looking out, she saw first Ted and little Johnnie running for all they were worth through the tall tangled grass, then her own Angela running as if her life were at stake. Angela had on a green dress, which she held up at the hips to run the better. Angela's blond hair flashed silver in the sun. Pursuing the three was a young Indian lad named Two Two. Two Two at fifteen winters was considerably taller than her ten-year-old Angela, and he actually towered like a man over Theodosia's Ted and Johnnie, who were six and two.

For a second, cold sweat broke out on Judith. A redskin chasing their children? Stars alive.

A moment later Judith heard wild, merry laughter burst from all four. And understood. Two Two had probably seen the children playing Indian and had joined them in the game. Two Two was whooping and making motions as if about to scalp Angela. A big smile opened Two Two's face. His teeth gleamed white. Judith let go a relieving sigh. Thank God it was only play.

Judith couldn't help noticing the sharp contrast between the young Sioux with his black hair and red-brown skin and Angela's silver hair and gold skin. There was a difference, all right, a big one.

The children playing Indian called something to mind. A few nights ago she had awakened out of a bad dream. She had dreamed that a tall, howling Indian had scalped a cowering white settler. The white settler was Vince, her husband. The dream had been so real, she could still see in her mind's eye Vince's scalped head: a long, narrow skinned place, red, with working arteries, and bloody hair to either side. She shivered, thinking of the bad dream again.

Then something off to one side caught Judith's eye. She turned her head slowly and looked up. Someone had been standing beside the purple hollyhocks and had been looking in through the window at her. The hollyhocks still were parted where the someone had stood.

Again Judith broke out in a cold sweat.

Judith just couldn't get used to the habit the Indians had of looking in on them through the window. It was probably true, as her missionary brother-in-law Claude often told her, that an Indian thought he was doing the white man an honor when he looked in on him, but to her it continued to be an unholy heathenish trick.

She blinked.

Before her, filling the doorway, stood a magnificent Sioux. He had one hand behind him, holding something. He was tall, well over six feet, with big bull shoulders, a large head, an aquiline nose, and black glittering eyes. He looked to be about thirty. He wore his black horsetail hair in the old manner, loose and falling to the shoulders. A single eagle feather, dyed scarlet, stood erect at the back of his head. The scarlet feather was slightly bent against the cabin doorhead. Except for buckskin moccasins and breechclout, he was naked. His skin gleamed a shining bronze in the sun. He had one face marking: a daub of yellow inside a circle of blue earth on his left cheekbone. The yellow daub was a sign to let the sun know that all men recognized that its light was needed to sustain life. The blue earth was a symbol of peace, like the blue sky above.

She recognized him. It was Scarlet Plume. She had first seen him about two weeks ago when he suddenly appeared in the new little Indian village across the swale. Word was that he was the chief's sister's son. His tall muscled physique and wide rich lips caught Judith's eye. When she asked her brother-in-law Claude about him, Claude told her that Scarlet Plume was one of the better Indians. "The pity is, though," Claude added, stroking his narrow chin, "the pity is, Scarlet Plume has resolutely refused to have anything to do with the white man or his Christian religion. He is an old-line Yankton Sioux. Just like his uncle, Chief White-bone. Pure heathen." Again Claude rubbed his chin. "There was once a time when I hoped to convert him. That was when his wife hanged herself two years ago. She was childless. Great was his grief. Yes. Scarlet Plume became a changed man overnight. And a strange man, I might add. He became very gentle with the children. At the same time he became more offish and distant with grownups. Yet his grief was not great enough to make his heart receptive to the Christian message."

A look of calm gravity lay upon Scarlet Plume's broad face. Too calm. His full, liberal lips were as if graven upon weathered copper. His breath came as if by afterthought, occasionally, barely lifting his powerful chest. Only his black eyes were alive. They were intent, brilliant, deep-set under the smooth dark eyebrow. His air reminded her of a picture she had once seen of a puma—full of pounce and just barely restrained.

Abruptly, for a fleeting second, hardly longer than the blink of an eye, a superior grimace touched his full carven lips. Then it was gone.

Almost immediately after, tears started in the corners of his eyes. A few of them ran down each cheek. And equally suddenly, the tears stopped. The quick tears made vividly real for Judith the story that in ancient times the Sioux chiefs were known to be great weepers, that they made much of letting their tears fall on the heads of those about whom they knew something bad.

Before Judith could wonder what next, Scarlet Plume's other hand came from behind him, where he had been hiding it all along, and he threw something at her feet. The thing was ashen gray, and fluffy, and rather large. It flopped over twice, and rolled under the oak table.

Judith stared at it. Why, it was a dead goose. Scarlet Plume had brought them a present. Something to eat.

"Why," she began, "how kind of you to—"

But when she looked up, the doorway was empty. Scarlet Plume had vanished as abruptly as he had come.

She got to her feet, hand to her brow. Her gray dress and apron fell to her ankles. She swept to the door and looked out. Scarlet Plume was nowhere in sight. Not even the grass was bent to show where he might have gone.

She went over to the table and bent down to pick up the whitish-gray fowl. The bird was quite heavy. It had a long, slim neck, and black bill and legs.

"Why, it's a wild swan. A young one. The kind Claude calls the trumpeter."

She examined the wild cygnet more closely. Its neck was broken. The bird had been strangled, and then, seemingly, its neck had been deliberately broken.

This meant something. She had heard Theodosia and Claude talk about Indian sign a number of times. Scarlet Plume had thrown the wild swan under the table for a reason. As a runner and newswalker, he probably knew something. Tribal custom, perhaps the grim soldiers' lodge, forbade him to speak of it. But the soldiers' lodge could not prevent him from leaving mute sign about.

As she was turning the dead bird over yet again, stroking its miraculously soft down, she heard footsteps on the path outside. It was Theodosia. Ah, her sister would know what the sign meant.

Theodosia stepped into the cabin with a swishing of long skirts. She wore blacks mostly: high black kid shoes, black dress, and gray sunbonnet. She was slender and quite tall, much like Judith herself. But where Judith walked with easy grace, Theodosia had stiff knees. And where Judith's cheeks had the clean pink glow of vigor, Theodosia's face was grainy and blotched over with freckles.

The eyes were the life of Theodosia. Hazel and gentle, they were full of Christian forbearance. They drew one with their sweet compassionate expression. They were the type men revered, would think of as mother eyes. Lust, passion, even simple man-woman love were foreign to them. Judith, in fact, had often wondered how Theodosia and Claude had ever gotten around to having children. Mavis Harder, more frank about such matters, had laughingly remarked one day that the two pure-in-hearts had probably cohabited while sound asleep, maybe while sharing the same deep dream.

"Theodosia, am I glad to see you!" Judith gave her sister a quick smile. "A strange thing happened. An Indian brought me this only a minute ago. Wild fowl."

A serene expression opened Theodosia's pale lips. "How nice. We've not had goose for supper in some time." She took the wild swan from Judith. "The Lord does provide, doesn't he?"

"But that's just it, Theodosia. It's not a goose at all. It's a wild swan."

"So it is."

"With a broken neck. See?" Judith described how Scarlet Plume had suddenly appeared in the doorway, how he had for a moment wept tears, how then without a word he had tossed the wild swan under the table. And disappeared.

At that, the serene expression slowly left Theodosia's face. She looked down at the wild swan in her hands. "A broken neck then."

"Yes. That means something, doesn't it? A sign of some sort?"

"Yes. It is a message. We had better call Claude."

"What does the sign say?"

"It means," Theodosia said, " 'The white man must fly or his neck will be broken.' "

Both women looked at each other. Both immediately thought of the Spirit Lake massacre. Theodosia's hazel eyes momentarily filmed over, and darkened with disappointment; Judith's blue eyes opened high and wide, and turned an almost hailstone gray. Theodosia stood calm and resigned, and her rustling black dress slowly fell silent. Judith swelled and rose, so that her gray skirt lifted off the floor a little.

Theodosia said, "May the Lord be with us in this time of extremity."

Judith said, "Hadn't we better warn the other settlers?"

"Of course."

Even as they talked, the sound of wild galloping came to them. Both women hurried outdoors.

It was Billy Vikes, bachelor. He lived in a sod shanty on the north point of the lake. He was riding a gray workhorse. The gray's harness had slid down and it dragged along on the ground. The skin over Vikes's cheeks resembled soot-mottled snow. The whites of his eyes showed stark.

Vikes had trouble talking. "Henry Christians. He's . . ." Vikes's teeth chattered like little gourds rattled together. "He's . . ."

"Yes? What is it? What about him?"

"He's . . . He's . . ." Vikes sucked quick shallow breaths. "Poor Henry."

Theodosia tottered a little. But her voice was calm. "Speak up, man. What about him?"

Vikes bit his teeth tight together for a moment to stop the chattering. Then he managed it. "I just found Henry Christians murdered on his front doorstep." Again Vikes had to bite down the chatters. "He was hit in the chest and scalped."

Again Theodosia tottered. "May the Lord have mercy on his soul. And his wife?"

"I don't know. I didn't see her anywheres."

Judith thought, "Dear God, Scarlet Plume's sign came too late for poor Henry. The Indians must have struck quicker than even Scarlet Plume expected." Judith shivered. "And they picked Henry off first because the Christianses live alone on that neck of land in the middle of the lake there."

Judith glanced over at Whitebone's village.

All seemed calm enough over there. The little children were playing in the deep grass, the squaws were out airing the buffalo-fur bedding, the braves were sitting in the morning sun, smoking and gossiping.

"It must be those renegade Indians living on the other side of the lake then," Judith said. "Mad Bear's band."

"Yes." Theodosia nodded. "It's just come to me."

"Or else some of the wilder ones from Pounce's band. From over the hill there by the mission church." Judith pointed toward a rise in the land which separated Whitebone's camp from Pounce's camp.

"But that can't be," Theodosia said. "Pounce and his group are all members of our church. They're friendlies. You know that. You've been teaching their children."

"I know. But I never did trust that scheming Pounce. Nor those lazy converts of his. They're candidate backsliders if I ever saw any."

"They're not lazy. They've learned to farm a little." Theodosia stood quite still. "Let's hope it's only a pet of some sort the Indians have fallen into, that it will soon pass away."

Both Vikes and his horse stood puffing above them. Vikes said, "There was an arrow right through Henry's heart. Slick and clean."

Arrow? That really did prove then it was Indians. But which Indians?

Theodosia said, "Yes. Well, I will hurry and fetch Claude."

Judith said, "And I'll hurry and find the children. God knows where they've gone playing by now." With a shudder Judith recalled that the Indian lad Two Two had been chasing them in play earlier in the morning.

Theodosia said briskly, "Billy, hurry and warn the other settlers." Theodosia stuffed the wild swan in the cooler against the north wall of the cabin. "Tell them they must all come here. At once. This cabin is the strongest. Hurry."

"I'll round 'em all up, ma'am. Don't you worry." Vikes set down his chin. "Poor Henry. Laying there scalped. My God, what's this world coming to, anyway?" Vikes picked up one of the loose tugs and walloped his horse over the rear with it. The heavy horse slowly gathered itself into a lumbering gallop and was off. Vikes rode with elbows flopping, whites of the eyes wild and high.

Theodosia hurried north across the swamp to get her husband. Despite stiff knees, Theodosia moved with surprising swiftness.

Judith scurried south toward a deep grassy meadow. Judith remembered that the children on occasion went there to play.

As Judith ran, the story of Abbie Gardner's rape and captivity came vividly to mind once again. Was another Spirit Lake massacre about to take place? Was it now little Angela's turn to be raped and tortured? Judith stumbled and almost fell at the thought of it.

As Judith breasted the first rise, she heard screaming on her right. It came from Jed Crydenwise's sod shanty at the edge of the woods next to a small field of barley. Crydenwise was a farmer in the summer and a trapper in the winter.

Judith stopped, and stared. Lord in heaven. Crydenwise had caught a timber wolf and had trussed it up on a wooden frame. The timber wolf's four legs were spread-eagled and Crydenwise was skinning it alive. Crydenwise was almost finished. The timber wolf's thick gray fur, still attached at the tail, lay at Crydenwise's feet in a pile of loose folds. Jaws wide, the timber wolf was yowling for all it was worth, its gleaming fangs and fierce eyes oddly out of place. The raw skinned wolf shivered in jerks, and humped up violently every few seconds, trying to free itself.

Glistening bloody muscles worked in spasmodic clutches all along its lean carcass.

Judith swayed. She touched her lips with her fingers. She had often seen her brothers skin out wild animals, and had often helped them with the fall butchering, but this—this was too much. "Mr. Crydenwise!" she cried. "What are you doing to that poor beast?"

Crydenwise hardly looked at her. He twitched heavy shoulders at her as if at a biting fly. "The son of a bitch," he growled. "I've been laying for him for months, and I finally caught him, ha!" Crydenwise's brown pig eyes glittered in triumph. Crydenwise wore boots, a pair of black trousers, and a faded blue shirt open at the throat. "This'll teach him to steal my fresh calves."

"But that's inhuman! Cruel. An awful thing to do."

"What is?"

"What you're doing. Why, it's bestiality itself."

"I know. I mean it to be." Crydenwise stuck his bristly chin out at her. "How would you like it if you brought a favorite prize-winning cow all the way from Ohio, walking, and with her bred there before you left because you knew there was no bulls in the new land, and then a sneaking son of Satan comes along and gobbles up that bull seed, ha? All the more so when that bull seed was twins, ha?" Crydenwise spat so forcibly that his cud of tobacco fell out of his cheek. His sailing spittle almost hit Judith where she stood.

Judith fell silent.

Crydenwise continued the grim skinning. The bloody naked timber wolf shrieked even more shrilly.

Judith covered her ears with her hands.

Crydenwise grumped, "I'll teach the son of a bitch to eat my twin calves."

It was with an effort that Judith remembered what she had come for, to look for the children before the risen Indians should have murdered and scalped them. She waited until the sound of the screaming lessened some, then she stepped closer and shouted, "I better tell you, Mr. Crydenwise, that somebody, Indians, killed Henry Christians this morning."

It took a moment for her words to soak in. Crydenwise finished skinning around the tail of the timber wolf, with utmost delicacy of touch, then slowly lifted away his long curved skinning knife and took a step back. Slowly his bare head came up and slowly the whites of his fat pig eyes began to show.

Crydenwise said, "How's that again, ma'am?"

"Billy Vikes just rode over on horseback to tell us he found poor Henry dead with an arrow through him." Judith had trouble shaping her lips to speak the words. "He was scalped too."

Crydenwise paled. The cruel, bestial expression around his mouth gradually changed to one of awestricken childish astonishment. His bristly chin took on the look of a slab of old bacon. "You don't say."

"I do say."

At that very moment the wolf quit yowling. It shivered convulsively, once, and died on its crude cross.

In the sudden silence the sound of Crydenwise's breathing was harsh and loud. "The redskins are on the warpath then?"

"I'm out looking for our children. You haven't seen them this morning, have you?"

"No, ma'am, I hain't."

Judith threw a look down toward the shore of the lake to see if she could spot any movement on the sandy beach. "My sister said for all of us to gather at her house. It's got the thickest logs. In case we have to defend ourselves."

Crydenwise took a trembling step toward Judith. His eyes turned like two little onions caught in boiling milk. "My God, they may kill us all, unh?"

Judith couldn't help but stick the hatpin in a little. "It's very well possible. You better hurry and round up your wife and kids."

"Ha! Lena and the kids're probably killed already." Crydenwise looked wildly around. "They went gooseberry-pickin' this morning."

"You better find them. Hurry."

"Yah."

Hurrying, breathless as much from fear as from exhaustion, Judith pushed along the top of a low ridge overlooking Skywater. In the lee of an island she saw what she took to be a half-dozen wild swans hovering under some overhanging willows.

Judith looked down every draw. She searched all the groves of oaks in the ravines. She hallooed through the waving wheat fields and the bristly barley stands. There wasn't a sign of the three children. Or of Two Two.

"Dear God, where can they be?"

She had visions of them lying slain in deep grass somewhere, their poor little bodies abused and mutilated. Terror clutched her vitals. She felt a sudden pressing need to relieve herself. Even before she could find a decent tree to sit behind, a spurt of hotness ran down her legs under her skirt. "Ohh." She caught herself, then sat where she was. She groaned miserably.

"Dear God, this is awful. Dear God, let them be alive. Please, oh, dear God."

Judith remembered there was one more family living to the south, the Joseph Utterbacks, just across the farthest ravine, on a spread of prairie. The Utterbacks were childless, but Angela and Ted and Johnnie often visited them to ride the Utterback pony, a pet. Judith nodded. Yes. That's where the children were.

Judith brushed through deep joint grass. The grass was sharp and it cut her across the shins when she lifted her dress to run. Goldenrod undulated above the grass. It hurt to see the lovely golden plumes.

She found a well-beaten path. It led toward a clump of ash trees. She next heard raised voices, loud, even snarling angry. Were the Utterbacks already fighting the Indians? There was even a kind of popping sound, as of small rifles being fired.

Wonderingly she stepped around the clump of ash. The Utterback farmyard lay directly before her: sod house, sod barn, hay-
rack and wagon, gleaming milk pails on a drying rack, beaver
traps on a pole, a dozen chickens timorously pecking in the grass
immediately in front of their little wooden coop. Beyond spread
the stubbles of what a month before had been a fine golden stand
of wheat.

The voices came from the middle of the yard where the deep
grass was trodden flat. There were the Utterbacks, Joe and his
wife, Maggie. And they were going at it hammer and tongs. In
fact, they were going at it with pitchfork and black-snake whip,
around and around, in a circle. Turf dust hung about them in a
small glittering fog. Only an occasional grunt and the snarled
words, "Bitch from hell," escaped Joe as he tried to get in a telling jab at his wife with the gleaming tines of his fork. Maggie
filled the air with curses hot enough to raise blisters on the devil
himself as she snapped and coiled the long black-snake whip
around and above her head.

Again Judith could hardly believe her eyes. "You people—
What in the world is going on here?"

Neither heard her. Around and around they went, hopping,
snarling, dodging. Maggie was a hand taller than Joe, and had
longer arms, and she kept Joe at bay with the long black-snake
whip. Joe, though stumpy and heavy, wearing only brown work
pants and boots, was the quicker of the two, and he made quick
little jumping feints at Maggie. Both were hatless, gray hair
tousled and wild. Their eyes glowed with a reddish fury.

Judith then noticed that Maggie had tied her long gray dress
in a knot at her waist, the easier to get around. Her long, skinny
legs shone plainly to view from the crotch down. Where Joe was
naked from the waist up, she was naked from the waist down.

"Maggie!" Judith was scandalized. "Aren't you ashamed of
yourself?"

Maggie finally heard her. Maggie's whiskery face took on a
man's mean look. "Ashamed? What fer? Are you seein' some-

thing you ain't seen before? I know Joe ain't, fer a fact." Maggie
was a ripper and had the gravelly voice of a mule skinner. "Him
askin' me if I had anything in the shape of dinner this early in
the day. The idee."

"Stars alive, you two. This is not a Christian way to act. Why,
you're acting worse than a couple of Red River breeds."

The dancing duel continued. Joe darted in, jabbed wickedly,
missed, dodged back. Maggie popped her black-snake whip with
a great cracking sound.

"This is terrible, you two," Judith cried. "In the name of
heaven, will you please come to your senses?"

Maggie took her eyes off Joe long enough to say, "We're going
to find out right here and now who's boss in this family. Today.
This cannot go on."

"Dear God."

There was more snarling and jabbing, and cursing and whip-
popping.

"Listen, you two," Judith cried. "Listen to me. Henry Christians
was found dead this morning with an arrow through his heart."

Joe and Maggie stopped dead in their tracks. Joe set his fork
down, Maggie let her black-snake whip fall to earth. Turf dust
floated slowly away from them.

"No!" Maggie exploded.

"Yes. You'd both better hurry over to my sister's house. We're
rounding everybody up so we can decide what to do. Hurry."

Joe's mouth slowly dropped open. "Red devils on the rampage?"

"Yes. Maybe just like at Spirit Lake. Hurry. And oh, yes—have
you seen our children around?"

"Indians killin' and scalpin'?"

"Has Angela been over to play with your pony? She was wearing a green silk dress."

Joe shook his head in a daze. "No, we hain't seen yer kit. No."

Maggie's jaw set out. "Joe, go get the guns. Both of 'em. I'll
dig up the balls and powder. Git."

Joe got.

"Then you didn't see the children at all, Maggie?" Judith asked.

"Naw, we didn't see your kits." Maggie gave her a sidelong darting look. "Judith, if I was you, I'd run and save my own skin. Because if it's really the Indians, the kits're long ago kilt."

"Oh, Lord, mercy, please no."

Judith ran back toward her sister's cabin.

Judith sweated. She panted. She ran with mouth open and eyes glazed. A dull flush suffused her cheeks.

The light breeze of early morning faded away. It became very still out, hot, oppressively humid. The far distances turned milky. Yellow butterflies fluttered languidly from aster to bull thistle.

Judith stumbled around the corner of Theodosia's cabin. She could not have run another step. She held her bosom in her folded arms.

She saw figures. Ah, there they were. They were coming across the swamp. The children, Angela and Ted and Johnnie, with Theodosia and her husband, Claude. "Thank God. Ohh, thank God."

Reverend Codman came on slowly. His light-gray eyes glinted with quiet determination. Reverend Codman was slight and wiry, with a large, even noble, head and a wide, thin-lipped mouth. A pink nose rode high out of his face, not unlike an Indian's. His complexion was pale, and where it had been exposed to the sun it was quite freckled. He gave Judith a reassuring look. "Are you all right, sister?"

"Yes." Judith caught a hand to her throat. "A little out of breath, is all."

"Good. Very good."

"The children?"

"They were playing with Two Two and his friends. In Whitebone's village."

Judith slowly got her breath back. "I was so afraid. I looked everywhere for them."

Angela slid to Judith's side. "We had so much fun, Mama."

Angela was a whitehead like Judith, and very fair. Her lips were naturally quirked at the corners and her blue eyes smiled, kittenish. Her green silk dress, too small for her, made her look a little like a slinking siren.

Judith lashed out at Angela. "Naughty girl! When I've told you time and time again not to play with . . ." Judith paused. She realized that what she was about to say next would not set well with her missionary brother-in-law. Also it was a lie. She had never told Angela anything of the kind. She finished, "Next time I want you to tell me where you're going."

Shadows appeared in Angela's eyes. "We were only playing, Mama."

Reverend Codman cleared his throat. "There is no harm done, sister." Reverend Codman's lips always moved a little before he spoke. He had the manner of a man who made it a point to first go over an idea thoroughly before giving voice to it. He looked down at Angela. "Fret not, child. Your mother means only for the best." A benign smile moved over his face. The smile was remindful of a late fall sun, having little heat or passion.

Theodosia breathed slowly. She made herself be firmly calm. She had Ted by one hand and toddling little Johnnie by the other. Ted was a towhead, with a single pale curl in front. Johnnie was a whitehead like Angela.

Judith smiled at her two nephews. "Thank the Lord your mother found you safe too."

Theodosia's blotchy freckles were more noticeable than usual. "Two Two had a new game to show them. A real Dakota game."

"Oh."

A puff of smoke showed above a far hill to the north. Almost immediately after, another far puff showed; then two quick ones.

Everybody stared at the puffs of smoke.

"Smoke signals," Judith said shortly. "Aren't they? Coming from the direction of Little Crow's band along the Minnesota River?"

"Yes," Theodosia said.

Reverend Codman's eyes half closed. His lips moved. "Yes." He nodded inwardly, once. "There have been rumors of Indian unrest along the Minnesota. Grave rumors."

More smoke signals puffed up. Slowly the puffs of smoke blended off into the milky distance.

Ted pointed, his pantaloons lifting on one side. "Look, there's some over there too."

All turned. Above the trees across the lake rose an answering smoke signal.

"That's the renegades," Judith said. "Mad Bear's bunch."

"I guess so," Reverend Codman murmured.

"What do all those signals say?"

Reverend Codman studied them, impassively, first looking at the signals to the far north, then at those across Skywater. The three children stared up at him, waiting.

Finally Reverend Codman said, "I do believe it's . . ." He looked down at the three children, and stopped.

Judith touched Reverend Codman's sleeve. "War signals?"

"I'm afraid so." Reverend Codman sighed. "Well, it seems we shall have to face up to it. May the Lord in his infinite mercy give us the courage."

"But why?" Judith demanded. "What have we done to them?"

"The way our traders treat them, I can't say as I blame them. Even our esteemed government agents have been guilty of cheating and defrauding the Indian."

A smoke signal next lifted from Pounce's village over the rise to the east. The smoke signal rose slowly. It resembled a slowly expanding toadstool.

"Now our fat Christian Indian seems to be joining in," Judith said.

"But that can't be," Theodosia said. "I'm sure of Pounce. His repentance is sincere."

"I never did like him."

Theodosia's eyes closed. "Oh, Lord, do have mercy upon us," she breathed. "It cannot be true, please, Lord."

Reverend Codman spoke almost musingly. "After we've had so much success too. More than a dozen adult Indian souls saved."

"Trapped," Judith whispered to herself. "Oh, if only I hadn't been so foolish as to come out here in the first place." She clutched Angela by the hand, hard. "What do we do now, Claude?"

"Pray. And hold firm in the Lord."

"Don't you have a gun?"

Reverend Codman shook his head. "God is love. It is in his name that I preach to the heathen savage. Not in the name of the god of war."

The smoke signals were soon seen in Whitebone's village and almost instantly it became a boil of activity. Braves jumped up from where they sat smoking. They ran to put on their war paint and pick up their war gear. Squaws called in the children with sharp warning clucks. Young boys ran to get the tethered ponies for their fathers. Door flaps snapped shut and were tied down. The sound of the drumming changed too. Quicker, harsher drumbeats came from the council lodge in the center of the village. One singer began a wild, exultant war song. Sharp whoops resounded against the thick grove of oak and hackberry along the lake. Finally smoke signals rose from Whitebone's encampment too.

In the midst of the wild goings-on, a vivid memory flashed through Judith's mind. It was the memory of her first days on the Skywater prairies, of how she had fallen in love with the frontier. She had arrived in late May and the rolling plains were an endless garden of wild roses, mile on mile of heady wild perfume. The air was so sweet it almost tasted of honey. And there were the dazzling flights of the multicolored carrier pigeons, purple and blue and pink, and the lake-skimming waterfowl, burnished green and rust and glancing black. The sound of all their multitudinous calling and quacking was that of a vast symphony orchestra warming up. Skywater had been an Eden on earth at last, a bewildering dream of a paradise.

Settlers began to stream toward them. From the south came Jed Crydenwise, then the Utterbacks. All three carried guns and powder and shot.

Next came Charlie Silvers, trader, with his Sioux wife, Tinkling. Silvers had a heavy belly and he moved across the ground with the sway of a heavy load of hay. He wore greasy buckskins and a torn wolf skin for a cap. His black beard was clotted with tobacco spittle. Beside him Tinkling looked like a child. She too was in buckskins. She wore her hair in two braids, one down either side of her face. There was a beaten, even old, look in her eyes and she stood slightly humped over. That summer she had lost her third straight child at birth. All three had been boys.

Mrs. Christians arrived. She had forced her way through some shallows in the arm of the lake and was soaked to the armpits. Wet garments accentuated the swinging of her gravid belly and swollen breasts. She was in hysterics. Her teeth chattered so hard, no one could make out what she was saying. She seemed to be trying to tell them something about her dead husband, Henry.

Merry widow Mavis Harder came skimming over from her store, green velvet dress gathered up at the knees, the better to run. Her dress matched the hue of the lush prairie grass exactly. She had the muscled legs and slim bosom of the ballet dancer. Her features were sharp, like a terrier's. Her eyes were gray, and she had gaunt hollows under her cheekbones. She came on breathless, wild-eyed. She threw her arms around Judith. "Judith! Oh! Am I glad to see you. After what just happened to me."

Judith embraced Mavis in turn. "Now, now. We are all safe here."

"Two young Indian boys just tried to attack me," Mavis said. "Can you imagine?"

"Not really."

"It was simply awful. Boys they were."

"There, there. Claude will have a talk with them later. Never fear."

"The nerve of them. Snotnoses!"

Billy Vikes came thundering back on his fat horse, one arm flapping, the other hand tugging a second gray horse along. Vikes pulled up short. "I tried to tell everybody, Reverend," he cried. The whites of his eyes were still wild and high. "But half are already murdered. The Wagners are wiped out. All five of 'em. There's feathers scattered all over the yard. Pigs and cows dead. Their dog murdered. Their garden all ripped up. Wheat stolen."

"What about the Magnus Olsons?" Reverend Codman asked.

"I don't know. Didn't see hide nor hair of them."

"And the Tallak Aanensons?"

"Here we are, Reverend," a voice growled from around the corner of the log cabin. A giant of a man, blond and red-cheeked, with blue eyes set unnaturally far apart, came striding up. A thatch of matted brown-gold hair stuck out where his shirt was open at the throat. His wife, Benta, came behind him carrying a baby. She was short, very thin, and had dark-brown hair. Beside her trotted three little girls, aged two, three, and four. The children, including the baby, were all goldheads like the father. All the Aanensons had glowing red cheeks.

Reverend Codman grabbed Tallak's hand in both of his and held it for a moment.

"Ain't run so hard since an old bull took after me in the old country," Tallak said.

Reverend Codman looked around at his flock. "Yes. We are all here but the Wagners and the Olsons. And Lena Crydenwise and children."

An Indian head appeared above the rise to the east.

Everyone turned to look.

"Ah," Theodosia breathed, "it's our good friend Pounce. He has come to help us. I knew he would stand by his new friends in Christ."

Reverend Codman rubbed his hands in relief. "So it is. Our work has not been in vain after all."

Pounce for all his fat belly came hurrying toward them with a quick light step. He had on a pair of black breeches and a gray work shirt given him by the mission. His hair was cut white-man style. His leathery brown face, deeply scarred by the white man's smallpox, had a worried look. His black eyes were bloodshot as if from lack of sleep. His thick lips were drawn back and down.

Pounce raised his left hand in greeting. The left hand was always raised upon meeting someone because it was nearest to the heart and because it had shed no blood. Pounce spoke in broken American. "Houw. I look at you. My heart is glad to see my friends."

Reverend Codman stepped forward with a smile and held out his hand. "It makes my heart glad to see you too, my friend."

Pounce looked away for a second. Then, bowing a little, and in the manner of the old-time Dakota weepers, he cried over Reverend Codman's hand. Tears fell on the back of Reverend Codman's wrist. "It is very bad. You must fly."

Reverend Codman drew back his hand. "What has happened? Why do certain of the red men show their anger? What have we done?"

Pounce shut off the ceremonial weeping with a single blink of his reddish-black eyes. "A runner has come to us. The bad Indians are killing at the Lower Agency. On the river the white man calls the Minnesota. The soldiers fly. All the whites are killed. Also the women and children."

A gasp rose from the settlers.

Crydenwise said, "That means we're cut off."

Vikes said, "Unless we can escape the other way."

"What other way?" Crydenwise asked.

"Why, toward Sioux Falls. We can take the mail carrier's route that way."

Reverend Codman asked Pounce, "What is the reason for smoke signals from our Christian brother's camp?"

Pounce scratched himself through his black trousers. His dark eyes roved through the crowd. His glance lingered on the women, in particular on Theodosia and Judith. "The white man must fly."

Theodosia stepped beside her husband. She gave Pounce a bright

Christian smile. "I see that our brother in Christ has come to lead us to safety."

Pounce's large sensual lips worked. "The young braves are hungry for the blood. The spirits of some of the dead fathers will not let the young braves sleep at night because enemy blood has not been found and spilled. It is very bad. The white man must fly. Or he will die like the rabbit when the wolf is hungry."

War drums continued to beat loud and clear. More smoke signals rose on all sides. Village dogs barked and howled. A fan-shaped flock of startled carrier pigeons flew past overhead and vanished into the oaks.

"Are you not the chief?" Reverend Codman asked. "Are you a woman that your young braves will not listen to your counsel?"

"Young braves make the war, old chiefs make the peace."

Reverend Codman managed to shape his thin lips into a kindly smile. "Has not the track of the moccasin and the footprint of the white man's boot lain side by side in peace these many years? Why must we shed each other's blood? Let the war trail grass over."

Pounce's eye fell on Theodosia again. "Tell the Good Book Woman she must fly. I have said."

"Our friend Jesus will not like this."

Pounce seemed to consider this. At last he too shaped his lips into a good smile. He went around shaking the hands of all the men. Next he patted the little children on the head.

"God bless," Reverend Codman murmured. Reverend Codman's fists were white over the knuckles.

Pounce also held out his hand to Theodosia and Judith.

Theodosia accepted his hand. Judith refused him.

Pounce threw Judith a darting, venomous look.

Judith glared right back at him.

Pounce next spotted Reverend Codman's white knuckles. He grunted, once, twice, then abruptly turned and started back for his village.

"Brother Pounce?" Theodosia called.

Pounce ignored her call and disappeared over the rise.

The faces of the whites, momentarily brightened, now turned darker than ever.

"That backslider," Judith whispered.

Silvers' bearded face worked with strangling emotion. "Damned summertime Christian."

Tallak looked down at Silvers from his great height. "That's what we get for lettin' you cheatin' trader fellers into our little town. Giving them poor red devils squirrel whiskey until they're so drunk you can steal their money and their land for nothin'."

Silvers gave Tallak a slow measuring look, then fell grudgingly silent.

Reverend Codman shook his head. "I fear that we may have to reap the whirlwind after all. Yes. Some of us have stolen from the red man."

Silvers sneered. "Reverend, beggin' your pardon, but you're a liar when you say the trader's cheated the red devil." Silvers shook his heavy fist in Reverend Codman's face. "Why, them red niggers desarve no better. They're hardly better than animals, in a manner of speakin'."

Reverend Codman's lips turned quivering white. Somehow he managed to keep from speaking. Reaching down, carefully, even meticulously, he selected a single blade of grass from between his feet. He began to pick his teeth with the pale green end of it.

Judith gave Silvers a withering look. The rank rutting odor of the man reminded her of an old boar she and her four brothers had once caught in the woods near their Davenport farm. She also recalled a remark Vince had once made, that many of the pioneers were not the best of people, that there were bounty jumpers, deserters, and thieves among them. Her eyes fell on Silvers' grease-spotted buckskin shirt front. "Hardly better than animals, eh?" She glanced around at Tinkling. "Who's this you married, then?"

Theodosia breathed quick short breaths. She took off her slat bonnet. "My, but it's close out." Sweat beaded Theodosia's pale forehead. The large freckles on her cheeks stood out like dark warts.

Silvers pushed back his fur cap, and a black forelock slid across his brow. "Yeh, and I say the gov'ment made a mistake when it gave you Christian willies permission to come out here. This is no place fer women."

Theodosia put her bonnet back on. "You don't seem to understand, Mr. Silvers, that my husband and I were called by the Lord to bring the gospel message to the heathen. We had to come."

"So you really think you can make a Christian out of a Indian, ha?" Silvers exploded. "Woman, it can't be done, any more than you can't make a house cat out of a weasel."

"Then you have no compassion for even the least of these? Even when they hunger for truth?"

"I wouldn't give them a stone to gnaw on."

"Not even your pretty little Christian wife?"

Silvers stomped his heavy boots. "Her, maybe yes. Because she's never said no to me in bed. But the rest of them red devils, naw. Let them eat grass. Or their own dung."

Tinkling jerked as if someone had cut her across the thin shoulders with a whip. She shied around to hide herself.

Joe Utterback had a word. "And if you want my honest thought on it, Mrs. Codman, this is what I say. It hain't right fer an ignorant savage to own so much land, unplowed, while the better white man is forced to live in want. The Indian never did use the land for what the Lord intended it fer—raisin' wheat. That's what I say."

Reverend Codman shook his head sadly. "Yes. How beautiful the Ordinance of 1787 reads. 'The utmost good shall always be observed toward the Indians. Their lands and property shall never be taken from them without their consent.'"

Angela tugged at Judith's sleeve. "When do we eat, Mama? I'm hungry."

Judith glanced up at the warm sun. "Stars alive," she said. "It's going on afternoon already. I completely forgot about dinner."

Maggie Utterback said, "Who wants to eat now? 'Ceptin' maybe that pig of a husband of mine."

The boy Ted gave his mother, Theodosia, a tug on the arm. "Make me some cornbread, Mama. I'm hungry. I surely like that new molasses you made."

"Shh," Theodosia said. "You'll have to wait awhile. Until we decide what to do."

Mrs. Christians covered her eyes with her hands. "Here I am, far in Indian country, cut off, and my husband dead." She cried bitterly.

Mavis put an arm around Mrs. Christians. "There, there. Now, now."

Mrs. Christians lashed out, eyes wild, throwing Mavis' arm aside. "Get your dirty hands off me, you whore, after what you done with some of our men."

Mavis turned white.

Billy Vikes and Jed Crydenwise gave each other wondering looks.

"Let us pray," Reverend Codman said. He bowed his head and folded his hands. His voice boomed loud and strong. "Our Father which art in heaven, we come to thee in the noon hour of this day, sorely troubled at heart and beset round about by—"

"Here they come!" Maggie Utterback cried. "Men, cock your guns."

Reverend Codman's light-gray eyes fluttered open. "Ahh," he said.

It was Pounce with a dozen braves. They came stalking toward them down the rise. Pounce had replaced his white man's clothes with a clout. His nose was painted a deep red and his chin a striped yellow. Daubs of white clay lay in swirls across his bare chest. He carried a long, heavy knob-ended war club. The braves with him were naked and daubed over with war paint too. Some of the braves carried bows and arrows, some guns.

Angela whispered into the silence, "They're coming to kill us, aren't they, Mama?"

"Now, now." Judith stroked Angela's silver-blond hair. "Shh." Judith could feel her own heart beating in her brain.

Reverend Codman said quietly, "Don't shoot. One shot and we'll all be plunged into eternity. There are too many of them. Instead we must try to persuade them to let us alone until help arrives."

Maggie Utterback lowered her gun. "Them fiends! Devils in human shape."

Pounce halted a dozen paces away. The young braves lined up on either side of him. All stood haughty, watchful.

Pounce raised his right hand. "Houw."

Reverend Codman looked from painted face to painted face. He said gently, "Have my red brothers forgotten the Good Book so soon?"

A sly grimace slid across Pounce's thick lips, then was gone. "We have come to protect our white brother from the bad Indians." With his war club, Pounce pointed in the direction of Mad Bear's renegade camp across the lake.

"Our friend Jesus will not like this."

Pounce went on smoothly. "Let the white brother put on the war dress of the Dakotas and we will make him our son. We will protect him. We will fight for him when the time comes." Pounce's glance fell on Theodosia.

"The sun does not rise in the west."

Cunning worked Pounce's lips again for a second. "Let the white man shoot his guns into the ground. That will frighten the bad Indians very much. They will think that the blue soldiers have come. They will run away."

Silvers gave Pounce a scornful look. "Does our red brother take us for fools? We will keep our guns loaded and cocked."

Pounce pretended grief. "The body of the white man named Christians, it will rot in the sun. Soon the wolves will devour it.

His spirit will not be happy. Let one of you come with us and we will bury it as the white man wishes."

Mrs. Christians began to wail again.

Silvers snorted. "The red chief thinks he will pick us off one by one."

"I want mum-mum," little Johnnie said. He reached up a grass-stained chubby hand. "Mama? I want mum-mum."

"Shh." Theodosia reached down and gathered Johnnie in her arms. She hugged him. "Yes, darling, yes, yes."

"Backslider!" Judith hissed.

Reverend Codman nodded. "Yes, sister, I'm afraid we have mistaken the red man's courtesy for conversion."

"Courtesy?" Mavis cried. "When he intended to rape and kill us all along?"

The settlers grouped themselves like a herd of horses facing a pack of wolves: males on the outside, females next, children in the center. Only Maggie Utterback broke the rule—she lined up with the men.

Judith thought: "It's like being caught in a terrible nightmare of some kind."

The leather door flap of the council tepee in Whitebone's village suddenly whipped open, and out ran two dozen armed and painted Yankton warriors. Two Two and other Indian boys hurriedly led up the war ponies. With a leap the warriors were mounted. They came on, directly across the swamp.

Silvers turned green. The giant Tallak shuddered.

Judith thought, "We're all going to die."

Joe Utterback whispered, "There's going to be some awful work now, boys."

Maggie Utterback would have none of it. She said loudly, "Joe, trouble with you is, you was born without sand in your craw."

Joe fired up at that. "Haw. Woman, I'll tough it out as long as you any day."

"That we'll wait and see."

Vikes was jumping wild.

Tallak tried to quiet him. "It's all right, Billy. With your first shot you become a new man."

Vikes cried, "But I ain't got no gun. Only a pitchfork, and I left that t' home."

Whitebone and his warriors spread out. They came on singing a monotonous, eerie chant, the Dakota death song. Each warrior had painted himself in his own individualistic style, celebrating personal coups and battle marks. Even the ponies were painted and decorated for battle. The warriors rode naked except for clout and war feather. Most carried bows and arrows, a few double-barreled shotguns. Compared to Pounce's Christian braves, Whitebone's war party had the old wild look. Whitebone's group had always kept pretty much to themselves, had never had much traffic with the whites.

Whitebone and his warriors came on. Their horses breasted through the rushes in the swamp in a wide line. In some places the growth was so deep, horse and rider vanished from view.

Reverend Codman stood calmly. But his fists were balled so tight they were white all the way back to the wrist.

Tallak shrugged twice, quick, then took command. "Boys, we've got to take cover. Ladies, take the kits inside and get under the beds and tables. Men, knock out the chinking from between the logs and we'll shoot them down as they come."

No sooner said than done. Women and children piled inside and hid as best they could. Vikes tied his team of horses to a wagon standing against the south wall of the cabin. Men looked to their guns and powder, and picked their spots inside along the log walls. Reverend Codman sat down in the old black rocker in the middle of the cabin. He fell into deep thought, eyes down. He rocked slowly back and forth.

Pounce didn't like the white maneuver of taking shelter inside the Codman cabin. He frowned. He had had other plans for them. And it was with an effort that he finally managed to clear his

pockmarked face with a benign smile. He pointed at Whitebone's oncoming band of warriors. "You see," he cried, "there the
enemy comes. Now you will see that Pounce is your friend. Pounce
will council with the chief known as Whitebone."

Tallak snorted. "That dirty devil Pounce. Look at him. Hair
cut off like a Christian. T'while his clout is shitty like the breech-
ing of a horse."

Theodosia spoke up near the door. "Remember, where the
baptized are gathered, there the Lord is."

Waggling his war club, Pounce strode off to meet Whitebone.
He met Whitebone just as the line of Whitebone's mounted,
chanting braves emerged from the deep grass.

Pounce held up his left hand, palm out. "Houw!" He spoke
loudly enough for the whites to hear.

Whitebone stared down at Pounce a moment, then, reining in
his war horse, held up his left hand too. "Houw."

The line of braves braced, and stopped. Slowly the eerie chanting faded away.

Pounce and Whitebone conferred. They were too far away for
the whites to hear much of what was said. Only occasional words,
spoken in sarcasm, drifted across the intervening space. Pounce
seemed to be talking big; Whitebone quietly and incisively.

Judith lay with Angela under the table near the door. Looking
out through a crack between the door and the doorpost, Judith
distinctly heard Whitebone say in Dakota, "I see my red brother
has removed the white man's pants and put on the breechclout."
A little later Whitebone laughed scornfully and called Pounce a
name. "Pantaloons."

Pounce defended himself.

Time passed. Hearts pumped loud. When the children whimpered they were pinched and told to shut up. The old black rocker
creaked as Reverend Codman rocked and pondered.

The two chiefs at last fell into a low murmuring discussion.
There was much looking toward the cabin by both of them, then
off toward the northeast in the direction of Fort Ridgely.

Judith could make out Whitebone's face quite clearly. The afternoon sun shone full upon Whitebone. He sat very erect on his spotted bay. He looked to be about fifty. He had a firm mouth, sharp nose, wide, high cheekbones, small glinting black eyes, forehead narrowing into black hair. His skin was dark, almost black. A fur-wrapped braid hung on either side of his face. He was the most primitive man she had ever seen, a true old-time savage.

Judith looked to see if Scarlet Plume, the tall Yankton who had suddenly appeared in their cabin earlier in the day, was in Whitebone's line of warriors. She examined the heavily painted faces, then the breadths of the shoulders. He wasn't. Apparently not all of the Dakotas were war bent. There was a chance then for the whites after all.

Judith recalled how only the previous week Whitebone had allowed some of the children of his band to join Pounce's little children in her sod-house school. There had been so many pupils suddenly, there weren't enough slates to go around. So she had taken them all down to the lake shore and had used the sandy beach to write on. She sat on a log, teaching them. The earnest dark little faces looked up at her, full of puppy trust. They were more intent on learning something from her than was her own Angela or her nephew Ted.

The whites in the cabin waited. The men along the log walls gripped their guns so hard they had to set the guns down every now and then and rub their hands to restore the circulation. Bellies rumbled. One of the women pinched off a squeaking private noise.

Movement on the trampled grass near the garden caught Judith's eye. She looked out. It was Theodosia's only cock and hen. That dratted pair. They and the mice and the babies had been in league all summer long to destroy what little flowers they had.

The cock was a gallant golden-brown fellow with a bright-red comb. The hen was small and modest. The two were pecking along together through the grass, here a seed, there a baby grasshopper, then a speck of sand, even a turf beetle. All of a sudden the cock made a whirring noise, dropped a wing hard to the ground, pranced around the hen once, then fluttered aboard. The hen was all too ready to acquiesce. Even before the cock dropped his wing she had squatted down and tipped her short tail up.

Cock and hen pecked along some more. A seed. A fly. A grain of sand. Again he dropped a wing, whirred, and fluttered aboard. Peck, peck, peck—then *urrr!* and in the saddle. In the space of a few minutes the gallant old boy had mounted her a half-dozen times.

The sight nauseated Judith. What a foolish chit of a thing the hen was to let herself be mounted so often. And at a time like this. Why didn't she peck him back a couple of times or two, to make him behave a little? Sharp and hard too. Where it would smart. Cocky men burned Judith.

The parley between the two chiefs broke up. Whitebone gave a signal, and his men fell back a little into the deep grass, he with them.

Pounce came lolling back, waggling his war club. A big smile cut his rough face in halves. He too gave a signal and his men fell back.

Pounce approached the door of the cabin. He called for Reverend Codman to come out.

Reverend Codman got to his feet hesitantly. He pushed the rocker back.

"Don't go," Tallak commanded. "It's a trick."

Tiny muscles over Reverend Codman's pale cheekbones twitched. "It is my thought that I should confer with him. He is after all a baptized man."

"Baptized? That baptism has long ago washed off."

"I must not overlook a chance to avoid bloodshed."

"Don't go. That is what I say."

Pounce called again. "Let the Good Book Man come outside. We wish to smoke the pipe with him."

Shadows passed over Reverend Codman's face. "Much hangs on what we do in the next hour. Someone should keep talking with them so long as they wish to parley. We need time." Then Reverend Codman hardened himself to the task. "It is my duty. I have decided. I have been chosen by God to be your temporal as well as your spiritual leader. You are all in my trust."

"Talk to him through a crack in the logs then."

"Let us smoke the pipe," Pounce called. "Come. The little hole in the pipe stem leads straight to truth. He who has a forked tongue cannot smoke the pipe."

Theodosia moved to her husband's side. She was sweating. She touched him. "Go. Talk to him, husband dear. And Christ be with you."

Reverend Codman smiled a Christian smile at Theodosia. "Yes. I must go. It is our only chance." Reverend Codman took a last look at all the white, haggard faces inside the cabin, then pushed Tallak aside and stepped outdoors.

Judith watched through the crack between the door and the doorpost. She saw Reverend Codman and Pounce sit down on the grass together. She watched Pounce fill the pipe carefully, with ritualistic gesture. She watched him light it with a fagot brought from his village.

Tallak shook his head. "How can our reverend let himself swap saliva with that dirty heathen?"

"My husband is a Christian," Theodosia said.

Reverend Codman sat calmly. His fingers hung free and limp.

Pounce smiled. He fawned in his most winning manner. Pounce's warriors stood back from them a dozen steps, forming a half circle. The warriors watched the smoking of the pipe narrowly. Sweat gleamed on their brown limbs.

Vikes let go with a low cry inside the cabin. "I see smoke to the north."

"Probably another smoke signal," Joe Utterback offered.

Vikes watched through his crack, eyes wild. "It's too dark for a smoke signal. It's a wood fire. Real wood burning. Somebody's house . . . My God, it's my own cabin!"

"No!" Tallak exploded.

Silvers was next to cry aloud. "Yep, there goes my trading post."

"Tallak," Vikes cried, "there goes your house. And there goes the Olson house. They're all going up in flames. Even the wheat and barley fields."

"Them fiends from hell," Maggie Utterback whispered, turning pale.

Crydenwise was next to speak up from his vantage point. "Well, Joe, old hoss, you can kiss our sod shanties good-bye. Two black plumes raisin' out our way too."

"They are firing the whole settlement then. Skywater is wiped out."

Mavis called from under her bed. "Any smoke out my way? The store?"

"Not yet."

Theodosia asked, "What about the mission church?"

"Still all clear there. So far."

Judith watched Reverend Codman and Pounce. The two were now exchanging sharp words. Reverend Codman was finally showing some fire. After a moment Pounce shrugged, and gave way. Pounce put on a smile. He agreed with whatever it was Reverend Codman said. Judith shuddered. That foxy backslider.

It became oppressively hot and close inside the cabin. Everyone breathed heavy.

Reverend Codman re-entered the cabin.

The men crowded around him, guns bristling.

"What took you so long?" Tallak demanded.

"There's nothing gained in hurrying an Indian, you know."

"What did he say?"

"Pounce says he and Whitebone have agreed not to molest us provided we agree to take refuge in the mission church."

Maggie Utterback spat in disgust. "That flimsy thing? Them clapboards wouldn't stop a fart. All them Indians has got to do is sit back in the tall grass and riddle it with rifle balls. And we're all dead. Beggin' your pardon, Mrs. Codman."

Theodosia pinched her lips together.

"No," Tallak said. "Them heathens won't respect the church any more than they will respect the reverend's cabin."

"Pounce says Whitebone has made up his mind that the white man must go. This is Whitebone's old hunting ground. Whitebone says all white lodges must be burned to the ground. Whitebone says only the white man's mission church can stay. Whitebone says he does not wish to offend the white man's god by burning his Good Book Tepee."

"No," Tallak said, "I don't like it. I vote to stay here. We are safe here now."

"Pounce says he and Whitebone have agreed to provide us with safe passage to the church. They will protect us from Mad Bear's bunch."

"Mad Bear's bunch? They ain't even showed up yet," Tallak protested. "What kind of talk is that?"

Reverend Codman spoke sadly. "I'm afraid Mad Bear's bunch has. While parleying with Pounce, I saw them sneaking through the woods behind our cabin here. Out of the corner of my eye."

The women gasped. The eyes of the children widened.

Crydenwise cursed. "Them devils. I'll bet it was them what fired the houses, then."

Reverend Codman said, "I'm afraid some of Pounce's band had a hand in that too. Pounce said some of his wilder braves got out of hand and joined up with Mad Bear's wild ones."

"Them sons of Beelzebub."

"And that is understandable, considering that both Pounce and Mad Bear are Santee Dakota," Reverend Codman went on to say. "Whereas Whitebone is Yankton Dakota."

Theodosia sighed. "Alas, how little do we know what lies be-

fore us. We know not what the hour, much less the day, will
bring forth."

Again Judith peered across at where Whitebone and his Yankton warriors waited in the deep grass. She could just make out
the tips of their war feathers and the ears of their horses. She
looked over at Whitebone's tepees. Where was Scarlet Plume? He
had given her and the whites a warning. A wild white swan with
a broken neck. Pray God that he might be at that very moment at
work somewhere trying to arrange for their salvation. Scarlet
Plume was their only hope.

"Well, what is your wish?" Reverend Codman asked them all
in a gentle voice. "What shall I tell Pounce?"

Every man panted. Sweat as big as gooseberries worked down
their faces. Cheeks became gray-edged. Some of the men trembled
violently, legs shaking, teeth chattering. Some buckled at the
knees as if weak from too much laughter. The crouching women
all had terror-circled eyes. The children waited, numb, looking
up at their elders.

Reverend Codman said, "Pounce reminded me that the red
man knows full well that the Union cause does not go well in the
South. Pounce knows that our great white father, Abraham
Lincoln, has had to call up old men and young boys to prosecute
the war. Pounce knows that not many men are left to protect
the frontier. Pounce said that perhaps the time had finally come
for the red man to rise up and throw off the yoke of the oppressor."

Everyone understood. There had been more than one report that
Fort Ridgely had lately been manned by a company of young
boys.

Judith thought, "Yes, even my husband, Vince, with his soft
hands and erudition, has been sent south." She thought, "We are
all going to die."

Blackness gathered on settler faces.

"Oh, if we'd only stayed in our clearing in Wisconsin," Mrs.
Aanenson said.

Tallak glared down at his little wife. "Woman, you know we

couldn't've kept on there. We didn't raise enough off that sand to feed our growin' gurls."

Reverend Codman asked, "Tallak, do you think this structure is strong enough to withstand attack?"

"Bullets, yes. Fire arrows, no. Just one burning arrow and *whoof!* up in smoke she goes. We can all be fried in it like sausages."

Judith got up from where she was hiding under the table. She brushed cobwebs off her gray dress. The other women and children also came out of hiding. They stood ringed around Reverend Codman. The little children—Angela, Ted, Johnnie, Tallak's girls —covertly touched the edges of the reverend's black coat. Body odors, some strong, some sweet, some musty, some soap-scented, began to drift about in the cabin.

Judith smoothed back Angela's silver-blond hair. Angela's hair felt as smooth as the fur of a pussy.

Tallak said, "I think we better all keep one bullet over. If worst comes to worst."

"What for?" Crydenwise cried. "I'd rather see it buried in a redskin."

"Ya, your Lena and kids are already dead, so you should talk."

Silvers snorted. "Well, my woman can take care of herself."

Reverend Codman smiled at the Indian wife of Silvers. "What does our sister Tinkling say? Will the Dakota respect the Good Book Tepee if we take refuge in it?"

With all eyes suddenly focused on her, Tinkling humped over more than ever. She threw a minklike defensive look at them all. The whites might be cornered by the redskins outside, but she in turn was cornered by the whites inside.

"Speak up, Mrs. Silvers."

The perfectly cut corners of Tinkling's lips trembled.

"Speak up."

Tinkling at last spoke. "Do not believe Pounce." She had a surprisingly squeaky voice. "Do not believe Mad Bear. Both are Santee Dakota."

"What about Whitebone?"

"He is a great Yankton chief and a true father of his people. He speaks with his mouth where his eyes look. He speaks true."

"Do you think Whitebone will respect our godhouse?"

Tinkling nodded, slowly.

Reverend Codman nodded too. "Yes, in matters of religion I've found the old-line Yankton Dakota to be as courteous as any people on earth."

Mouths panted. Hearts bumped, wildly irregular.

Crydenwise moved. Before Mavis could defend herself, he slipped his hand about her waist and kissed her roughly on the lips. Then Crydenwise threw Mrs. Christians a smirking look. "Since I been accused of takin' liberties with the widder I might as well be guilty of 'em, ha."

Mavis slapped Crydenwise. Her eyes flashed. Her face took on an even sharper terrier-like look.

Reverend Codman frowned. "My beloved in the Lord."

Mrs. Christians' lips, already thick from her near lying-in, took on a child's pout. "That's what my Henry said. That's what he said. And you wouldn't want to go against a dead man's word, would you?"

"Children!" Reverend Codman said sharply.

"Mama," Ted said, "when are we going to have some mummum?"

Theodosia stroked Ted's wild blond hair. Her hazel eyes were calm. "In a little while, son."

Far in the distance, barely within ear range, there was a low rumble of thunder. Almost immediately after, a wild whoop rose from the woods along the lake.

Reverend Codman looked kindly at Tinkling. "Sister, I ask it again. Do you still think Whitebone will respect the Good Book Tepee of the white man?"

"Let's go," Silvers exploded. He threw his trembling wife a scornful look. "Don't pay her no mind, Reverend. She don't know from nothing."

Reverend Codman persisted.

Tinkling stood straighter. She took heart. "We go."

There was a roar of relief inside the cabin. Everybody quickly got ready to make a break for the mission church.

Tallak held up his big hand. He blocked the door with his huge frame. "Wait a minute, everybody. Whoa. That's one thing you can't do. Run across to the church like a bunch of scared rabbits."

Reverend Codman agreed. "We go as men or not at all. Calmly. Showing no fear. After all, we are Christians, are we not?"

The settlers steadied. Of course. To show fear was to invite instant massacre.

Joe Utterback handed his wife, Maggie, a skinning knife.

"What's that fer?" Maggie Utterback exclaimed.

"Wal, if them red devils should happen to forget theirselves and attack you, wal, you know what to do. It's sharp enough."

Maggie Utterback almost blew up in disgust. "I will not." She knocked the skinning knife out of her husband's hand. "I ain't afeard. Besides, what's the difference? A bull man is a bull man whether he's red or white. Or even blue. Ain't he? You men are all a bunch of lazy good-fer-nothin' boar pigs, the lot a ye."

Joe Utterback flushed around his eyes. "I was only thinkin' of your good." He picked up the skinning knife and thrust it into his belt again.

"The Lord be with us, that I pray," Theodosia whispered, hugging Ted and Johnnie.

Tallak turned to Vikes. "Billy, are your horses afraid of Indians?"

"Huh? Who, mine? Naw. They're used to Pounce's bunch. I can't say, though, for the others."

"Good. I want you to quick hitch them to Reverend's wagon behind the cabin there. We're going to need it for Mrs. Christians. She's already walked too far. And there's food and powder and extra clothes we need to take along. We better load on all we can. The Lord only knows how long it'll be before help arrives. We may have to live in that church a week."

"Before we go, let us offer up a prayer for a safe journey,"
Reverend Codman said.

All of the womenfolk knelt on the circular rag rug in the center
of the cabin. Of the children, little Johnnie knelt too. And of the
men, only Tallak got down on his knees. The rest stood with their
heads bowed.

Reverend Codman used the back of the black rocking chair as
though it were a pulpit of the Lord's. "Father, here we are, on
this earth, sorely troubled. We who have ventured much stand to
lose all in an instant. Much labor in thy service, many many
months of it, both spiritual as well as temporal, is in danger of
being lost if Thou dost not soon send us help. O Father, we
pray Thee to consider us in our great and sudden extremity. Come,
hear our cry. We are thy humble servants. Hear, hear our cry. We
plead, yea, we beg of Thee, not for our sakes, since we by ourselves are sinful and utterly deserving of utmost condemnation,
but for thy sake out of grace granted by Thee, to save us. In
Jesus' name, amen."

Another drumming of thunder sounded, far in the southwest.

A guttural sigh rose from them all. Silvers had a tear in the
corner of his eye. Vikes's eyes were awash like melting hailstones.

Little Johnnie at last seemed to understand that all was not
well. He began to cry. A wet spot slowly spread down the side
of one of his pants legs.

Theodosia swept him into her arms.

"All right, Billy," Tallak ordered, getting to his feet. "Get
them horses hitched to the wagon. Mrs. Codman, tell us where
things are so we can quick get them loaded."

Canned food, clothes, blankets, the thick Bible, a keg of gunpowder, mission records were all hastily carried outdoors. Tallak,
the tallest, placed them in the bottom of the wagon. A feather
tick was spread out on the floor near the rear end. Tallak hoisted
Mrs. Christians up and settled her on it. Mrs. Christians wept un-
controllably. She held a fresh loaf of brown bread to her breast.

Tallak next placed the children on top of the load up front. Theodosia carried Johnnie. Johnnie's eyes were crossed in fear and Theodosia decided to carry him snuggled warmly in her arms.

Silvers, Crydenwise, Maggie and Joe Utterback stood on guard, guns cocked.

"Look at that smile all of a sudden on Pounce's face," Maggie Utterback muttered.

" 'Pears to be in high feather at what we're doin', all right," Joe Utterback said.

"Gassy pigs," Maggie Utterback said. "Wish there was some way of taming them. Like dogs."

"The only way you can tame a Indian," Silvers said, "is to fill him up with white blood. Like I been tryin' to do with my woman Tinkling."

"Whoever thought the Indian had a soul must've surely lost all his buttons," Joe Utterback said.

Reverend Codman frowned.

"Ha. Ever try to domesticate a wolf?" Crydenwise said. "Try it sometime and see what you get. I know. A wolf'll snap at anything that comes near him even after he gets used to livin' with you. Same thing goes fer a red devil."

Reverend Codman shook his head as if at wrongheaded children.

"Preach, I tell you," Silvers said, "someday you'll larn that it was a mistake to be tenderhearted with the noble red savage."

Vikes finally had the horses hitched up. "Everybody ready?"

"Let her go."

Vikes climbed up on the wagon seat. He snapped the reins. "Giddap. Colonel. Duke. Get!"

The grays picked up the urgency in Vikes's voice and their ears rose. They leaned into it and the wagon began to creak away.

Pounce and Whitebone exchanged hand signals. Pounce's group immediately formed a moving wall on the south side, Whitebone's warriors came out of the grass and formed a moving line of mounted men on the north side.

The caravan moved slowly toward the mission church. The church was still out of sight over the rise. Reverend Codman strode ahead alone, pale, bold nose in the lead. Those not riding walked behind the wagon.

They had gone but a dozen rods when Mad Bear and his bunch of renegades came whooping out of the timber behind the cabin.

"There they come!" Maggie Utterback yelled. "Shall we shoot?"

"Hold your fire!" Tallak roared.

There were at least thirty renegades. They were even more ragged than Pounce's band. Some wore white-man breeches, some blankets, some feathers, some plug hats, all mostly stolen goods. Their yelling was wild, unearthly, more like the erratic crazy chirps of prairie dogs than war cries. Mad Bear was in the lead. He carried an old-time longbow. He was a squat, muscular devil some forty winters old. He had a naturally deep-set scowl and wild, rolling black eyes. He wore a grotesque necklace.

Whitebone galloped over. He saluted Mad Bear.

Mad Bear saw Whitebone's raised left hand. Mad Bear signaled and his marauders held back. They danced in the grass, barely restrained, brandishing shotguns, knives, spears, bows and arrows.

There was a further cry from the woods, higher, shriller. Out poured Mad Bear's squaws, fat and thin both, all of them squalid. They made straight for the cabin. They clawed and squealed their way inside. In a moment all that had been left behind was in tatters—clothes, sheets, bedding, feathers, books, papers. Two heavy, snarling squaws fought over a jar of pickles. One of them became so wrought up that when she finally got control of the jar she whacked the other over the head with it. Pickles and glass and juice flew everywhere. Another pair of squaws fought over the dead wild swan with the broken neck; head and neck went one way, body and legs the other. In the midst of it all, one of Mad Bear's braves came running up with a burning torch and set fire to the cabin.

The faces of all the whites took on the hue of scorched clover.

Judith almost fell down. She caught hold of Angela's reaching hand from the wagon. She pinched Angela's hand so hard, Angela whimpered. Again Judith had trouble controlling her bladder.

Reverend Codman called from up front. "Courage now. Be of good faith. The Lord is with us and not with them."

Whitebone made another decisive gesture, and Mad Bear held up his hand again to hold his savages in line.

Mavis let out a cry. Gasping, she pointed toward a new plume of smoke rising beyond the hill. "There goes my store and post office."

Houses, haystacks, fields of grain were blazing everywhere. The roaring red flames, the towering plumes of smoke, the demonic yells of the renegades, the hellish shrilling of the squaws, with behind and over it all a slowly gathering cloud bank full of snapping thunder, made it appear that Judgment Day was surely at hand at last. Terrible. Yet somehow grand and tremendous.

"I think," Tallak said, "I think we better keep one bullet over."

"The church!" Reverend Codman replied. "Keep your eyes on the house of God. It is our only hope and our only salvation."

A single stout plum tree stood halfway up the rise ahead. An Indian with ripgut tied to his head rose out of the grass beside it. It was one of Pounce's men. He had skulked through a swale to head them off. After a moment other Indians, also camouflaged with ripgut tied to their heads, rose out of the prairie, blocking their path.

Reverend Codman up front, to avoid setting off a shooting affair right then and there, veered slightly to the right, going along the edge of a wide slough. Rushes in the slough stood head high.

The Indians were quick to spot the weakness and pushed the whites even further into the slough.

The settlers pressed on. The ground became rough with potholes and grass tussocks. The wagon jolted heavily. Mrs. Christians groaned.

Crydenwise played his cocked musket around. "Boys, I think we've been worked."

"No shooting now," Reverend Codman warned over his shoulder. "Steady."

Theodosia said, "Remember, friends, sweet will be our rest in heaven when all this is finished."

Theodosia carried Johnnie high against her bosom. His little feet dangled with each step. She walked slim and stiff and looked straight ahead.

Except for the slough directly ahead, the settlers were soon surrounded by the Indians. Whitebone and his soldiers' lodge rode silently on the settlers' left. Pounce and his dark, lowering savages walked mostly along on the right. Mad Bear and his renegades cut off all retreat behind them. Whitebone's face was expressionless. Pounce was all smirks. Mad Bear frothed at the lips.

Ted asked from the wagon, "Mama, will we eat when we get to the church?"

"Yes, my darling son. All of us. After we've thanked the Lord for preserving us."

Tallak's face was ashen white. He stalked along with high steps. "By gol, if it wasn't for that damn Mad Bear and his devils, I think we could make it."

Silvers nodded. "They're no good. No good to anybody. Even the Indians hate 'em." Silvers swung his gun around menacingly to protect their rear. "You should hear some of the stories I've heard about 'em. Turn your stomach inside out."

"Ya, I suppose."

Theodosia said, "As long as the least of these have souls, we must do everything within our power to save them."

"Souls, hell. When they're so rotten they've been known to sleep with wild animals fresh killed?"

The old wagon lurched heavily. Then the reach cracked underneath. There was a sound of splintering wood.

It could not go on.

Reverend Codman turned and held up his hands.

Vikes reined in his grays. "Whoa, there, whoa. Steady now."

It came over Joe Utterback and Crydenwise what they had to do. It was mole under or lose hair. They took one wild look around, then plunged toward the tall rushes in the center of the slough.

A half dozen of Pounce's braves tried to head them off. They were too late. Both whites vanished.

Maggie Utterback was outraged. "That dirty skunk. That coward." She swore. She spat after Joe. "Joe, come back here and fight like a man. Fat lot of good that knife's gonna do me now, stuck in your belt."

No answer. Nor was there any stirring in the green rushes to indicate where the two benedicts might be lying secret.

Mad Bear's band rushed up close, brandishing guns, howling, yelling, dancing. Pounce's bunch joined them. The din was unearthly. Sight of so many roaring wild Indians made the children on the wagon cry. Random shots whistled over the heads of the settlers.

Reverend Codman approached Pounce with his raised left hand. "Brother in Christ, what is this? Did you not grant us safe passage to the Good Book Tepee? Is your tongue split?"

Pounce's heavy lips turned down at the corners.

Reverend Codman said sternly, "It seems my brother's word has as much worth as an empty corn shuck."

"It is the young braves who make the war."

"Is this what my eyes see?"

"The young braves make me go to war." Pounce rubbed his heavy belly in a circular motion. "But I will shoot up, over your heads. Do not fear."

Mad Bear danced up, black eyes rolling, mouth foaming. He roared, "The white man must die!" He had a big yellow circle painted around his right eye. It meant he was his band's best shot.

Close up, it could be seen that his grotesque necklace was made of fingers chopped from the hands of his victims. "The white man must die!"

Reverend Codman continued to address Pounce, ignoring Mad Bear. "I have lived with you twenty winters. A whole generation has grown up since I set up the first Good Book Tepee in your village beside Skywater here. My wife and my children and I have lived with you as one of your own blood. We have never done you any harm. We have tried to show you the true path." Reverend Codman pointed toward a field of burning corn just visible across the slough. "We have taught you how to plant corn in a furrow. We have given you plows. We have been your true friend at all times. Your grief was our grief, your joy was our joy. Why do you want to kill us?"

"The white man must die!" Mad Bear continued to roar. "The white man has stolen our land. He has killed our sons. He has counted coup on our daughters in his dirty dog manner. He has defiled our wives."

Pounce said, "I can do nothing. The soldiers' lodge has decided you must die. I cannot spare your life. Their orders are to kill all white men. You are a white man. I cannot save you."

Reverend Codman was finally beside himself with Christian rage. "Then you have lied to me."

"I promise to shoot up when the time comes."

"When . . . the . . . time . . . comes?"

"I must shoot my gun a little or the soldiers' lodge will punish me."

"You have lied to your Christian brother."

A blush blackened Pounce's pocked face. "We are very poor. You have stolen our hunting grounds. You have stolen the graves of our fathers. You have stolen even the place for our own graves. We have no place to bury our dead."

"What!" Reverend Codman rose on his toes in the deep grass. "From this spot when I look north or east or south I can see neither house nor store built by the white man. It is only along the shore of Skywater where I see white-man dwellings."

"You take our money and give it to this trader"—Pounce threw Silvers a snarling look—"and he touches the pen to the books in a false manner and then he says we owe it all to him."

Silvers stuck his chin into it. "You goldurn lyin' red nigger. Why, I've given you and your bunch credit for years so you could buy blankets and hoes and plows. That's why you always owe me out of your annuities when they arrive. I wasn't put into this world to feed and clothe you red devils out of my own pocket. And that's why as far as I'm concerned you and your whitewashed bunch can go eat grass. And if you're really as hungry as you pretend, you can go eat your own dung."

Pounce's eyes whirled, flashing, black. Gone was all pretense that he ever was the white man's friend.

Reverend Codman turned on Silvers. "There is no need to swear. The Indian never swears."

"Never swears?" Silvers ejaculated.

"Never. The worst he ever says is, 'You are a dog.' That is all."

"Never swears, does he?" Silvers was jumping mad. "Well, maybe he ain't human enough to swear. Did you ever think on that, ha?"

Pounce boiled. He turned toward his men. He held up his hand. He held it high until their howling fell away, until only the sound of their hate-thick breathing could be heard. He spoke in a fury. "Dakotas, attend! Before the sun sets across Skywater and the moon rises above the eastern rim of the earth, I will lead you against the stinking hairy-faces, against the fat men who have come to cheat us and take our lands away and put us in the pen for not helping them rob our women and children. Attend!"

Mad Bear addressed his men in turn. "Attend, Dakotas! This is what I say. Are we to starve like the buffalo who has fallen into deep snow? Are we to let our blood freeze like the waters of a little stream in the middle of the Hard Moon? This is what I say. Let us make our mother red with the blood of the white man."

Whitebone, however, held his men back. He and his soldiers'

lodge meant to keep their word that the white settlers were to have safe passage to the church.

One of the older squaws from Mad Bear's bunch approached. She gave a low trill. The trill set off a wild roar in both Pounce's and Mad Bear's bands.

Silvers said mockingly, "Well, Reverend, you're a deep-read man; what do we do now?"

Bitter disappointment smoked in Reverend Codman's eyes. It hurt the good reverend grievously to see his Christian Indians go berserk, while the heathen Indians did not. The defection of Pounce and his men, the killing of Henry Christians, the burning and pillaging of the settler homes and fields meant the total collapse of a world he and Theodosia had spent most of their adult lives building. Both he and Theodosia had often tried to explain the sinful greed of the white man to the red man. Both he and Theodosia had time and again tried to explain the nature of Stone Age people to the church back east. After much labor he had somehow got a few of the savages to listen to him, had somehow raised funds to build a church. But all was now for naught. It had turned out just as cynics predicted.

Judith recalled the time when she had once applauded Pounce. It was when she had first arrived. Services were being held in the new little clapboard church. Both whites and Pounce's band were present. Toward the end of the sermon, Reverend Codman asked rhetorically, "Who has not stolen sometime somewhere?" All of a sudden, weeping, one after the other, Indian women got to their feet and began to confess. When finally even Pounce's wife, Sunflower, rose to confess, Pounce broke in, growling, "Who knows how many times my wife has stolen? The Dakotas are a nation of thieves according to the white man's laws, that I can see. I have said." It had broken up the meeting.

Reverend Codman tried once more to avoid bloodshed. Sweat stood out on his nose. He said to Pounce, "Brother, remember when you touched the pen to the paper and signed the peace treaty with the white man? Well, let us remember that peace."

Mad Bear brandished his longbow as if to cleave Reverend Codman in half with it. "Treaties of peace with the white man," he
raged, "are as worthless as ropes of sand." He turned to his men.
"Dakotas, hear me. It is time to harvest the blood. Our slain
fathers cannot depart in peace!"

A double-barreled shotgun went off, twice. The back of Reverend Codman's head broke inward above his neck. After a
moment the insides of his head tumbled out like yellow clay being
pushed out of a hole by a pocket gopher. The face that was
left slowly closed over in peace. Then the body of Reverend
Codman toppled backward into the deep grass.

A squaw lifted the high quavering trill of victory.

Judith sucked, and sucked, and sucked for breath. The Indians
were at last killing them. Actually.

Theodosia, still carrying Johnnie, staggered, then cried aloud,
"God is the refuge of his saints!"

A single stroke of lightning flashed beyond the trees. Then
came a drum of thunder. The forward sheeting edge of a cloud
bank began to cover the sun. Brightness gradually dimmed off.

The white women gaggled in terror.

Vikes tumbled down from the wagon seat and scrambled in
between his grays. His eyes rolled wild, from side to side. His
mouth hung open like a zigzag rectangle. He grabbed hold of the
hames and hung on. He shook in such fear, the grays leaned away
from him.

The boy Ted jumped down from the wagon and ran to his
mother and hugged her around the legs. Theodosia settled to her
heels, her slat sunbonnet folding over Ted and Johnnie like
spreading wings.

Angela was next to leap off the wagon and run to her mother.
Judith knelt in the grass. They threw their arms around each other
and cried aloud in one voice.

Maggie Utterback let go with her gun. The ball popped through
the painted chest of a brave, felling him.

Both Mad Bear and Pounce leaped for Silvers with a yell.

Silvers fired from the hip. He missed them both.

Pounce caught Silvers over the head with his war club, crunching his skull.

Mad Bear let go with his longbow, *whung!* The arrow passed completely through Silvers' heavy body and fell unbloodied on the ground behind him.

Silvers teetered momentarily, caught between the smash of Pounce's war club from behind and the force of Mad Bear's arrow in front, falling neither one way nor the other. Silvers' eyes closed over. At last Silvers' legs caved in, parting at the knees, and he fell in a heap at their feet. Slowly he undulated over on his back.

Pounce dove for him. He sunk his war club into Silvers' brain once more, this time with such force it caused Silvers' body to bound from the ground. In a flash Pounce had his knife out and scalped him. Mad Bear had his knife out too in a whip and scalped what was left of Silvers' hair. Blood filmed over the round skinned skull. Red streamed into the green grass. Pounce and Mad Bear jumped up and began to dance in the grass, waving portions of Silvers' hair in triumph. Both claimed first coup. Both their scalp yells quavered on the thick air.

Tinkling, humped over, stared at the slain body of her white husband. With trembling fingertips she pressed the sides of her brown face. A low brokenhearted tremolo broke from her. Silvers had been her great man husband. It was hard to believe he was so suddenly dead. She stood keening a moment; then, ducking, she ran for the deep cattails in the slough, vanishing from view.

Pounce snatched up a handful of sharp grass and stuffed it into Silvers' open mouth. Pounce laughed down at the dead Silvers, mockingly. "So the white man is eating grass, is he? Ha, ha. Is it not good? Does it not fill the belly? Do you like it better than a horse likes it? Or shall we fill your mouth with your own dung instead? Ha, ha."

There were sudden wolfish barks. A crazy, howling roar rose from the blood-maddened braves. The roaring slowly increased in volume. Deep within it, there next surged up a dark, bellowing counterpoint as if coming out of the earth itself, from a thousand mud lizards, a throaty *rhu*ing undertone.

Angela quivered in Judith's arms. "Are they ready to kill us now, Mama?"

"There, there, darling. Everything will be all right."

"Mama, you won't let them kill me with those knives?"

"Angela."

A heavy squaw made a grab for Angela's soft limbs. She screamed something at Angela.

"Mama, what does she want?"

Judith shook. Judith understood. The squaw said the child's white flesh would taste very good stone-boiled.

"What does she want, Mama?"

"Shh, child. Never mind her. She's crazy."

Vikes still cowered between his grays, eyes flicking from side to side. One of Pounce's warriors, a lean starved wolf of a man, crept on quick light feet behind Vikes and aimed his musket at Vikes's head. He fired. Bullet and eyeball flew paired out of Vikes's right eye socket. Vikes's other eye cocked off to one side. Vikes slid from sight between the grays. The lean wolf of a savage let go with a triumphant war whoop and was upon Vikes to count coup and lift scalp.

The giant Tallak shook himself. And took command. "Head for the deep grass!" he bawled. He grabbed up his three little girls from the wagon like a woman gathering up underwear from a clothesline on the run, and jumped for the slough. His leap was so powerful it carried him beyond the wagon. He landed on his elbows and knees, the three little tykes still tucked close. With another lunge, grasshopper fashion, he vanished. His wife, Benta, carrying the baby, bent low, screaming, scurried behind him. She too vanished into the tall growth.

Judith and Angela, and Theodosia and her two boys, also dove for the slough. Bullets whistled around them. Some shots cut down rushes neatly and crisply, as if the work of an invisible

scythe. A ball ticked Judith's shoulder. The brush of its velocity
hit both her and Angela like the light slap of a lath.

Maggie Utterback and Mavis Harder scrambled after them, also
on hands and knees, gasping, trembling violently.

A bullet caught Maggie Utterback a glancing flick through the
crotch. She yelled, scrambled faster.

"Joe, curse you, where are you?" Maggie Utterback cried. "I've
been hit where you won't like it."

Tallak whispered hoarsely, "Quick, Maggie, load your gun
again. One of us has always got to be ready to fire. So they won't
dare come poking into the slough."

Tallak and Maggie Utterback took turns firing at the Indians.
When Mad Bear's braves climbed to the highest part of the rise
and aimed their shots just under their rising puffs of smoke, both
Tallak and Maggie held their fire.

The children couldn't help but wiggle when bit by an occasional
mosquito. The children's least movement stirred the tops of the
rushes above. Instantly shots rang out, balls cutting through the
thick growth, striking dangerously close. The spent balls fell with
a *plak*ing sound in the muck beyond.

"Tell your kits to lay still!" Maggie Utterback hissed. "Don't
make a move. Not even a finger."

"You can't ask children to lay quiet," Judith protested. A headache began to crack in her head. The headache made a noise like
a door with a rusty hinge. "At least not for very long."

"They've got to. Until it gets dark. Then we'll all try to make
a run for it and head for Fort Ridgely."

Mad Bear's ragged renegades spotted Mrs. Christians in the
wagon. They grabbed her by the heels and dragged her out
through the endgate. She fell with a burdened bounce on the
ground. Her soft face opened in a terrified scream. She still
hugged the loaf of brown bread to her bosom. The lean savages
grinned down at her. She pinched her eyes shut, still screaming.
She appeared to scream on and on without taking breath. Vainly

she tried to have her free arm everywhere at once to protect her belly, around and up and down. One savage knelt and laid his war club across her throat to shut her up. A gargling screech still came from her. Another savage knelt beside her with a flashing knife. He made a single swipe across her mounded belly, cutting through cloth and flesh. He reached in and took out her unborn babe. He cut it from her. Blood squirted everywhere. Mrs. Christians' body lashed up off the ground like the doubling up of a tormented inchworm. She broke free from the war club on her throat. An enormous scream burst from her. Her free arm and both legs flailed out.

The mud-lizard *rhu*ing counterpoint in the howling abruptly changed. It became a merciless triumphant shrilling.

The lean savage stood up and held the bleeding fetus for all to see. The lean savage grinned wickedly. The cross-legged purple fetus shuddered at the sudden touch of air upon its glutinous skin. The fetus resembled a curled-up giant crayfish. An odd rhythmic convulsion shook it. It shat a tiny ball of glistening black dung.

The grinning red devil spotted the single plum tree halfway up the rise. He ran toward it, carrying the fetus by the nape of its neck. He broke off one of the plum tree's prickly branches near the trunk. Taking hold of the fetus by its neck and its crossed feet, he impaled its soft body on the stub of the branch. The soft body jerked, jerked, jerked.

Both Judith and Theodosia saw it from where they lay hidden.

"Animals! Monsters in human shape." Judith shuddered violently. "Worse than wolves even."

"It cannot be true," Theodosia said.

"Hellish outrages." Numbness moved into Judith's brain.

Tallak groaned. "Ya, I should have kept one bullet for Mrs. Christians."

"It cannot be true."

Worse was yet to come. Two other renegades, wearing stolen

stovepipe hats, with clouts dropped and phalluses erect, pushed
aside the arm with the loaf of brown bread and mounted Mrs.
Christians' riven body and raped her in turn.

Mrs. Christians hardly noticed them. She lay staring at her
baby impaled on the plum tree. Popped eyes a ghastly purple, she
slowly stretched her free hand toward her crucified issue. With her
other hand she still hugged to her side the loaf of brown bread.
The bread was saturated with blood.

Judith whispered, "It's enough to make one's eyes want to
vomit."

Her movement stirred the tops of the rushes above. Immediately shots rang out. Balls narrowly grazed her.

Theodosia rose a little on her knees. She stared at the scene,
hazel eyes now black with horror. "May God in his infinite mercy
forgive them."

Pounce ran over and squatted beside Mrs. Christians. With one
chopping swing of his war club he crushed her skull. White brains
instantly pudged out behind, oozing through her hair. Pounce
turned in his squatting position. With two quick slashes of his
knife he scalped her private parts. He rose and held his new
trophy up for all to see. He danced the victory coup. "The white
man may count coup in his manner when he debauches the wives
and daughters of the red man. Well, now it is the red man's turn
to count coup in his manner. Houw!"

"Our prize pupil in Christ," Theodosia murmured.

"Theodosia," Judith whispered. "Shhh."

"Our covenant red child."

"Sister, now."

"Such terrible filthy doings."

"Theodosia."

"Vilest of reptiles."

Whitebone and his soldiers' lodge decided to hold a council of
war on the far side of the meadow. They smoked the pipe. So far
they had not joined the massacre. Quietly they gestured among
themselves, every now and then looking over at the screaming

shooting melee. After more talking and looking, they rode in an orderly manner to a knoll near the plum tree. One by one they slid off their ponies and sat in a row on the ground. They watched. Whitebone smoked his gossip pipe meditatively.

The cloudbank in the southwest moved up. It thickened all along the horizon. Soon a black roll formed under it. Lightning spangled down, then thunder boomed dully with long, slow detonation.

A brush of wind came up. It came from the direction of the burning Utterback sod house. On it rode thousands of fine bits of white fluff down.

Maggie Utterback cursed where she lay. She beat the ground. "All them years of picking goslings. Lost, all of it. A handful at a setting. It took years to fill one quilt. Let alone our featherbed."

"They look to me like they're crazy with whiskey," Tallak said. "Somebody must've sold them a barrel of squirrel whiskey last night."

Judith remembered the time she had asked Charlie Silvers what was meant by squirrel whiskey. Silvers sold it. Smiling, Silvers told her squirrel whiskey was made of cheap alcohol, very raw, colored artificially and tinctured with turpentine and the ground-up leaves of fresh tobacco. "It really makes them redskins jump around," Silvers said. "Makes them think they can run up and down a tree like a red squirrel."

There was a rush of squaws and red children over the rise. The squaws raided the wagon, carrying off the canned goods, boxes of clothing, blankets. Ledgers and records exploded into flying bits of paper. The Indian boys latched onto the waiting grays. The grays snorted at their Indian smell, and jerked away, but the Indian boys unhooked them anyway and led them joyfully to their camp. Pounce secured the keg of gunpowder and ordered his braves to lug it to his village. Other braves came along and toppled the wagon over on its side. The wagon made a perfect barricade.

An older squaw, Sunflower, Pounce's squaw, poked quietly

through the rubbish left by the other squaws. She found something. She stooped over and picked it up. A thick book. The lettering on it shone gold.

"Isn't that our Bible?" Judith whispered.

"Yes." Theodosia sighed. "Ah, who knows, perhaps Sunflower will at last be the one true believer we have been looking for."

"What fools we were to leave the reverend's cabin," Tallak said. "This is a perfect trap. They don't have a better slaughter pen in St. Paul. A regular slaughter slough."

Angela touched Judith's arm. "Mama, what is that Indian doing to Uncle Claude?"

Judith looked. "God in heaven."

"Surely there cannot yet be more for my husband to endure?" Theodosia cried.

"Don't look."

But Theodosia looked. The brave who had killed Reverend Codman with a double-barreled shotgun had removed the reverend's heart and was sitting on the ground solemnly eating it slice by slice.

"Animal's Voice," Theodosia said. "One of Pounce's band. He would never come into our mission church. He once shot at our bell while we were holding service. He was always a stubborn blanket Indian. A pagan."

A cannibal. Also a communicant eating a piece of holy bread at a Lord's Supper. Flesh of my flesh. Blood of my blood.

It became very quiet out. The heavy cloud could be heard moving up. There was also the soft sound of lightly threshing rushes. The sweet smell of vegetable decay hung in the hot and sticky air. Dust sifting off the standing reeds made it hard to breathe.

The children whimpered for water. The hummocks were too prickly to sit on and the soft ground between slowly gave way under their bodies. Soon everyone had wet knees and seats.

A grasshopper flicked out. A skink glinted at the edge of a patch of muck. A single red ant kept climbing up and down a slender cattail. An occasional mosquito settled on the back of a hand.

One of Angela's feet fell asleep. She rubbed it. The drowsy look of a lazy kitten came into her blue eyes.

A frog leaped up from near where Angela rubbed her leg. It hit a few rushes, stirring their seeded tops. Immediately shots rang out from the rise.

Mad Bear and Pounce and their men sat down to wait the settlers out. They lolled on the short grass halfway up the rise, guns across their knees.

Presently a few squaws came over the rise carrying food: boiled buffalo meat, flat bread, some of the white man's canned goods. Many of the braves raided the stout plum tree of its yellow fruit. Some of the yellow plums were spotted with blood from the impaled fetus. The fetus was at last dead. The braves spat the plum pits into the grass.

Pounce mocked the whites from where he sat. "My arm is lame from killing so many stinking hairy-faces. Houw."

Mad Bear's body twitched, hungering for something to do.

"Perhaps we should set fire to the slough," Pounce said. "That will drive them out."

"I want the Good Book Woman for my wife," Mad Bear said.

Someone moved in the rushes.

A half-dozen braves instantly lifted their guns and fired. The barrage slapped into the slough.

Mad Bear called down, "If the whites will send up the Good Book Woman we will let the rest of you escape."

Pounce laughed. "Mad Bear, the Good Book Woman is mine. I must have her to help me enter the white man's heaven."

Laughs of derision broke from the long line of waiting braves.

The black roll under the heavy cloud rushed toward the slough. There was a blast of lightning. Thunder.

"Hurry," Pounce cried, looking up at the threatening sky, "hurry, Good Book Woman, come out of the grass or it will rain on your black dress."

Ted asked, "Is Papa truly dead now, Mama?"

"Oh, my child."

"Is he in heaven by now, Mama?"

"Yes, my child."

"Then it won't do any good to make him a birthday cake now, will it? With maple-sugar frosting?"

"Oh, my child."

Again someone made the mistake of stirring in the rushes. Two volleys of flying balls whacked into the muck.

"I'm hit," Mavis said calmly from where she lay hidden.

"Bad?" Tallak called.

"Just tore my dress."

"You sure?"

"Well, there is a little blood."

The cloud bank came on, a high arching cave.

Tallak said, "When it starts to rain pretty soon, I want you all to scatter out some. Everybody. They won't see the grass moving so easy in the rain."

There was a sudden yell on the other side of the slough. Shots followed. There was the sound of hard running.

Judith turned on her heels in the soft oozing muck. Cautiously she peered out.

Mad Bear's men had flushed Crydenwise. Crydenwise was running for his life across a low slope. An Indian named Bone Gnawer, a fine runner, was chasing him, war club raised and ready to smash in his brains. The two made a complete circle of the slough. The seated redskins cheered them on. The two ran directly in front of the hidden whites. Bone Gnawer was so close upon Crydenwise that he stepped in Crydenwise's tracks before the bent grass could rise again.

One of Mad Bear's men slithered his bow through the grass at the running Crydenwise. It was perfectly done. Before Cryden- wise could leap to avoid the bow, it got tangled up between his legs and tripped him. Crydenwise went down. Bone Gnawer overran him a couple of steps, stopped short, turned. Crydenwise rolled

over on his back and began kicking his legs furiously at Bone
Gnawer. Crydenwise held up his hands to ward off the coming
blow. Crydenwise showed his teeth and a low gargle like that of a
cornered mink crackled in his throat. Crydenwise's dark whiskery
face was drawn taut in a final snarl. Bone Gnawer feinted with
his war club; then, before Crydenwise could recover, let it fall
true. There was a sound as of a squash being broken open. Next
came the flash of a knife, the quick twist of a wrist, and Bone
Gnawer came to his feet with a triumphant cry of coup, holding up
a bleeding scalp. There was a roar of triumph from the watching
braves. A series of tremolo whoops rose from the squaws.

Whitebone and his soldiers' lodge sat observing it all, silent,
smoking the pipe.

"There goes our church!" Tallak called out.

Everybody looked. Over the rise lifted a pouring column of
black smoke and snapping flames.

"Now there finally is nothing to show for all those years,"
Theodosia said.

"Them oak beams I cut by hand," Tallak said.

There was no wind. The black smoke rose straight up. It slowly
turned yellow as it towered higher and higher. Gradually it blended
off into the overcast.

Redwings and meadowlarks flew by overhead and hid in the
slough. One redwing hid but a step away from Judith.

The dark roll under the heavy cloud rushed toward them. It
churned rumbling across the prairie. Lightning worked through it
like a dozen burning sparklers. The front edge touched down on
the south arm of Skywater.

Squaws came running with buffalo hides to shelter certain of the
armed men. Rain would soften the taut bowstring and wet the
powder. The rest of the braves scurried for shelter in Pounce's
village.

"We better keep our powder dry too," Tallak advised in a low
voice.

"I've already got mine under," Maggie Utterback said.

"And remember, when the rain starts, everybody scatter out."

"Can we drink the rain, Mama?" Angela whispered.

"Of course, darling."

"I'm hungry too, Mama."

"I know, my kitten, I know. We all are."

Judith slowly shook her head. This was not really happening. It could not be true.

Soon the roar of the storm was upon them. Huge drops fell with plashing thwacks. A wrestling wall of wind rolled over them. Then came buckets of water. The tall grass bent under it. The stiffer cattails kept bending down, then springing back.

The whites scattered out. Judith and Angela moved apart one way, Theodosia and her sons moved another way. Each group became invisible to the other.

A slowly traveling roar came to their ears. Presently hailstones began to pelt into the slough around them. Pieces of ice the size of robin eggs hit them over the head and shoulders and arms. Tallak's children cried out. So did Johnnie Codman.

Angela smiled under the irregular plunking. She quickly caught up a few hailstones and put them in her mouth. "Look, Mama. Mmm, they're good."

Ted scrambled through the rushes and gathered up a handful of hailstones too.

As suddenly as it had come the storm was over. There were no afterdrops.

Sioux children rushed about on the rise, eagerly gathering up hailstones in parfleches. They chattered about the clear cool drink they could now have.

The smell of the swift storm was rinse sweet. It didn't seem possible after such a beautiful rain that people could be skulking for their lives in a green slough. Where was the lovely morning when everybody was still at peace and the gardens and little fields were fat with produce?

The warriors again came out in force on the rise. They checked the powder in their guns. Some fired off their guns to make sure, blasting random shots into the slaughter slough.

"I'm hit!" a voice called out.

"Joe, is that you, you cowardly devil?" Maggie Utterback cried. "So that's where you hid out."

"Yeh. Worse luck."

"Are you hit bad, Joe?"

"A right smart clip over the cheek. It's put my nose out of joint a little."

"You far off, Joe?"

"Stay where you are. I'll bandage it myself."

"Joe, I want you with me when I'm killed." Maggie Utterback's voice softened. "Joe."

"Woman, if you know what's good for you, for godsakes stay put."

More random shots smashed into the muck.

Benta screamed. She screamed and screamed. Presently she began to cry in a strangled manner.

Tallak tried to comfort her.

Judith called across to them. "Is she hit bad, Tallak?"

"They got her in the bowels."

Benta groaned. From the sound of it she was dying. Benta moaned, "Stay where you are, Judith."

"Ya," Tallak said. "They will see you move through the grass."

Theodosia prayed. "Father in heaven, look down upon us in thy infinite mercy. Thy servants are—"

"Ahhh," Benta gasped, and died.

The four Aanenson girls began to wail.

"Kits!" Tallak bawled. "Shh! They will shoot us all."

"Is Mama dead?"

"Shh." Tallak sobbed. "Poor Benta. She never blamed nor blabbed."

More balls snarled through the rushes. Seed tops spilled open.

"God!" Tallak groaned.

"Tallak?" Judith called. "Tallak!"

"They got me, missus."

"Tallak?"

There was a long low moan. The moan tailed off. Silence.

The oldest Aanenson girl stopped crying. "Now Papa is dead."

Dogs from Pounce's village came trotting over the rise, pink tongues out and lolling. They had smelled blood and got loose. They ran down to where Reverend Codman and Silvers and Crydenwise lay. They sniffed the bodies, hesitated, then, stiff-legged, ruffs rising, backed away. After a moment, slinking, moaning a little, they ran back to the village.

"How be you now, Joe?" Maggie Utterback called.

"Like an old beaver, I can still wag my tail."

"It sure is fierce the way things worked out."

"It surely is."

"Them fool red devils with their overdeveloped war bumps."

Some of the braves began to use Mrs. Christians' body for target practice. The body jumped on each shot and slid down the rise an inch or so. The braves jeered the dead woman.

"The whites are the greatest fools I have ever seen," Pounce taunted. "Dakotas, look at the whites puffing there in the grass, where it is hot, while we sit here in peace on the rise, where there is a breeze."

Bone Gnawer sat on his heels and looked at where Crydenwise lay. "It is fun to kill the white man. The white man runs away and leaves his squaws to be killed by the enemy. He is a coward." Bone Gnawer's spotted clout brushed the ground as he rocked on his heels. "One Dakota can kill ten white men without trying."

"Good Book Woman, come out," Pounce called. "We will not hurt the women and children. It is only the cowardly white men we want to kill."

Silence.

"Come out."

"Pounce?" Joe Utterback called weakly. "Come down here."

Pounce snorted. "Ha, you are surrounded and cannot escape. You come up here."

"I'm about done in. I can't come up. I'm soon gone under."

"Joe!" Maggie Utterback cried. "You can't leave me now."

"Maggie, old gal, if I had a tail like a dog, you know what I'd do. I'd wag it to show you how much I luv you."

There was the sound of scrambling in the rushes. Footsteps squished in muck.

The Dakotas spotted Maggie Utterback wriggling through the grass. Immediately shots rang out.

Maggie Utterback found Joe. "There you be. Why, man, you're mortal hit."

"Yeh." Joe Utterback spoke in gasps. "That last bullet . . . put a hump in my back. I feel like a cat . . . that's et too much glue."

"Joe."

"Bye, Maggie. Sorry I stomped you . . . when we first got married."

A short passage of heavy breathing followed; then ended.

"He's dead," Maggie said, flat.

Mad Bear called down. "Good Book Woman, you must be my wife."

Theodosia at last staggered to her feet. "This has gone far enough," she said. "We shall all be killed if we remain here much longer. We shall have to throw ourselves upon their mercy." Theodosia stepped onto a wobbling hummock and waved her arm. "Pounce, brother in Christ, I am coming out."

Pounce stood up. He held up his left hand to halt the rifle fire. "It is good. Let the Good Book Woman come up."

Theodosia took Johnnie in her arms. She led Ted by the hand.

"Where is your sister?" Pounce asked. "The woman with the sunned hair? She must be my wife also. I have need of many wives, now that the white man has been chased off the red man's hunting grounds."

Judith hugged Angela close.

Theodosia looked back. "Sister, I think you'd best come too. Let us accept this cup for the sake of our children. If we do it for the children, it will perhaps after all not be a fate worse than death. Christ will understand. He will forgive."

Dumb, Judith got to her feet.

"Judith, you fool," Mavis cried, "don't you see it's another trick? They will kill the children and then you two will be slaves for the rest of your lives. Slaves to a squaw."

"I'm afraid Theodosia is right," Judith said. "It is our only chance to save the children. Our men are all dead now. We have to look at it practical."

"It's a trick."

Judith took Angela by the hand. Judith tried to smile; found her lips frozen stiff.

Theodosia stepped up the rise, stiff, erect.

Pounce held up the flat of his hand against Theodosia. "Wait. We wish to make sure the white men are all dead. Tell us if they are dead."

"They're dead, all right. May God have mercy on their souls."

"Bring the guns with you. Go back and get them."

"You see me with my children. I cannot bring the guns."

"Where is the loud woman who has the voice of a man? Let her carry the guns."

"Maggie?" Theodosia spoke calmly, utterly resigned. "Comply with his request, won't you? We are in no position to argue. Come out with all the guns."

"Comply, is it?" Maggie raged from her hiding place in the rushes. "When they've killed my Joe?"

"Please, Maggie."

"No, and be damned to you."

Theodosia sighed. "All right." Again she started up the rise, tall, erect.

Pounce took her hand when she reached the top of the rise and shook it. "Look," Pounce called down to those still hidden. "You see? We do not kill the women and children. Hurry out or soon the young braves will set the grass on fire."

"Set the grass on fire?" Maggie snarled back. "After the rain we just had?"

Pounce smiled. Tiny muscles worked under the skin of his pock-marked face. "Come out. We have promised not to touch the women and children."

Judith fought off the terrible headache cracking in her brain. "Mavis? Take Tallak's children with you. We shall perhaps all be spared, at that."

"Spared, my arse," Maggie Utterback said.

After a moment Mavis appeared, carrying one of Tallak's girls. The other three blond heads followed her. Mavis limped badly. There was a mat of blood over her thigh.

The braves of both Mad Bear's and Pounce's bands came running up. They formed two lines from the slough to the top of the rise. The women and children walked up through the gauntlet.

Whitebone and his men sat watching, impassive. They had put the pipe away.

Pounce also held out his hand to shake hands with Judith. The swirls of white clay on Pounce's chest and the red paint on his nose and the yellow stripes on his chin had run some in the rain.

Judith, numb, was about to shake Pounce's hand, when her eye caught something. Pounce was wearing a pair of leather work gloves. The gloves were those her brother-in-law Claude often wore when he worked in the garden. Judith shuddered. Judith could only wonder at what Theodosia's thoughts were when she shook the gloved hand. Judith drew back her hand.

Angela's deep-blue eyes opened like that of an animal suddenly alert to extreme danger. A little fire had come alive in her eyes. "Mother, now?" Angela spoke with thickened lips.

"Child."

Mad Bear came stomping up. His big mobile lips were drawn back. His eyes boiled wild and worked in spasms. "Let us count coup on the women the white man way. Let us take them into the bushes and abuse them. I have said."

Pounce held up his right hand. "Let my Dakota brother remember that the Good Book Woman and her sister are spoken for. They are mine to wive. The loose woman with the blood on her hip and the woman who talks like a man, those my Dakota brother can have."

Mad Bear stood stock still. He swelled. The big yellow painted circle around his right eye gave him the look of a devil incarnate. He trembled to strike Pounce. "Let us count coup on all the women the white man's way!"

Theodosia spoke up. "This you cannot do with me. The time of the red flowers has come upon me, and I must withdraw from the presence of men." A blush stole over her freckled face. The blush made her look quite becoming.

Both Pounce and Mad Bear saw the blush. A knowing look flashed between them. The Good Book Woman was one of those who could not lie with a straight face.

The crazy squaw broke through the braves circling the two white women. She headed for Angela to pinch her again. Judith quickly stepped in front of Angela, shielding her. Blocked, the crazy squaw began to rage. She grabbed Pounce's war club from him and turned on Ted instead and hit him over the head with it. Ted, stunned, almost toppled over. Blood began to stream down his face. He screamed for his mother. Blinded by blood, he groped around for her. He staggered past her, unseeing.

That was all Pounce needed. He grabbed Theodosia so hard by the arm, he parted her from little Johnnie. Johnnie fell to the ground with a thud. Before Johnnie could begin to cry, the crazy squaw hit him over the head too, crying, "The soft flesh of the white child will taste very good stone-boiled." Blood whelmed over Johnnie's baby face. Ted staggered around until he fell over Johnnie's body. The two towheads recognized each other and, still unseeing, hugged each other.

Pounce gave Theodosia another jerk, hard. Then he forcibly led her away to a small patch of wolfberries. He hit her over the back of the neck and she disappeared from sight. Drawing aside his clout, he also sank from sight.

Mad Bear grabbed Judith by the arm and tore her away from Angela.

At that, Bone Gnawer caught hold of Angela.

Two Two appeared from nowhere. He was crying. He put his arms around Angela's middle and sought to wrest her from Bone Gnawer. Two Two cried, "What! Can a grown man desire to wive a little child who still plays with dolls?"

Bone Gnawer sneered at Two Two. "Little Brother, a war has come. We have lost many braves to the far-shooting wagon-guns of the white man. We thirst for the blood of the white man so that the spirits of our dead may depart happy. The spirits of our dead braves weep for the blood. We wish to be free of the weeping spirits. Thus the white man must die. He has stolen our land. He is losing the fight in the South. We will strike the coup the white man's way. We will teach him what he has taught us."

Two Two still clung to Angela. "But this child is a virgin."

"Ha. Can it be that my little brother wishes to play at wiving in the bushes with this child virgin and thus at last learn the way of a man with a woman? Ha ha." With that, Bone Gnawer bumped Two Two aside so hard, Two Two fell to the ground.

There was a roar of ruttish whoops. All was confusion. Angela vanished. Other braves grabbed the bleeding Mavis and threw her upon the ground. The crazy squaw clubbed all of Tallak's little blond girls until they were dead. Still other braves ran down into the slough to flush out Maggie Utterback and Tinkling.

Judith felt herself being led along so swiftly she couldn't get her heels set into the ground to resist.

It was all a dream. It had to be.

Suddenly Judith fancied she could hear her mother calling her. "Judith! Judith!" She remembered how her mother used to stand in the door of their old farmhouse near Davenport, gazing toward the broad mighty West with her deep and yearning eyes. Her mother had often wondered what life was like for her daughter Theodosia.

"Angela!" Judith shrieked.

Mad Bear threw Judith down. Sharp grass worked through Judith's dress. It prickled into her back and buttocks. Mad Bear caught her by the throat with one hand and shook her like a mad dog shaking a doll. With his other hand he ripped up her clothes. A sudden punching knee and he stunned her in the belly so that her legs flew apart. He was already erect outside his clout. She gasped for breath. Mad Bear's phallus resembled the neck of a wild swan. Judith scratched him. She clawed him. She tried to knee him in turn.

Judith's struggling only helped Mad Bear. He was brutally, fiendishly strong. Through her mind shot the wish that oh! had she only taken to wearing bloomers. Bloomers had lately become quite the style. She remembered the advertisement she had seen in *Harper's Weekly* just before coming down to Skywater. Bloomers would have given her a wee bit more time to fend him off.

Mad Bear's big yellow-painted eye was immediately upon her. It glowed with an unholy fire right in her eye. She felt his necklace of human fingers tickling her. She felt him make entrance. For a moment it was cold. An urgent thrust or two and it became quickly warm. For a moment it also hurt. But then it became easier. Part of her body was betraying her.

Judith heard a child's last cry on earth, piercing, desolate; choked off.

"Angela!"

Judith fainted.

Judith was already sitting up when she came to. Mad Bear was hurrying off toward the patch of wolfberries where Pounce had taken Theodosia.

There was loud laughter and japing behind a cluster of braves. It was where Judith remembered Two Two had fallen to the ground.

"Angela!"

Animal's Voice came running for her.

Judith backed away, bowing deep at the waist. "Oh, God. Not you." She could still see Animal's Voice eating Reverend Codman's heart slice by slice.

Animal's Voice came on. He grabbed her by the hair and jerked her head backward. He wrenched her so hard she almost broke at the hips.

Judith closed her eyes. She whimpered.

Someone bellowed in outrage beside her. It was Pounce. He roared something in Dakota. Animal's Voice let go of her.

Judith opened her eyes. She saw dimly.

Animal's Voice looked at Pounce, amazed. Were not the white women to be used as the white men had often abused the Dakota virgins?

"I have spoken for both the Good Book Woman and her sister," Pounce raged. "They are mine." Pounce's big belly quivered. The white clay on his broad chest was now a smear of gray. "They will sit at my fire."

Animal's Voice gave Pounce a glitteringly envious look.

Pounce said, "Where is Mad Bear?"

Animal's Voice said with a sneer, "He lies in the bushes with the Good Book Woman. Where you left her weeping bitterly."

Pounce grabbed Judith by the wrist and started to run with her toward the wolfberry bushes.

"No!" Judith cried. "Where do you take me?"

"I wish to save your sister. Come."

Even as he spoke, Mad Bear erupted from the wolfberries. Mad Bear adjusted his clout. He came straddling toward Pounce. His yellow-painted eye glared furiously. It seemed to protrude from his head. It resembled a ball of fire.

Mad Bear said, "Does my brother Dakota wish for something?"

"The Good Book Woman will sit at my fire. Not yours. Also her sister. I have said." Pounce put his arm around Judith the white man way. He tried to nuzzle her cheek affectionately.

Judith ducked her head down and away. Pounce's face was as rough as a warty potato.

Mad Bear snarled. "Ha, what is left of your Good Book Woman lies there a broken cornstalk on the ground."

Pounce's rough face slowly blackened over. The crazy squaw stood near and Pounce grabbed his war club back from her. He waggled his war club menacingly. It worked up and down like the snapping tail of an angry tomcat.

Suddenly Pounce was surrounded by members of Mad Bear's war party. All carried clubs.

"What is this?" Pounce cried.

Mad Bear whipped off his clout and hit Pounce in the face with it.

Pounce seemed to constrict. "What is this?" he repeated.

Pounding hearts.

Then Pounce knew. Mad Bear had once more decided to turn on his own kind. "My father often warned me never to trust a Santee Dakota who is a Sisseton," Pounce sputtered, "they of the fish smell. I see now that an outcast Sisseton is even less to be trusted." Pounce had been a fool to align himself with the smeary Sisseton renegade killer. Pounce's hair slowly rose on end like the quills on a porcupine.

Mad Bear's painted yellow eye looked like a burnt hole in a blanket. He gestured, curtly.

Pounce was suddenly clubbed from all sides. One of the blows broke his left arm above the elbow and immediately the fingers below it splayed out as if paralyzed. Another blow caught him over the head and teeth sprinkled out of his mouth like kernels of wild rice threshed from a sheaf. He was killed on the spot.

Mad Bear grabbed Judith by the elbow. Mad Bear spoke to Bone Gnawer. "You, Gnawer of Bones, take this white woman to my tepee. Also the Good Book Woman lying in the brush."

Bone Gnawer took hold of Judith and led her to one side. Bone Gnawer commanded another brave named Born Without Testicles to get Theodosia.

After a moment Theodosia appeared. With a great effort of will Theodosia managed to walk erect. White clay was smeared over the front of her dark dress. With her free hand she straightened out her slat bonnet.

Theodosia kept looking for something. Craning her neck, she finally saw it. Her husband, Claude. She said to Born Without Testicles, "I wish to weep a moment over the body of my dead husband."

Born Without Testicles suffered her.

Theodosia knelt beside the mutilated body of Reverend Codman. She ignored the great bloody rent in his chest. She ignored the blasted back of his head. With her fingertips she touched his face, lightly, tenderly. She stroked his bold nose. She kissed his closed eyes, each in turn. Finally she kissed his cold, fallen lips.

"He was a man of God," Theodosia said. "He would never lock the door of his home. His church was always open to the stranger, heathen or infidel or Christian. Often when we arose in the morning we found our friends the Dakotas camped on the floor." Theodosia's hazel eyes were calm. Her many freckles seemed to have faded. She shed no tears. "Husband, I have been outraged. Yet I have remained faithful in mind and heart to our redeemer Jesus Christ. Soon I shall be with you in heaven and we shall sit together on the right hand of our Lord and Saviour." Theodosia put a hand on her knee and stood up. She turned. She looked to where her Ted and Johnnie lay bleeding together. "Treachery, thy name is Dakota." A film slid over her eyes. "And yet, remembering Christ, I am commanded to forgive thee. I do forgive thee."

There was a boiling of young braves nearby.

Judith turned to look.

The young braves were standing around someone lying on the ground. Their backs were toward her.

Off to one side Two Two lay quivering on the grass. Of a sudden he sat up. His black eyes rolled. He remembered. He panted for breath. His young mobile lips worked. He sprang to his feet.

He grabbed a war club from the nearest warrior and in blind rage began to beat the coppery backs of the braves in front of him. His wild fury opened a path into the center of the japing braves. He cried a name.

Then Judith cried the same name. "Angela!"

With a desperate twist of her body, Judith broke free of Bone Gnawer. She gathered up her skirt and ran into the middle of the snickering braves. She stopped short, and rose on her toes. She covered her mouth.

What she saw not even the devil should see. It was all a scarlet nightmare.

Angela was lying on her back, slim child arms and golden legs staked to the ground and silver-blond hair outspread upon the grass. Her green dress was torn to shreds. She had been opened with a scalping knife and afterward had been outraged by God only knew how many bullish savages. Her child lips hung wyed off to one side in a last fixed grimace and her kittenish eyes still stared unseeing at the blue sky above.

Angela. Her sweet belly violated. And dead.

2

A silence spread around Judith. Even the boyish bellowing of Two Two was stilled.

Judith turned stiffly to look where the others looked.

A horseman was coming. He came swiftly from the northeast, from the direction of Fort Ridgely. It was an Indian on a spotted red-and-white stallion. The Indian rode hard. The spotted stallion was almost spent. The Indian rode naked except for a clout. A moment of sunlight made his body gleam, coppery, shining from the passing rain.

Judith blinked, blinked.

The naked Indian wore a single scarlet feather. It was Scarlet Plume.

Numbly Judith watched Scarlet Plume pull up in front of where Whitebone and his band of soldier Dakota sat. She watched Scarlet Plume slide to earth. She watched him sit on the ground in front of Whitebone, the others gathering around. She watched them light the pipe and pass it—the inviolable Dakota custom of never taking measure without first smoking the pipe.

Presently they finished the pipe and solemnly put it away. And at last Scarlet Plume spoke. He spoke shortly, a few words.

Whitebone bounded to his feet. He harangued his soldiers' lodge with strong gestures, speaking rapidly. He reached down and picked up a pinch of dust and threw it into the air.

All of his braves instantly leaped to their feet and ran for their war ponies. A succession of sharp wolfish barks and they rushed straight for Mad Bear's and Pounce's bands. The dark riders came on with such ferocity, they scattered the standing savages. Both motley bands ran for the slough. It was only then that Judith saw there had been three other snickering clusters of Indians, each of them standing around prostrate women staked to the ground: Mavis, Maggie Utterback, and Tinkling. A dozen of the dark riders dropped to the ground and freed the three women.

Scarlet Plume came walking over. His exhausted spotted stallion followed him like a tame dog.

Scarlet Plume's grave face was cracked with grief. He still wore the yellow dot inside a blue circle on his left cheekbone. The wind had combed his loose black hair back behind his ears. His single eagle feather glowed scarlet. Rain lay drying on his broad shoulders.

Scarlet Plume went straight for Two Two and put his arms around him. He murmured something to him. Then he turned him away and with a gentle brotherly shove started him toward Whitebone's village.

Eyes averted, with delicate consideration, Scarlet Plume stooped down and straightened out Angela's green dress. He drew his knife and cut the thongs binding her to the stakes. He composed her limbs. He gently touched her eyelids in the corners, and her eyes closed of themselves.

He rose, turned, and stood towering over Judith. The low sun struck a glancing rainbow off his red-brown chest. He held out his hand the white man way. He spoke. There was thoughtful regard in his voice. It was almost impersonal. "The white woman feels sad. I want to shake hands with her. That is all I have to say."

Judith, numb, let him take her hand and shake it.

"We shall bury your daughter in the proper manner."

Judith nodded.

Mad Bear was the only one of his band who had stood his ground.

Whitebone rode directly up to Mad Bear. Six of Whitebone's stern armed soldiers' lodge rode with him. They surrounded Mad Bear, bows and arrows drawn.

Without ceremony Whitebone said down to Mad Bear, his voice full of contempt, "Hear me. Scarlet Plume brings the news. The white man with his wagon-gun wins at the fort called Ridgely. Hear me. The Bad Talkers with their forks also win at The Place Where There Is A Cottonwood Grove On The River. New Ul-m. What was begun in foolishness now ends in foolishness. We must fly. Hear me. Your people have taken away the riches of the whites in this place. Well, we shall take what is left, the white women. You are neither a true Dakota nor a cut-hair Christian. You are worse than a white fool. Once again we must drive you away from the council fires of the good Dakota. You are a bad creature. You have the black hungers of an evil spirit. You count a bull's coup on the white women like the white fool. You marry your relations. It has been told that some of your men cohabit with animals freshly slaughtered. Therefore we shall take the white women from you and keep them safe from your bad warriors. Also we need them."

Mad Bear heard him out with slowly mounting rage. He foamed at the mouth like a wild beast.

Whitebone waited.

There was nothing Mad Bear could do. He stood alone. His cowardly men, and Pounce's shabby warriors, had been scattered into the prairie slough like frightened quail.

Mad Bear looked at Judith. He looked at Theodosia. He looked at craven Tinkling. He looked at cursing Maggie Utterback. He looked at bleeding Mavis. Finally he said, "I will take the shot-up white woman there." He pointed at Mavis. "She will be a burden to you as you fly across the prairie. But to me she will be better than two dead squaws."

Whitebone reined in his restive war pony. He sneered down at Mad Bear. "We will take all the white women. You cannot have the shot-up woman. We will keep them all. We will also keep the trader's wife, the red woman with the bent neck. Go. Join your cowards in the deep grass. I have said."

A sudden loud wail of lamentation rose nearby. It was Sunflower. She had just found Pounce, her husband, dead. She still carried the Bible under her arm and the gold lettering on it glinted in the falling sunlight.

Then another squaw set up a death cry. The second squaw had just found Angela lying dead upon the ground. The second squaw was the sister of Sunflower. From her lament it was apparent she had planned to adopt Angela to replace a lost daughter. "My white daughter. Why were you killed? Now I shall miss you as much as I miss my own red daughter."

Light faded in Judith's eyes. She fell on the prairie grass.

PART TWO

Dell Rapids

Young hands tugged at her. They were urgent. A young boy's voice in a strange tongue called to her again and again. "Woman With The Sunned Hair, arise. The time has come to hurry."

Judith opened her eyes. It was Two Two. His earnest Indian face almost touched hers nose to nose. He was weeping over her.

"Where?" she whispered.

"Come. Hurry. The camp removes to another place. My father has said."

Judith sat up. The rose of a lingering sunset tinged the grass and the trees. The sky above bloomed with a luminous pink. Everything seemed to have been rinsed in warm blood.

"Come." Two Two took her by the hand and helped her to her feet.

It was as if Two Two were breaking her out of a cast of ice. Her whole skull still cracked with the terrible headache. She also felt beaten deep in the seat. Someone must have kicked her many times while she lay unconscious.

"You must hurry. The great wagon-guns come and they will kill us." Two Two tugged at her hands.

Dazed, Judith stumbled along beside Two Two. She saw White-bone riding ahead. Warriors of his soldiers' lodge rode on either side of him. Theodosia was being led by Scarlet Plume, Mavis was being led by Scarlet Plume's brother Traveling Hail, Maggie Utterback was being led by a brave named Bullhead. Tinkling walked alone. All were headed straight for Whitebone's camp.

An evening wind from the west had come up and the deep grass rolled in pink waves toward them. The smell of sweet rain still hung in the grass.

Whitebone stopped in front of his tepee and slid off his horse. Two Two ran to hold the bridle. Judith stood alone. Whitebone called a name. An old man known as Walking Voice, the village crier, emerged from a nearby tepee. He came over in a shuffling run. Whitebone spoke to him quietly in a low voice.

Walking Voice listened carefully. His old rheumy brown eyes looked from side to side. Slowly his old eyes lighted up with intelligence. Walking Voice was being given something to do. When Whitebone finished speaking, Walking Voice turned and, again in a stiff, shuffling run, made the rounds within the camp circle, proclaiming aloud in a clear, deep voice so all could hear: "Hear me. The white man has a new weapon. Where once he wore a long knife, he now shoots a wagon-gun. It is a terrible weapon. It kills many women and children at one time. He is coming with it. We must flee. Game is now a long distance from our camp. Therefore make ready to remove immediately. We will journey in the dark until the moon rises. It is late in the day yet it must be done."

The dusky people came out of their tepees. They looked to where an emblem adorned the top of Whitebone's lodge. The emblem was part of the jawbone of Unkteri. Two great teeth, the size of teacups, were still left in the jawbone. The two teeth together were just enough to suggest what had once been the grin of an ancient terror, the dinosaur. The white emblem was White-bone's medicine, after which he had been named. No female was allowed to touch his great medicine. It was said to be fatal if she did.

Whitebone took hold of one of the loose lodgepoles of his tepee, the one to which the white jawbone was attached, and gently lowered it. He pointed the emblem southwest, away from the wagon-guns. He hung the emblem near the ground on a tripod. It meant the journey would be a long one.

Whitebone settled on a stump for a last smoke on his gossip pipe. Other braves also sat down near their homesites for a last smoke.

"I ache so," Judith said.

No one heard her. Each of the four white women was encased in her own desolation.

An old woman came out of Whitebone's tepee and set out a papoose wrapped in a buckskin cradle. The old woman leaned the cradle against the stump Whitebone sat on.

Squaws boiled at their work in the lingering pink twilight. Tepees collapsed, and were rolled up almost as if by magic. Tailless dogs were harnessed to short travois and given light loads. Tame ponies were harnessed to long travois and loaded down with heavy goods. The womenfolk worked grimly, swiftly.

After a bit, Whitebone noted that Judith wasn't helping the old woman take down his tepee. Also the papoose squalled beneath him. A gathering frown pinched his old lips, making his sharp cheekbones jut out even more. Removing his short red pipe, he finally said to Judith, "Woman, can you not help her?"

Judith mouthed soundless words.

"Woman?"

Judith licked dry lips.

"My wife has taken the south road. She is gone and my little son cries. Therefore the old woman of my lodge, my mother, Smoky Day, has come to live with me to care for my little son. But my mother is very old and feeble. Therefore you must help her with the lodge."

Judith glanced around. Theodosia still stood with head bowed

where Scarlet Plume had left her. Mavis, still bleeding down her
thigh a little, was trying to take down a tepee for Traveling Hail
and getting herself all tangled up in the folds of the hide shelter.
Maggie Utterback stood balky in front of Bullhead's lodge.

The papoose squalled and squalled. It struggled to be free of its
bonds.

"Woman?" Whitebone asked again.

"I can't," Judith said helplessly. "I know nothing of this."

"Have you milk? Perhaps you can give him breast to pacify
him." Whitebone threw her a turtle's wrinkled look.

Judith started. It was as if someone had ripped her dress from
the neck down, exposing her bosom. She looked at the little brown
face sobbing its heart out on its cradleboard.

"Have you milk?"

Judith kneeled beside it, her seat and hipbones aching so
sharply she thought she would break. "There, there," she crooned.
"There, there, little one." She rocked the cradleboard gently.

The little mouth fell silent and the little black eyes opened. Two
trickles glistened under its nose in the pink dusk.

Smoky Day smiled an old cracked grimace. "The child's name is
Born By The Way." Smoky Day puffed as she rolled up the lodgepoles in a bundle. "Have you milk?"

Judith shook her head.

Whitebone next spotted Tinkling standing alone, head bowed.
Again removing his gossip pipe, he said, in a kind voice, "Has no
one taken you to wife? Come then. Help my old mother with the
lodge. You will live with us until some warrior takes you to wife."

Tinkling was as one forgiven of a crime. She awoke from her
standing trance, shook her head to clear it, then rushed to help
Smoky Day.

Whitebone went back to puffing his gossip pipe and contem-
plation.

Judith rocked the papoose.

Bullhead, smoking his pipe, big head held meditatively to one
side, soon saw that his tepee wasn't coming down. Instead his new

wife, Maggie Utterback, was standing in the grass as stiff and as unmoving as an old gooseberry bush. Bullhead reared back on his seat, greatly offended. He grunted. "Woman That Walks Ahead Of Her Man, it is late. Soon the blue soldiers come to shoot us. Take down your tepee. Hurry."

"Go to hell," Maggie Utterback growled, hands on her hips and a sneer on her whiskery face.

Bullhead did not understand the white words. But he understood the intonation. He leaped to his feet in sudden wrath. "My woman was killed by a horse. I have taken you to replace her. She was a good worker. Now it is your turn."

"The nerve of these brutes," Judith thought. "Yet if we don't act like their way is dead right, we'll be killed too. Like my poor Angela was."

Maggie Utterback glared at Bullhead. "My turn? Why, durn you, after what them squaws done to me there in the slough, it ain't never gonna be my turn. Not never." She began to froth at the lips over the outrage she had suffered. "Getting that durn dog to run his tongue into me, and then trying to have him line me, with me staked to the ground, that was awful. Awful. Why, it's enough to make a body gall-sick to think she might've had a litter of pups. And the worst was when them durn squaws laughed at me that I was no good that even a dog would not use me." All of a sudden Maggie Utterback's hands came off her hips and she swung a fist at Bullhead with all her might. She caught him full on the jaw, and he went down as if cut off at the ankles by a scythe. He lay stunned on the ground.

Work stopped. Everybody stared. A gasp went through the camp. Even Whitebone removed his gossip pipe from his lips a moment.

Maggie Utterback said, "By God, I never let my Joe boss me around. So I sure as hell ain't gonna let you start, you filthy red nigger."

Bullhead recovered his wits. He bounded up from the grass, war club in hand. His big head seemed to swell to twice its size.

His cheeks burned black. Maggie Utterback had put a bad face on him. Unforgivable. Bullhead spoke in a tight, choked voice. "Once I saw a white man strike another white man with his hand made up into a club. But never have I seen a white woman strike a man in this manner. Also you walk ahead of a man. You must be one of those whom the gods gave a wrong spirit at birth. I do not want you for a wife. I put you away. Also you have offended the memory of my wife. She was a good worker. Therefore you must be punished." Bullhead rose up on his toes and with his war club hit Maggie Utterback over the head with all his power. She plunged more than fell to the ground. She was instantly dead. Her head lay open on the grass like a decayed pumpkin stepped on by a horse.

Another gasp of astonishment went through the village. This time all eyes turned away.

Judith sat as one who was sightless. A lullaby mummed on her lips.

Bullhead looked around. He spotted Theodosia standing alone, head bowed, waiting for the inevitable.

Bullhead stepped across to her. Bullhead said, "Good Book Woman, has Scarlet Plume taken you to wife? I saw him leading you to our camp."

Theodosia did not move.

Bullhead looked toward the center of the encampment. "I see that Scarlet Plume helps the soldiers' lodge take down their tepee. I see he does not want you. Come with me. All that I have is yours. All that was my wife's is yours. I will hunt every day for you. I will bring you many scalps and much honor. Come, take down the tepee. Read in your Good Book if you do not know how. Also, I will help you the first time."

Theodosia finally looked up. Her face was as an ash leaf in winter. All color had faded from it. She looked up at the high red sky of dusk above. Her lips moved in silent prayer. Then she stepped toward Bullhead's lodge and set to work.

Bullhead helped her. To Bullhead's surprise, Theodosia knew

much about the tepee. Neither one looked at the slain Maggie Utterback lying to one side in the deep slough grass.

Walking Voice, the camp crier, continued to make his rounds, urging the people to hurry. They had a far way to go before the moon rose.

When all was ready, Scarlet Plume strode over and stood in front of Whitebone. Scarlet Plume's sweaty body gleamed a deep red-brown in the purple dusk. "The people and their tepees are all afoot. They stand to go."

Whitebone knocked the ashes out of his gossip pipe. He got slowly to his feet. "Where is my horse Snort?"

Two Two came running with a black-and-white spotted pony. "I have him ready, my father."

Whitebone smiled. His old face crinkled with it. "My son, take the horse to Traveling Hail's new wife. Tell her that she must not walk with her bleeding limb. We wish her a long life with her new husband. Tell her that Snort will carry her safely if she will nŏt sit the white woman way, with both legs ready to jump down, but as a man with legs apart. I have said."

Two Two beamed a wide boyish smile. It made him glad to see that his father wished to be kind to a stranger. He ran over with the restive pony and helped Mavis get on. Traveling Hail seemed pleased too.

"I will walk at the head of my people as in the old days," Whitebone said.

But something still was not right for Scarlet Plume. Scarlet Plume's black eyes glittered. He towered over Whitebone. His head jerked every now and then to one side, shaking the loose black hair on his shoulders. The yellow dot inside the blue circle on his left cheekbone was almost worn off. A tremble shook his legs.

"Why are your eyes black, my son?" Whitebone asked.

Scarlet Plume looked over at where Maggie Utterback lay dead in the grass. "We cannot let her be eaten by the wolves. She also had a people who once loved her. Even as the girl child of Sunned Hair."

"My son, do as your heart tells you. But afterward, you will guard the rear of our marching camp?"

"Traveling Hail, my brother, and two others will help me. He has a robe which we shall wrap around her body. We will place her on a scaffold. Will this offend the Good Book God? We do not wish to offend Him, but to save her bones from the wolves. Her spirit will weep in our dreams if we do not help her.

"Have you spoken with the Good Book Woman about this?"

Scarlet Plume considered. "It is a good thing to ask." He went over and talked to Theodosia in a low voice. For a quick moment the trace of a wan grimace came to Theodosia's lips.

Scarlet Plume returned to Whitebone's side. "The Good Book Woman says it is a good thing to do. I have said."

"Afterward, guard the marching camp well, my son."

A muscle twitched in Scarlet Plume's left cheek. He still seemed agitated.

"Well, my son?"

"Father, you are my mother's brother. You know that nothing lies between us. We have no secrets from each other. I ask this. Is it not time we removed Bullhead from our camp? When he becomes angry he is like one demented. He is like some of the whites, wild without reason. Father, he belongs with Mad Bear's renegades. Let us throw him out."

"My son, he is a good fighter. He brings in the game. He feeds many mouths. He is a great stealer of horses. All this I cannot forget."

"He will kill the Good Book Woman before we reach the game in a new place. This will be a bad thing. She has never done anyone harm. She has shown us many times that she loves the red man."

"My son, I will watch him. I will see that he treats her as a good Yankton should treat his woman. He is a sad man, even as you and I are sad. He too has lost a good wife on the south road."

Scarlet Plume's eyes half closed in reverie. A sad expression touched his large, mobile lips; then, willing it, he put it away.

Whitebone took up the weathered jawbone of the dinosaur. Great age and much drying had caused the emblem to become as light as a wasp nest. Even the two ancient teeth were light, like white puffballs. Slowly Whitebone led the way. The emblem seemed to give off a soft phosphorescent glow in the purpling dark. Four venerable headmen walked with Whitebone.

Women, children, old people, dogs followed the leaders. Camp soldiers walked guard along either side. Judith carried the papoose. Smoky Day had helped her shoulder it onto her back. Smoky Day rode on a travois, sitting on her packed goods. Theodosia led Bullhead's pack horse. Two Two led Mavis' horse. The dogs with their loads snuffled along silently. They more than the merry children seemed to realize that danger lurked in the rear.

All eyes followed the softly gleaming white-bone emblem.

A baby cried; was given breast; fell silent.

Stars came out as thick as grass seed. An occasional falling star speared across the black sky.

Soon the trail turned straight west, past the south point of Skywater. Sometimes the prairie grass was head deep. It was still sweet with the day's rain.

A brave went ahead and shot a fire arrow into the air. The fire arrow would help the stragglers in the deep grass keep to the true path.

"A pillar of fire by night," Theodosia said.

Judith started. She hadn't been aware that her sister was walking beside her in the dark.

"And a cloud by day."

The papoose on Judith's back seemed to have suddenly doubled in weight. Judith guessed it had finally fallen asleep. Yet the heavy walking was good for the deep ache in her seat and thighs. She shuddered, remembering the terrible thing Mad Bear had done to her, remembering how his necklace of shrunken fingers had tickled her as his body pounded into hers.

"Judith?"

"Mm?"

"Do not hate God for this."

"Mm."

"Even if we do die in a far place somewhere unremembered."

A sudden sob escaped Judith.

"God shall be our refuge and our strength."

Judith inwardly pinched her brain to keep from remembering and seeing terrible things.

"They may ravish our bodies, but never our souls."

Judith pinched her brain even more, to the point where she saw dazzling blood stars.

"Judith, please, do not hate God for this."

"Mm."

"Your husband, Vincent, was a doubter, wasn't he?"

Another sob broke from Judith. Judith thought, "Yes, Vince also have I wronged. It was my doing that sent him off to the wars."

"God has something in mind. There must be a divine purpose behind all this. There has to be."

Judith thought, "My poor poor family. Gone."

Theodosia sighed. "Well, I did not choose to be killed by the Indians either. But if the Lord wills it, it is all right. And that should be your thought too. Because remember, someday we shall see Claude and Angela in glory."

Two Two spoke suddenly beside them in the dark rustling grass. There was in his voice the sound as if he too had been weeping private tears for Angela. "Bullhead does not like it that the white sisters speak overmuch in the white tongue. He thinks all whites are bad talkers."

Both women fell silent. They trudged on. They followed the sounds of creaking leathers ahead. Far in the lead, the pale-white jawbone wavered from side to side.

The trail led over rough ground. Sometimes the going was over gravel hummocks, sometimes across wartlike clumps of buffalo grass.

Judith bent forward from the hips, the better to carry the

papoose. She followed in the steps of the pack horse led by Tinkling. The tops of her high black shoes began to cut her across the calf of her legs. A small corn on her left toe began to sting.

Judith thought, "Where did I make the wrong turn, that fatal mistake, which led to this walking horror? When I left the farm near Davenport? Because I was too prideful to marry a farm boy? Rear a raft of country kids?"

Judith thought, "Yes, even Theodosia. Her path too led in a straight line toward destruction. She married Claude, then was assigned by the church to help him build a mission station at Skywater. Why couldn't the Lord have spared her, after all the savage souls she had saved for Him?"

Judith cried to herself.

Yes. Marrying Vincent Raveling had been her first mistake. She had known it from the beginning. He was exactly as her father had once described him. "A lily-fingered city clerk who'll always have his nose in a book. No good."

Marrying Vince had meant so much to her at the time. Vince had just been assigned to St. Paul as head clerk for Western Shipping. St. Paul was a new and fast-growing city. They would grow up with it. They would hobnob with the best people right from the start.

Well, it had not worked out. Vince hated social doings. He preferred his pipe and Lucretius to parties. Also, the wives of General Sibley and Governor Ramsey, jealous of her blond-gold, statuesque beauty, had snubbed Judith at every turn, considering her an upstart from the country. Judith soon found herself making friends instead with a merry widow named Mavis Harder.

Judith stumbled through a tangle of wolfberry bushes. Tinkling had apparently chosen the wrong path. Some dogs laden with parfleches broke out in a snarling wrangle. Tinkling talked to them like they might be persons, and the dogs soon quieted.

But even then all might have been well, Judith thought, if she had only remained content with her lot in St. Paul.

Actually it had been a fairly good life. Both she and Mavis had joined a women's club where gossip was frowned upon and improving one's mind was encouraged. She and Mavis participated in the new feminist movement then sweeping America. They went to the theater together. They read the new books together. They became fast friends.

The tip of Judith's tongue strayed over the edge of her upper lip and pushed at the stubs of the four pesky black hairs. Ah, so they'd grown back again. She'd plucked out the four black hairs but two weeks before.

She'd never discussed the four black hairs with Vince. She'd always made it a point to keep them plucked so he wouldn't remark on them when they kissed.

In her mind the four hairs were associated with an odd demand Vince often made of her when they made love. Making love had never really meant much to her, it was perfunctory with her, so when Vince asked her to submit the Lucretius way, well, that she didn't appreciate at all. Not at all. As a self-respecting woman she just couldn't let herself submit to such indignity. Especially not just as she was all fired up with the feminist dream of freedom from male domination.

She had to admit, though, that submitting to Vince's odd demand wasn't nearly as awful as being ravished by a filthy Mad Bear. That horrible tickling of Mad Bear's necklace of dead brown fingers on her chin . . . Oh, God.

She could feel, even hear, Vince's letter crackling where it was hidden in the bosom of her dress. "My precious pet," he had written. Yes, precious pet. Yes, yes. "And precious dear man wherever you may be tonight, fighting Johnny Reb in the deep, dark South."

"Forgive, forgive," she murmured aloud in the dark. "It's my fault Angela is dead. I should never have come out here."

"Judith?" Theodosia called.

Judith thought, "Well, we're all going to die anyway, so in the end it really doesn't matter."

"Judith?"

Judith thought, "It's all still like a dream to me. Like it never happened, actually."

"Sister?"

Judith held her tongue.

"Do not hate God for it. Please, my sister. He has a purpose."

Angela had come to Judith after a long and difficult labor, giving her much pain. But from then on Angela had been her precious love. Dear sweet darling girl with her flowing silver-blond hair and her kittenish blue eyes and her golden legs.

Theodosia threshed through the tall grass beside Judith. "You are saved, aren't you?"

A short, wild laugh broke from Judith.

"Remember. We are all God's children. All of us. Red as well as white."

"The black man too?"

"Sister."

Judith bumped into the rear of Tinkling's pack horse. Tinkling and the horse had suddenly stopped dead still. The horse flourished its tail in Judith's face in irritation, and stomped the ground hard, once.

The rest of the caravan—squaws, children, dogs, horses—had stopped too. Whitebone and his white emblem had vanished from sight. All stood immobile, absolutely unmoving. It became difficult to make out anybody in the prairie dark. Something was wrong.

They waited.

There were shots. One, two, three, four.

They waited.

Finally the sound of running came. Behind them. It was a runner. He went straight for Whitebone ahead.

There was another interval of waiting, and then the softly glowing white emblem rose out of the deep grass again.

"We are safe," Tinkling whispered from where she stood holding her horse's nostrils.

Word came back that Scarlet Plume and Traveling Hail had

spotted enemy skulking in their rear. At least so it seemed at first.
There was a grayness about the skulkers which made Scarlet Plume
think they were white scouts from the great enemy army coming
down from Fort Snelling. Scarlet Plume and his brother and the
two other guards lay down in the grass, waiting, watching. Soon
they noticed that the skulkers, quiet as they might be, took no
pains to hide themselves. This was surprising. Then the four rear
guards saw what it was and they smiled to themselves. Antelope.
Curious antelope. Antelope were known to approach things they
did not understand. Four shots followed and four antelope lay
dead.

"Ah," Smoky Day cried from her travois. "Now we shall have
fresh meat at our next stopping."

The caravan moved on.

An hour later there was another alarm in the night, this time
up front.

Whitebone's emblem was being jiggled about with agitation.
There was also a sudden wild cry, followed by much lamenting.

Everybody hurried forward to see what it was. The entourage
piled up, became a mob of redskins and horses and dogs.

They had come upon a small creek of running water. Beside it
grew a single sweet cottonwood, a young tree about the height of
a telegraph pole. The moon revealed a gruesome sight. An old
Yankton woman hung from a limb of the young tree. A young
Yankton wife lay on the ground beneath her, wailing her heart
out. The old woman had been hanging from the limb for some
time. The withered, gaunt face of the dead woman had a strangely
eloquent expression in the moonlight. The arms hung straight
down like sticks attached to a bundle, while the shadowed eye
sockets seemed to glance from side to side.

Everybody stood staring at the scene. All remarked on the fact
that the old woman had not fallen apart in decay but had dried up
into a mummy instead. She had been too tough, too leathery, to
succumb to maggots.

Smoky Day told Judith and Theodosia about it. On their last

remove, Snow On Her, aged mother of Alighting Goose, had been left behind to die. Snow On Her knew she was a burden to the band. Abandonment was the same thing as ordinary dying. Nothing could be done about it. She had become infirm, knew death was near, and had asked to be left behind to be eaten by the wolves. The wish was respected. It was a reasonable wish. It was right. When the band was at last out of sight, Snow On Her had instead taken thongs and hung herself. It was less painful than being gnawed to death by wolves.

Walking Voice, the village crier, came along and spoke in a low voice. "Attend, Yanktons. The moon has now risen and the enemy can see us moving in the grass. We will remove yet a short distance. We will follow the stream south to where it turns near certain ripe plums. There we will pitch our tepees. After the tepees are up, let the smudge fires against the mosquito be but small fires. I have said."

The band took up its burdens and followed the winding stream south. The stream ran swollen from the day's heavy rain. The wailing of Alighting Goose was gradually left behind.

Whitebone stopped a mile farther on. He looked around in the gold, dusty moonlight. He liked what he saw. The low, flat place behind a cutbank in the turn of the stream was a good camping ground. The grass was rich. There was much running water. He stuck the pole of his white emblem into the ground in an upright position. Instantly the squaws tumbled out the lodgepoles and unfolded the leather tepee coverings.

By the time Judith had unhooked the papoose from her back and had set its cradleboard up on end, Tinkling and old Smoky Day had the tepee half up. All around them, in a neat exact circle, other tepees were swiftly going up too, each according to its allotted place as determined by the rank of the man of the house.

Two Two watered and hobbled the horses, then with skins got in a supply of water. Tinkling and Smoky Day finished lashing down the tepee covering, then brought in the parfleche traveling bags. Whitebone hooked his emblem on a loose lodgepole and tied it upright to his tepee. The ancient jawbone shone above them in the moonlight like a soft white flag. Smoky Day set up a tripod just inside the tepee on which to hang Whitebone's shield and spear. Tinkling built a small smudge fire with willow twigs. And home was ready.

The papoose Born By The Way began to cry just as Judith carried it through the flap door. Something had frightened it.

Tinkling cast a number of buffalo robes on the grass around the fire. Smoky Day showed Judith where to sit, on the left as one entered, or the women's side. Baby in arms, Judith settled on her robe, knees to one side.

Judith was dead tired. She looked down at the crying baby. It would no doubt grow up to be another violator of women, white women. Gladly would she have thrown it to the wolves outdoors if she dared. But she was now a captive and if she wished to survive she had no choice but to keep it quiet, even to comfort it. So she rocked the baby, and hummed to it, all the while that she hated it. Her own humming made her belly leap.

Whitebone leaned in. He stopped behind Judith. His old face wrinkled up momentarily in a great cry. Tears fell on her gold hair. Then, abruptly composing himself, he proceeded to his place across from the door on the other side of the little pinking fire.

Two Two sat on the right as one entered and near the door. A place was left for Scarlet Plume when he should return from his camp duties.

Whitebone took a pinch of sweet grass and sprinkled it over the little pyramid fire. Instantly a smell of wild, smoky incense filled the tepee. It obliterated the smell of sweated leathers for a moment. The little fire cast a soft circle of pinking light. Shadows were black and abrupt along the circling wall. Brown faces and brown hands hung upon the air as if painted onto the shadows.

Whitebone got out his stone gossip pipe. He filled it with prairie tobacco and lighted up with a twig fagot from the fire. He offered a puff to the six great powers, then took a deep puff for himself. He sighed from the depths of his being, and lay back on his slanted lazyback. The woven willows creaked comfortably under his shoulders.

Born By The Way still whimpered a little. Judith rocked the baby in its buckskin cradle. The rocking made the porcupine quill-work glint in the soft light: blue, yellow, red.

Smoky Day rustled in a deep parfleche and brought forth pieces of dried beef. She passed each member of the family a strip and signified they should eat. "It is too late for soup. There will be time in the morning for boiled meat. It is hoped this will quiet the growlings of your belly until you sleep."

Judith took a sniff of her strip of beef. It looked dirty, un-appetizing, resembling the leather sole of a shoe. But the smell was good. It had an aroma not unlike dried halibut. She bit into it. It was tough. A couple of chews and to her surprise a wonderful flavor spread over her tongue. Her mouth flooded with moisture. It was good to be eating again. She chewed heartily with the others. After the terrible events of the day, and the long, tiring march carrying the papoose, Judith couldn't help but admit the nomad lodge felt cozy.

Around them outside, the other Yanktons settled in for the night too. The sounds were comfortable. It reminded Judith of a flock of chickens settling down for the night on its roost. She hoped Theodosia was being treated kindly by Bullhead. And poor Mavis by Traveling Hail.

The papoose continued to whimper. It stirred in discomfort inside its bound cradle.

Whitebone stroked his two fur-wrapped braids, first one and then the other. The braids reached almost to his navel. His won-dering turtle eyes took on a few more wrinkles. He crossed his legs and rubbed them against each other. He scowled down at his toes.

At last Whitebone looked across to the women's side and said to Judith, "The child is not happy. Can you not give it something to eat?"

Smoky Day's old eyes flicked blackly from Whitebone to Judith

and back again. She laid aside her strip of leathery meat, and getting to her knees, reached across for the papoose.

Judith, feeling stupid, handed the baby over.

Smoky Day unlaced the buckskin covering of the cradle and
took out the baby. She removed a few handfuls of soiled cattail
fluff, and tipping up the baby's cherry-red bottom, carefully cleaned
it, much as a white mother might clean her baby with the corner
of a soiled diaper.

Watching, Judith couldn't help but be drawn a little by the
chubby little brown creature. Without thinking, she reached across
and tickled it under the foot.

Smoky Day quickly drew the child around and away from
Judith. "Do not tickle the feet of the child," Smoky Day scolded,
"or its legs will not grow down. It is the same with patting a
child on the head. There it will not grow either, up."

"This I did not know. Forgive me."

Smoky Day dug out a stalk of cattail from a storage parfleche.
Two quick twists and the brown cattail exploded into a handful
of light, wispy fluff. A few of the seed fluffs lifted up, like mosquitoes, took a lazy turn about the circular tepee, abruptly were
sucked down into the little pink fire.

Smoky Day packed the fresh fluff around the little papoose's
bottom and then placed the papoose in its cradle again. Smoky
Day next dipped a hand into the wide sleeve of her deerskin tunic
and lifted out one of her paps. She handled her wrinkled old pap
like it might be a stretch of bread dough. With a motherly smile,
strangely young for so old a face, she gave suck to the baby. Presently a drop of milk appeared in the corner of the baby's pink-
brown mouth. The baby's black shiny eyes slowly closed over,
contented.

Judith was astounded. So old a woman giving suck? Judith shot
a high blue look at Whitebone, then back at Smoky Day. Had
something heinously private transpired between mother and son
that her breasts should run again? Thoughts as wild as wolf tails

whisked around in Judith's mind. Well, suppose it was conceiv-
able that mother had slept with son, should she at her age still
have been able to produce milk? Let alone bear a child? No. It
was unheard of. Impossible. Unless a savage mother was capable
of miracles where a white woman was not. There was of course
Sarah in the Bible, Abraham's wife. She had had a baby in her old
age. "Who would have said unto Abraham that Sarah would give
a child to suck, bearing him a son in his old age? And the child
grew, and was weaned."

Judith finally couldn't resist asking it. "Surely Born By The
Way is not your child?"

Smoky Day's withered old lips flashed a smile. "He is my grand-
child, as it was told you. The child's own mother died a winter ago
when the band was on the way. I have nursed it ever since."

"Is it a common thing for Dakota grandmothers to have milk
for their grandchildren?"

"The baby cried. To pacify it I placed my old pap in its little
mouth. Also, I gave it warm meat soup, drop by drop with a little
wooden ladle. I continued to play-nurse it until, behold, one day
milk flowed from me. The little orphan smiled with joy when
the ma-ma appeared. Yet the other pap remained dry."

Judith fought down a gulping motion in her throat.

Smoky Day said, "Come, play-nurse the baby. Surely milk will
return to your bosom since you are still young."

Judith shook her head.

Whitebone continued to rub his crossed feet against each other.
He coughed roughly, twice.

Smoky Day said, "The father of this child wishes that someone
would dress his feet."

Tinkling sprang up out of the shadows. She took up a skin of
water and set it beside Whitebone's feet.

Whitebone coughed again. This time there was an angry grump
in it.

Smoky Day looked meaningfully at Judith. "Come, it is for you to do. You are to be his new wife. A chief who is a good provider always expects to have his feet washed and soothed by his wife's hands after a long journey."

Judith started. Wife? No. My God, no! Judith suddenly found herself panting for breath.

"Come, it is for you to do."

Judith bowed her head. Bitterly she reminded herself that she was a prisoner and had no choice. For the time being she had somehow better try to get along with her captors.

Judith removed Whitebone's moccasins. She chafed his ankles and the sides of his feet. She saw that his feet were surprisingly young-looking. Strangely too the smell of his feet was not offensive. She washed his feet with water, well up his bony leg, and then dried them with a handful of grass plucked from the ground under his buffalo robe.

When she finished, Whitebone wiggled his toes, removed all of his garments, and, naked, lay down on his fur robe. He lay with his feet to the fire, head away. His pudendum lay in a puddle between his thighs. It reminded her of the liver of a freshly butchered sheep. Two Two behind Whitebone already lay snoring on his fur. He too lay naked. His pudendum resembled three freshly popped mushrooms.

Judith couldn't resist several furtive looks at both males. Lord. Lord. What she hadn't all seen in the space of one day.

Sitting on her own fur again, Judith was further startled when Smoky Day beckoned for her to take over the baby and once more urged her to give it suck. "It is still hungry. See, its little mouth still nibbles at the night much as a small fish does. Let him suckle your breast and soon milk will also return to you. It is what a dutiful wife must do for the orphan child of her new husband." And before Judith could protest, Smoky Day placed the child in Judith's lap.

Judith stared down at the brown face. Its two black robin eyes stared up at her.

Presently the pink-brown mouth pursed up for more milk. And

automatically Judith found herself unbuttoning the top of her gray dress and cupping out her left breast, white and gentle, and giving it to the papoose. The child's little lips quickly found her light-brown nipple.

The pink-brown lips were warm. They were tender and perfect. The papoose pulled at her teat like a cute little pig. Its brown touch spread into her. Judith twisted her head to one side. "Angela," she whispered. She had no milk.

At last the baby fell asleep and Smoky Day took him from her. Smoky Day slung him in his cradle from one of the slanting lodgepoles.

Smoky Day next motioned for Judith to lie beside Whitebone.

Judith blazed up at that. "What? Not again? God, no! I thought you Yankton Dakotas were different."

Whitebone had been watching affairs all along and he now lifted his old head from his pillow. "Come," he said. "You have washed my feet and you have given suck to my child. Thus you have married me. I am now your husband. Come under the blanket with me." Whitebone coughed lightly. "If you do not wish to cohabit the first night, I will not press thee. I am not as the white husband, who would force himself upon thee. It is only that my legs become chilled in the night. Also, my thin belly is sometimes cold. A woman with her soft, warm flesh helps to keep away the chill of the prairie night. Later, when you have become used to our ways, we can cohabit if the need arises. Come."

Judith didn't know whether to laugh or weep. "The gall of these people." She swallowed. She swallowed again, "And yet, in their own way, I suppose they really mean well. Because there just is no question in their minds that theirs is the right way. And, as a captive, as a slave, I'd better make up my mind to obey him, or die." When in Rome do as the Romans do.

Judith crept over on all fours and lay beside Whitebone.

Whitebone still wasn't quite satisfied. "Woman," he said, "with the Yanktons the wife also removes her clothes. Learn this. Unless the time of the manner of woman is upon thee?"

Judith burned a fiery red. "No."

"Come then. There is no warmth unless we sleep skin to skin."

Judith thought, "After what Mad Bear did to me, I don't suppose I can worry much any more about a fate worse than death." She lay very still. "I hate them enough to kill them for what they did to my poor Angela. Even if they aren't the same Dakota." She lay very still. "Oh, God, I'm so tired. So dead beat. Why should I care what happens to me any more? They can kill me for all I care now."

Judith removed her clothes in the shadowy half-light of the falling pink fire. She placed her shoes, her stockings, her dress, her underclothes with Vince's letter to one side. She wore no bloomers. Naked, she sat shivering.

Whitebone had heard something. He sat up. He looked at where her underclothes lay. His black eyes glittered suspiciously. "Do you carry dead leaves in your clothes? Is this the white custom?"

"No."

"What is it then? There was a sound as of cottonwood leaves cracking."

"It is a message from my white husband."

Whitebone held out his hand for it.

Judith knew there was no use to protest. She handed Vince's letter over.

Whitebone studied it uncomprehendingly a moment; then put it away.

The skin over Judith's bare back shivered of itself. "That's my letter."

"Come," Whitebone said gently. "Another time."

At last she let herself settle against Whitebone's side.

Whitebone immediately relaxed and fell asleep. He was warm.

Judith lay awake for a long time. A drum beat somewhere in camp. She could hardly believe she was who she was.

The incense from the burned sweet grass died away. The Indian smell of Two Two came to her. It reminded her a little of the way a puppy might smell after a run in the rain.

She recalled a funny thing her mother had once said: "It's shocking to think that after a woman dies her person will be exposed to the eyes of an undertaker."

A draft of cool air breathed down through the smoke hole. Automatically, in his sleep, Whitebone drew up a robe and covered his old body. Judith drew on the robe a little too to cover herself.

She watched a star slowly slowly move across the smoke hole. She fell asleep.

Her left side felt cold. She awoke. She saw stars through the smoke hole. Moonlight struck directly down in a pillar of gold. The fire in the hearth appeared to be out. Someone snored on the women's side.

She lay dazed, trying to understand where she was.

The nipple of her left breast hurt. It was where the papoose had pulled at it like a cute little pig. Her thighs and seat also hurt. She recalled the events of the day before.

A sob gathered in her belly. She drew at the fur robe to cover her nakedness. As she did so she discovered Whitebone no longer lay at her side.

She was thankful he had kept his word not to force her to cohabit with him.

A piercing death cry cut the night. It came from some distance. It was the cry of an old man.

Judith lay very still. She knew right away who it was. Whitebone. What could he be howling about so in the middle of the night? His dead wife?

The snoring on the women's side stopped. All except the papoose seemed to have awakened.

The howling continued.

Presently the camp around them began to stir. A few people poked their heads out of their tepees and began to wonder aloud what had gone wrong with their old chief.

With a groan, Smoky Day got to her feet. She stirred up the

embers, dropped on a few dead leaves, built a little pyramid of twigs over them, blew carefully, and finally had a licking flame.

Judith reached for her dress.

Smoky Day looked at her gravely. "Sleep, my child. This does not concern thee."

Whitebone continued to wail piercingly outside. He seemed to be pounding the earth with something.

"Is it because of his former wife?" Judith asked.

"Scarlet Plume and the headmen will attend him. Once each month he is overcome with grief. It is fated."

Judith saw deep love for her son in Smoky Day's black eyes. The little winking fire gave Smoky Day the look of an ancient mother of Israel. "Mother, your son will forget her after a time."

Smoky Day looked to one side. "It is not a good thing for a mother-in-law to talk in this manner with the new wife of her blood son. Yet we do not know your people. You are alone. You are without a mother. Therefore I will serve as your own blood mother and befriend you." Smoky Day's gnarled black hands rubbed over each other with a husking sound. "My son weeps because Bluestem, the mother of his baby, threw her life away. You saw the old woman Snow On Her hanging from a single cotton-wood. Well, there is yet another single cottonwood along this stream, a dead one. It was from this dead tree that Bluestem also hanged herself. Whitebone knows now that his wife was unhappy with him for many winters. Yet she never told him. He did not know. The thoughts of a chief are often more with his people than with his family. This makes his grief doubly heavy. Also, he misses her."

The wailing continued. The sound of men's voices offering the old man comfort came to them.

Smoky Day listened carefully. "He does not heed the good words of his headmen this time. I will go. Also, we do not have a medicine man. On our last remove through Hole In The Moun-tain, the good Sky Walker died mysteriously. I will go. Watch the lodge." Smoky Day hobbled out into the night.

Judith saw Tinkling look at her from under her robe. Tinkling's black eyes and the fur over her made her look like a mink. Two Two also looked at her, wonderingly. The papoose slept, head hanging, in his gently swinging cradleboard. The baby's even breathing gave the cradleboard its motion.

Judith decided to have a look for herself anyway. She slipped into her dress and got up. "Watch the lodge," she said to Tinkling, and ducked out through the leather flap door.

The moon was directly overhead. A soft radiance, almost like a gold fog, seemed to be drifting through the encampment along the ground. Thin wisps of smoke rose from the guest lodge in the center of the camp.

Beyond the camp circle and downstream a short distance stood a group of braves. In their midst was Whitebone. Whitebone was naked and he was kneeling on the ground. The limbs of a dead cottonwood spread spectrally over them.

Judith drew near, hesitantly. She heard Scarlet Plume's even, murmured words. Smoky Day stood off to one side, head down, listening. Even Bullhead gave the old chief counsel in surprisingly soothing tones.

Whitebone had dug a hole in the ground with his bare hands. Looking closely, Judith saw that Whitebone was handling some human bones in a fond manner. His old face was twisted with deep grief. Bitter tears fell copiously. It took Judith a moment to grasp what she was looking at. The skull he wept over and the rib case he clutched to his bosom—they could only be his dead wife's. Bluestem.

Judith stole back into their lodge. She slipped off her dress and, naked, lay under their fur robe again. The soft fur against her skin was warming, comforting. She stroked her chin against it.

Presently Smoky Day came leading Whitebone home. Whitebone's face was once again composed, grave and impassive. There was no sign whatsoever that grief had only a few minutes before ripped it open. He lay himself down beside Judith, naked, skin to skin. Quietly he drew a fair share of their robe over his thin belly and thin legs and gaunt chest. He did not even sigh.

He lay breathing, slow. She lay breathing, slow. They warmed each other's sides.

Sleep came back to Smoky Day and soon she was snoring again. Tinkling and Two Two also slept. Scarlet Plume did not come to his fur bed.

In her mind's eye, and benumbed as if caught in a spell, Judith saw herself lying beside the old chief: gold hair next to his fur-wrapped black braids, blue eyes next to his brown turtle eyes, white, still young body next to his aged brown body, gold-tufted pudendum next to his grayish-tinged milkwort puddle.

She noted the sweetish Indian smell of him. The smell of him was like the inside of an empty perfume bottle.

"Sweetish?" she thought. "O Lord, how far have I fallen!"

He stirred beside her.

At that she held her breath.

After a moment he turned toward her. Then his hand lay upon her naked belly.

The trail to love for Whitebone was short and straight. He rose over her, with a hard bump of his knee divided her legs, charged, and, erect, was upon her.

Judith lifted up on an elbow to push him off.

Too late. With a lustful grump of a sound he made partial entrance.

O Lord, then it was to be again. She fell back, giving up. After what Mad Bear had done to her, and what Mad Bear's braves had done to poor Angela, what was the use? She was a prisoner of a strange people in a cruel land. She let Whitebone split her legs even farther.

A dozen thrusts, a lingering groan of pleasure, and Whitebone was done. He lay dozing in pleasure upon her a few moments and then, receding, rolled off and stretched out beside her. Soon he was sound asleep.

She thought, "I must surely be out of my mind to let him do this to me."

She threw a quick look around in the dusky tepee to make sure Scarlet Plume still hadn't come to bed.

2

Judith awoke to a red dawn. It bled through the gray leather of the tepee, suffusing everything with a rosy hue. A small aromatic smudge fire burned at her feet. There wasn't a fly or a mosquito around.

Judith turned her head. Whitebone, Two Two, Smoky Day, Tinkling, even the papoose were gone. It was time to get up.

Judith lay all tired out. Nausea worked in her belly. Slush ice seemed to have formed in her skull during the night.

Smoky Day came in with the papoose. "I have given him ma-ma. Do you wish to play-nurse him again?"

Judith could only stare at her.

"Play-nurse him?" Smoky Day urged.

"Where is everyone?"

Smoky Day was startled by the question. "The chief and his son Two Two bathe in the stream in the men's place, as is the custom each morning. Tinkling bathes with the maidens in the women's place."

Judith slowly sat up. She hugged her white breasts close. "Each morning?"

"In winter as well as summer."

"You bathe in a stream in the winter?"

"It is even so, my daughter. The Dakotas have axes."

"You chop a hole in the ice and bathe?"

"Yes, my daughter."

"The babies too?"

Smoky Day smiled down at her. She was as wrinkled as neglected leather, yet her smile as always was that of a young woman. "The Yankton baby is always given a dip at birth. This is to see if he is a true Yankton."

"Even in the dead of winter?"

"Even so."

"Do not the babies freeze? Catch their death of cold?"

Smoky Day smiled. "I am here. Whitebone is here. Two Two and Born By The Way are here."

Judith was astounded. That accounted then for the cleanish smell of the Indian lodge despite all the grease and smoke and worn leather about.

"Do you wish to play-nurse with Born By The Way in bed?"

Judith felt dirty. Filthy. "Can someone show me where to bathe?"

"Find Tinkling and she will show thee. It is near the dead cottonwood." Smoky Day handed Judith a twist of wild tobacco.

"What is this for?"

"You must throw the tobacco in the stream as a gift to the water god. It is the custom."

"I must?"

"You must."

Judith reached for her clothes, only to discover they were gone, even her high leather shoes.

Smoky Day smiled at Judith's surprised look. Smoky Day set the papoose against a lodgepole, and brought forth a pair of moccasins, a pair of deerskin leggings, and a long deerskin tunic. She placed them in Judith's hands.

Judith stroked them. They were all beautifully decorated, sharp angular designs done in beads: blue, yellow, green. The leather was well worked, and soft, and as white as a bunny's tail.

"Are these for me?"

Smoky Day looked shyly away. "If they please my daughter."

"Where are my other clothes?"

"They have been put away. You are now the wife of a great chief and must dress accordingly. Also, some of the warriors grumble that we have whites in our camp. They wish to kill all the whites. They say we will be punished by the terrible wagon-guns when the white soldiers find that we have white women in our midst. Therefore you must dress as a Yankton woman. Go, bathe, and then we will clothe thee in the proper manner."

Judith threw a light wolfskin over her shoulders and drew it close around her middle. She stepped outside. The upper half of the ball of the sun lay on the eastern horizon. For a moment it looked exactly like a flaming prairie fire. A heavy dew, almost like a light rain, had fallen in the night and the grass in the slow turn of the creek sparkled with a million jewels. The air was as sweet as cider. She took a deep breath.

Judith heard the merry sound of female laughter beyond a fringe of red willows near the dead cottonwood tree. She could just make out Tinkling and other maidens playing in the stream.

Judith threw a hasty glance at where Whitebone had been digging in the earth during the night and then resolutely looked the other way. She shuddered, abruptly, when she thought of how Whitebone had first hugged the bones of his dead wife, Bluestem, and then had cohabited with her, Judith.

Hesitantly Judith approached the bathing Yankton women. She parted the willows and stepped through. Various tunics and chastity ropes of soft deerskin lay piled at her feet. Tinkling and the other naked young women were chasing each other through shallow silver water. The creek bed was perfect for bathing, sandy, clear.

Judith marveled at the way Tinkling had suddenly become happy. Tinkling played and scampered about like a child. She had been released at last from an intolerable burden. Having been married to the brute Charlie Silvers must have been torture for her.

"Yes," Judith thought, "and now it is my turn to become all humped over like that. Unless I can somehow escape."

Judith wondered how Theodosia and Mavis had made out during the long night. She looked around. They were nowhere in sight.

Judith, shy, had trouble understanding how Tinkling and the Yankton maidens could run around stark naked, unabashed. She shivered inside her wolfskin.

Finally, feeling a little funny about it, she cast the twist of tobacco in the water and stepped in. The stream ran warm over her toes. It was as clear as good drinking water. Multicolored sand sparkled on the bottom. A pair of minnows hardly larger than two short threads of black yarn nosed up to her toenails. They tickled her.

She listened to the others play and splash. After the first moment they no longer looked at her. Presently, willing it, she dared to shed her wolfskin and settled in the water. She bathed herself harshly. She scrubbed her limbs with fine sand, scouring especially where Mad Bear and Whitebone had touched her. Then she rinsed the fine sand off. The water was fresh, soothing. After a while she lay back on the sandy bottom to enjoy it. She laved her bruised body with cupping hands of water.

The menfolk were waiting for her when she and Tinkling returned. Whitebone, Two Two, and even Scarlet Plume sat each on a pink rock around the cooking fire outside the lodge. They were obviously savoring with delight the rich smell of the boiling antelope meat in the family black kettle.

Judith entered the tepee, where Smoky Day awaited her. Smoky Day took up Judith's hair and examined it closely. "Ah," Smoky Day said, "you do not have the louse."

"Of course I do not have lice."

Smoky Day explained. "You have been with Mad Bear. He and his band are known to be very lousy." Smoky Day smiled at her. "A good Indian does not have the louse. The Yanktons are a clean people. Also, we have a grease for the louse."

Smoky Day deliberately rubbed a wad of soft tallow dyed with tannin into Judith's gold hair. Judith's hair changed color reluctantly. Smoky Day next braided Judith's hair, the tallow making both braids as stiff as whip handles. Smoky Day painted the parting down the middle with red vermilion. Smoky Day rubbed brown ointment over Judith's face and neck, and placed a red dab exactly under each eye. Last, Smoky Day helped Judith into her tunic, leggings, and moccasins.

Tinkling broke out in merry girlish laughter when Smoky Day

had finished. "Except for the sunned hair, Whitebone's new wife has truer Yankton skin than Whitebone himself."

Smoky Day laughed too. "Whitebone will not know his bride." Smoky Day dug out a trader mirror from a parfleche traveling bag. "See your image."

Judith looked at herself in the mirror. After a bit she couldn't resist a grudging smile at the figure she cut. And she had to admit she did look quite Indian, even with the stained braids. Smoky Day had done a good job. It was too bad she couldn't go to a white man's masquerade.

"Yes," she murmured to herself, "and I'll never see St. Paul again."

Smoky Day caught the sad intonation of the words. "Do the clothes bind thee?"

The deerskins felt wonderfully comfortable against the skin. Judith had the curious feeling she now had two skins.

"Do they bind thee?"

"The clothes are good. I am glad to have them. I thank thee."

"This old mother is pleased. Come. The meat is boiled. The men await us." Smoky Day, hobbling, led the way outdoors.

The three men looked at Judith, amazed. Yet they said nothing. And after a moment, in fine delicate courtesy, they looked everywhere but at her. It was evident from the way Whitebone sat on his rock that he was pleased. Even the face of the silent Scarlet Plume smoothed over.

Smoky Day and Tinkling handed out wood chips for plates. With a long wooden fork Smoky Day fished up slabs of meat from the bubbling black kettle and handed them around to the men. After offering the first bite to the six great directions, all three males pitched in, eating with their fingers. Whitebone had a way of eating in which he first lifted the meat slowly to his mouth, then suddenly his mouth snapped at it and the meat vanished.

Judith had to wait until the men were nearly finished. It was impolite for a woman to eat with hungry men about.

Finally Smoky Day handed Judith a choice cut of meat too.

Judith was ravenous. She tore at the meat like the men did. It was good. Smoky Day had put some native herbs in the boiling water. Judith hoped Smoky Day would save the water for soup later on. Mmm, the meat was good. At least there was that.

The baby suddenly let go inside the tepee, bawling with all his might.

Two Two's white teeth gleamed like a beaver's. "Ha, ha, Born By The Way already wishes to eat with the men."

Everybody smiled.

Tinkling was about to bring the papoose out, when Smoky Day frowned. "It is for Sunned Hair, the new wife, to do. He is now her baby."

Judith, somewhat to her own surprise, found herself getting the baby. And the moment Judith sat down beside Whitebone the papoose fell silent.

A smile cracked Whitebone's old turtle face. "Perhaps the little one wishes more ma-ma."

Judith blushed. She found herself shy about exposing her breasts in front of Scarlet Plume. She hated the old man and his leering turtle eyes.

Scarlet Plume sat forward, elbows on his knees, black eyes intent on the cooking fire. He was wearing buckskins and his single scarlet feather. He had washed off his face-painting in the morning bath. His otherwise compassionate face seemed unusually severe and distant, Judith thought. Judith decided it was probably because he was still worried the wagon-guns would overtake them. She felt more than a little drawn toward Scarlet Plume. She admired his powerful face, his brooding eyes, his large, warm lips. Why couldn't it have been he instead of Whitebone who had taken her over? If such it had to be.

Judith noted a little buckskin bag tied high on the baby's cradle-board. It was diamond-shaped and decorated with a beaded design representing a turtle.

Two Two saw where her eyes were looking. "My little brother had to be chased out by a turtle."

Judith looked at Two Two with questioning blue eyes.

Smoky Day spoke up. "When Born By The Way was struggling to be born, it did not go well with the mother. Sky Walker, the medicine man, was called. What he did was wakan. He told a small turtle to chase the baby out."

"Oh."

Just then the papoose smiled up at Judith. The bright, wide grimace on the little one's otherwise dark solemn face startled her.

Two Two was overjoyed. So was Smoky Day. Two Two cried, "See, already he regards Sunned Hair as his true mother. Even as I do."

Whitebone reached down and touched the little one's dab of a nose. "Does Sunned Hair please thee, brave one? Do you like her new garments?"

Judith wyed her head to one side. The stiff braids lying on her bosom moved like a pair of long sausages. She was jealous of the baby. She thought, "Why couldn't Angela's life have been spared, instead of this pagan's?" A flash of hate suffused Judith. Her eardrums cracked with it. She thought of throwing the cradle and child into the cooking fire.

But of course she couldn't very well take it out on the child. The child did not know. It had no fault in the matter. And it was sweet and adorable.

Judith shot a question at Whitebone. She wanted to hurt him. "There is a thing that has been sticking into my heart ever since the Dakotas arose and killed the whites at Skywater. A brave named Animal's Voice butchered out the heart of my brother-in-law, the Good Book Man, and ate it as if it were pemmican." Judith's voice almost broke at the memory of it. "Animal's Voice was not a cut-hair Indian but one of those who refused to shed the buffalo robe. He was one like you. My heart was stabbed to see this. Why was this done?"

Whitebone drew back, affronted. His old eyes flashed black fire.

Judith persisted. Male dominance infuriated her. "It is true. Claude Codman, the Good Book Man, was a good man. He was a most kind man. He meant nothing but good for the Dakotas. Yet his heart was eaten as if it were but the heart of an antelope." She threw a look at the black kettle, where some antelope meat still cooked over the fire. "This is bad."

Whitebone turned to Scarlet Plume. "What troubles this woman? Can you tell? Does she not see that when Animal's Voice ate the heart of the white man it was an honor for the white man? When a red man eats the heart of another red man, it is an honor. But when a red man eats the heart of a white man, then it is a great honor." Whitebone coughed in a disdainful, superior manner. "The Good Book Man was of an inferior people, the whites."

"Inferior?" Judith exclaimed.

"It is a true thing. The white man is a woman. He is the greatest fool under the sun. In a battle he stands up straight and lets himself be shot at. He is a liar and a swindler. He cannot tell the truth. He is born with a white heart. Thus his heart cannot be like the heart of the red man, which is red and sweet." Whitebone bent a chief's grim look upon her. "Therefore it was a great honor for the Good Book Man when Animal's Voice ate his heart. Animal's Voice found the heart of the Good Book Man red and sweet. The Good Book Man was a brave man and Animal's Voice wished to acquire that bravery." Whitebone snapped his head down, once. "Also, Animal's Voice slew him as a sacrifice to appease the manes of his slain relatives. Animal's Voice's dead relations needed the blood to depart."

Judith lowered her eyes before the old man's eloquence.

Scarlet Plume's face remained distant, expressionless.

Born By The Way began to babble happily in Judith's lap. He too wanted to talk like a chief.

Smoky Day, Tinkling, and Two Two smiled.

Presently Whitebone couldn't resist the baby's happy babblings either. He relaxed, began to smile a little.

All the while, Whitebone's words continued to work in Judith's mind. They moved in her like a dawn coming in. After all she had gone through, it was only now coming home to her, truly, how far apart, how terribly far apart, the red man and the white man really were.

Whitebone again touched the baby's tit of a nose. "Before he was born I had a dream that he would enter the world deformed. This made me feel very sad. When a child is born deformed it is considered a curse from Wakantanka. Such a child is always left behind to die."

"Aiii," Smoky Day cackled, "and now I see our chief playing with his son. Aiii, and was it not a good thing that the old woman of your lodge did not listen to you when it was requested that the little one be interred with its dead mother on the scaffold? His little cries would have followed us through the night across the prairie, until long after he was out of sight. His spirit would have followed us forever. This your old mother knew. You are a good chief for your people, ai, but not when you are possessed by the madness of grief."

Whitebone's old head came up. "But my wife that was, she was not happy in the spirit land without her child."

"Aiii."

Whitebone turned solemnly to Judith. "I have thought on this very much. Listen. You are now my wife. I am happy in thee." Whitebone placed a soft hand on Judith's sleeve. "This is what I desire of thee. Listen. When Wakantanka shall have summoned me away, I want my nephew Scarlet Plume to kill you so that you may become my attendant in the spirit land. I am happy in thee. In the night that is now past, had not the thought of my new wife lying waiting for me in my tepee come to me, ai, I might well have thrown my life away. Such was my grief."

Judith sat stunned.

Then a change came over Whitebone's face. He set his wooden plate aside. He reached inside his leather shirt. Slowly he drew out the letter he had taken from her the night before. "Tell of this again."

Judith blanched.

"Tell it."

"It is a message from my husband."

"Where is he now?"

"He fights the bad whites far to the south."

"What does the message say?" He next drew the letter out of its envelope and spread it out for her to read. He kept fast hold of it.

Through tears Judith read him the first paragraph. It dealt mostly with the fact that Vince was profoundly lonesome for her and Angela.

Whitebone with his finger pointed to the start of the paragraph again. "Tell of this yet again."

Judith did.

Whitebone watched her eyes narrowly at the same time that he kept an eye on the handwriting word for word.

After a moment Judith caught on. Whitebone was slyly trying to trap her into making a mistake by getting her to repeat over and over the reading of certain marks. A sour smile touched her lips. "Does not the great chief wish for me to read all of the message? There is nothing in it about the white man's war against the red man."

Whitebone jerked back the letter. He stared at her a moment, then at the letter. Slowly an equally acrid smile touched his lips. Then he leaned down and slid the letter and its envelope into the fire.

Everyone watched it burn. The letter rapidly curled up into fragile black wisps, and vanished.

The sun rose behind them. Light turned yellow, then flashing clear, then warm.

Whitebone next turned to Scarlet Plume. "My son, a thing is troubling thee. Tell us what it is while we sit around the cooking pot. Or is it a thing that must be told of in the council lodge?"

Scarlet Plume set his plate aside. A large red ant ran across the knee of his buckskin legging. After a moment he gently picked it up and set it in the grass behind the pink rock he sat on.

When Scarlet Plume did not immediately answer, Whitebone turned to Two Two. "Little son, you know where your father's gossip pipe is kept. Get it. You know also where your cousin's pipe is kept. Get it. Attend."

Two Two got the pipes.

"Little son," Whitebone said next, "call your young friends and run to water the horses. Then let them out to graze in a new place. Attend."

Again Two Two ran to obey.

Whitebone lit up with a tiny brand plucked from the cooking fire. Scarlet Plume also lit up. The two men smoked together. It was a silent smoke, leisurely done, full of good taste and content.

The two men finished their smoke at exactly the same time and together clapped out their pipes.

Again Whitebone spoke to Scarlet Plume. "My son, a thing is troubling thee. My ears, even my red heart, are open. They all listen."

Scarlet Plume turned and fixed glittering black eyes on Whitebone. His loose black hair moved where it touched his shoulders. "My father, with the cooking pot between us, I can perhaps speak of it. It concerns one named Bullhead. You know him. I have spoken of him before. It is bad in his lodge. He will hurt the Good Book Woman."

"Has she not made him a good wife?"

"There were heavy words in Bullhead's tepee in the night."

"What?" Whitebone ground his old teeth together. "Does the son of my sister spend his nights with his ears to the doors of his friends?"

Scarlet Plume ignored the sarcasm. He threw a look at Bullhead's lodge five doors down. "Neither Bullhead nor the Good Book Woman has appeared for the morning bath. The door is still lashed tight from within." Scarlet Plume glanced up at Bullhead's smoke hole. "Nor has a fire been lighted within. There is bad trouble there."

Whitebone forced a jovial smile to his lips. "My son, it is now two winters since you last bedded with a wife. Perhaps you have forgotten the morning pleasure a man may have with his wife before he arises, even before the household awakens." Whitebone gave Judith a turtle's bland wink. "My son, it is time you found a new wife, even as I have done. You have forgotten what it means to be a married Yankton man."

"The Good Book Woman was not made for childbearing. Children came to her, yes. Yet the Good Book Woman is wakan. She is one of those chosen by the white man's Wakantanka to read and to teach out of the Good Book. She will never be content to be the wife of a brute named Bullhead. He is a bad man. I have said."

"He is also a brave man in battle. The Yankton nation dwindles. We need the brave man."

Scarlet Plume held his eyes steadily on Whitebone. "My father, listen. What Bullhead does with his wives is not done in the Yankton manner. He has the bad heart of the renegade. He belongs truly with Mad Bear's band. I spit on his tobacco. I will not smoke it. The blood of the innocent is in it. He kills without measure. He should be banished. Do the Yanktons have need of murderers to increase their kind?"

"My son, we have touched on a matter that has been much in my thoughts. It is this. You are much alone. Yet it seems you do not wish to marry again. This is not a good thing. You shun the women much as some medicine men do. Sky Walker, who took the south road, was one of those. My son, it has been much in my thoughts that if you do not like women, then you should become our new medicine man. You know much of such matters. I do not. We do not even have a keeper of the time. Thus consult your heart, seek a vision, and see what Wakantanka has to say. It was told us that you turned over in your mother's belly before you were born. That was a great thing. It was a sign. We could see then that Wakantanka had set you apart for a special life. Consider this."

A tiny smile quirked at the corners of Scarlet Plume's lips and a glint appeared in his obsidian eyes. "I have sought this vision you speak of."

"You have had this vision?"

"I have."

"What does it say?"

"It says nothing of being a medicine man."

"What does it say?"

"I have had a vision of a different thing."

"What does it say?"

"I will speak of it at the proper time."

"Does it speak of marriage?"

Scarlet Plume shook his head.

"Does it speak of women? White women?"

Scarlet Plume crossed his long legs. Still another single red ant had found its way up his leg and again Scarlet Plume very gently picked it up and set it down in the grass behind the pink rock he sat on.

An uneasy silence fell between the two men. Everyone in the household noted it. Black eyes, and Judith's blue eyes, flicked at each other and then looked away.

Afraid of becoming involved in a possibly violent family quarrel, Judith turned her attention to Born By The Way. The little papoose had got one little brown hand loose and was playing with one of her white fingers.

A slow drumbeat boomed on the far side of the camp, steady, insistent, jarring.

Presently Judith's eye fell on a dusky young woman sitting just across from her in the gate or the horns of the camp. Her name was Squirts Milk and she seemed to be nursing two little ones, twins, at her ample bosom at the same time. This in itself was unusual enough, until Judith noticed that one of the nurslings was abnormally hairy. Judith couldn't help but stare and stare, until of a sudden the hairy nursling gave a kick. The hairy one wasn't a baby at all. It was a puppy. The puppy's little eyes were closed in bliss as it suckled at Squirts Milk's soft tan pap.

Smoky Day smiled. "The puppy's mother was eaten yesterday. There was so little meat that some of the camp dogs had to be eaten."

It had always given Judith pause to see that Indians considered dog meat a delicacy. "Surely now, when this puppy comes of age, he will not be eaten?"

"It is fated. When the pa-pa is scarce there is no other way."

"Pa-pa?"

"Pa-pa is the meat of the buffalo."

Smoky Day's remarks were like strange stones sending ripple after ripple through Judith's mind. Wasn't it remarkable that to the Dakota "ma-ma" meant milk from the mother and "pa-pa" meant meat brought home by the father—almost the same as to the Anglo-Saxon?

Judith looked at Bullhead's tepee five doors down. Things were still quiet there. Judith longed to stroll over and ask her sister how she was doing. But she didn't dare. There just was no telling how Bullhead would take it.

But Mavis was up and about six doors down. Mavis seemed paler, though she did not limp as much. She had boiled some antelope meat for her handsome savage husband Traveling Hail. He seemed content enough as he chewed heartily away.

The Yankton women passed to and fro, busy with the morning chores. Clouts and leggings, thoroughly scrubbed in the sandy stream, were hung out to dry. Old men sat talking, and smoking their gossip pipes. Braves were busy repairing bows. An arrow-maker sat just outside the horns of the camp, flaking out a new supply of arrowheads. Older boys sat at the feet of grandfathers, listening to tales of great exploits, their faces strained with yearning for the day when they might be hailed as brave warriors, the only path to distinction for the Dakota. A pair of young wives took turns biting on lead bullets with their strong teeth, the better to make enemy wounds big and ragged. A fat squaw brought food to a damsel sitting alone in darkness in a menstruating hut beyond the camp circle. On the other side of the dead cottonwood, Two

Two and a dozen young lads stood guard on the grazing horses. Across the stream some maidens chatted merrily as they gathered fruit in a clump of plum trees. Apart from the grieving white women, Whitebone's band was generally a happy and contented one.

"Darling Angela."

With a fine groan of pleasure, a hand to each knee, Whitebone got to his feet and toed over to the front of his tepee. He picked up the lodgepole, to which the white jawbone of Unkteri was fastened. Everyone in camp watched to see in which direction they would remove that day. With proper ceremony, Whitebone pointed his emblem west, then placed it on a forked branch. All squaws instantly got busy, taking in the spears and guns standing by the lodge entrance, loosening the lodge stakes for swift striking, calling in the children, tying up the dogs and puppies.

Judith watched Smoky Day and Tinkling bustling in and out. It irked her to see so many bowed-over women in camp. Her resentment came out on her like an emanation from her blood. "What a self-constituted lord of creation the Dakota woman has let her man become," Judith muttered to herself. Aloud she said, "What a strange thing I see in the Yankton camp. The women do all the work while the men sit on their behinds doing nothing but eat and smoke and gossip."

Whitebone stiffened on his pink rock and his old head retracted like an angry snapping turtle's. He was suddenly so mad, Judith could smell him from where she sat.

Scarlet Plume was offended too. And it was he who spoke in defense of the Dakota customs, not Whitebone. "Listen carefully to what will now be said. This is what the Dakotas hold. Wakantanka means for each to do his own work. The men must hunt the meat, fight the enemy, steal the horses, and teach the boys." Scarlet Plume gave Judith a direct look. "The women must cook the meat, make the clothes, build the tepees, have the babies and feed them. Who else can have the babies and feed them?" Scarlet Plume's voice softened some. "All this is just. And it can be seen

that it is just when it is noted that the horses and the weapons and
the honor feathers belong to the men, and the tepees and the
parfleches and the food belong to the women." Scarlet Plume
paused a moment. "Also, Whitebone is a great chief who must
carry the burden of much thought for his people."

Whitebone finally found voice. "My other wife that was, she
was a good woman. Yet it must be also said that she was one of
those who could put out the lodge fire with the wind of her angry
words." Whitebone shook his head in memory. "Sometimes at the
end of her moon she could be as crabby as a crazed she-wolf. I had
much regard for her, yet her black madnesses often darkened my
spirit." Whitebone glared at Judith as his voice took on the
crackling hardness of a man who meant to have his own way.
"Let not my new wife be as one of those wolf women often seen
in the white village. I have said."

"Aiii," Smoky Day cackled.

Judith flushed under the paint over her cheeks.

Then something caught Scarlet Plume's eye down the line of
tepees.

Judith, relieved to have the attention shifted from her, looked
too.

A glinting thing had suddenly poked through the leather wall
of Bullhead's lodge, just under Bullhead's emblem, the painted
brown head of a buffalo bull. It was the point of a knife. The
knife jiggled a moment, then, desecration of desecrations, it
whipped up, slitting directly across the middle of the emblem.
Two pale hands took hold of each side of the long rent, pulled
them apart, and out stepped Theodosia.

"Sis!" Judith cried.

"Ah," Theodosia said, "there you are. I worried all night what
might be happening to you." Theodosia spoke in a tight voice.
Her sunbonnet was gone and her face was a sight. It was shock
white, even the large freckles, and her eyes were like the eyes of a
swamp specter seen from a distance. Tottering a little, Theodosia
started toward Judith.

Bullhead emerged roaring from his tepee door. He stood a moment beholding the gaping rent cut through his emblem, then, brandishing his war club, he came after Theodosia.

"Theodosia, what happened?" In her excitement, Judith threw the little papoose to one side.

The papoose landed in the cooking fire, almost upsetting the boiling kettle. The papoose's little brown face closed down like a scared puppy's, then opened in a tremendous bawl.

Smoky Day and Scarlet Plume leaped to save it.

But Theodosia, already moving in a half-staggering run, got there first. She plucked the papoose and cradle from the fire before the flames could take hold. She brushed off a few live coals and gray ash. "There," she crooned, "there, there."

Trembles broke out all over Judith. She could feel whiteness blanching over her breasts inside her tunic. The devil had been in her to let her do such a terrible thing.

Theodosia cradled the baby, and murmured to it, and slowly the baby quieted.

Still bellowing, still waggling his war club, Bullhead stomped out his rage on the grass behind Theodosia. He didn't quite dare to hit Theodosia as long as she held the chief's son in her arms.

Theodosia gave the little baby a kiss on its nose, and handed it back to Judith. As Theodosia did so, she had her first good look at Judith. She started. "Judith, why, what have they done to you?"

"Me?" Judith cried. Judith's heart leaped up. Even now, concern for others was still uppermost in Theodosia's mind. Greater love could no woman have. "What about you, Theodosia?"

"Sister, rescue is on the way. Remember, under God all things are possible."

Judith couldn't say further. She saw in a swift glance that Theodosia had been through hell. Theodosia's clothes had been torn off her during the night. Somehow she had managed to patch them together with thorns for pins. There was a large blue lump on her forearm and a deep red mark across her throat.

Bullhead raised his club for a swing at Theodosia.

Scarlet Plume moved, stepping between Theodosia and Bullhead. Scarlet Plume's eyes were dancing wild. He caught Bullhead's club and stayed the blow. Holding the end of the club, he pushed Bullhead back.

Theodosia hardly noticed the two men. Her gaze wandered off, abstracted. She began to babble a little. "The heathen rage. Yet when one of them shames himself with his rudeness to you, you must make it appear that you deserve it." Theodosia had to set her feet apart to keep her balance. "I know that my noble Claude lives. He resides on that farther shore where he has joined the multitudes of them who have gone on before. While I remain behind in this vale of horror." Theodosia staggered, almost falling to the ground. "Oh, how I long to be translated to that upper world so that I may join him."

"Sis!"

"Life is made up of shadow and shine. Oh, I pray God that He in his infinite mercy may grant me removal of all memory of this time so that it may pass from me forever. I cannot bear it." Theodosia leaned down to look Judith in the face. "Sister, can you tell me of a place of refuge where this poor soul may go to hide? The Bible speaks of such places in Israel, cities where tormented souls could go and be safe from those who would oppress them."

"Why . . ."

"I wish for such a place of refuge."

Scarlet Plume's voice crackled. "There is such a safe place for a guest among the Yanktons. Let the Good Book Woman go to the council lodge. There you will be received as one of the land."

"But she is a woman," Bullhead roared. "Have the Yanktons become women that they welcome a woman in their council lodge?"

Smoky Day, Tinkling, Squirts Milk, and all the people, even pale Mavis, stood by their tepee doors and watched with slowly darkening brows. Some even stood with their hands clapped over their mouths at what they heard, their eyes directed to one side in consternation. Yanktons were known never to interfere in man-and-wife squabbles.

Theodosia leaned nose to nose into Judith's face. "Verily, we are like poor hens, being attacked again and again by mad cocks. But face must be saved, and first of all the face of others."

"Theodosia, oh, my dear."

"Do you know what my brute did to me last night? My brute— may God forgive his poor savage soul—who thinks himself my husband. Yes; he staked me to the ground in what was supposed to be my own house, and gagged me with a buckskin thong over my throat so that I could not cry out, while he perpetrated the most shameless, most horribly outrageous, acts upon my person. Why, he even poked a hot stick under me to make me come up to his go-down." Theodosia shuddered at the memory of it. "The Lord only knows how I lived through it all. Again and again and again. Like some buck goat gone mad. When all my life I've considered my body a vessel of the Lord's. Holy. Oh, God, oh, Claude, forgive, forgive, but the raw liver of the Indian way of life I cannot eat."

Scarlet Plume's eyes rolled like a furious wild stallion's.

Judith handed the papoose to Smoky Day, and went to her sister and took her in her arms and comforted her.

Theodosia murmured on Judith's neck, voice muffled. "May the name of my husband be held in everlasting remembrance for his effort to bring these miserable sinful natives knowledge of Christ. Because what my husband did was beyond the call of even Christian duty."

"Yes, sister, yes, yes."

"Claude meant nothing but good for them."

"Of course he did. We all know that."

"Come hither and I will show unto thee the judgment of the great whore with whom the inhabitants of the earth have been made drunk with the wine of her fornication. And I saw a woman sit upon a scarlet-colored beast."

"Theodosia!"

"Yet though my sins be as scarlet, they shall be as white as snow."

Bullhead was beside himself. He was so mad spittle sprayed out of his nose. His black cheeks quivered in sheets. The little row of honor eagle feathers at the back of his head worked like the snapping tail of an angry turkey cock. He lowered his big head at Scarlet Plume and swung it from side to side. He pawed the ground like a mad buffalo bull. Yet he did not quite dare to charge Scarlet Plume.

Whitebone stepped between Bullhead and Scarlet Plume. He held up his old hand in peace. "What is this? Are my children squabbling over a white squaw? The Yanktons hate the white man with a hot heart, and yet this comes about?"

"Kill the whites!" Bullhead bellowed. "Let us kill my white woman! Let us kill your white woman! Let us kill Traveling Hail's white woman. They are all good for nothing."

Theodosia recovered her calm. She freed herself from Judith's embrace, and turning on her heel, staggered straight for the council lodge.

Bullhead jumped around Scarlet Plume and bounded for his tepee. He danced in; danced out. He came carrying something else besides his club. In his right hand was something that looked like a silver quirt, which he swirled around and around. He leaped in front of Theodosia just as she reached the door of the council lodge. The dark-browed guards standing in front of the door jumped out of his way. Bullhead roared, "Kill all the whites! It is fun to kill the whites." Then Bullhead lashed Theodosia in the face with the silverish thing. "You cannot enter the men's lodge. It is where the sacred symbols of power are kept."

The lashing did not hurt Theodosia, only stung her. Yet she stopped as if clubbed. She cried a name.

Judith heard the name. She ran up. Her eyes followed the swirling silverish thing as Bullhead lashed Theodosia once more in the face. Then Judith saw it as it momentarily came to rest. She too cried a name. "Angela!"

Mavis stood before Traveling Hail's tepee as one shaped into a graven image.

Scarlet Plume rushed up. He also saw what it was. Angela's silver hair. Her scalp. And at last Scarlet Plume's control snapped. He picked up a log and waggled it in Bullhead's face. "What you have done is a terrible thing! The gods will punish us for what you have done!"

Whitebone walked over. "What is this? What has he done?"

Scarlet Plume snarled around at Whitebone. "After all were gone, the after guard and I buried the child Angela in the proper manner beside the lake. At that time her hair had not been troubled." Scarlet Plume jerked spasmodically, he was so outraged. "This Bullhead that you wish to keep in the band because you think he is a brave warrior, he has scalped the body of a dead child after it was buried."

Whitebone fixed glittering eyes on Bullhead. "Is this a true thing? Speak with a single tongue."

Before Bullhead could answer, Theodosia let go with a strangled scream. She dove for the door of the council lodge.

Bullhead was determined to block her. He tucked Angela's silver-blond scalp in the belt of his clout, and crying, "This is your die day," hit Theodosia an awful wallop over the head with his war club. The blow rocked Theodosia back a step. Her head suddenly seemed to be lopped over on one side and the level of her brows broken. Her hazel eyes slowly sharpened, and darkened, slowly became like the eyes of a fire-crazed mare determined to re-enter a burning barn. Again she lunged for the door of the council lodge.

Again Bullhead clubbed her. This time her head seemed to bulge out on the other side and the level of her eyes became even more broken.

The people stood beside their lodges, hands still clapped over their mouths.

Blood began to ooze through Theodosia's light-brown hair. Her whole head seemed to work like a mound of stirring bread dough. It rose to a peak. And her eyes slowly became popped as if something were pushing them out from behind.

Theodosia stood tottering a moment. "Sister?"

"Yes, oh, my pet."

"They will not let me enter the place of refuge as promised."

"Oh, Sis."

"I shall have to strike out for myself. I shall walk to the fort on the Minnesota River. God will help me."

"Sis."

"God keep thee until I return. For I will return with help. I am determined that at least you and Mavis shall be saved."

Mavis broke out of her stiff trance and ran to embrace Theodosia.

A stern-eyed warrior blocked Mavis' path.

"Good-bye, sister. Good-bye, Mavis. Help will soon be here." Theodosia looked at the rising sun, got her bearing, and, staggering, headed directly northeast.

"Good Book Woman," Scarlet Plume cried, "the wild wolves will devour thee if you travel alone. They will smell the blood and come from the four quarters of the earth."

Whitebone held up a hand. "My son, let the Good Book Woman go. It is a good thing. We must not quarrel over her. The band must survive. We are the Shining People. We are they who live in the center of the world and carry one of the seven sacred fires of the Dakota. This we must preserve."

Bullhead was not satisfied with the turn of events. "The manes of my dead wife need the blood!" he cried, and he started after Theodosia.

A signal passed between Whitebone and the dark-browed guards. Two of the guards stepped forward to block Bullhead's path.

Judith caught the signal. She gasped. "Ahhh." She understood suddenly. Whitebone had been in control all along. He had perhaps even arranged what had come to pass.

Theodosia staggered to the cutbank across the narrow meadow. She started to climb the cutbank. She scrabbled up through clumps of bluejoint grass. Gravel rattled down.

Theodosia had almost reached the top, and made a grab for a final clump of grass, when she lost consciousness. Toppling back-ward, she fell to the bottom, her head landing on a pink rock with a mashing sound. She lay still.

Judith pushed past the stern armed guards. Running, she fell upon her sister.

Theodosia was dead.

Whitebone gestured, sharp, once.

Four guards went over and stood over the two women.

There would never be any escaping Whitebone's band.

3

Walking Voice went crying around the circle of the tepees. "Strike the lodges. We remove to the foot of a high place where there has been built up a man of stone. We will rest beside the River Of The Rock while the scouts climb the high place to see if the enemy follows. Make haste. Strike the lodges. The sun rises in the sky."

Down came the tepees. Bundles were loaded onto horses and dogs and squaws. Braves emptied their guns, muzzles close to the ground to deaden the report, and reloaded with fresh powder.

The Yanktons started out with an impromptu parade in the old-time way. Whitebone and three elderly men mounted their horses and in solemn ceremony made a slow circuit of the camp, going out through the horns. Whitebone carried his emblem and the three elderly men carried the fire of the village. The four elders went ahead to select the places for resting and smoking en route. Behind them rode the various soldiers' lodges and war societies in paint and feathers, singing their favorite war songs. Spear points and guns flashed in the sun. Old women cried out the names of the warriors as they rode past and recited their glorious deeds. Maidens looked shyly down. Boys got themselves willow sticks to represent horses and rode behind the warriors. Some boys barely managed to keep their willow sticks from running away. Other boys pretended to be brave warriors afoot, fighting a running battle, jumping from side to side as they had seen their fathers do, dodging violently, hard to hit, slapping their mouths with the palms of their hands and lifting their voices into high, thin cater-wauling cries. One youngster pointed toward the far-off enemy whites and offered as ultimate insult the jerking away of his clout in their direction. Naked bodies gleamed a deep rosy brown in the morning sun.

Judith saw Bullhead riding by. He wore Angela's flowing silver scalp at his belt, deliberately flaunting it so that she would see it. His black eyes burned straight ahead. He was still gorged with rage. He had had to take his own tepee down.

Judith walked along as one numbed. Once again she found herself weighted down with the papoose.

Mavis walked beside Judith. Smoky Day and Tinkling had also dressed Mavis out as a squaw: moccasins, doeskin tunic, leggings, two heavy larded braids, a painted face.

After a last lingering drink in the clear, purling stream, the band headed straight west. Leathers creaked. Dogs whimpered. Children romped through the deep grass. Squaws gossiped and laughed as they walked along. The Yankton heart beat in magic unison with the heart of the earth. The sun had come up again and it gave them good light and they were happy.

Slowly the band straggled out.

When they came to a rise in the land, Judith looked back.

She could just make out the dead cottonwood beside the cut-bank. Something seemed to be caught in the cottonwood's branches that wasn't there before. It reminded her of a squirrel's nest. Then it came to her. The Good Book Woman had been put up on a tree scaffold, buried according to Stone Age rites. A mile behind the band rode the afterguards—Scarlet Plume, Traveling Hail, and two others.

Mavis' face, stained brown, was sharper than ever. Mavis made a perfect Sioux woman. She had exactly the right features and the proper form and height.

"Judith?"

"Yes?"

"Now it's just the two of us."

"Yes."

"That was awful back there."

"Yes."

"I feel so guilty about it."

"You?"

"I just couldn't move to help her. I tried and tried but I couldn't."

"Yes."

"I was perfectly paralyzed. All those terrible things—they were of the devil himself. Hellish."

Judith held her stomach. Her womb hurt. With her free hand she adjusted the pack strap over her forehead. Born By The Way had fallen asleep on her back.

"You think we'll be able to escape?"

"I don't know."

"What's going to happen to us, Judith?"

"I don't know."

"What are we going to do—just go along as if everything is as nice as pie, and let them do with us whatever they want?"

"I guess so." Judith managed a wan grimace with her cracked lips. "Where there's life there's hope."

"Ha."

They walked side by side.

Judith soon learned that moccasins made for easier walking than did high leather shoes. Her legs felt solid and tireless.

Breaths of wind moved across the grass in silverish waves. Wild flowers lay on the surface of the prairie like flecks of iridescent scud—asters, goldenrods, brown-eyed susans, wild onions. Perfume cloyed the breath at every step. There were myriads of prairie birds. Song sparrows spurted from underfoot. Meadowlarks flew in a dipping motion from wolfberry bush to wolfberry bush. And the deeper wet grass exploded even more birds—yellow head blackbirds, redwing blackbirds, plain blackbirds. Bird song cloyed the hearing on every side.

There was a sudden shrill call from the rear. Then came four quick sharp barks as from a coyote.

Everyone disappeared. Horses, squaws, dogs, children, all dropped into the deep grass.

Judith and Mavis were astounded. It was like watching partridge vanish into a slough.

Two Two crawled toward them in the deep grass like a very fast blue-runner snake. "Hide!" he cried in desperate whisper up to them. "Hide, or the camp soldiers will kill you. Hide in the grass."

Judith and Mavis dropped. It was harder for Judith because she also had to think of Born By The Way on her back.

"Who is it?" Mavis asked.

"We do not know," Two Two whispered.

Judith hoped it might be white soldiers.

Two Two gave them a troubled look through the grass. "Please do not talk together in the white man's tongue. The braves murmur against it. Also, prepare to die should it be the blue soldiers. It will be bad for the Yanktons should the blue soldiers find white women captives in our midst."

Judith heard rustling. She looked. Through the tips of the deep grass she could just make out Bullhead and another brave, their guns aimed at them. Judith pushed herself down as low as she could in the grass. So did Mavis. They lay as still as scared prairie chickens. Not an eyelid moved. Even Born By The Way hardly seemed to breathe.

They waited.

There was a second shrill call. This time it was a call as from a high-flying eagle. The alarm was over.

Everyone jumped up. Horses, half-gagged by boy hands, desperate for air, snorted and cavorted about. Dogs snapped playfully at each other. All the people danced in the grass.

"What was it? Can you tell?" voices called to each other.

Presently Walking Voice, the news walker, came along. "There were some horses. They were not spotted horses. Therefore it was thought they were mounted white soldiers come to get us. But soon it was made out that the horses were some of those which escaped a white man's camp many moons ago. It is well. Do not fear. Soon we will be at the foot of the hill where there has been built up a man of stone."

They walked.

The band straggled out again, became almost a mile long and half that wide.

The children thought it an endless picnic. There were sleepy jackrabbits to scare up. It was fun to see the crazy jacks bound from left to right in great leaps. There were meadowlark nests to discover, cozy, with a secret tunnel entrance, and four chestnut speckled eggs. There were the sweet wild onions to suck on. There were tricks to play on each other, hair-pulling, tripping, scaring. The younger ones, even up to five winters, could always run to mother for a little ma-ma. A suck or two on the always available brown nipple and off they would go again, galloping through the grass. The Indian children, Judith decided, were the happiest in the world.

A meadowlark, perched on what appeared to be a stalk of wild sumac, sang a song. "Let the people beware," it whistled, flashing its lemon breast from side to side, "let the people beware!"

Two Two laughed, full of pride. "You see the Sioux bird of fidelity. He is always full of cheerful warning for the Yanktons." Two Two's smile was as clearly cut on his brown face as a quarter moon on a dark sky. "He is warning us now."

"Ha," Judith said, short. "What is he warning us about now?"

"He is sitting on a bush called the thunderwood. It is a bad thing. Touch it with a finger, and the finger will swell up and then rot and fall off. See, look at the bush he sits on. It is so ashamed of itself for being evil that it hangs its white berries in a sneaky way, beneath where the leaves have white undersides."

"Let the people beware," the meadowlark sang.

"Perhaps he also sings a certain song for the white man," Mavis said.

Two Two laughed. "Then the white man is a fool not to listen."

The women walked pigeon-toed under their burdens. The men walked straight-toed. The footprints of the women lay turned in one after the other. The footprints of the men lay parallel to each other.

A single hackberry appeared. The tree stood some thirty feet high, had a fine grayish trunk, delicate greenish leaves, and over-all perfect symmetry. It cast a gentle round shadow and the wind soughing under it was cool.

Whitebone and the three elders looked up at the sun almost directly overhead and decided that the whole band could rest awhile near the tree. They would have a bite to eat and then a fine smoke.

Quickly the squaws sent the children scurrying out over the prairie to dig up turnips and various other prairie roots. Horses were staked out to graze. Dogs were commanded to lie down.

Judith thought the single hackberry a godsend. She removed the papoose from her back with a sigh of relief and set it against the foot of the tree.

Soon the children came in with handfuls of roots. The four old men dealt them out to each family in equal shares. The wild vegetables were eaten raw.

Smoky Day came up with a full gourd of honey. She mixed it with water in a small bladder and passed it around. It made for a most delicious reviving drink.

A snake was discovered underfoot. It raised its head and hissed its red tongue at them all. It was a big one, some seven feet long. There were cries of fright from the children. Scarlet Plume made sure it was not a deadly rattler, only a bull snake, and then sat back to let it find its own way out of the resting place.

The bull snake's flickering red tongue put Whitebone in a re-flective mood. Eyes wimmering, elbows on knees, he mused aloud. "I am here by the will of Wakantanka. He has made me a chief.

Because I listen to the will of Wakantanka, my heart is red and sweet. I know it is red and sweet because it seems that whatever passes near me puts out its red tongue to me."

Smoky Day's old she-dog Long Claws smelled something. Long Claws sniffed and sniffed. Suddenly she jumped up, burden and all, and nose to the ground, headed straight for a clump of blue-joint. A cottontail popped up. Instantly Long Claws took up the chase. Other dogs and many puppies came alert too and took off after the bouncing cottontail.

Smoky Day and Tinkling, and all the other squaws, immediately bounded to their feet. They shouted and cursed at the dogs, trying to call them back. "Come here, you bad dog you! Come here. Here! here! here!" A chase could be disastrous. In the heat of a good run dogs were known to scatter precious cargo all over the prairie. The squaws ran heavily after the dogs. The children joined them, hooting and hollering.

The men sat back and smiled. This was a trouble the squaws for once could handle alone.

Soon the bobbing cottontail vanished down a badger hole. The dogs piled up around the hole in a howling rage. Some of the dogs tried to dig the hole wider, some snapped at each other. They had a snarling good time.

The squaws caught up with the dogs and belabored them with sticks. Several bundles had fallen apart, and various articles— buffalo-horn spoons, wooden chip plates, sticks for firewood—lay scattered in the thick grass. Painstakingly the women gathered them up and retied the bundles to the dogs. Then they all came trooping back, laughing, sweating, all out of breath.

Long Claws lay down in the middle of Whitebone's family circle in a sheepish manner. She had received the worst beating.

Mavis, feeling sorry for the old she-dog, reached out to pet her. "Poor doggie."

Long Claws showed her teeth. The muscles of her old legs still quivered from all the blows.

"I'd be careful," Judith said. "Indian dogs make poor pets.

They're always being chased out of the tepee, kicked and hollered at, all day long. They don't understand kindness."

There were a few nose flies about and the horses kept shaking their heads up and down, rattling their reins. A few of the nose flies flew orbits around the older men. When one of them began to pester Whitebone and his big bold nose, Smoky Day dug out a homemade fly swatter, a buffalo bull's tail. Whitebone took it and laid about him. But he missed.

Scarlet Plume, sitting near, snapped out a cupped hand, and the nose fly was gone.

Sweat bees with their striped yellow bellies appeared too. They hovered in front of the eyes like motes. One of them buzzed but a finger's length from Smoky Day's forehead. After a moment Smoky Day retrieved the bull's tail from Whitebone and whacked about as if at phantoms. This time it was Two Two's hand which flicked out and extinguished the pest.

"Look," Mavis said, "ah, look what I see."

Judith followed her glance. Something golden gleamed in the grass at the edge of the hackberry's shadow. "Yes." Judith leaned over and parted the hair-thick grass. "Why, it's a dandelion."

"Seems so queer to see a lonesome dandelion way out here," Mavis said, "when the lawns in St. Paul were always full of them."

Judith's clublike braids hung heavy against the sides of her face. The grease in the braids had begun to have a rancid smell. "I thought at first it might be a gold coin somebody lost here. That some white settler had gone by here."

Whitebone heard her. "Gold!" he snorted. "The whites always think of the gold." Whitebone stuck out his gray, coarse tongue, and lifting a ham, let go a noble fart. "A good Yankton considers gold to be the dung of the gods. Goddung."

"Houw, houw!" cried some braves sitting near.

Judith threw the old man an angry look. The gassy old brute.

There had never been much squaw-stealing in Whitebone's camp. But this hardly kept Bullhead from trying. Bullhead needed a wife to run his tepee and during the noon rest he began to make overtures to Squirts Milk, wife of Plenty Lice. The big smile he gave both the baby and the hairy pup as Squirts Milk breast-fed them wrinkled up his usual black countenance grotesquely.

Squirts Milk was onto him and, suffering him, gave him a bland moon smile even as her eye roved over to where her husband, Plenty Lice, stood guard.

Bullhead took her smile to mean encouragement. He sidled up to her. And finally he gave her a good firm pinch.

Squirts Milk had enough. She withdrew her breast from the suckling mouth of her baby, and taking it full in her chubby hand, squirted him in the face.

Bullhead reared back, sputtering, wiping milk out of his eyes. Blacker in the face than ever, he retreated to his pony and goods.

Two Two and his friends laughed in derision. "Ha, ha," they cried, "the great Bullhead's heart has been wiped out."

When all was quiet again, Whitebone turned around. He turned so far, a web of wrinkles appeared along the side of his neck. He bent kindly, inquiring eyes on Scarlet Plume. "My son, you will make the divination for the pa-pa? You will learn where the buffalo will be roaming?"

"I will, my father."

"It is good." Whitebone poked up his head and beckoned for Walking Voice to come near. "Ho hechetu! Old one, tell the people we will remove to the next resting place. It will be the place of the evening camp. Where there has been made up a man of stone."

It was almost sundown when a fringe of willows and ash trees appeared in a wide valley ahead.

Walking Voice went crying through the line of weary marchers. "You see the running water with the little trees. It is the River Of The Rock. It is still a young river at this place."

The gently meandering stream was gorged with beaver dams and swimming holes. Beyond, the plains lifted abruptly into the flank of a long hill.

Judith's eye ran along the brow of the long hill, from north to south. There was no cairn of stones that she could see, nor the odd chance that the Indians had a stone statue of some sort.

Two Two saw Judith's wondering look. "My mother with the sunned hair, do you look for something? What is it?"

"The man of stone."

Two Two's face turned solemn. "It is wakan, my mother."

"I would like to see it."

"It is not for a woman to see."

"What is it like?"

"It is wakan. It was made by the old ancient ones. These ancient ones were of another old time, beyond even the time of the grand-father of the grandfather of my father, beyond even those who were given the seven sacred fires of the Dakotas. They lived be-yond the count of many grandfathers. We do not remember." Two Two pointed. In the bloody sunset a single bronze horseman mounted the high hill. The horseman stopped to look for sign in all directions. After a moment the horseman slid off his spotted pony, and walking over, kneeling reverently, seemed to be scatter-ing something on the evening wind. "You see? It is Traveling Hail. He brings a small sacrifice of tobacco to appease the gods of the old ancients. He drops it at the foot of a stone effigy in the grass. The effigy of the man is made of sacred white stones. If the man of white stones could stand up, he would wear moccasins the size of my father's tepee."

The red solemnity of the lonesome scene moved Judith to moist eyes.

"I have spoken. My father calls me to unburden the horses."

Around them all was business. Lodgepoles were raised, leather coverings were shaped into cone dwellings, stakes were driven into the ground to hold down the tepee against storms, cooking and smudge fires were kindled, horses were watered and put out to grass, dogs went for a sopping swim, and certain of the stern-eyed camp soldiers were set out as guards. Soon the living of one night solely for itself was begun again.

Judith did her share. She removed Whitebone's moccasins and bathed his feet. She changed the baby with fresh cattail fluff, then fed him, letting soup trickle into his puckered mouth drop by drop from a little wooden spoon. She scurried about for sticks under the ash trees.

Last she picked up a pair of bladders and went to get a supply of fresh water. The River Of The Rock was but a half-dozen steps wide but it ran full to the brim, pinkish clear over clean red stones. She rinsed out each bladder thoroughly and then filled them.

She knelt down and with a cupped hand gave herself a drink. The water was cool. It was good.

She was about to rise, when she heard an awful groan in a clump of swamp willows behind her. Scared almost out of her wits, she dropped in the grass, face down, hiding herself as flat as she could.

She waited.

Nothing happened.

She wondered what it was. Someone had to be in great pain to moan so.

There was another groan, not of this earth, as if coming from a womb about to give birth.

Judith ticked off in her mind all the squaws in the band. None seemed to have been pregnant that she could remember, at least not far enough along to notice.

Cautious, Judith raised her head a couple of inches and peered through an undergrowth of ground cherries.

Scarlet Plume.

What? Judith stared and stared.

Scarlet Plume was sitting on his heels inside the clump of willows, in a tiny clearing. He was alone. He was wearing his single scarlet feather, and had repainted his left cheek with a yellow dot inside a blue circle.

He had also made a rough contour map in sand: there was a meandering river, then a long, bold outcrop of cliffs, then a flat plain beyond. Off to one side stood what looked like a toy buffalo, an effigy. It had been carved out of a piece of wood, then painted and properly tufted with bits of brown hair.

Great beads of sweat stood out on Scarlet Plume's brow. His penny-skin features, otherwise warm, were tinged with a sickish gray. His cheeks were fearfully indrawn. His lips were quivering and pulled down at the corners as if in extreme penitence. His eyeballs, staring and enlarged, arteries pulsing, were fixed on the buffalo effigy.

He spoke in a low murmur. Though his eyes remained fixed on the effigy, he actually seemed to be talking into an open pouch at his belt. He was communing with his secret helper.

Judith had to quick clap a hand over her mouth to keep from crying out at what she saw next.

The effigy began to jump around on the sand. And it jumped without any help from Scarlet Plume. Scarlet Plume's hands were folded over his belly, his feet were firmly planted on the sand. There were no puppet strings attached to it. Nothing. Yet the wooden effigy was jumping around as lively as any real buffalo. Not only that; the effigy buffalo was gradually advancing toward the line of cliffs Scarlet Plume had shaped in the sand. Finally, with a little higher jump than usual, the effigy buffalo leaped over the edge of the cliff, and tumbling in the air, fell below.

Stars and saints alive. What devil's doings were these? Judith sat frozen, sat as one hypnotized.

So this was what Whitebone had meant when he asked Scarlet Plume to make the divination for the pa-pa.

Scarlet Plume was wakan. Truly. No wonder Whitebone wanted him to become a medicine man.

The effigy lay very still where it had fallen.

Gradually Scarlet Plume's face gentled over and the old warm liberal expression returned to his large carven lips. His eyes half closed in a musing smile.

Scarlet Plume spoke low to himself, satisfied. "The Yanktons will see plenty pa-pa at the Buffalo Jump two days hence."

Scarlet Plume picked up his effigy reverently and stood up,

stretching to his full height, and in the waning red sunset made his way out of the clump of willows.

Judith sucked in a long, slow breath. A mild shock set in from what she had seen.

A divination. Truly.

4

The next day the Yanktons removed to a place where much cold water flowed out of blue mounds. The leather village was set just above the springs and inside a thin loop of scrub oak. Across from the running springs, on a small plateau, lay sign of what once had been an ancient village: broken potsherds, a grassed-over kitchen midden, loose piles of chipping stones, animal bones so old they collapsed at a touch, and many strange-shaped arrowheads.

There were dozens of springs, and they all came together to form a small stream that flowed east into the River Of The Rock. The River Of The Rock itself flowed south, to the left of a red rock ridge. The red ridge kept lifting out of black earth until it became a considerable frowning escarpment. Two miles south of the springs, the red rimrock curved around to the west. Here the highest outcroppings were colored over with greenish-gray lichen, giving them a blue look from a distance. The curving escarpment made a perfect setting for a buffalo surround or buffalo jump. This was the place the Indians called the Buffalo Jump At The Blue Mounds.

At dark all flares and fires were extinguished. A cold supper was served. Camp soldiers patrolled the village and kept close watch. No one was allowed to go wandering off alone to leave scent about and scare off any chance buffaloes grazing nearby.

Late in the night, Judith awoke to find herself sleeping alone. Whitebone was not beside her. She listened. She heard Smoky Day and Tinkling snoring lightly on the women's side. She raised

her head. In the dim pink light of the fallen embers she saw that
Two Two was also gone.

She heard drums, faintly. Ah, the men were holding a secret
meeting of some sort.

Her sleeping robe had slid off a little, and Judith felt cold
along her hip. The touch of chilly air had awakened in her a call
to nature.

She decided to repress the night call, make it go away. She covered herself again and nuzzled her head in the fur. She crossed
her naked legs to help them warm each other.

She listened to the steady drumming. The drumbeat was urgent,
alive. She wondered what was going on. Probably the men were
holding a ritual dance of some kind, full of smoky ancient mystery.

After a while the night call became stronger than ever. She saw
there was no use to fight it. Sighing, stiffish, she got up. She threw
the sleeping robe around her shoulders and stepped outside. She
found a place behind the circle of tepees. There was a gentle hiss-
ing in the grass under her. A soft sigh broke from her.

The beat of the drums came down wind, from the north. She
could just make out a weak orange reflection on red rock across
the stream. The dance was being held around a fire in a hollow to
keep down the sound as well as the light.

She couldn't resist one little peek. She had to look. She had seen
a few ritual Indian dances at Skywater, but the trouble with them
was that they had been held for the benefit of the whites. She
wanted to know what a real Dakota dance was like out in the
wilds.

Cautiously she stepped through the soft, deep grass. She walked
soundlessly. She pushed through a cluster of grazing ponies. She
passed unheard within a dozen steps of a camp guard. She had to
part some prickling gooseberries. At last she stood on the rimrock.
To the left, and below, there it was. A dance. Some twenty men
and boys were slowly winding around a small stick fire, around
and around on beaten grass, toe down first and then the heel, a
bird step, drums striking *tuk-tak tuk-tak,* mouths lifted up and

bellowing. Each brave had tied a buffalo tail to his buttocks and fetlocks to his heels. A few braves wore black horns to represent buffalo heads. And one of the braves actually had put on a huge dressed-out buffalo head with horns and hair and whiskers. Otherwise they were stark naked. Around and around they pranced. *Tuk-tak tuk-tak.* They bellowed. They crouched on all fours. They pawed the earth. They butted each other. Some mounted each other. *Tuk-tak tuk-tak.*

A little closing of the eyes, Judith thought, and one could see them as actual buffalo bulls. They were truly dancing up the buffalo.

Judith spotted Two Two, Bullhead, Traveling Hail, and Whitebone. Walking Voice and another old man were at the drums, both of them crying their hearts out. At their feet lay a white buffalo skull, fired sweet grass smoldering in front of its bony nostrils. It was heathenish, pagan, savage, barbaric, all these things, and yet at the same time Judith couldn't help but admit it was more profoundly moving, soul-rousing, than any Christian rite or ceremony she had ever witnessed in her life. Only the Roman Catholics and the Episcopalians had anything like it. In their own minds the Yankton men had been transformed into buffalo. They were the buffalo. It went beyond mere belief.

It struck her that the white man had things backward. The white man, both her brother-in-law Claude and her sister Theodosia, believed that all things spiritual were heaven-sent. They weren't. The real truth was they were earth-born. Stone was not just stone, dust was not just dust, grass was not just grass, savages were not just savages, but all of them were manifestations of something profound, utterances dark and from far out of the deeps of time. They related back to some ultimate seat of truth. A truth was emanating out of dreaming stone rather than out of indifferent pan-Spirit. The dancing and the crying, the butting and the bellowing, the drumming and the singing, were voices out of the heart of Matter.

Then she recognized Scarlet Plume. He was the dancer wearing the huge dressed-out buffalo head.

His dancing was magnificent. A true re-creation. His movements were truly the motions of a real butting buffalo bull. His horns hooked up on the left, gutting a rival bull, then his horns hooked up on the right, gutting another rival bull. His bellowing, resounding out of the huge hollow skull he wore, was tremendous, deafening. He kept butting away the rival bulls. Slowly he made his way to his favorite buffalo cow. Already he was prepared for her. His phallus was erect, resembling the head of a bull snake straining to lift itself off the ground. He was buffalo.

Judith backed away. As she retreated, she kept looking at the dancing risen Scarlet Plume until she could see him no longer.

It was only when she lay down again by her tepee fire that she remembered who she was: a white woman captive.

At dawn the form of Traveling Hail loomed a golden copper in the leather doorway. He was naked except for clout and bow and arrows.

Whitebone was instantly awake. He reared up from his fur pallet. "What is there, my son?"

"My father, a big dust has appeared in the air across the plains. It is the buffalo."

"What is the direction, my son?"

"They come from the northwest."

"Where lies the wind this morning, my son?"

"It comes sweet and warm from the southeast."

"How many buffalo are there?"

Holding up both hands, Traveling Hail bent down each finger in turn. When all ten fingers were down, he let them spring up like geese flying away. To remember each ten, he kept down a finger. He counted his ten fingers ten times and then added six. "Six and ten bending downs, my father."

"Ah. They are the buffalo Scarlet Plume saw in his divination. It is good. Hoppo! Up! Awake the people."

"They are already awake, my father." Traveling Hail smiled down at his uncle in a slow, sober manner. "We await you and

Two Two. Also the Woman With The Sunned Hair. Hurry. The people tremble at the thought of the great day before us." Traveling Hail was careful not to look at Judith as she lay beside the old man.

"Have they all had the morning bath?"

"All, my father. Already they wear freshly washed moccasins. My brother warns we must be very careful not to leave any scent in the grass for the wise bulls to smell."

"You speak well, my son. Have the women tied up the dogs?"

"They have, my father."

Whitebone turned and placed his hand on Judith's belly. "Awake, woman. Be ready to run far. There will be no time to warm the wake-up soup. First the chase. Ho hechetu, the buffalo awaits us. He wants us to catch him so we can all eat fat pa-pa again and be merry."

Whitebone was quickly out of bed. He grabbed up his robe and stomped off to take his morning dip. Two Two followed him, hopping along lightly.

Judith and Smoky Day and Tinkling also got up and hurried off to take their required baths.

Returning, Judith slipped on her tunic and freshly washed leggings and moccasins. The buckskins, having become rounded to her form, fit her perfectly. Never in her life had she worn such comfortable attire.

She stepped outside. Sparkling lemon light brought out the deeper greens in the grass and the subtler reds in the rocks. Her stomach gnawed in hunger; nevertheless she felt extraordinarily alive, ready to run miles.

Yanktons who were to make up the two wings of the human corral were gathered under the oaks: camp soldiers, young mothers, boys and girls. Traveling Hail was giving them some last-minute instructions. They listened, eyes flashing, flushed to their chins. Some ran about not quite knowing what they were doing. Some touched the hard elbows of oaks for strength.

Judith found herself assigned to the south wing, the one which would form along the rim of the escarpment far to the south. She and Two Two, and others, would hide behind rock outcroppings.

Scarlet Plume stalked in among them carrying his buffalo effigy.

Judith couldn't help but shiver at the sight of him. Several times already she had caught herself daydreaming about him, and in a way to make her blush.

Scarlet Plume looked each member of the chase in the eye.

All fell silent.

Slowly Scarlet Plume's calm face changed. A great weep took possession of him. Copious tears ran down his red-brown cheeks. He let the sparkling tears fall on his buffalo effigy.

Scarlet Plume spoke. "This we do in memory of all the pa-pa who will die for us today. We are of their blood. We weep for them now because we already know their fate. Ho-ha. Listen at all times to my brother Traveling Hail. He has been appointed the master of the surround. Remember, it is very bad to disobey him. I have said."

Scarlet Plume's tears abruptly ceased. He covered his little effigy with a parfleche, and turning on his heel, disappeared behind the scrub oaks.

The Yanktons hurried. Each carried a scaring blanket. Sometimes they ran skulking, sometimes openly. The land rose under them like the slanted deck of a vast ship. They toed through patches of buffalo grass, its blades curly and crinkly. They raced across islands of sage, its silver dusty and muted. Sprigs of wild onion and lonesome bull thistles speckled solid stands of goldenrod.

As much as possible they kept to the exposed red rock. The soil was so thin that in spots whole acres of absolutely naked red rock lay open to the sky. The open red rock made Judith think of the time when as a child she had badly barked herself falling out of a tree. There were skinned areas on her thighs as big as peeled beets, red flesh showing. The exposed red rock was sometimes so glassy slick she had trouble keeping to her feet. Across the face of one such exposure ran long, wavering lines, as if some cosmic groom had run a currycomb across it.

Judith ran easy in her Indian garb. She ran lightly up the hard rising plateau. She seemed to have endless breath that morning.

She came across a tumble of rocks where the quartzite still seemed to be in a state of violent boiling. Mad scarlet and bruised blue and veined purple and raw pink swirled underfoot. She couldn't resist pausing for a look.

"Why do you stop, my mother?" Two Two called.

"It's this rock. Like flowing blood."

"It is Boiling Rock you are looking at."

At last Judith found herself hidden behind an outcropping. The outcropping resembled a family of blue buffalo snoozing in the morning sun. The outcropping was reddish along the edges near the grass, but thick blue lichen bearded over the rest of it. Some of the edges, about waist high, shone as if polished with a lapping rag.

Two Two was stationed not far off, west some fifty steps. He also lay hidden behind a tumble of rocks. The Yanktons once again seemed to have vanished into the ground.

Judith allowed herself a cautious look around. To the south, the escarpment dropped away in a series of rock shelvings, until it leveled off into a prairie. The view beyond was stunning. She could see miles and miles across an expanse of valley. A spacious sky arched high over a sweeping land. The valley lay like the palm of an open hand. Down it ran a life line, the River Of The Rock.

"The prospect from Summit Hill in St. Paul can't compare with it," Judith thought. "Not even the hills west of Davenport." She nodded to herself. "I see it now. This is why men have westered. Yes. Beyond the ridge of every horizon lies a new Eden prairie. Each new valley is a virgin in itself, and if a man is any kind of bull at all, he has to possess it, he has to fulfill it."

Judith wished she were a man.

She looked down. At her feet she spotted the purple flowers of a cluster of wild onions. There seemed to be three of them in a bunch. Kneeling, she dug out the pale bunched roots. The ancient turf was tough and it took a firm forefinger to pry them loose.

She nibbled at all three until they were gone. The wild onions were strangely sweet. It made her think of what she had seen the night before, Scarlet Plume dancing naked and risen. Some dirt had gotten under the nail of her forefinger and she sucked it out.

"They come," Two Two called over in a piercing whisper.

Judith turned to look.

"Do not show yourself," Two Two warned. He smiled at her from behind his rock and tilted his head in such a way as to show it wasn't his fault the laws of a buffalo surround were hard.

Judith looked cautiously around a corner of her rock.

Blinking, she saw them, lumps of dusky brown against a shimmering morning green. Except for their color they reminded her of a herd of cattle. The cows and yearlings were up front, the bulls behind.

They came grazing. A crop here at a better tuft of grass, a switch of the short tail, a half-dozen steps forward, then a crop there. They grazed through little gardens of golden aster. The soft wind blurred the brown hair over their humps. With every step they loomed a bit larger, sometimes all at once, sometimes in varied groups, sometimes singly. Dipping swallows caught insects on the fly above the herd. Bolder cowbirds sat on the backs of the bulls and dug out the larvae of botflies.

"Scarlet Plume comes," Two Two whispered low along the ground.

Judith slid around the tumble of her rocks and looked from the other side.

At first she couldn't find him. All she saw was yet another buffalo, a bull, grazing alone. Then she noted the single bull was smallish. Scarlet Plume. He had put on a buffalo skin and head. She guessed instantly what was up. He was the decoy, a Judas buffalo.

Scarlet Plume grazed quietly along. Every now and then he

lifted his shaggy head to sniff the air. He switched his tail. He stomped a foot at a fly. He grazed.

When the herd was yet some distance away, Scarlet Plume sang a song, softly:

> Come, buffalo. Come, pa-pa.
> You are one of the Yankton gods.
> We wish to eat you.
> Hohe! Give us your strength.
> We wish to eat you.
> Hohe! Give us your succession.
> We wish to draw closer to the gods.
> Wana hiyelo.
> This is a very good song I sing.
> Listen to it, buffalo.
> Hohe. I have said.

The herd came on, cropping at ease. All the buffalo were fat.

Scarlet Plume grazed through an island of rippling sage. His brown fur took on a blackish luster against the silver leaves.

Judith watched Scarlet Plume, fascinated. She forgot where she was.

The calves cavorted in and around the cows. The calves had fluffy yellowish hair, remindful of just-hatched chicks out for their first perky walk.

Certain of the bulls walked a step behind the cows. Every now and then an old bull would mount a young cow, and he would be so heavy for her she would almost collapse under him. When a young bull mounted a cow, usually an old one, he could scarcely make connection. Sometimes the young bull missed entirely and his charge of seed floated on the air like a liquid arrow.

The rest of the bulls formed the rearguard. Sometimes they stopped to rub themselves on the edges of the taller rocks. They gave themselves a good scratching. Their vigorous rubbing explained the polished lapped edges.

There was one very old bull. He trailed along far in the rear with the yellow calves. He had hair on his forelegs and chin so long it dragged through the grass. From a distance his hair resembled shadows trailing under his body and tapering off to wavering points.

Immediately behind the herd traveled a small army of jackrabbits. They moved along in erratic bounds. Still farther behind came a pair of spying wolves.

Scarlet Plume sang another buffalo song. His voice was low, persuasive. Out of the midst of the song there occasionally broke the urgent grunt of a bull mounting a cow.

> Come, friends. Come, pa-pa
> We belong to you.
> Ungh. Ungh.
> You belong to us.
> Ungh. Ungh.
> This is a good song I sing.
> You are walking into our trap.
> You like this.
> Ungh. Ungh.
> We like this.
> Ungh. Ungh.
> See, the ghosts of our dead ones
> Come along to share the fun.
> They will feast with us tonight.
> Come, pa-pa.
> We have you in our power.
> Hohe. We thank you.
> Wana hiyelo.

The tufted buffalo drifted farther and farther into the trap. The sun rose to the midpoint of the morning sky. The wind continued warm and sweet from the southeast. Flowers opened. Perfumes hazed upon the air. Bumblebees flew about drunk. Meadowlarks cried their cheer that all the skies were clear.

The two trailing wolves were the first to smell trouble. They stopped, sat on their haunches a moment, sniffing the air with lifted noses, laughing with long red tongues, then up and with a twirling whisk of brush tails were gone. The jackrabbits were next to sense it. They abruptly began to bound away to the left and the right.

Traveling Hail stood up from his hiding place. He gave a high, clear coyote call. It wavered over the entire plateau. Instantly the heads of all the Yanktons popped up from behind stones and boulders and, making even lines, formed the wings of a human corral. There was another clear call and the ends of the wings ran toward each other, closing the corral. "Yip! yip! yip!" everyone hallooed, waving their scaring robes.

The buffalo didn't scare immediately. They were fat, lazy. The laggard bulls in back turned their great heads about in mild curiosity. They chewed, and wondered.

But the old bull with the long shadow hair knew. He let go a great snort.

The snort galvanized the entire herd. Up came their heads, they stiffened, and then, tails in the air, they broke into a heavy run. They headed into the wind. They went straight for the highest dropoff of the escarpment, Buffalo Jump.

The Yanktons hallooed, "Yihoo!" and waved their robes, and shrilled and barked and hooted. "Yihoo!" The stampede was on.

Scarlet Plume up ahead appeared to be the least concerned of all the buffaloes. He casually grazed toward a grayish-red boulder. When the rampaging herd was almost upon him, he deftly stepped behind the boulder. The buffalo thundered by, going as fast as they could hump it. When the last one was well past him, he stepped into view again. Gone were the buffalo head and buffalo skin. He was sweating and in the sun his limbs shone like freshly burnished copper. With the others he ran after the buffalo, shouting, waving, hallooing.

Judith found herself running with the others. Her two heavy braids clubbed her over the back and arms. The running and hallooing reminded her of the children's game pump-pump-pull-away.

Judith gathered her tunic up around her waist and ran hard. She ran swiftly. Her long legs enabled her to keep up with the swiftest of the Yanktons. She was one of those women who could run fluid and elastic off the hip, not as though hobbled at the knees.

The buffalo thundered on, tails up. The faster cows and heifers took over the lead. Then came the bulls. Then came the yellow calves. All ran blindly. All ran scared. All ran with heavy grunting bounds.

There was a slight fall in the land just before the brink. The buffalo gathered even more momentum.

Then they poured over, somersaulting, the cows with their legs still galloping in air, the bulls bellowing, the calves bawling. Trees cracked below. Pillars of red rock tumbled over. There was a heavy thunder of many thumps. There was a moment of swallowing silence; then, dying miserably, all splashed to pieces, all the fallen buffalo let go with a rising massive moan.

The Yanktons ran so hard after the stampeded buffalo, they almost took the jump too. They had to lean back to stop at the brink.

The Yanktons peered down. From below rose a slow cloud of dust and hair and threshed-out milkweed seed.

Scarlet Plume lifted up both hands. "Yanktons, you see the power of the divination. You see all the killed buffalo. They have consented to die for us so that we may eat."

The women trilled cries of thankfulness.

Scarlet Plume turned to Two Two. "Brother, run to the village for pony drags. We are ready for the butchering. Tell them not to forget the many parfleches. We will need them all. There is very much meat."

Two Two ran to obey.

Scarlet Plume sniffed the air. "The smell of buffalo blood is sweeter than the smell of a Yankton rose." He looked down. Buffalo bellies still stirred and buffalo limbs still crackled. "Friends, let us descend. Hohe."

They filed down a pass in the red cliff, eyes popped and shoulders humped in anticipation. They surrounded the great tumble of broken buffalo. There were splintered hoofs, cracked spines, split bellies, running green anuses, limp tails, dying hearts, bitten tongues.

The Yanktons waited for Scarlet Plume to speak again.

At last, in reverent manner, Scarlet Plume took a pinch of dried sweet grass from a pouch he carried at his belt and touched the nearest buffalo with it. That done, he scattered the rest of the sweet grass in the direction of all the broken buffalo. He took a knife from his belt and placed his moccasined foot on the head of the nearest buffalo. "Friend," he said down to the dulled-over half-closed eyes, "we thank you for letting us catch you. Friend, we too were animals before we were people, hence we must apologize now that we have killed you. Friend, we will not forget this. We thank you. I have said." He made motions with his knife as if to lay open the hairy hump of the buffalo, then on the fourth and sacred motion finally did cut into it. Flesh parted, blood flowed.

The Yanktons piled in with their knives and teeth and fingers. They were like thirsty weasels. They drank the blood of the buffalo before the heartbeat faded away. Each cut for himself a choice tidbit. The Yanktons believed that like parts of animals nourished like parts of man. Some fancied raw purple liver seasoned with a drop of green bile. Some desired certain portions of raw kidney. Others declared raw brains were the best. Young wives anxious to have more children craved the silky envelope of the embryo. Mothers who wanted powerful runner sons fancied the soft feet of the fetuses. Old men hoping for a return of virility cut themselves slices of raw testicles. There wasn't a part of the beloved buffalo but what some Yankton didn't fancy it. The Yanktons crawled in and out of the mass of flesh like beetles investing the dead carcass of a super mammoth. Soon they were all covered with blood from head to foot. Red blood for red men. Even Scarlet Plume.

Judith and Mavis were revolted. They turned away. They retched. Their empty stomachs pumped and pumped. The one's retching led to more retching by the other. Gall burned bitter on the lip and smell of it cut the nostril. The human beast was no better than the wolf who lived from kill to kill.

Judith and Mavis started back for the village by the springs.

The Yanktons were amazed at the behavior of the white women. Enough food had been given them by Wakantanka to last them all of a bitter winter and a mother turned sick at the thought of it?

Scarlet Plume and Traveling Hail hurried to block their path. Both men were gory with the blood. It trickled from the corners of their mouths.

Traveling Hail said to his wife, Mavis, "Shot-up Woman, what is this? Are you not happy with our great kill?" Traveling Hail was trying not to be angry. "Tell me."

Mavis retched yet once more.

Scarlet Plume spoke soothingly. "You have run very far without food. The white woman has not done this before. There is a fruit nearby that will quiet your belly. Come." Scarlet Plume stepped over to a patch of wild roses and picked a handful of orange hips. He gave Judith and Mavis each four. "Eat them. They are often given to mares to quiet their bellies after a hard run."

Judith and Mavis stared at the proffered hips. Both women gave each other tormented, even strangled, looks.

"Eat."

Judith nibbled at one of hers, found it surprisingly good. Finally she ate all four. So did Mavis.

Traveling Hail said to Mavis, "I will help the Shot-up Woman. Come. This is your first buffalo kill."

Scarlet Plume said to Judith, "Come. I will help you get the meat for my father's tepee. The day will come when your tongue will relish raw liver sweetened with a pinch of gall."

Remembering their captivity, swallowing their bile, the two went back to the place of slaughtering.

After the best meat had been separated from the mass of broken bodies, and green hides removed and folded up, it was found that one of the yellowish calves still lived. This became a source of much astonishment to the Yanktons.

Scarlet Plume helped the calf out, and set it on its feet in the grass. The yellow calf stood stunned awhile.

"The calf is wakan," Scarlet Plume said, "to live after such a great fall. He is protected by the spirit of the Buffalo Woman herself."

Judith's heart went out to the yellow calf. She gave it two fingers to suckle.

Soon it was seen that the yellow calf was drawn to Judith and would not leave her side. This astounded the Yanktons even more.

"See," Two Two cried, "the yellow calf is also related to the Woman With The Sunned Hair. We can now see that the white woman is a Yankton truly. She is my mother. Ho hechetu!"

The yellow calf nosed after Judith wherever she went. It reminded her of calves she used to feed on the farm. Only its head appeared to be different from the usual domestic calf.

Judith became a bit more reconciled to the buffalo kill that evening when the hunters brought home the game. The shrilling, wildly exultant welcome the little children gave them was one of the most moving things she had ever seen. "Oo-koo-hoo! Oo-koo-hoo!" the children cried. "Now there shall be a great feast." There would be dancing and mimicking, and singing and drumming, and heroic tales told. The blood, the blood, the blood. The time for rejoicing had come. "Wana hiyelo. Houw!" The children proclaimed aloud the names of the heroes: Scarlet Plume, Traveling Hail, Bullhead, Two Two, Plenty Lice, all those who had been in the buffalo surround. They were the great ones, all of them.

But the name the little red children sang the loudest of all was that of Whitebone. Whitebone went carefully about through his entire village looking for the poor and the unlucky, and those without a hunter in the house. Whitebone gave them heaps of meat, and many fresh buffalo hides, until at last even the poorest of the

Yanktons appeared to have more than he himself. Through it all yellow tears ran down his seamed face.

Judith's heart was wiped out.

Judith retired early. Born By The Way hung asleep in his cradle. A twig fire bloomed pink at her feet. Smoke rose in a silky line straight for the smoke hole and vanished against the faint glow of the Milky Way. The only discomfort in the curved cone of the tepee was the flatness of the ground under the bed robe. Back in St. Paul she and Vince had always slept on a featherbed. Prairie sod, while not as hard as rock, certainly wasn't any feather mattress. It just didn't give enough in the right places.

Outside, the Yanktons were still celebrating the great kill. Booming drums echoed off the red rock walls. Various dances were going on at the same time: buffalo dance, scalp dance, victory dance. Singers opened their throats to the stars. This night the Shining People Living In The Center Of The World were very happy.

Roasted buffalo hump had tasted good, delicious, gamy. Judith's mouth still watered at the thought of it. She recalled Whitebone's wonderful remark when he had finally had enough. "My belly was folded up. My teeth were long. But now, look, after this feasting I am a fat man again." Judith smiled as she ran a hand over her own stomach. She too had eaten too much. She had gorged herself.

Out of the camp revelry there gradually arose a discordant note. There were occasional violent words said. Some of the braves were arguing. One of them seemed to be roaring mad.

She heard mice gnawing at the parfleches near the door. She knew she should get up and chase them out, but decided she was too tired. The Yanktons could use a few cats. Their dogs were worthless when it came to mice.

Smoke smells drifted around her. Smell of jerked meat on the drying racks outside came in through the door. Her braids lay rancid on her breasts.

Suddenly the door flap swung open and Bullhead jumped in.

Two great strides and he loomed over her. His big face was fearfully worked up. His bloodshot eyes glared down at her from behind an ambush of black hair. Angela's silver scalp hung over his ear like a woman's extra switch of hair. He carried a globe-shaped club in his right hand. He was stark naked.

Judith lay petrified under her fur robe. She tried to scream; couldn't. She tried to swallow and scream; couldn't. She tried to collect spittle on her tongue and scream; couldn't.

Bullhead settled on his heels beside her, the head of his phallus bobbing between his thighs. He grabbed her arm with his left hand. "Get up, white woman," he said thickly, giving her a jerk. "I wish to count coup upon thee the white man's way. I know a place behind a rock."

Judith quivered at his touch. Then she jerked free.

His big hand closed around her slim white neck. He pinched thumb and forefinger together so hard she couldn't move. "Come, white woman, I wish to play bull and cow."

A puff of his breath touched her cheeks. Then she knew she was really in for it. His breath stunk of alcohol. Of wine. Bullhead had somehow managed to get hold of liquor.

He waggled his globe-shaped club in her face. "Come, or tonight the blood of the white woman shall run like red rain."

"No!"

"Come."

Judith got off a piercing shriek. "No-o!"

There was a face in the door. It was Two Two. Two Two looked; was gone.

Bullhead grabbed Judith by the braids, gave her a neck-cracking shake; then, glancing at the door where Two Two had just looked in, he let her drop back on her fur bed. Balked, swearing vengeance at the interruption, Bullhead stalked out heavily.

Judith panted for breath. "Ohh. Ohh." At last she managed to sit up.

Another face appeared in the leather door. It was Scarlet Plume. He sprang in, puffing, hair in his eyes.

"Good Lord, what now?" Judith cried, clutching the bed robe around her shoulders.

Scarlet Plume swept her from head to foot with a single piercing look. "Two Two came to tell me. I ran very fast. I was afraid you would be killed."

"You scared me half to death, coming in like that."

"He did not touch you?"

"No."

Scarlet Plume let down a shoulder.

"That lunatic," Judith cried, "coming in here like a crazy boar."

"Bullhead has been drinking the white man's push water. He kept it hidden all this time. It was a jug he stole from the Good Book Tepee. Tonight before the victory dance he drank it all, alone. The spirit water from the Good Book Tepee is not good for him. An evil spirit has entered his stomach and he wishes to kill. He has become as one apart from himself."

"Terrible."

"He is not a good Yankton."

"He is not a good anything, if you ask me. That beast. Why!"

"I will speak to Whitebone about this."

"Terrible."

Scarlet Plume moved; was gone.

The silken thread from the twig fire steadied again and found the opening out through the smoke hole.

Judith sat gasping until she got her breath back. Finally she lay down. Her heart beat in her throat like the gallop of an irregularly running colt. Her stomach, still full of buffalo hump, lay in her like she might have had a log for dinner.

"It's almost more than I can bear," she murmured. "One day I shall surely go insane. Oh, God."

Singing and drumming and dancing continued outside.

She had lain alone for perhaps another hour, when again there was an outcry among the braves. This time the singing and drumming stopped. Instantly. Utter quiet followed.

Judith rose on her elbow. The fur robe slipped off her pear breasts. She leaned her head toward the door, listening, all ears. Something had happened out there that had shocked all the Yanktons into silence. There had been a grave offense of some kind. Judith was sure it was Bullhead. Mad drunk, he had attacked some other poor female, no doubt. Squirts Milk or perhaps even Tinkling.

Or Mavis. She was the other white woman in camp. Of course.

Judith scrambled to her feet, slipped into her moccasins and tunic, rushed out. She called aloud. "Mavis!"

The big fire in the center of the camp burned brightly. So did the dance fires below along the running springs. No one was around. The dancers, everyone, had run to their lodges.

"Mavis?"

Judith saw movement downstream. It was just beyond where Mavis had erected her husband Traveling Hail's tepee. Lifting her tunic, Judith ran for it, across the camp circle and past a red outcropping of rocks, and then around in front of Mavis' tepee. There, some dozen yards beyond, on the ground, lay the figure of a woman. It was Mavis.

Scarlet Plume and Two Two stood over Mavis. Off to one side, sitting on a rock, Smoky Day and Tinkling were weeping softly to themselves. There was just enough light from the center camp- fire to make out their faces.

Judith kneeled beside Mavis. "Mavis?"

Mavis was partly covered by a sleeping robe. Her face was gaunt, and so white she looked dead. A trail of fresh blood glis- tened in the grass and it led toward a patch of wolfberries. There were signs of a violent struggle in the wolfberries. A war club, its handle bloody, lay to one side.

Judith threw back the sleeping robe. Blood was pushing out of Mavis' vagina in soft, even pulsings.

Judith whirled on Scarlet Plume. "What happened here?"

"The bad Yankton has done this thing."

"Bullhead?"

"He will be banished. The warrior council meets even now."

Judith stared at the bloody handle of the war club lying to one side. "Did he outrage her with . . . that?"

Mavis stirred under Judith's hand. Her eyelids fluttered like a pair of gray butterflies about to open wings. Her voice was a husky whisper. "He took me into the bushes. I kept fighting him off. Out of a crazy kind of loyalty to Traveling Hail." Breath lifted her small chest irregularly. "So he finally gave me a whack over the head with his war club, then did it with the handle."

"God in heaven."

"Yes."

Judith whirled ferociously on Two Two. "Son?"

"I am here, my mother."

"Do you know where the cattails are kept?"

"I do, my mother."

"Get them. And also bring a woman's belt."

"I will, my mother."

Mavis rolled her head from side to side on the grass. "It's no use. It's too late, I fear."

"Shh. Some cattail fluff will help stanch it."

"It's no use. Bullhead pushed it through me. Into my abdomen."

"God God God."

Two Two came flying back with the cattails and belt.

Quickly Judith exploded the cattails into handfuls of fluff, then packed them between Mavis' thighs.

Mavis stirred. "It's no use."

"Shh."

A long silence followed.

Presently Mavis fixed her eyes on Judith. "There's something I want to ask you."

"Go ahead."

Mavis sucked for breath. "Do you think heaven will blame me for having slept with all those Indians?" I meant to ask your sister Theodosia but she was gone before I had a chance."

"Blame? Not if you resisted."

"Are you sure?"

"Well, what about me? I'm just as guilty. If there is guilt."

A pensive smile touched the corners of Mavis' lips. "Well then," she panted, "well then, for once I've had my fill of sleeping with men without offense to God."

"What an awful thing to say."

"But it's true. It's the way I really feel."

"Mavis."

"But I did worry about it. Because you see, even when that first Indian did it to me, and I saw there was no use in resisting, I told myself something that was wrong."

"Never mind all that now." A sob broke from Judith. "Please. And don't talk." Yet Judith couldn't help but wonder what it was that Mavis had told herself.

Mavis' eyes slowly closed. Her cheeks seemed to collapse inward. She hardly breathed.

Maddening thoughts worked in Judith's mind. All this blood. This terrible slaughtering. This living from kill to kill. First Claude. Then his children, Ted and Johnnie. Then Angela. Then Theodosia. So that all that was left now was herself and Mavis, two torn bleeding lambs at the mercy of wild devouring wolves. And Mavis about to die.

Judith packed fresh cattail fluff between Mavis' thighs.

Very weak, Mavis went on. "I said, 'Well, if it has to be—welcome, pleasure.' And that was wrong, I think. I guess I got started wrong with my white husband. Because I surely enjoyed doing it with him. When our church says that is wrong."

"But you had no choice when the Indians attacked. Even Theodosia gave herself up to the brutes trying to save the children."

"Yes. I know. That's why I was hoping that maybe I hadn't done such a wrong after all."

Poor, poor Mavis. Oh, Lord. From sweet sixteen in St. Paul a few years ago to this. Judith recalled Mavis' remark about herself when she got married. "I was only sixteen, and really too young to marry, you know, but nothing would do my lover John Harder but

I must marry him. I suppose many another woman from her own experience knows how it is." Amen.

Marriage to John Harder had led from one thing to another. After John was killed in the First Battle of Bull Run, Mavis found herself a much-sought-after widow. She had been pestered to death by men who now thought she would be that much the easier to seduce. . . .

There was the time when Mavis through some mistake found herself with two dates on the same night. Luckily she had made one for early in the evening and the other for later in the evening, the first with storekeeper Fat McGrath and the second with Lieutenant Davy Knight. Fat McGrath had to go to a meeting at nine, and Davy came off duty at Fort Snelling at eight-thirty and would be over on horseback an hour later.

Fat McGrath had made up his mind he was not going to leave until he had had a man's way with her even if he did get late to his meeting.

Mavis was of a different mind. She had decided that if it was to be, then it would be with handsome Davy. So she fought off Fat McGrath with all she had. She said she had a headache. She scratched him. She said that "those" had come upon her. As a dancer she had strong legs and managed to catch him once in the groin with her knee.

Fat McGrath, purple with desire, persisted.

When Mavis saw by the clock that Davy would soon be along and so catch her two-timing him, she decided to give in and let Fat McGrath have his way. Quickly. And God forgive. Then she hurried Fat McGrath out of the house, pleading a real headache at last.

Tired, somewhat dispirited, Mavis changed her mind about how she would spend the rest of the evening with handsome Davy Knight. She would be cool to him instead. Once was bad enough. A widow's reputation was easily ruined. Those damn men always talked. Doing it with two different men on the same night—unthinkable.

Davy came along some ten minutes later. Davy in his bright-blue uniform was his usual charming self. He brought along a bottle of choice French cognac. He toasted her. Mavis made sure she drank very little. She was pleased to see Davy drink a lot. She hoped he would soon be too drunk to want her. They built up a hot fire in the fireplace, and had a gay time chatting together.

Around midnight all that choice cognac suddenly seemed to hit Davy, and instead of making him too drunk to do anything, it changed him from a correct gentleman into a hot-eyed satyr. Davy picked her up from the chair where she was reclining and wrestled her down to the floor in front of the blazing fire, and without even removing his bright-blue uniform, proceeded to attack her. Rough and brutal.

She bit him. She scratched him.

But each defensive move seemed to play right into his hands. And the truth was she really loved Davy best. So, alas, yes, she let him have his way too. God forgive.

Just about then the clock had struck one. As she told Judith later, "Actually, you see, by the clock it was a new day and so I really didn't do it after all with two men on the same day. Because that's the one thing I didn't want to do. . . ."

Judith stroked Mavis over the forehead.

Mavis was cold. In the light of the flare Judith saw that Mavis had gone. Mavis had passed away so gently Judith had missed it.

Judith drew back. She covered her face with her hands. The ends of her heavy braids lay on her knees.

Thoughts worked in Judith like night crawlers gone crazy. So near did she border on insanity, she felt like singing.

The door flap to the council lodge opened. Traveling Hail stepped out. His face had a distant, even high, look. Six stern

armed warriors came out behind him. After them came Whitebone.

The six warriors went directly to Bullhead's tepee. Two of them
secured Bullhead's ponies, another two began to take down his
tepee, and the third two stepped inside the tepee. After a moment
the last two led Bullhead out, each holding him by the arm. They
led him to Whitebone. Angela's silver-blond scalp flashed in Bullhead's hair.

Whitebone was very sad. Fur toga wrapped around his shoulders, he spoke slowly and gravely. "Yanktons, this is what I say.
We have forgiven this bad Dakota many things. We needed the
brave men. But now he has gone too far. Yanktons, hear me. Seize
his goods, and his horses, and take them out through the horns of
the camp and set them well out in the wilderness. We cast them
out. Yanktons, hear me. Seize the bad Dakota by the arms and
lead him out through the horns of the camp also and set him free
well out in the wilderness. We cast him out. I have said."

It was done.

Traveling Hail came over and held out his hand to Judith to
shake it the white-man way. But before she could accept his hand,
he broke completely apart, and crying bitterly, fell to the ground.
He put his arms around a red stone and wept on it.

Judith went back to Whitebone's tepee as though she were
sleepwalking.

5

It was the Moon of Scarlet Plums, early September.

The Yanktons removed to the Place Of The Pipestone. The
Yanktons were short of horses and dogs. Thus it was decided to
quarry some pipestone and make pipes with which to trade with
the Teton Dakota. The Tetons across the Missouri River were
known for their wonderful spotted ponies and their dogs bred to
wild wolves.

The Yanktons made camp west of the quarry across from a trickling stream. The Place Of The Six Strange Boulders, where the spirit Two Maidens lurked, lay to the south. Water gushed over the Falls Of Winnewissa. The low places were thick with rose hips.

Certain of the men, Scarlet Plume among them, were chosen to do the quarrying. They took the sweat bath, and purified their rose-brown limbs with silver sage, and made the proper sacrifice of tobacco to the Two Maidens, then pried up the slabs of soft, fleshy pipestone.

The quarry was an old one. It was believed to have been the site of a battle between contending brother tribes of the Old Ones, as the color of the pipestone had the appearance of dried blood. It was thought that the petroglyphs under the Two Maidens had been made by the winning Old Ones to ensure good quarrying. The quarry was now known as a sanctuary where the bitterest of enemies could meet in peace.

Scarlet Plume made the best bowls. He was the expert. He also made the best pipestems, out of ash. An ash twig had a pith that could be easily removed. Sometimes Scarlet Plume started a wood-borer grub at one end of the ash twig and harried it through the pith by holding the twig near a hot coal.

Judith, still stunned, numbed, went for a walk over the prairie. She had her heart set on a cup of tea and was out looking for certain dried leaves.

She found a blackberry bush. She picked a few of its drier leaves. Chewing one of them, she found it tasted exactly like a tea leaf. Ah, these would do. Too bad it wasn't spring. Young leaves, dried, steeped best.

She parted her way through a clump of fruited red haw. She spotted some wild sorrel underfoot and sat down to eat a few of its lush green leaves. Its sourish taste was pleasant. She dug out one of the roots, a bronze bulb. The bronze root had the flavor of a roasted acorn.

Nausea caught her in the belly. She retched. A trickle of white curdles slid into the grass. "Oh, Lord," she wept aloud, "let there be no half-breed child conceived in me." It would be a miracle if she wasn't pregnant.

What one glad thing ahead could she look forward to, fasten her mind on, to save her sanity?

A flock of passenger pigeons flashed by overhead. Then another. The skies were sometimes darkened by them. Sometimes the pigeons flew over so thick it was as if bluish-slate hail clouds were driving over. The wings of the pigeons clattered on the rising swoop. Their calls were hoarse. *"Klek-kluk. Klek-kluk."*

As she wandered on, meadowlarks rose out of the grass like the spontaneous whimsies of a carefree child. They sang, "I am the bird of fidelity. I love the Yanktons." Redwings dove through butterflies defting back and forth. There were white butterflies, and blue butterflies, and butterflies resembling flying clots of blood.

She found a single purple aven, prairie smoke. Again she sat on her heels to take comfort of a kind from its solitary beauty. She cupped her hand just under it, not quite touching its crumble of smoky styles. Yes. God's handiwork could be lovely at times.

She came upon a patch of small asters, blue petals with gold centers. She considered it miraculous that there were so many kinds of asters on the wild prairies while in the cities flower lovers spent hours and hours trying to raise the domestic variety.

A new day and a new garden. There were as many glowing flowers in the day as there were gleaming stars at night. Clouds of perfume by day and pillars of fire by night. It was comforting to read God's handiwork, more so than to read God's revealed Word. The simple psalms of life did more to keep reason from being dethroned than all the impassioned gospels of the Bible.

The wind is my shepherd. I shall not want. Perfumes make me to lie down in green prairies. Butterflies lead me beside still waters. Singing birds restore my soul. The bird of fidelity leads me in paths of righteousness for its name's sake. Yea, though I walk through the valley of the shadow of savages, I fear nothing but their kindness. The birds and the flowers comfort me.

She looked back at the camp. It gave her a start to see how far she had wandered.

She was alone at last. If she wanted to she could actually escape. Whitebone probably figured that by now the white settlements had been left so far behind she'd given up all thought of making it back alone.

All she had to do now was to get down on her hands and knees and crawl behind some dried bluejoint and then, bending low, run down a gully. Should the Yanktons begin to look for her before she could get completely out of sight, she could hide in the grass like a partridge. Her buckskins made a perfect camouflage.

She had kneed along a dozen feet or so, when abruptly two stern armed Yanktons rose out of the dried bluejoint, blocking her path.

Caught. Still a prisoner. She instantly realized that that wily old Whitebone had ordered the two guards to watch her all along. One of the guards was Plenty Lice. He had been elected to take the place of Bullhead in the warrior society which only the day before had been designated to police the village for the next moon.

Plenty Lice motioned for her to hustle back to the village. He menaced her with a globe-ended club.

Meekly she got to her feet and headed back for camp. As she trudged along she let the blackberry leaves slip through her fingers. The dried leaves fluttered on heat waves rising out of the grass. The wafting leaves reminded her of wool moths.

It was sundown. Supper was over. They were all out on the grass around the cooking fire, enjoying the evening. Judith, having washed her feet, was trying to trim her toenails with the sharp edge of a clamshell. Two Two sat with one foot in his hand, sucking his big toe while he stroked the lobe of his left ear with a thumb and forefinger. Judith remembered that Angela had sometimes sucked her thumb. Humpneck Tinkling was busy repairing moccasins. Smoky Day sat on a red rock combing out her old hair with her fingers. Smoky Day's hair was very long and coarse, smoke-white at the roots and as black as a horse's tail at the ends. Whitebone sat apart on a pile of folded green hides, a piece of buckskin caught over his old shoulders, wrinkled turtle eyes almost closed. Whitebone was brooding and thinking on his people.

The tepees of the camp stood around them in their neat and appointed circle. A booming dance drum filled the air with even knots of sound. Young maidens came out to adjust the ears of the tepee so they might catch the love glances of a favored boyfriend. Little boys were practicing their shooting beside a small prairie pond. With grass stalks for arrows, they fired away at frogs. When they hit the mark they laughed with glee to see the white-bellied danglelegs turn somersaults in the air.

After Bullhead's banishment, Scarlet Plume had taken to sleeping in Whitebone's tepee again. Scarlet Plume lay on his back, on a robe, playing with Born By The Way. He was holding Born By The Way up by the arms. Born By The Way took a chubby step on Scarlet Plume's groin, wobbled; took another step onto Scarlet Plume's narrow, hard belly, slipped off; took yet another step onto the mound of Scarlet Plume's huge chest, stood solid for a moment.

"See"—Scarlet Plume laughed, white teeth flashing—"already he walks up a hill. He will be a very brave warrior."

"Aiii," Smoky Day cackled. "He will be bad medicine for the enemy when he grows to be a man."

Judith looked up from trimming her toenails. It was the first time she had seen Scarlet Plume so relaxed and pleasant. For once he seemed to be enjoying his role as second father to Born By The Way. Judith couldn't help but steal a glance now and then at his handsome face, broad and compassionate. His rich, wide lips were those of a lover, graven upon weathered copper. He was all man. A god among men. He made her think of the old Greek heroes: Achilles and Ajax and Odysseus. She found it difficult to think him a deadly enemy, a Cuthead Sioux.

Born By The Way soon tired of his baby walks and Scarlet Plume placed him on the ground to let him crawl around in the grass.

Scarlet Plume stretched. "It is a good thing to rest. I am glad that another warrior society guards the camp tonight." He sighed, full of content. His eyes closed as he nuzzled the back of his head into the robe. "It is a good thing to lie down with the people of one's own mother."

The cutting edge of the clamshell was rough and Judith had to make sure she didn't cut too close. "Lord, yes," she thought. "I'd give anything, anything, to be lying beside my husband Vince right now, with Angela asleep in the next room. Disgusting as Vince sometimes was."

Of a sudden Two Two, sucking his big toe, leaped up off the ground with a strange choked cry. He fell back and lay rigid in the grass. Little rhythmic quivers rippled through his groin; at last ebbed away. His face was flushed, purplish, his eyes turned under.

The family took it in stride. But Judith was astounded.

Smoky Day parted her hair into two tails and began to braid them up. She explained to Judith. "Two Two has done this thing since he was a child. Sometimes Born By The Way also takes his toe for ma-ma. It is a thing their mother did when she was a child. I remember it well. This is true. Aiii."

Normal color gradually returned to Two Two's face. Presently his eyes came into focus. He sat up. He sat back relaxed, even limp, smiling vacantly at the cooking fire. The lobe of his left ear appeared to be longer and more swollen than the lobe of his right ear. Presently he picked up a puzzle made of human finger bones and began to play with it.

Then it was Born By The Way's turn to make an outcry. Everyone turned. Born By The Way had crawled too close to the cooking fire. He had jerked back, and tumbled up into a sitting position. Holding up his finger, he was bawling his head off, eyes shut, tongue ululating, his mouth as wide as he could stretch it.

Judith hurried to comfort him. "Now, now," she murmured, "so our little boy burned his fingers, uhnn?"

Scarlet Plume smiled at Born By The Way. "So the fire has bit thee, little warrior, eh? Well, it is a good thing. Today you are wiser. And tomorrow the pain will have gone away."

"It was my fault," Judith said. "I should have been watching to keep him away." She gave Born By The Way an affectionate shake. "Bad fire. Stay away. No, no. Do not come near the fire."

Scarlet Plume regarded Judith with amused eyes. Finally he sat up. "Hear me. The Yanktons do not use the white man's no-no. The Yanktons let the children discover for themselves that sometimes there are sharp teeth about. The Yankton child thus by himself grows up watchful for the enemy and he never comes to hate his father or mother because they have said no-no to him."

Judith threw him an appreciative glance.

Tinkling gave Born By The Way a rattle made out of a bull's scrotum to play with.

Scarlet Plume got out his gossip pipe and filled it. He reached over and plucked a coneflower. He shredded it of its narrow leaves and crushed them between thumb and forefinger until juice appeared. He rubbed his thumb and forefinger carefully in the juice, then reached over and took a hot coal from the cooking fire. Unhurriedly he lighted his pipe, and unhurriedly put the coal back.

Born By The Way continued to cry.

Whitebone stirred nervously on his pile of hides. The child's cries were distracting his deep thoughts. He bent his black eyes on Judith. "This crying of the child, it is not the way of a good Yankton. Cannot my sit-beside woman give him some ma-ma?"

Smoky Day interposed. "There is another way." She took the child from Judith and lightly pinched Born By The Way's nose and mouth shut. The baby's face slowly darkened. Just when it seemed he would suffocate, Smoky Day let up and let him breathe again. She repeated the treatment until the baby quit. Smoky Day said, "It is the old way as done by the ancients. The child must learn never to cry or the enemy will know where the Yankton lies hidden."

It burned Judith a little that Whitebone was always so ready for her to give the baby ma-ma. She had never been able to resist giving Vince the needle and she couldn't resist giving it to Whitebone now. "The Yanktons consider themselves the Shining People, yes? A people who refuse to count coup on a woman the whiteman way? Yet our great chief was slow to punish a certain Yankton who outraged my sister, the Good Book Woman. This I cannot understand."

Whitebone's head came up a little.

"Our great chief next permitted this certain crazy Yankton to remain until he had raped the wife of Traveling Hail with the handle of his war club. This also I cannot understand."

Whitebone slowly turned his head around as if looking for someone. "Where is this Yankton?" he inquired mildly. "I do not see this crazed one that my sit-beside woman speaks of." Whitebone then nodded once, emphatic. "You saw him banished."

Judith snorted. "There is already another such Yankton to take his place."

"Where is he? I do not see him."

"It is Plenty Lice."

Whitebone blinked. "Ha. It is true then. There is but little difference between a white wife and a red wife. Both can be crabby at times."

Scarlet Plume put his pipe away. He threw a small twig on the fire. He spoke in a grave voice. It was plain that he was much affected by what Judith had said, that he could see there was justice in her biting words. "The Yankton brave is taught even as he suckles his mother's breast that the body of a woman is a precious thing. He is born from her belly and he is given milk from her ma-ma. The place from which he is born and the place from which he feeds cannot help but be a sacred place. The Shining People cannot be born from a foul place. They can only be born from a

good place. And a good place is a sacred place. We worship all
sacred things. We worship the buffalo. We pray to the Buffalo
Woman and we receive her permission to take some of her flesh to
eat and some of her skin to have shelter. She is our mother and
our god. This is also true of the maidens. We worship the virgins.
We pray to them. We cannot mistreat a sacred thing. The gods
will punish us if we do. Thus it is that as long as our maidens
remain virgins, the Buffalo Woman sends us much meat. This is
true. I have said."

Silence.

Judith stole a look at Scarlet Plume. It was just dusk enough to
give his skin a bronzy glow. For the first time Judith noted he had
a pair of gray scars on his chest. Ah, medicine-lodge scars. Scarlet
Plume had had his vision in youth then, had danced his sundance
ordeal. She looked over at Whitebone, saw that he too had a pair
of old scars on his chest. She threw a look at Two Two. He had
none. Two Two still had not cried on a high hill in lonely vigil
to discover what his mission in life was to be.

Scarlet Plume threw a few more twigs on the fire. Little flames
leaped up after a moment. Highlights came out so clearly on every
face that the faces appeared to be translucent.

The firelight made Whitebone's big nose more prominent than
ever. Looking closely, Judith saw something she had not noticed
before—a big blackhead on the very point of it. The blackhead
reminded her of the eye of a potato. She stared at it. She had always had a penchant for pinching blackheads. Her father had had
a lot of them in his neck and she used to squeeze them out regu-
larly. Vince, her husband, had such soft baby skin that he never
had any. She had to repress an impulse to go over and take hold of
Whitebone's old nose and give it a hard squeeze.

Whitebone turned his old eyes on Scarlet Plume. "My son,
I have spoken of a certain thing before. It has been much in
my thoughts that you should become our medicine man. We do
not have one. This is bad. What does your new vision say of
this?"

"My father, I will speak of the new vision at the proper time. The meaning of it has not yet become clear to me."

Whitebone probed slyly. "It seems that my son has had a vision which has told him he should become a heyoka, one of the Contraries. Perhaps that is a good thing. We need someone who can pacify the wrath of the thunderbirds when they come out of the west."

Scarlet Plume closed his face against his uncle Whitebone.

Whitebone sat musing to himself for a time. Then, just as it was about to become pitch dark, he suddenly got to his feet and took up his war club and sacred shield from the tripod outside the door of his tepee and strode toward the council lodge. He struck the bloodied pole in the center of the village and lifted his voice for all to hear.

"Yanktons, hear me. It is time your old chief spoke of certain things. I have thrown my spirit back to the old times and this is what I see. Once there was a people with only one great council fire. This fire was kept alive through many winters without number. This people prospered and multiplied. One day there were too many families for the game. The braves of this people began to fight each other. At last a great council was called. After much smoking and much silent thought, one great chief rose to his feet. He spoke with one tongue and from one heart. The vision of a divination had come to him. He was told to take the hot coals of the single council fire and divide them into seven portions, one each for the Six Great Powers and one for He Who Has A Secret Name. It was done. These people then called themselves the Friendly Allies, the Dakotas. The people who lived in the end village, the Yanktons, were given the portion meant for He Who Has A Secret Name. You see the descendant of this same fire burning here at my feet beside the council lodge."

All the faces around the camp circle turned to look.

"Thus it is we are known as the Center People. This fire is sacred. We must keep it alive or the Center People of the Dakotas will fail and die away. All the other six Dakota tribes look to us. Many Yanktons have already cut their hair and put on the white breeches of the Bad Talkers. Soon their blood will be lost amongst the whites much as a rain is lost in a lake. When the sun shines again can anyone tell out the raindrops from the waters of a lake?"

The people sat in front of their tepees as still as wondering jackrabbits.

"It is for this reason that the old chiefs of this band have forbidden you the use of the white man's woolen blanket, the white man's pipe hat, his breeches pants, his silver spoons, his strange stone plates, his iron needles, his push water, his wagons. It is not for us to like the things of the white man. We belong to the old medicine lodge of the Center People. We are the only ones left of the old Yanktons who live in this manner."

Light from the council fire struck the old chief from the side. His shadow going out through the horns of the camp slanted up gigantic into the night sky. The little children sat as still as graven dolls.

"Your old chiefs have wondered at times if the Yanktons should not return the white man's iron guns and iron cooking pots. Perhaps He Who Has A Secret Name is angry with us because we keep the iron guns and the iron pots. Perhaps that is why the heart of Bullhead was corrupted. I do not know. I have pondered on this much to myself."

A baby began to cry; was immediately silenced.

"The iron of the white man is a bad thing. He uses it in his wars, not for the game. The white man's war is just shooting. He shoots his small guns and he shoots his wagon-guns. He kills and kills. When the white man gets mad he wants to kill everyone. There is no honor in it. It is just killing. The Great White Father who lives in a village known as the Washing Town cannot stop it. It goes on and on. White brothers delight in killing white brothers, and red brothers and black brothers. How can this strange thing be? I have thought much about this. It is in my heart that the Yanktons should think of moving farther west. Perhaps the Yanktons should remove to the other side of Great Smoky Water where our brothers the Teton Dakotas have pitched their tepees. Then we can let the white man shoot his big wagon-guns. We will laugh at him because it will be like the bang-bang on a big drum for all the good it will do. It will only make a noise."

Farther west?

"Dear Lord," Judith thought, "then I'll never get back to St. Paul."

"We do not like to leave the Place Of The Pipestone. It is our old home. It is a good place. It was given to us so that we might protect it for all the red brothers. It will be a bad thing if the white man comes and touches it. The day the white man begins to quarry the pipestone, a hole will be made into our flesh and the blood will run out and we will never be able to stop it. I do not know. We must consider together to see how we can save the old ways of the Yankton council fire. There is much to be thought on. I have said."

Whitebone turned and gravely retired to his tepee.

Deep night came. Cooking fires were allowed to die. Tepee doors were lashed shut. Only the single council fire continued to burn brightly, without smoke.

Early the next morning there was a nervous cough outside the door. The three males sat up—Whitebone, Scarlet Plume, Two Two.

"What is it?" Whitebone called. "Who calls? Can you not wait until the tepee fire is kindled?"

"Bullhead has arrived at the Place Of The Pipestone." It was Walking Voice, the camp crier. "Bullhead has pitched his tepee beside the Rock Split By Thunder. He is alone. The camp police believe he has refused to offer a sacrifice of tobacco to the Thunderbirds. In ancient times another brave who refused to offer this sacrifice on the Rock Split By Thunder was struck down by the Thunderbirds."

Scarlet Plume looked at Whitebone with a slowly darkening face. "My father, here is another bad thing. We did not burn and utterly destroy the goods of this banished one. We did not follow the sacred custom. You see now that he still has a tepee to live in. Soon others will pitch their lodges beside his. Our band will be broken in two."

Whitebone sat very still. He scratched the sides of his gaunt old chest.

There was a clap of thunder to the west of the camp.

"See!" Walking Voice cried outside. "Already the Thunderbirds utter their displeasure."

Whitebone spoke. "Ai, I have failed my people. I could not be cruel to Bullhead. He was a brave man. Aiii."

"The Thunderbirds come with many beating wings," Walking Voice cried. "I see a great wind rising in the west. The smell of rain is not in it. It is a very strong wind. The people must rise quickly and hold down their tepees."

Smoky Day, Judith, Tinkling sat up, drew on their buckskins, and rushed outside.

It was brown out. The front of a line storm had already rushed past overhead. Shreds of a second roll of clouds flew by like arching shrapnel. The butt of the storm, black and unusually high, was but a mile away. The cloud butt was long and narrow. It churned and twisted. It resembled a river hanging upside down in the sky, full of whirlpools and cataracts.

There was a tick in the earth beneath the cloud butt, then an enormous explosion of zigzagging yellow light.

All the Yankton women in camp rushed about hammering down the tepee stakes. Even Bullhead, a half mile off to the east, could be seen flying about his tepee. One of the Keepers Of The Center Fire scooped up the red ashes of the council fire and brought it inside.

"Look," Two Two cried. "Traveling Hail does a strange thing."
Everyone whirled around to look.

Traveling Hail came out of his tepee walking on his hands, toes pointed to the sky. Traveling Hail had painted a face on the soles of his moccasins while his real face was covered by a mask.

Scarlet Plume spoke in an awed whisper. "Ahh, I see now that it is my brother who has become the new Contrary. He has fasted and this is what he has seen in his vision."

Whitebone looked pleased. "It is a good thing. The Yanktons have been without a heyoka for many moons. Now we have one in our midst who can keep the lightning away. Now we will not need to fear the wrath of the Thunderbirds." Whitebone threw Scarlet Plume a wily look. "Perhaps soon we will also have a new medicine man."

Walking on his hands, Traveling Hail made a complete circle of the camp, going from tepee to tepee.

The Thunderbirds overhead appeared to be baffled by Traveling Hail's new medicine. The black butt of the storm came on without further flicker. The Yanktons watched it churn by.

When it became apparent that the storm cloud would not strike the camp, the women began to trill songs of thankfulness for the presence of their new heyoka.

The thwarted Thunderbirds, however, did let go with one last flicker of power. Just as the tail of the cloud passed over Bullhead's single tepee beside the Rock Split By Thunder, the Thunderbirds struck. They threw a yellow spear of fire down Bullhead's smoke hole. His tepee seemed to explode into bits, then was gone.

"Aiii!" cried the Yanktons. Many covered their eyes as well as their mouths.

The Thunderbird cloud drew in its tail and passed on.

After a time Whitebone sent out the camp police to see what might have been the fate of Bullhead.

To everyone's surprise, the camp police returned carrying Bullhead on a litter made out of the remains of his tepee. The camp police carried him to the door of Whitebone's tepee. They placed him carefully on the grass.

All looked down at him. A great burn lay across his thigh where the lightning had grazed him. The Thunderbirds had bit off his testicles. Bullhead's big face was pale, of the color of scorched leather. He was conscious. A piece of hide, burned to a crisp, smoked in his hair. It was all that was left of Angela's silver scalp.

Bullhead's eyes moved slowly from face to face. Finally he saw Whitebone. "My father." Bullhead's voice was low, like that of a ghost speaking out of a hole in the ground. "My father, I wish to speak with you."

Whitebone sat down beside Bullhead. Whitebone called for his special pipe. He filled and lighted it. He smoked it. All the people watched him in silence. Finally Whitebone held the stem of the pipe toward Bullhead. "Speak, my son. You live. Come straight for the pipe."

"My father, the Thunderbirds have spoken to me."

"What did they say? Come straight for the pipe. The pipe does not lie."

"They said I have done much wrong."

"What did they say? Come straight for the pipe. Think of the helpless women and children who await to hear what you have to say."

"They said I must change my ways."

"What did they say? What did you see? Come straight for the pipe."

Bullhead sat up on his litter with a great groan. He took the stem of the pipe between his lips while Whitebone held it. He drew on it. He let out smoke with a gradual, collapsing breath. "My father, my heart is wiped out. I am changed. The Thunderbirds say I must follow the path of a medicine man. Well, there is much to learn. I must pray. I must be purified many times. Perhaps by the time another Moon of Scarlet Plums has come along I shall be a true medicine man. Let the people have patience. Perhaps they will learn to love me. There is much to learn." Bullhead fell back on his litter exhausted. The big purple burn on his thigh began to bleed.

Whitebone stood up. "Yanktons, a great thing has come to pass. The man who was once known as Bullhead has changed hearts.

Therefore he must be given a new name. From this time forth let him be known as Center Of The Body. Yanktons, once again we are a complete People Living In The Center Of The World. Yanktons, let us take the morning bath of purification and begin the new day. Groom the head. Let there be no lice. I have said."

That same day, when the sun was halfway down the slope of the afternoon, Smoky Day fell on her face in the grass. She had been about to bring in the sleeping robes for the night.

Tinkling, who was with her, immediately began to wail.

Judith rushed to Smoky Day's side. So did Scarlet Plume and Whitebone. Together, and gently, they rolled Smoky Day over on her back. Smoky Day still breathed but her eyes were closed. As Judith leaned over her, she caught a whiff of rotting flesh. It was the first time she had noticed the smell on her. She had often wondered how Smoky Day managed to keep smelling so young. Among the white people an old woman often smelled like the inside of a pisspot.

Scarlet Plume gave Smoky Day a smile full of the warmest love. His single scarlet feather wiggled as he spoke. "Where does it hurt thee, Old Woman Of The Lodge?"

"My breath departs." Smoky Day's whisper seemed to come from behind and above them. "This is my die day."

"Open your eyes, old mother."

"My eyes have seen enough."

"Come, you are the mother of my mother. I wish to look upon your loving eyes once more."

"My sons, remove to a new camping site. Do not think of me. I do not wish to be a burden to you." Her old twig fingers threshed lightly on her buckskin dress. "I am an aged tree. My branches are all knocked off. Not even the Thunderbird cares to alight on my stumps."

"We will never leave you behind to die alone. Come, open your eyes."

"My eyes have finished with their work. They will never see

again. I choose to fall asleep in this sacred place. I have spoken."

Presently, as they all waited, He Who Has A Secret Name permitted her one more lingering breath, and Smoky Day was dead.

It fell to Judith to dress the body in a new white doeskin tunic. In so doing Judith found the cause of the strange rotting stink. A big sore, the size and shape of a rose blossom, ran pus at the root of one of Smoky Day's paps. It was the same pap the baby Born By The Way suckled. Judith recognized the sore as a cancer. Judith placed the dressed body in a tanned robe, then wrapped the whole with an untanned hide secured by thongs. Smoky Day's favorite bone awl was buried with her. Scarlet Plume meanwhile cut a lock from Smoky Day's whitening hair and rolled it up in a spirit bundle. The spirit bundle was placed on a special tripod at the back of Whitebone's lodge, the place of honor.

Scarlet Plume built the burial scaffold and together with the family gave Smoky Day's body to the power of the sky. Both Scarlet Plume and Whitebone scarified themselves and cut off part of their hair in mourning.

All the Yanktons wept. The harsh cries of the braves were like the screams of eagles: "Eeee. Eeee!" The strident shrieks of the squaws were like the yowlings of wild wolves: "Owooh! Owooh!" Even the children screeched in sorrow: "Iiii! Iiii!" Yankton tears glistened in the green grass.

What happened next stunned Judith. Whitebone not only gave away all of Smoky Day's belongings, he also gave away all of his own, everything, because she was of his family. While two drummers boomed out the slow Giveaway Dance and certain young braves bird-stepped around the drummers in a circle, the women of needy families came by, one by one, to take the gifts from his hand: tepee, lodgepoles, robes, armor, bedding, stores of food, clothes, moccasins, until at last Whitebone, except for the old shiny breechclout he wore, stood naked and alone in the grass. Receiver as well as giver wept unashamedly.

Finally even Judith wept. But she wept for another reason. She had just then come to appreciate fully the meaning of what was done at Blue Mounds when Whitebone went through his village to make sure that the lowliest and poorest of the Yanktons had sufficient to eat, heaping fresh meat and new buffalo skins upon them until they had even more than he did.

"Where does the red man come from," she cried aloud, "that he gives instead of takes?"

No one answered her.

She thought, "The white man and the red man will never, never get together. One or the other has got to go under." She shook her head sadly. "I see it coming. The givers shall all be destroyed. Even if there were to be deliberate intermarriage, a mingling of the bloods, the giver shall still be wiped out. It is apparent that the white man's stronger God loveth the cheerful taker."

The two drummers struck a new beat, quicker, happier. As if to show that even the needy and the unlucky also had their code of giving, a foursome of the very poorest squaws went about the village retrieving most of Whitebone's possessions, not Smoky Day's, and returned them to him. The brown faces of the four poor squaws glowed from within, their black eyes sparkling with happiness at what they were doing.

It bewildered Judith even more. "What fools you are," she cried aloud again. "This is the very thing that will surely destroy you."

Scarlet Plume moved in the grass beside her. "You do not consider this a good thing?"

"All I can say is, Jesus Christ himself must have been an Indian. Give, and it shall be given to you. Lay not up for yourselves treasures upon the earth, where moth and rust doth corrupt, and where thieves break through and steal, but give to him who hath need. No wonder Theodosia came to love the red man."

Later a woman's society known as the One Only Wives held a feast. Smoky Day was one of those who all her life had been with only one man and thus was an honored member.

6

The Yanktons obeyed Smoky Day's request and removed to a place known as Where Part Of The River Turns Through A Red Cut In The Land. Judith called the place simply Dell Rapids. A fork of the River Of The Double Bend ran through a deep and beautiful red rock gorge. In one turn the red gorge widened out and formed a natural amphitheater. The amphitheater had a sandy floor and made a perfect spot in which to hide a village. The stream ran slow and clear, and formed many pink swimming holes. The looming columnar walls of the amphitheater were covered with grapevines and scarlet sumac. Plums grew in wild profusion both on top and along the bottom. Farther along, where the amphitheater shaped off into a narrow gorge again, the Yanktons sometimes used the west wall for yet another Buffalo Jump.

Judith was out gathering ripe plums when she became aware that "those" had at last come upon her. She let go a big relieving sigh. "Thank God I am not mother again." By her reckoning she had been a good week overdue. She had had the whites quite bad the last few days and these she had heard always preceded conception. It had happened the time she'd had Angela.

"All that awful work done to me must have thrown them off. Well, they're here and thank God for that at least."

She put aside the parfleche of plums and gathered a lapful of cattails from a swampy spot upriver. She would catch the flow with their tender fluff.

When Judith returned to Whitebone's lodge she said nothing about her "those." According to strict Yankton taboo she was required to retire to a retreating lodge or menstruation hut. She made up her mind she was not going to conform to this. She would be obedient to the old chief in some things but not in this. She was from St. Paul, where women knew how to handle "the curse" and still be free like men. The Yankton taboo in this matter belonged back even before the time of the Old Testament. She would cover her "those" with the perfume of juices squeezed from wild flowers. At night she would so arrange it that Whitebone would not find out. Somehow for five nights she would avoid his nosy hands.

She spent the evening getting water, washing out the cooking pot, and mending moccasins. She made a point of presenting a face without guile. The corners of her lips would not give her away. She was the dutiful, seemingly pregnant wife interested in keeping her nest neat and orderly.

Later that evening Walking Voice went about the village handing out invitation sticks to a Virgin's Feast. It would be held the next day. Everyone went to bed looking forward to a day of showy ceremony and much good eating.

Judith got ready for bed only after she was sure Whitebone was sound asleep. She decided she would go to bed with her dress on. This also was not the usual custom with the Yanktons. But Whitebone was snoring so hard she was sure he would not catch her at it. And she would make certain to get up before he did in the morning. Wearing a dress in bed would help hide her difficulty. She scented herself thoroughly with wild perfumes, then carefully slid under the sleeping robe beside him. She was careful not to let cold air touch him. She was also careful to stay well on her side of the fur bed.

She lay still. In between Whitebone's slow snores she could hear the gentle regular breathing of Scarlet Plume and Two Two. Tinkling slept soundless. So did Born By The Way. The stick fire slowly turned to ashes. Stars moved across the smoke hole.

The sand under the fur bed for once gave in just the right places and Judith had just about sunk away into the first fluff of sleep, when Whitebone, snorting, awoke with a start.

Judith stiffened awake. Her heart instantly began to pound, shaking her breasts. "Dear Lord," she breathed to herself, "dear Lord, please let him fall asleep again."

Whitebone lay very still. Only his breathing appeared to be off. He seemed to be quietly sniffing the air.

"Dear God, please let him fall asleep again."

Whitebone spoke suddenly. "What is this I smell?"

Judith lay frozen.

"Woman, what is this I smell?"

"Wh-what?"

"I smell the crushed juice of many flowers. Have the mice gotten into the parfleche where the perfumed bear grease is kept?"

"Perhaps." Judith let herself relax a little.

"Where is the dog Long Claws?"

"She sleeps."

"Wake her and let her chase the mice away."

"Ah, she is good for nothing but chasing rabbits. A mouse and a mosquito are all one to her."

"Hrmm." Whitebone continued to sniff the air. "It is pleasing to smell all the perfumes, but is it a good thing to waste it all in one night? Perhaps someone should arise and chase away the mice."

"Yes, my lord."

Whitebone grumped. "What is this 'my lord' you speak of?"

"It is only a manner of speaking among the whites."

"Wagh. Is this because the white husband believes he has the right to knock down his wife like she might be a warrior?"

Judith recalled the fighting Utterbacks. She could feel her lips smile at the corners. "Perhaps."

"Hrmm."

They lay very still, each in their place.

Scarlet Plume and Two Two continued to sleep soundly.

Stars moved across the smoke hole.

Of a sudden, with a grunt, Whitebone rolled over on his side. He reached across and placed a hand on Judith's belly.

Judith stiffened again.

"Woman," Whitebone inquired mildly, "are you chilled that you wear a dress in bed?"

Judith quickly seized on the suggestion. She feigned a shiver. "A down draft strikes me from the smoke hole where I lay."

"Can you not adjust the ears of the lodge to prevent this?"

"It is not a pleasant thought to get up in the cold night."

Whitebone sniffed the air. This time as he did so his hand slowly stiffened.

Judith held her breath.

Whitebone drew in a long, long breath, his big nose carefully going over every atom of it.

Judith waited.

All of a sudden Whitebone let out a terrified scream. He convulsed into a ball and bounded up. He went up like a dog that her accidentally lain down on hot coals. He tumbled to one side of their bed. He groaned a great groan. He flopped up and down four times, then stiffened out like a board.

Scarlet Plume and Two Two came alive like two startled panthers. Born By The Way let go with a loud bawl. Tinkling threw a handful of bear fat on the fire and immediately the pink embers in the hearth exploded into high dancing flames. The sudden light was dazzling.

Judith was struck dumb. She turned and stared at Whitebone.

Whitebone's old eyes slowly turned up into his head. His coppery face turned ashen gray. His whole body seemed to be gradually turning to stone.

Scarlet Plume jumped over. He stuck his broad face into Judith's face. "What have you done to offend our father?" Scarlet Plume's cold squared lips were those of a hated male.

Never had she seen such outrage in a man's face. Husband Vince's rages were laughable by comparison. A hot smell radiated from Scarlet Plume. She recalled her father once saying that when a wild boar really got mad one could smell the mad in him a mile off.

"What have you done to offend our father?" Scarlet Plume cried again.

Tinkling knew. She shrank back from Judith as far as she could on the women's side.

"Tell us, what have you done to offend our father?" Scarlet Plume reached out as if to shake Judith.

"Do not touch her!" Tinkling cried to Scarlet Plume. Tinkling covered her mouth and her eyes. She shuddered.

Scarlet Plume drew back. "What is this?"

Tinkling whispered, "The white woman has done an evil thing." Tinkling couldn't resist throwing a spiteful look at Judith through her fingers.

Scarlet Plume stared at Tinkling. "What evil thing do you speak of? Our father dies and we wish to know what it is that we may save him."

Tinkling spoke one word. She more hissed it than spoke it.

Scarlet Plume's eyes opened in terror, and he jumped all the way back to the slanting wall of the tepee. Two Two also jumped back. Both stared at her as if she were some fearsome monster from the other side.

Judith felt horrid. It was her flaunting of a Yankton taboo that had thrown the old man into a seizure. In the eyes of the old chief what she had done was wickedly obscene. For a Yankton man to touch a menstruating woman was to invite some kind of ultimate barbaric curse. In all her life she had never seen grown men show such shock.

Humpneck Tinkling was the first to recover her wits. She ran over and knelt beside Whitebone. She touched his arms, his legs. "He turns cold. Quick, dig a hole under the hearth. The heated sand will restore warmth to his limbs."

Scarlet Plume dropped to his knees, scooped up the fire with his bare hands and set it to one side, then dug out a shallow trench. Sand flew between his legs like he might be a dog digging for a gopher. Then together Tinkling and Scarlet Plume lifted the stiff chief into the trench. They crossed his arms over his chest and covered him with warm sand. Scarlet Plume quickly painted

Whitebone's face with vermilion to give him the color of seeming health.

Tinkling next snapped around at Judith. She grabbed a knife and cut a slit up the back of the tepee. She held the edges of the slit apart. "Step through this," she said to Judith. "We cannot let you defile the front door with your going."

Judith did meekly as she was told. She slipped out into the night.

Tinkling hissed at her. "Stand still until I can attend thee. When we have brought the old father back to life, and we have purified the tepee, then I will help thee put up the separation lodge." She added more kindly, "Understand this. The Yanktons consider the woman spirit a powerful thing. If it is not kept in bonds it will destroy the man, perhaps even destroy the woman. When blood flows from that place where the child is born, it is a sign of the terrible power for harm in the woman. Therefore you must stay in the separation lodge until all danger is past."

A picture of home in St. Paul flashed through Judith's mind. She remembered how ardently she and Mavis had once argued in favor of equal rights for women: the right to vote, the right to own property in their own name, the right to appear in public without a hat, the right to nurse the wounded on a battlefield. In fact, both she and Mavis had taken the extreme feminist point of view in these matters.

A wild, hysterical laugh broke from her. "To think that I once got so excited about all that, and now I'm standing here." Then she fainted and fell upon the pink sand.

Later, when she came to, she found herself in a little hut alone.

The tepees went to sleep. Only the center council fire burned on the pink sands. Guards dozed in the wolfberry brush on the far hills above the gorge.

The next morning from the darkness of her separation hut, looking out through a slit, Judith witnessed a wonderful thing.

It was the unfolding of the Virgin's Feast in the natural red rock amphitheater. It reminded her of the playhouse in St. Paul. There was the bright light shining down on exotically costumed players, and she was the audience sitting in the dark. Earlier it was explained to the Yanktons that Sunned Hair was temporarily lame and so could not appear for the ceremony.

Walking Voice made the rounds of the tepees after all had taken the day's purification swim. "The woman known as Four Only wants all to know that her daughter Drowsy Eyes wishes to hold a Virgin's Feast. Some gossips in the village have spoken bad words about her daughter. The mother wishes to show before all the Yanktons that her daughter is pure. All pure maidens, and all young braves who have killed an enemy but who have not yet lain in the grass with a woman, may eat at this feast. Yanktons, hear me. We worship the virgins. We pray to them. We cannot mistreat a sacred thing. The gods will punish us if we do. Thus it is that as long as our maidens remain virgins the spirit of the Buffalo Woman will send us much meat. This is true. I have spoken."

The new medicine man, Center Of The Body, once known as Bullhead, placed a sacred stone on a slightly elevated drift of pink sand. Center Of The Body, gaunt, slate-cheeked, moved with slow, uncertain steps. He painted the stone red and ornamented it with specially selected feathers. He planted a long knife in the ground in front of the sacred stone. He scattered some dried sweet grass and silver sage on the ground around the stone and the knife. Then Center Of The Body retired to one side. Whitebone, restored to warmth and health, watched all that his new medicine man did with narrowed, intent eyes. It was apparent at the end that he approved of Center Of The Body's performance.

Drums boomed out a steady beat.

Walking Voice cried, "Let the mothers with their pure virgins step forth."

A dozen Yankton women led their daughters to the sacred stone. The maidens were all neatly dressed in white doeskin tunics.

Each maiden had a red dot on both cheeks and vermilion painted down the parting of the hair. The hair was combed to a luxurious jet-black shine, hanging down straight and stiff to the shoulder. All wore a single yellow coneflower over the ear. One by one the maidens touched the sacred stone and looked to the power of the sky to declare their purity with a solemn oath. Done, they then stepped back a dozen paces and sat down on the clear pink sand in a semicircle. The mothers deposited gifts for the feast at the foot of the knife: venison, flatcake, boiled duck, sweetmeat made of buffalo brains, plum broth, and that rarest of all delicacies, choked pup cooked whole.

Walking Voice called aloud again. "Let the young braves come forth."

A dozen handsome young men dressed only in clout and moccasins stepped from beside the stream, where they had been working on their toilet. They had made their faces savagely beautiful with fresh red paint and they carried the courting robe.

One by one, with flashing eyes and impassioned words and gestures, the young men related how they had killed a hated enemy and scalped him. This one had overcome a Pawnee, that one a Chippewa, that one an Omaha, and one even a white man. After all had spoken they formed a line facing the maidens.

Walking Voice turned to the rest of the Yanktons, assembled to one side of the ceremony. A few of the young boys had climbed up on a rocky ledge for a better view. Walking Voice cried, "If anyone among you knows of anything to say against any maiden sitting in this sacred circle, say it now."

All were silent. For a single fleeting second the Shining People sat very stiff, as still as statues gleaming in a sculptor's marble shop.

"It is good. Now let the feast begin."

Four Only dished out the food on big pieces of ash bark and served all the virgins and their mothers. Four Only also dished out food for herself and her daughter Drowsy Eyes. From time to time Four Only flashed a black, suspicious look around at the assembly. Four Only was living with her fourth husband, her first three having been killed by the enemy.

Drowsy Eyes was comely, plump, and had a soft, languorous manner. She had the look of one who might very well have lain in the grass with a brave.

When the last one had been served, the virgins began to eat in a leisurely fashion, unconcernedly, looking to neither the right nor the left.

Silence. Everyone waited to see if there would be a challenge.

The young braves stared down at the maidens. The morning sun shone on their naked skins, some rose-brown, some penny-brown, some rust-brown.

The maidens continued to eat unconcernedly.

From her vantage point in the darkened separation hut, Judith was momentarily distracted by still another play. Up on a slope above where the Virgin's Feast was being held, the she-dog Long Claws was behaving strangely. Long Claws was frolicking about alone in the tall grass like a young bitch in heat. Then, even as Judith watched, a wolf came slinking out of a patch of wolf-berries. At first Judith thought the wolf meant to harm Long Claws. But then she saw that the wolf, a splendid male, had more the look of a lover than a killer. The male wolf's phallus protruded glistening and pink in the sun. Long Claws seemed delighted to see the male wolf, and after frisking about a little more, presented herself to him. He promptly mounted her and made connection. Slowly he pumped her out of sight into the bushes.

"Disgusting."

And only then did it come to Judith why it was that some of the Indian dogs had that crazy wild look.

When Judith looked back at the Virgin's Feast again, she saw that the mood of the ceremony had changed. Whispering had sprung up among three of the young men. The three were known as Moldy Clothes, Large Organ, and In A Hurry To Become A Copulator. The last was better known as Copulator. Moldy Clothes and Large Organ seemed to be urging Copulator to speak his mind. Copulator apparently had once told them a certain story.

Copulator was tall, long-limbed. He impatiently flicked an elk-horn quirt against his leg. He had proud, thick lips. He had know-ing eyes. It was apparent he had come to understand the way of a man with a woman.

Poor haggard Four Only glared hard at Copulator, then shot a worried look at Drowsy Eyes. Four Only feared the worst.

At that moment the new Contrary, Traveling Hail, wandered into view, walking on his moccasined hands. His head was hidden by the long fringe of his buckskin hunting shirt. His feet were covered by a hood on which was painted a grotesque face. He was throwing the influence of the spirit of heyoka into the assembly to counteract whatever was about to happen.

Copulator finally made up his mind. He stepped boldly in front of Drowsy Eyes. He pointed a belittling finger at her, a sneer on his thick lips. "You have been made pregnant by a snake. One I know saw the snake enter you. You are not a virgin. Why are you sitting in this sacred circle? I have said."

Drowsy Eyes looked Copulator in the eye. Her face slowly darkened over. She was so angry that for a moment she couldn't talk. She was beyond putting on the usual maidenly act of injured innocence.

All eyes narrowly watched both accuser and accused.

Copulator glared at Drowsy Eyes, imperious.

Drowsy Eyes glared at Copulator, steady.

Soon it was seen that Copulator was nervous.

The assembled Yanktons, noting the nervousness, immediately began to cry in unison, "Swear by the sacred stone! Swear by the sacred stone!"

Drowsy Eyes took courage. She rose to her feet. With queenly bearing she stepped forward and knelt on the silver sage strewn on the pink sand. She embraced the sacred stone.

"Ahh!" cried the crowd. It was apparent that Drowsy Eyes was innocent. Immediately they began to jeer and howl at Copulator.

The accuser slowly backed away.

Drowsy Eyes looked him in the eye with blazing scorn. Her
lips were squared in contempt. She said scathingly, "Ha! So you
are the great copulator, eh?"

Copulator flushed purple. The elkhorn quirt in his hand began
to whirl around and around.

Drowsy Eyes had more to say. "The only woman who will
have you is your own hand. Well, lie in the grass with your own
hand then."

Some two dozen men and boys closed in on the would-be great
copulator. They jeered him to the skies with high Yankton
ridicule.

Copulator turned and fled up the Dells. He bounded like a
scared jackrabbit being pursued by a pack of howling wolves.
Sticks and stones flew after him. "Ha, ha!" cried the little boys.
"See him run. Now he is truly in a hurry. Ha, ha!"

A thrilling shriek of triumph went through the camp. It was
the mother Four Only. She was overjoyed. She shrilled once more,
then collapsed on the pink sand.

Six days later Judith wandered downstream to take her purification bath. She knew of a lovely beach where the branch made a
leisurely turn deep in the Dells. It was private, the pink sand was
very fine, and the high red rock walls kept out the wind.

She slipped out of her doeskin tunic and leggings and moccasins. Kneeling naked at the edge of the slowly sliding stream,
she scrubbed her clothes clean with pink grit, then draped them
in the sun over a large boulder.

A small hollow of water gleamed beside the large boulder. It
was a place where birds might come to drink and bathe. It was
perfectly smooth and shone like a polished mirror.

She stood looking down at the hollow of water. She saw her-
self on its surface. Her blue eyes, she saw, had a lost, beaten look.
Her hair, done up in two heavy braids, was strangely darkish.
Her cheeks and neck were also strangely dark-skinned. She was

quite thin, even stringy looking. The rest of herself she could recognize—a pink skin with a faint golden fuzz.

She shuddered. "Thank God I am not mother again."

She undid her braids. With her fingers she combed them out. She looked for lice; found none. Her hands became greasy with tallow.

She toed into the water. It was surprisingly warm for September. The sun was directly overhead. She went in over the ankles, then the knees. The pink bottom shelved downward slowly, deeper. She cupped up water in both hands and let it run down her arms and off her elbows. She cupped water to her face. She cupped water over her pudding belly. She loved it. She waded in deeper. Water welled up her thighs. Water touched the gold tufts of her pudendum.

"Oh! It's so good."

Water lapped around the paired loaves of her buttocks, then up around her hips.

The bottom seemed to shelve off steeper and she decided to swim for it. She slid forward, her breasts going under and then her shoulders. She paddled along gently. She nosed into the shadow under the south wall of the turn. The darkened water seemed a bit forbidding to her. After a moment she turned and paddled back to sunny waters. She swam leisurely, slowly. She luxuriated limb for limb in the warm branch water.

"O, it's good, so good."

Her fingertips touched bottom and she stood up. She stretched to her full height. Her chest lifted, her belly shrank, her seat arched back. She looked around to make sure no one was watching. She saw only a fox squirrel playing in a gnarled oak high on the south wall. She stretched again.

"Wouldn't Angela have loved this. So beautiful here. So by one's self."

A wave of gall-like nostalgia misted up in her. Never again would she sit with Angela and Vince around their once happy table. St. Paul was the dearest spot on earth to her and never would she see it again.

She fell to her knees. Her lips shaped a prayer. She thought this strange. She and Vince had never been much on religion. "Oh, Christ Jesus," she prayed, "thou who art able to save souls from hell-fire, come save my body from fiends. I am lost in a far place. Amen."

The fox squirrel chattered at her from the very tip of a twig in the gnarled oak.

Embarrassed by the sudden need to pray, she moved into shallower water and began to scrub herself thoroughly with handfuls of pink grit. She cleansed herself between the thighs. Not only would she purify herself, but she would also rub off all touch and memory of what the Indian studs had done to her. She scoured her face. She filled her hair with pink sand and rinsed it out. Again and again. A frenzy of scrubbing and scouring and washing possessed her.

Gradually the tallow and tannin came out of her hair. Slowly its original color returned. In the sun her hair became a sun-whitened gold again.

She rinsed her hair until it made a squinching sound between her fingertips. She threw her long hair over her shoulders this way, then that way.

She laved her limbs with the warm, clear water. She poured handfuls of water down her shining belly. She felt renewed. She felt clean again.

She ran. She skipped across the pink beach. She pirouetted on her toes. Eyes half-closed, dreamy, she let the sun make love to her skin.

She let her tongue play along the edge of her lips. The tip of her tongue touched four black stubs of hair on her upper lip. Goodness. She had completely forgotten about them. They had grown back. She recalled again how she had always been careful to keep them pulled so Vince wouldn't see them. Well, she had no scissors with her and would have to let them grow.

A pebble fell from high off the south wall, plunked into the dark, deep part of the stream.

She glanced up, wondering what the playing fox squirrel was doing.

She stiffened. Someone had been observing her all along. Whitebone. Old face of the same color as the weathered red rock, he sat in a crevice in the shadow of the gnarled oak. He sat immobile, so fixed that the fox squirrel played unconcernedly just above him in the green leaves of the oak.

Judith dove for the deep water. She stood in water up to her neck. A delicate crimson came and went on her scrubbed cheeks.

Whitebone stood up. He spoke in a low, grave voice, full of awe. "White woman with the white sunned hair, know this. I have seen a great thing today. You are sacred. I see that I have done a bad thing. It was wrong for me to wive a sacred white being. You are wakan. This I did not know. You belong in the company of the spirit of the Buffalo Woman, she who lives behind the braiding waters at Falling Water. From this time on, you shall live in a sacred tepee apart. No man shall touch you again. Wakantanka reveals his presence in all white creatures. Your presence shall make the Yanktons a great people. This is true. This is right. Bathe in peace, white woman with the white sunned hair, this is your sacred bathing place. I have said."

Judith listened to it all with gradually widening high blue eyes.

With a groan Whitebone got to his feet and stomped back to his camp.

By the next night Judith found herself living the life of a white goddess. She was given a white doeskin tunic, white leggings, and white moccasins, all exquisitely worked and decorated with porcupine quills. The Yankton women set up a new buffalo-hide tepee in the center of the camp circle where she was to live alone. The new tepee was nearly white and translucent. She was given a sacred white buffalo fur for a bed, a white wolf fur for a sleeping robe, and a pair of white weasel mittens for cold

mornings. As a special favor, the new medicine man, Center Of
The Body, instructed her to wear her hair loose and flowing. The
people were to see and to take heart from her sacred sunned hair.
She was also instructed to avoid walking or sitting in the sun
unless fully clothed so that the skin on her hands and neck might
regain its former pristine whiteness. Whitebone himself took his
sacred white emblem, the weathered jawbone of a dinosaur, and
adorned the top of her lodge with it. Two guards stood outside
her door.

Judith liked the privacy. No longer would she have to fend off
urgent savage studs. But she saw too that she was now more
trapped, more prisoner, than ever. There was no escaping the
Yanktons.

There was one small piece of justice done. Whitebone took
the poor humpnecked Tinkling to wife so that the papoose Born
By The Way should have a mother. Tinkling was wildly happy
over the turn of events. Once her own housework was done,
Tinkling hurried over to work in Judith's tepee. She fawned over
Judith, held her more in awe even than Whitebone. At least once
each day she held up both hands and bowed her head in the
Indian gesture of thankfulness.

The Yankton children, naked, rose-brown, hovered around
Judith's lodge. They were as persistent as bumblebees around a
white rose. They tried to peer at her from under the skirts of her
tepee. They poked their black hands in at the door. When the
guards chased them away, they stood to one side whispering
together and made up lively stories about her. When she strolled
down to her sacred bathing place they scampered behind her like
a pack of curious puppies.

"Give them a long tongue," Judith thought, "and they'd lick
my hand."

Once one of the bolder boys came up to her and said, "I see
the white woman looks sad. I want to shake hands with her."

Judith let him shake her hand.

Yet it could not go on. She was no goddess.

Her new role was false. She was only too human and soon would once again do something offensive to the savage mind. And the next time something was bound to happen. A certain turning, and there it would be. Death.

"Yes. There's no doubt of it now. I'm going to die out here."

One evening after dark, as she lay alone in her white fur bed, Judith heard many footsteps passing by her tepee. The footsteps were those of men. They all led to the big council lodge nearby.

The night was windless. The least sound came to her magnified. She could hear the braves shift their feet in the sand inside the council lodge. The small stick fire in the center of the lodge burned with a sound as though a continuous breath were being expelled from an open mouth. Light coughs sounded almost as if inside her tepee. A sacred council pipe was being smoked and passed from hand to hand.

At last Whitebone spoke in the quiet. "My son, come straight for the pipe. We wait."

Scarlet Plume spoke. "My father, at last the time has come for me to speak of the new vision that was given me."

"Come straight for the pipe. The single hole in the stem does not lie."

"My father, a white ghost came to me in the night. It woke me in my sleep and it spoke to me."

"What did the white ghost say? We wait."

"The white ghost said to form a new society. The white ghost warned that many of the Yanktons would not like the new society, that perhaps no one would join it, that perhaps I would be the only member in it. The white ghost warned that even my father would be unhappy with it."

"Come straight for the pipe. What did the white ghost say would be the name of this new society?"

"The white ghost said it should be called Return The White Prisoners Society."

Silence.

A single pair of moccasins squinched in the sand.

When Whitebone spoke next, his voice was a snarl of just barely controlled fury. "Come straight for the pipe!"

"The white ghost said that the Woman With The Sunned Hair must be returned to the white people." Scarlet Plume's voice resounded strong inside the leather lodge. "If Sunned Hair is not soon returned, all the Yanktons will be destroyed. That is all I have to say."

"But Sunned Hair is wakan. She is white and sacred. She is now a Yankton goddess."

"The white ghost has spoken. I wish to form this society."

Whitebone snorted with ridicule. "This society of yours, it is a crazy fool society."

There was another silence. Even from where Judith lay she could feel blackness gathering on the warrior faces.

"Come straight for the pipe." There was a sound of flaming hate in Whitebone's voice. "Speak truly. What did the white ghost say?"

Scarlet Plume continued to talk strong. He believed in a certain thing and it was in complete control of him. "The white ghost says that if we do not return the white woman to her people, the Thunderbirds will strike us. Even the new Contrary, my brother Traveling Hail, will not be able to help us."

"My son, we have spoken of a certain thing before. It is that you turned over in your mother's belly before you were born. It was a great thing. It was a sign. It was told us that you were favored by the gods and would do a great thing for the Yanktons someday. Is this now the great thing you would do?"

"My father, I am helpless. I know only what the white ghost has told me."

"A white ghost? Why was it not a red ghost? Are not the Yanktons red? White. White. You know that one does not climb a hill for water nor listen to a white man for straight talking."

"My father, the white ghost says that if we do not soon return the white woman, some other bullhead warrior will rise in crazy anger and kill her."

"My son, does not the law of the Dakota say: Justice for our red people and death to all the whites? Let my son say if that is not true."

"My father, why should this young innocent woman be killed by a bullhead? Has she not always been kind to us, smiled upon us? Has she not washed your feet as a good wife should? Did she not give her breast to suck to our child Born By The Way? Even when she had no milk to give? Do not all our children love her as a tender sister? Why must a crazed Yankton be permitted to kill her?"

"My son, she is now a sacred person. No one shall touch her. We all worship her, even the new bullhead, Plenty Lice."

"My father, I smoke the pipe and cry to you—let her go free."

"Who will help her return to her people?"

"The white ghost says that certain members of the Return The White Prisoners Society must accompany her until she has safely arrived in the Fort Of The Snelling."

Whitebone snorted. "Who are these certain members?"

"Your son waits for others to join the society."

"Ha. Are there any here present who wish to join this crazy fool society?"

Silence.

Judith was suddenly filled with a wild exultation. If Scarlet Plume had his way, she was going home! The mention of Fort Snelling thrilled her so profoundly she shuddered from head to foot. Going home. St. Paul. In her extremity, in the midst of desolation, one man, a savage, had suddenly arisen to plead for her freedom.

She had always admired Scarlet Plume, had even had a love dream about him. How right she had been about him. Once in the long, long ago he had thrown a dead white swan at her feet to warn her that she must fly to save her neck. And he still wished

to save her. Yes. Yes. He was more than just a simple red man.
He was a great man.

Whitebone spoke tauntingly. "We see then that there is only
one crazy fool in your society."

"I wait for others to join this new society."

"My son, why is your mind set on this girl? Can she work
moccasins better than others? Can she carry a heavier pack? Can
she dress a buffalo skin better?"

"My father, you took her to wife. I did not. Why did you take
her to wife? Why this one?"

There was a pause, a long one. When Whitebone finally spoke,
it was in a startlingly soft voice. "When I looked upon the
Woman With The Sunned Hair for the first time, I knew she
was buried in my heart forever and my wife she had to be. It
was done to appease the manes of my wife that was."

Scarlet Plume spoke courteously. "This I ask again. Why this
white woman? You have now declared her to be wakan. How can
this be when she is buried in your heart and she has slept with you
skin to skin? I wish to know. It is a strange thing."

Whitebone jumped to his feet. His heels ground into the sand.
"The whites, ha. The white man does not deserve this sacred
woman, no. The white man does things for gold, for goddung,
ha. He tries to sell the earth to his brother, yes. Who can tear
our mother into small pieces and sell her?" Whitebone raged in
a slow, clear, incisive voice. "The white man knows how to make
things but he does not know how to share them. The white man
is one of the lower creatures. He is an animal. Look at him carefully. His face is covered with hair. His chest is covered with
hair. His legs are covered with hair. Only animals are that way.
What can one think of a creature that has short hair on his head
and long hair on his face?"

Scarlet Plume continued in a quiet, insistent voice. "This I ask.
Must we believe then that Sunned Hair is a daughter of a hairy
dog?"

Whitebone snarled, "Ha! We see now that Sunned Hair is also

buried in the heart of my son. Does the only member of the crazy fool society wish to lie with her in the grass when he returns her to the Fort Of The Snelling?"

Scarlet Plume bounded to his feet. His heels hit the sand with a thump like that of an angry buck rabbit. "Wagh!"

Judith quivered. The two were sure to come to blows over her. She almost cried aloud in torment at the idea.

Then another thought shot through her. "Scarlet Plume loves me."

A tired voice interposed. It was the new medicine man, Center Of The Body, once known as Bullhead. "Brothers, Dakotas, let the feast-makers serve the meat. Later we shall have a further smoke on the matter of the Woman With The Sunned Hair. I have said."

While the council ate meat, Scarlet Plume stepped outside and walked down to the pink stream.

Judith got to her knees and peeked out of her tepee door. She saw Scarlet Plume in the vague starlight. His head was high, long black hair flowing to his shoulders. Presently he began to pace back and forth. The sound of his footsteps on the strand was firm and crisp in the night. He moved tall and muscularly powerful. The single scarlet feather upthrust at the back of his head quivered at his every step.

"Yes, those two are bound to kill each other," she whispered. "And after that? A hell on earth. The whole band will fall to killing each other in a wild blood bath." It was chilly. She drew her sleeping robe around her body. "I know this much. If I don't get out of here right away, escape right now, I'm dead in any case."

And there was something else. If Scarlet Plume were to touch her, she was dead in another way. She would never be able to resist him. She would have to go savage, eat raw liver.

She made up her mind to go. She had to go.

Quickly a plan formed in her mind. She would head south, toward a settlement called Sioux Falls. To go north, to backtrack to Skywater, would be exactly what the Yanktons would expect her to do. Rollo, the mail carrier, made the trip from Sioux Falls to New Ulm once a month. She would catch a ride with him to New Ulm. From there she could take a steamer to St. Paul. It was the long way home. But it had to be done. Someone had to get back to civilization to tell what had happened at Skywater.

She put on her leather clothes. She also picked out a parfleche and hurriedly packed some pemmican, an extra pair of moccasins, and some Indian toilet goods.

She waited until Scarlet Plume returned to the council lodge, then slipped stealthily outdoors. She skipped across the stream and treaded her way up through a crevice to the plateau above.

She carefully steered a course between the guards on the far hills. She ran, stooped.

She hoped they would find her gone just soon enough to keep from killing each other, but not soon enough to catch up with her.

PART THREE

Lost Timber

A warm hand touched her.

Judith didn't want to wake up. She liked sleeping. She was in the middle of a lovely dream and wanted to keep on with it. Four loaves of bread freshly baked stood in a row on the kitchen table. Ma had just dropped a dab of butter on their hot, bulging brown crusts and the butter was running down the sides. Mmm, they looked good. And there on a sideboard stood a basket of the fattest cucumbers she had ever seen, waiting to be sliced and pickled.

"Ma, can I have some?"

"No."

A warm hand touched her.

She resented the warm hand. She didn't want to wake up. Lying flat on her back, she snuggled her shoulders deeper into the matting under her. It was so fine to be back with Ma and Pa.

A drop of dew landed exactly in the corner of her left eye. That did it. She looked up.

It was day. The sky was blue. The sun was straight overhead. Crystals of light came glancing down through the leaves of the brush under which she lay snug and warm.

She remembered. Last night she had escaped the Yanktons. She had run and walked, and walked and run, straight south by the stars, toward where she thought the village of Sioux Falls lay. At last, chest burning, with dawn just beginning to show in the east, she had crept into a patch of what she thought were wolf-berries.

She yawned, and stretched. Her throat worked, and swallowed. She wet her lips with the tip of her tongue. Time to eat.

She fumbled for the parfleche, and in so doing found herself covered with a thick blanket of loose grass.

Loose grass? She lifted her head. Yes. She was lying under a pile of haylike grass. She stared. She couldn't recall having scratched up long grass the night before. But there it was. She must have done it while half asleep.

She thought again of Whitebone and his Yanktons. By now they would have discovered she had flown the nest. She could almost see them making casts all around the Dell Rapids encampment to find her trail.

She lay very still, listening, so still that not even the loose grass rustled. No, there wasn't a sound. No stealthy footsteps. No neighing ponies. No creaking leathers. The only thing audible was the odd croaking beat of her heart.

Poor Scarlet Plume. He was sure to get the devil from Whitebone for having called a council meeting. It made her smile to think that while the council discussed Scarlet Plume's vision of restoring the white woman to her people, the white woman had escaped. Yet Scarlet Plume was powerful. Whitebone would not dare to punish him. Scarlet Plume was probably at that very moment already searching for her, along with the rest of the braves. She feared Scarlet Plume's hunter eyes more than she did the eyes of the others. Very little ever escaped him.

She found the parfleche at last and dug out a skin of pemmican.

She broke off a small piece of the pemmican, put the rest back. God only knew how long it would be before she got to Sioux Falls. She nibbled on the mixture of pounded meat and ground-up chokecherries. The pemmican was perfect. Not sweet. Not sour. Exactly like treated meat should taste, with a slight nutty flavor. She chewed it all thoroughly to make a little go a long way. A piece of broken pit got caught between her two front teeth. With her fingernail she pried it out.

She longed for a drink of cold water. Her eyes happened to light on berries hanging in the silvery leaves of the bushes above her. The fruit was a brilliant crimson, not grayish-blue. Also, the berries resembled tiny rabbit noses. Ah, they weren't wolfberries after all. They were buffalo berries, and good to eat. She reached up from where she lay and picked a few. She bit delicately into one. Mmm, sweet and very juicy. A touch of light frost had made them very flavorsome. Their bouquet was perfect. She reached up for more. Wonderful. She reached up for still more. Finally she picked all the crimson berries within reach before both her thirst and a suddenly aroused craving for them was satisfied.

She lay back. She snuggled under the blanket of loose grass. Deliciously she slid her shoulders back and forth on the soft turf. She felt sweetly tired. She decided not to stir out of her grass nest. She would rest, and nap, and rest some more, and then when it got dark she would get up and once more run and walk, and walk and run, straight south. As long as the Yanktons had not found her she had a chance. She was free.

She napped.

Judith dreamed. A stark-naked savage had just scalped her soldier husband, Vince. Bloody knife and bloody scalp in hand, the naked savage turned and came toward her. A warm smile lay coiled on his full lips. His black eyes were half closed. He spoke to her in resonant Sioux. A knob-ended club swung from his belt. The club stuck up like a third hand might be holding it by the handle. He began to dance. His horns hooked up on the left, then hooked up on the right. He let go a tremendous bellow. Slowly his head changed into a buffalo bull's head. He came toward her. He butted away rival bulls. He took hold of his short knob-ended club and threw it at her. It hit her between the legs. At that very moment a warm hand on her brow awakened her.

She opened her eyes. It was dark out.

She lay very still for a few moments, trying to collect her wits.

Her heart beat hard and fast. The dream had been so real she could still feel where the small club had struck her, hot, stinging. The silhouette of the naked bronze savage hung before her in the dark like a glowing sunspot. The touch of the hand on her brow was the most real of all.

She shook her head, and shuddered. Lord in heaven. It had been high time, all right, that she escaped Scarlet Plume and his Yanktons.

She scrambled to her hands and knees. Cautiously she raised her head above the buffalo-berry bushes and looked around. In the deep dark she could make out nothing. There were no stars. The sky was overcast. She wondered how she would find her way without the North Star. It was easy enough to lose one's way in broad daylight on an open plain.

Her stomach grumbled. She sat down and dug out the skin of pemmican. She broke off a piece and nibbled small bits, careful not to lose any crumbs. The chewing awakened a really ravenous hunger in her. She nibbled and ate and nibbled. She weighed what was left of the pemmican in her hand, decided she might as well clean it up. After her long run of the night before, the village of Sioux Falls couldn't be too far away. By dawn she should find it, where she was sure to find a friendly door, and food, shelter, sleep.

Memory of a conversation between Scarlet Plume and White-bone came to her. They had talked of the river making two big loops before joining the Great Smoky Water, the Missouri. That's right. That was why the Yanktons called it the River Of The Double Bend. The Yanktons spoke of a mystery, wakan, in connection with the two loops of the river. It had something to do with a guardian spirit named the Buffalo Woman living behind some braiding waters. A falls? Of course. That was why the whites called the place Sioux Falls. She recalled then that the white name for the stream was the Big Sioux River.

She decided to strike west until she came upon the Big Sioux, then follow it until she hit Sioux Falls.

A dozen steps, and she realized both of her moccasins were worn through. Rummaging through her parfleche, she found the extra pair of moccasins. She slipped on the new pair and stuffed the old pair into the parfleche, thinking to repair them come daylight.

She felt her way along in the dark. The land fell slowly underfoot. Twice she stepped into natural dips in the land, jarring herself hard enough to rattle her teeth.

She noted that her white doeskin tunic glowed some in the dark. This was dangerous. Both wild beast and the enemy might spot her. Coming upon a dry coulee, she stopped to scratch loose some black earth. She took off her tunic and her leggings and rubbed them in the black earth until she could no longer make them out in the dark. She thought it a shame to dirty the lovely white garments, but it had to be done. Later perhaps she could clean them. She vaguely hoped to be able to save them until she could show them to her friends in St. Paul. The workmanship in them was the best she had ever seen.

She went on. The land continued to slope away underfoot.

She stumbled into a dropoff. There were deep rushes, and some wet sluck. She pushed through to the other side of the rushes. Soon a fringe of trees loomed over her, a darker patch of black in the night.

She stopped to listen, head bent, loose and flowing hair hanging to one side. Somewhere ahead, water was running over gravelly shallows. Ah. The Big Sioux River.

She moved through the trees. Once she bumped into a leaning trunk. Its bark was as smooth as a table top. She stepped on grass, then gravel. Stooping, hand on the ground, she toed ahead until she touched the edge of running water.

She drank from cupped hands. She bathed her face and arms, then her neck under her flowing hair. She drank again.

There were stealthy creeping sounds behind her. She listened. She listened. When she heard nothing further, she guessed it was only an owl floating through the trees looking for field mice. "I fear I've become too notional, after all I've gone through."

She dug out a primitive currycomb, something Smoky Day had once made for her out of a prickly slab of dried buffalo tongue. She combed her hair, from the forehead back and then down to the ends hanging about her hips. Little crackling sparks spit in the dark on each stroke. She combed it this way, that way.

"Thank God I am not mother again." There would be no half-breed child after all.

She considered putting up her hair in a big bun; finally decided to put it up Danish style in a tight crown of braids instead. She used twigs for hairpins.

Neat at last, groomed, she began walking south.

She followed the Big Sioux, sometimes on sandy stretches, sometimes on high banks, sometimes through thick underbrush.

Several times she came upon sloughs too mucky to cross. She was afraid of trying to cross the river in the dark, so she skirted the sluck instead. It took time to circle the sloughs.

She bumped into another tree with smooth bark. Her hand happened to touch a tuft of hair. She pulled up some of it, sniffed it. The familiar odor of a dusty buffalo hide came to her. Ah, the trees had been rubbed smooth by buffaloes shedding hair. Pa's cattle back home were always rubbing themselves on tree trunks too.

She ran when she could, walked when she had to.

She went back over the days since the massacre at Skywater. There was the night when Whitebone gruntingly took her to wife. Dear Lord in heaven. There was the day when Bullhead murdered Theodosia. Pray God Theodosia might now be safe in the arms of her Lord. There was the evening when Scarlet Plume, sitting alone in swamp willows, caused a wooden effigy of a buffalo to dance on a mound of sand. Such devil's doings. There was the night when Scarlet Plume danced up the buffalo. Sight of him naked had been even wilder than her craziest dreams. After that the days blurred off into each other.

Counting from the last day spent in the separation hut, her best guess was that it was around the twentieth of September. Also there had been only one light frost so far. First frosts were known to come to that part of the country around the twentieth. By hard walking, and some luck in catching Rollo, the mail carrier, she could be in New Ulm in about two weeks. And then in St. Paul by the end of another week.

She made up her mind to keep track of time. Just to make sure she wouldn't forget, she jerked off one of the doeskin fringes of her sleeve and carefully tucked it into her parfleche. It would stand for the twentieth of September. Tomorrow she would jerk off another one for the twenty-first. Not to know the time of the year made one feel more lost than ever.

She stopped for another drink at the edge of a rippling shallows. She bathed her forehead. She dried her hands with swatches of grass.

She came to a place where the river took a big turn west. This disturbed her. She looked up. It was still cloudy overhead, no stars. If she struck out across the prairies to catch the river where it came looping back, she might miss it. Then she would really be in trouble.

She decided to play it safe, follow the bank of the river no matter where it led. The village of Sioux Falls had to be along it somewhere.

She pushed on. She ran; she walked; she ran.

A side-ache began to stick her under the heart. It cut her breath. She came upon a round boulder and sat down to catch her wind.

What to do. What to do. If there were only a man along to

help her. A pair of strong shoulders and keen eyes she could rely on. Show her the way. Even comfort her. Because maybe the river went west for miles in a really big looping bend.

The side-ache gradually throbbed away. Her breath came evenly again. She got to her feet and hurried on.

The bend did turn out to be a big one. Slowly too the footing became squishy. There was little or no sand, mostly caked mud, with the surface stiffish like thin frosting on a spongecake. Her moccasins began to slap on her feet.

Her cheeks itched. Then her neck. Then the backs of her hands. Once it seemed something bit her. She slapped at the itches. On one of her slaps her fingertips brushed against something wispy. Spider webs?

Mosquitoes. Dear Lord. There were millions of them. The air was suddenly stuffy with them. She felt tickles in the back of her throat. She coughed. Puffing with her mouth open, she had been breathing them in by the dozens.

Then she saw it. Something was following her. A gray shape.

Coyote? She hoped it was a coyote. A coyote was not as ferocious as a wolf. A coyote was also known to run silently after its prey.

Her heart began to pound. She held her hand to her throat. She had to work to get her breath. It was a wolf, she was sure.

She turned to face it. If it was going to jump her, she would at least meet it head on.

The gray shape, or whatever it was, stopped too.

Or was it a mote in her eye? Because when she turned her head a little to hear the better, the shape seemed to move too.

She listened, all ears, trying to catch the sound of its breathing. Were it a farm dog following her, tongue lolling, it would be breathing with happy, audible puffs.

She waited. She breathed shallow breaths. Her own heart shook her. Soon trembles shook her thighs. She had to let her mouth hang open to keep her teeth from chattering. She almost wished she were back in the safety of her wakan white tepee.

Darkness became heavy. The gray shape stood out even more clearly.

It became very hot out, close. Sweat trickled down her face. Mosquitoes trailed across her cheeks with a thousand tickling legs.

A tremor beginning in the calves of her legs moved up until it made her neck crack. Her breasts shook.

"O Lord, if it be thy will, let this pass from me."

Almost as if in answer, a blast of lemon light exploded above her. She bowed under it. She sank involuntarily to her knees. A split second later, thunder came out of the ground. She steadied herself with a hand to the earth. The sudden stroke of lightning and thunder completely took her breath away. Chest caught, squeezed tight, she sucked and sucked for air.

At last, willing it, working the muscles of her belly, she managed to make a pinched wheezing sound, then take a tiny breath. It took a while before she could resume her shallow, rapid breathing.

Rain dropped from the skies like a bucket overturned on a hot-air register. It hit her like a blow with the flat of a hand. It pushed her down. The mosquitoes vanished.

She cowered under the storm. She tucked the parfleche under her. She sat on her heels, crouched. Huge drops fell on her back like little fat pancakes.

The rain was cold. Water poured in around her neck and down inside her tunic. She could feel her nipples harden. Goose pimples swept over her like wild measles. Water trickled into her ears. Every now and then she had to hold her head to one side, first this way, then that way, to let the water run out. She shivered. She waited. She worried that the gray shape might jump her. Blood boomed in her temples.

"Enemies and much adversity ring me about."

Rain came down in varying sheets, drenching, with weight.

"A woman sitting upon a scarlet beast."

Another dazzling blast exploded above her. The ground under

her shook like a rickety table. She fell on her side, hugging doubled knees to her chest.

"Though my sins be as scarlet, they shall be as white as snow."

Abruptly there was a sound of great rushing high above her. Rain began to hit around her like water being spilled out of a whirling pail.

"Baby Angela a year old and in my arms again. Please, yes."

The wind swooped down and began to move along the ground like a vast broom. It snapped the leather fringes on her sleeves. Rain hit her like the stickles of a scrubbing brush. It was cold, cold.

"Just some little child's body I could hug and hug and hug."

Warm tears mingled with cold rain on her cheeks.

"Something to love up."

The rain stopped. Presently the wind let up too. Thunder and lightning moved slowly into the northeast.

Wonderingly, she opened her eyes in the new silence. Stars were sparkling merrily above her.

She sprang to her feet, ready to fight off the gray shape.

The gray shape was gone.

"Mercy me."

Then in the starlight she saw that her doeskin tunic could once again be seen in the dark. Rain had washed it clean, back to a light gray. She herself was now a gray shape in the dark night.

Lightning far in the east gradually gave way to a buttermilk dawn. A meadowlark peeped single sleepy notes in a beard of willows downstream.

Judith was exhausted. It was time to think of sleeping through the day again.

She stood on a steep bank on the east side of the river. Ahead, another big bend meandered off to the west. A hogback directly south kept her from seeing where the river doubled back. The tops of the hills to either side were sandy, with short tufting grass.

A breeze from the southeast came fresh and sweet over the hogback. The smell of water was in it.

She heard it. A low, steady droning sound as of pouring, rising and falling, and rising again. She held her head to one side the better to hear. Yes. There it was, all right, a sound as of a little stream falling on a leather drum.

Looking around, she wondered where the little waterfall could be. The river below her ran silently between steep banks, so it couldn't be that. Nor was there any sign of a small stream trickling down the hogback.

She listened intently. The sound was unmistakably that of falling water. It came on the wind. It was some distance away. Perhaps a couple of miles to the southeast.

Waterfall. Of course. It was the falls on the Big Sioux River. Sioux Falls.

A half-dozen miles at the most, and there lay safety. A warm fire in a cookstove, a kind white face, a white smile. Home. Civilization. Thank God.

She climbed a mound halfway up the hogback for a better look around.

The river had risen during the night from the heavy rain. Water was slowly flooding across a slough on the inner side of the fan-shaped bend. Looking ahead, she could make out where the river turned south again as it curved through a wide, deep valley. She could almost see where the river headed back northeast toward where she believed the falls were. By cutting across the country she could save miles and much time.

Carefully she examined the gullies, the riverbanks, the willows, the deep grasses to all sides for sign of skulking animal or enemy. Nothing moved. No wolves or coyotes, no Yanktons or renegade Sioux. She was alone.

She decided to risk going across open country in daylight. It shouldn't take her too long to go a half-dozen miles. And then she'd be safe.

Parfleche tucked under her arm, she hurried up the rest of the hogback. Near the sandy top the grass became prickly. Twice she had to step around prickly-pear cactus.

She hurried.

Gophers whistled at her. They sat at a safe distance, erect beside their holes. The gophers reminded her of asparagus grown fat and tall overnight, of a lazy husband stirring sleepily on a Sunday morning.

She was winded when she reached the top of the hogback. She stopped to catch her breath. She listened, head bent sideways. The sound of braiding water to the southeast now came to her very clearly. Again she examined the prairies to all sides. Still nothing.

She began to run, bowed slightly at the hips, covering the ground with loping, swinging strides.

"Dear God, please let Rollo, the mail carrier, be there when I arrive. Amen."

The sun coming out of the cloud bank on the eastern horizon was an eye being gouged out of a skull. Presently it bathed her in a light tinctured with blood.

Judith had to set herself to keep from plunging down a steep bluff. Her hand came up and lightly she held her throat.

Below her, green grass sloped down to a huge bed of exposed red rock, and there, down through the middle of it all, tumbled a full-size river. Water rumpled across zigzag cataracts, then dropped off a stiff fault in the red rock, then in a series of whirl-pools chased itself down a tortuous channel. The wild, twisting waters reminded her of a pack of dogs milling about and snapping at their own and each other's tails. Farther on, the river flattened out and flowed serenely across broad shallows of pink sand.

It was a noble waterfall. Even in her extremity, Judith noted the wonderful primitive colors: grass as fresh as lettuce, rocks as red as just-butchered buffalo flesh, water the color of newly brewed green tea. And the year's first frost had turned the leaves of the ash to gold and the grapevines to wine. It was stunning to find such a lovely spot on the lonely prairies. Miles and miles of monotonously rolling flat land, and then suddenly this, a little green paradise beside a waterfall.

A faint mist hovered over the maeling waters at the foot of the falls. The little dancing mist took curious shapes in the light wind. Watching it, she understood why the Yanktons believed a guardian spirit, the Spirit of the Buffalo Woman, lived behind the braiding waters.

She looked upstream. And there they were. A dozen log cabins and sod dugouts surrounding a little cluster of stores, all built on a bench overlooking the cataracts and the falls. Sioux Falls. At last.

She angled down the face of the green bluff toward the village. She hurried, full of expectation, face radiant, heart beating with joy. She was home at last. Soon someone would spot her coming and then they would all come out on their doorsteps to greet her with happy, excited voices, glad for her that she had been saved. There would be white faces and the sweet sound of white tongues.

"Easily might I have been lost, but I was not, for Thou wast beside me. Amen."

She hurried toward the first cabin. Sumac burned scarlet all around the base of it. A gnarled scrub oak flung an oblong shadow on the grass in the yard. The garden beside the house was dug up and littered with dried-up potato stems. She passed through the neat white picket gate, went up a pink gravel path to the log stoop.

She was about to knock when, looking at the doorknob, she saw a heavy bronze lock hanging in the door hasp. The lock was snapped shut. There was no one home.

"Probably out visiting. I'll try the neighbors next door."

She hastened to the next brown cabin. This time she didn't have to go through the white gate to find the front door locked. She could see the closed lock from the street.

She took a few hesitant steps farther down the rutted pink

street, and stopped. She stared down the line of dwellings, not wanting to believe, not being able to believe, what she then saw. All the cabins and dugouts, even the stores, were locked tight. Most of the windows were boarded up. The city fathers, everybody, had flown the nest. Deserted. That explained why there were no children or dogs out playing.

"And after all I've gone through."

She sat down on a red rock just off the street. Her pulse beat strangely, so trippingly swift she thought she was going to have heart failure.

Gradually she began to understand what had happened. Of course. Rollo, the mail carrier, would have brought the news to Sioux Falls that the Sioux were on the warpath. And, from the looks of things, with not a single house or store or barn burned down, the whites had all escaped alive. Thank God for their sake at least.

She wondered if one of the storekeepers might not have left a back door open. Methodically she made the rounds. She climbed over a pile of lumber, skirted a mound of stacked empty boxes, stepped across splashes of broken glass, pushed through a patch of head-high ragweed. Everything was locked tight.

She peered through the windows of one of the stores. The shelves and counters were bare. Everything that could be moved had been taken along. That explained why there were no wagons or runabouts around.

Dejected, she trudged back to the first cabin. She stood looking at it.

Need for sleep finally made up her mind. She would get in anyway. There was no point lying on the cold ground as long as there were empty beds around.

She picked up a stone the size of a clam and chinked it against the bronze lock a few times, hoping the spring would let go. But the lock was rusty, and stubborn.

She went around to the window on the south side, then to the window on the east side, to see if she could pry them up. Peering

PART THREE / *Lost Timber* 215

through the dusty glass she saw they were nailed to the sill. She flipped the stone in her hand a few times, weighing the idea of knocking out a windowpane with it. Glass was precious out on the frontier, a real luxury.

She stepped around to the front door again. She studied the door hinges. They were iron, also rusty, and very heavy. The pins in the hinges had heads at either end and couldn't be punched out.

She found herself a heavier stone and chunked it, hard, on the bronze lock. Teeth set, she hit the lock a good dozen times, each time harder than the last. Finally she gave it one last big whack, on its flat side.

That did it. The lock clicked, let go, sprang open.

She gasped in relief, and rushed inside as if it were her own home she had at last managed to enter. She closed the door behind her, barring it.

The morning sun streamed through the east window, casting a square shaft of saffron light across a large single room. The light fell on an oak cupboard, revealing shelves full of glistening glasses. On the pantry shelves gleamed blue dishes and a handful of silverware. A black, well-polished cookstove stood near the chimney. A fallen mound of yellowish ashes lay between the andirons in the fireplace. A multicolored hook rug covered most of the puncheon floor.

In a far corner stood a four-poster with a creamy gray wolfskin for a bedspread. She went over and sat on the bed. She almost sank to her waist in a feather tick. She reached under the quilt and found actual sheets, clean and white. There was also a pillow with a white case. She nuzzled her face down in the clean white linens. The smell of lye soap was in them. She stroked the creamy wolfskin.

"Poor woman, whoever she was. After having brought these lovely things all the way out here somehow, prized precious possessions, then she had to run and leave them."

Searching through a wooden bin she found a few measures of

flour. In a tin box she discovered a few leaves of black tea. And in a stone crock she found a slab of smoked bacon. Food. White food at last.

She found a tin bucket and got some water. She gathered up an armful of wood and soon had a fire going in the black stove. She put on a kettle of water for tea. She fried herself a mess of bacon, then a round dozen flapjacks. She ate, at first ravenously, then more sedately, chewing all thoroughly to make it go the further. The smoked bacon strips made up for the lack of molasses.

Fatigue moved in her like a fog, engulfing her mind until sight blurred. She undressed, hanging her gray doeskin tunic and her leggings over a three-legged stool. Naked, she rose on her toes, stretching to her full height, arms out. She held her breasts in the palms of her hands and fondled them. They seemed less full than usual, she thought. She'd been starving them the last while. Well, when she got back to St. Paul she would take care of that. She'd eat nothing but ham dinners for a while. She cast a glance at the sunken mound of her belly, then at the golden brush over her privates. Sighing, allowing herself one last luxurious stretch, she crept into bed. The sheets felt delicious to her skin. The sheets were like sweet ices on a warm tongue. She curled over on her right side. She could feel the creamy wolfskin bedspread slowly embracing her. The sound of the steadily pouring waterfall outdoors made her drowsy.

"A body rests all over when she lies down in a feather bed."

Even before she could straighten out her under leg, she was sound asleep.

A squeaking sound woke her.

She roused enough to realize where she was: in a featherbed in a deserted cabin in Sioux Falls. Squeaking? Hadn't everybody left town? She looked around. There was nobody that she could see.

She went back to dreaming again, picking up almost exactly where she had left off.

A gray shape with a kindly wolf smile touched her on the brow.

He had a warm paw. The touch woke her, though she really knew she was still asleep.

Gray Shape said in Sioux, "The white woman feels sad. I want to shake hands with her. That's all I have to say."

She smiled in joy.

"The white woman must flee or her neck will be broken. Come, I will lead the white woman back to her people in safety."

She smiled ecstatically.

Gray Wolf took her white hand in his penny-skin paw and led her to a river. He helped her across the stepping-stones to the other side. Scarlet waters flowed in silence at their feet. A waterfall poured with a roar just out of sight behind an arch of rocks. The arch of rocks was covered with wolfberries.

Gray Plume, still leading her by the hand, took her to a house. He opened the oaken door. She entered ahead of him. Together they looked at the deep bed in the far corner, then they looked at each other. They stepped toward the bed hand in hand. They lay down beside each other. He fondled her breasts with one hand and with the other—

She sat up out of sleep. This time she was sure the door had creaked.

Heart tribbling in her throat, she threw a look at the door. It was barred. No one could have gotten in that way. She looked at the windows. They too were still nailed down tight.

With a sigh she lay down again. Perhaps it was only the tin in the stovepipe cracking after the fire had gone out. She stretched her limbs inside the clean white sheets. She let her eyes rest on the brown raftered ceiling.

The light in the cabin was different. She turned on her pillow and looked. A shadow slanted across the south window. It meant the sun was setting beyond the bluffs to the west. Evening shadows were rising out of the earth. A whole day of sunshine had gone by.

"What a sleep that was."

She had slept so long and so deep she only now began to realize how tired she had really been. Yes, and had been since Skywater.

That horror at Slaughter Slough had almost slipped from memory, so long ago it seemed now. And looking back at it, it actually did seem more nightmare than true fact. But the worst was she had taken to dreaming in Sioux, not American.

She scrambled out of bed and moved from window to window, cautiously looking for sign.

The street was still empty. The pink paths were still silent. No dogs barked. No wolves lurked in the wild hemp.

She felt a call to nature. She picked up the creamy wolfskin from the bed and draped it over her shoulders. It did not quite come far enough around to cover her. But it would have to do. She unbarred the door and stepped out. The sinking sun hit her full on with its big red eye. She ducked her head, almost shyly.

The trail to the privy went around behind the cabin. She entered and closed the door after her. The only light came from a quarter moon cut in the door. In the dimness she could just make out where the seats were, a big one and a little one. She couldn't help but feel thankful for the luxury of a privy. It was the first time since Skywater she had decently gone to a toilet. The former owners had been considerate enough to nail up a swatch of wrapping paper on the wall within easy reach of the sitter. Even the thought that a spider might have woven a web across the big seat was a comfort of a kind.

Stepping outside, she became aware of the river once more. The Big Sioux, sliding golden green across the red cataracts in a thousand little separate brooks and then over the falls in one huge splash, was a wonder.

The sparkling water looked so inviting in the falling sunlight, she just had to have a quick dip. She skipped down a pink path. Close up, the roar of the waterfall hurt the ear. Humps of water-honed red rock fit the arch of her bare foot exactly. They reminded her of well-licked blocks of pink salt in Pa's cattleyard. She watched the flooding green tea tumble over and around and down the haphazard cataracts. She watched the sliding flood drop over the fault in the rock and splash in the maeling pool below.

She climbed to a shallow pool higher in the cataracts. The bottom of the pool was as smooth as the socket of a just-butchered buffalo's hipbone. She threw her wolfskin aside and knelt in the river and cupped herself a drink. The water was warm. She sat down in the pool. The water rose over her hips to her navel. She splashed herself, cupping water with both hands over the slopes of her pear breasts. She took down her golden hair and unbraided it and rinsed it from side to side in the gently rivuleting water. She turned over on her belly and doused her face. She lolled in the water from side to side with only the back of her head and her buttocks showing.

She sat up. She combed her hair with trailing fingers. She looked directly into the red eye of the setting sun and sang a song:

> Aura Lea, Aura Lea,
> Maid of golden hair;
> Sunshine came along with thee,
> And swallows in the air.

She gathered a handful of reddish sand lying in a curl of the stream and scrubbed herself. She wrung the water out of her hair.

When the sun set she snatched up her wolfskin and scampered naked up the path toward the brown cabin. She felt marvelously refreshed.

It was dark inside the cabin. She gathered more wood and lighted a fire in the hearth.

She decided not to put on her Indian garments again. Instead she searched through a closet to see if the woman of the house hadn't left some clothes behind. To her delight she found a shimmering purple petticoat and a green dress. On the floor beneath them stood a pair of black button shoes. She held the petticoat and the dress up to the light, then held them against her body. A perfect fit. She slipped them on, then sat down on the three-legged stool and slipped on the high black shoes.

She paraded up and down the cabin. The clothes weren't new.

But they were civilized. What a joy to be wearing decent white things again. With all her soul she wished she were back, right then, in St. Paul and wearing her own clothes. How moldy they must smell by now in the closet behind the fireplace. With a yearning hotness, she wished she were standing, right then, in the little corner of their bedroom where she always dressed.

She searched some more in the closet. She found a comb, a little scissors, a round box of aromatic pink powder, and a mirror. She set the mirror up on a shelf and examined her face. Her complexion was perfect. Yet she couldn't refrain from powdering her nose a little and around under her ears. The perfume in the powder made her think of a Paris she had often imagined but never seen. She combed her hair until it spat tiny sparks. She found a folder of hairpins and put up her hair in a pyramid of golden circles one above the other. She examined her hands. The palms were calloused, crisscrossed with small cuts, wrinkled. A rose thorn festered in the tip of her ring finger. But the worst were the fingernails. With the little scissors she trimmed the nails carefully, neatly, and with the point of the scissors cleaned out the blue funeral rings under the nails.

Well-groomed at last, feeling quite dressed up again, she set about making supper.

She found herself a gay blue apron and tied it on over the green dress. She made herself some unleavened bread with what was left of the flour. She found a jar of wild plums on the top shelf of the cabinet.

She recalled the potato patch in the garden outside. "There's bound to be a couple of spuds left in the ground. Digging with a fork you sometimes overlook a few."

It was as dark as Egypt out. Stooped over at the hips, she scratched through the crumbly humus. Halfway down the third row she found a root still tight in the ground. She probed along it and found four lovely fat tubers. One of them was almost as large as a piglet. Happily she gathered them up in her apron and hurried back into the cabin. She peeled the potatoes and dropped them in boiling water. She set the water for tea. In place of steak she cut herself several thick slabs of smoked bacon. She set the table for one, with her chair facing the fireplace. She hummed to herself. It was so good to be at home in a wooden house again.

She ate in a leisurely manner, pretending she was among fashionable people. She spooned her plum dessert in style.

As she sipped her tea, pinkie lifted, she spotted a newspaper in a magazine rack on the wall. Avid for news, she got it. It was an old copy of the St. Paul *Press,* a triweekly, dated September, 1861, at least a year old. As she read, it came to her that she had seen that issue before, beside her own fireplace in St. Paul. Rollo, the mail carrier, must have brought it down long ago on one of his trips to Sioux Falls. The newspaper was worn and much fingered, indicating it had been passed from hand to hand. There was an odor of old straw in its creases. She even read the editorials, which before she had ignored. Finally, finished reading, she put it back where she had found it.

Nostalgia set in. She wept when she thought of her dead Angela. Never, never would the two of them sit down to a good meal again. She wept when she thought of her soldier husband, Vince.

It was night and time to get on. She cleared off the table, washed the dishes, put things away just as she would have done in her own home.

She made the bed, tightening the sheets and fluffing out the pillow and straightening the quilt. She respread the wolfskin cover.

She sat down on the edge of the bed a moment to catch her breath. What a change the furnishings of a white home were compared to those of a tepee. She leaned down to take a last sniff of the pillow. The smell of soap in it was as precious as the aroma of any perfume she'd ever known. The woman of the house was a good housekeeper.

She let her hand trail across the creamy gray wolfskin cover. She settled back against the headboard.

She jerked awake. Her heart beat in her chest like a pounding fist. Red inchworms galloped across the line of her vision.

She had been dreaming of husband Vince. She had just dodged out of his reaching arms, running to her corner in their bedroom, with Vince following close on her heels. He was angry with her, demanding his rights as a husband. "It is your duty to submit," he said. "It is God's will that you be the good wife." He reached for her throat with both hands, intending to shake some sense into her. Surprisingly she found his hands warm. She had hoped they would be cold and clammy so she could hate his touch.

She shuddered when she thought of the dream again. The after-effect of it was like too much smoke in the nose. And the worst of it was that Vince's American tongue had sounded strange to her Sioux ears.

Warmth touched her hand. Looking at where her hand lay on the pillow, she saw why she had dreamed of a warm touch. The sun was just up, and from where it came in through the east window, it had caught her precisely across the throat and the hand.

Her glance went back to the window. What? The sun coming up? It had only gone down a bit ago.

"Stars alive, I've slept around the clock."

It was hard to believe. But there the sun was, rising in the east.

"I better skedaddle. I don't like the idea of traveling in the day-time but I can't stay here forever either. I'll just have to be doubly cautious, is all."

She jumped to her feet. She took off the other woman's clothes, putting them neatly away in the clothes closet, and slipped into her gray buckskins again. Indian clothes were best for roughing it. She rebraided her hair and pinned it up in a rope around her head.

She snapped off two fringes from her sleeve for the two days idled away in Sioux Falls, and stored them carefully in her parfleche.

"First thing a body knows, old Whitebone and his wild bulls will stumble onto this village. Or maybe even that fiend Mad Bear will find it, coming down Rollo's buggy trail."

She ate a cold potato left over from the night before. She sliced up what was left of the smoked bacon, and after eating several raw strips, put the rest away in her parfleche. She also helped herself to a supply of matches from the tin box over the stove.

She sat down at the table and with a stub of a pencil wrote a note on a piece of brown wrapping paper.

Dear friend, whoever you are: I was lost. But just when I was about to give up, I found your home. I wish to thank you very much for the use of your stove and things. Someday we shall meet and then I will be able to thank you in person for your hospitality. I hope when you come back you will find everything all right. Pray God the red devils do not find your lovely village here by the falls. You have worked hard to make yourself a cozy home, truly, and you deserve not to have it destroyed. I know about this. I saw all the homes at Skywater burned to the ground. I saw grown men killed, and women and children outraged. I myself was taken captive and have only now escaped. Now I must hurry on and try to get back to my own home in St. Paul. God bless you. Sincerely, Judith Raveling.

P.S. To get into your house I had to hit your lock with a stone, but I think it will work again and no harm done.

She placed the note on the table and weighted it down with a stone. She had a last look around, then resolutely set her face and left.

The spring lock did work again when she snapped it shut, and that was good.

2

Judith stuck close to the Big Sioux River. Somewhere along the line she was bound to come across Rollo the mail carrier's tracks.

Noble hills, like great loaves of brown bread, lay one behind the other on her left. She was careful to make her way along the bottoms, staying to the underbrush as much as possible. When the river ran naked of trees, she walked along the water's very edge, staying well below the crumbling black bank.

She learned to take a quick jerking look around to all sides, furtive, like that of any savage in the wilds.

It was straight up noon when she came to where the Big Sioux angled south. The time had come for her to strike out across the open country, northeast toward Skywater and New Ulm. She took a last drink of water, washed her hands and face, then started up the side of the steep bluff.

A soft wind greeted her when she topped the rise. It breathed out of the east, damp on her cheek. Ahead lay a prairie the color of wolfskin.

As she stood looking, little white mushroom scuds appeared in the sky.

Presently, breath caught, she headed out across the flat land.

The white scuds began to build up into cumulus clouds immediately ahead of her. She watched the clouds merge into towers of cream and gold.

She walked.

The undersides of the highest cloud towers turned black, and shafts of purple shadows began to trail to earth. The clouds moved with slow, massive silence ahead of her into the northeast.

She walked.

The sun shone hot on her neck and back. She stepped through undulating sweeps of gray-green grass. She could feel the soles of her moccasins thinning and wearing through.

She had tramped for perhaps two hours when she came upon a patch of bare, sandy ground. Across the middle of it, like a series of well-wrought brush strokes on yellow canvas, lay innumerable pairs of buggy tracks. And down the middle of each of the paired tracks lay the prints of horseshoes. All of the tracks were old.

Her face lighted up. Rollo's trail at last. Now all she had to do was follow it and she would eventually arrive at New Ulm.

She walked.

Sand gave way to grass again. The trail was sometimes difficult to follow through deep grass. By keeping a sharp eye out for occasional broken stalks of joint grass, she managed to make it out.

Not even a shoot as big as a riding whip could be seen. She sometimes had the impression that she was making no headway whatever, that she was trudging on an endless grass treadmill.

The towering clouds ahead continued to merge, at last formed a mountain range of dazzling cream-gold peaks. Every now and then lightning rumpled the cloud bank. The entire mass seemed to move at about the same speed she walked, a couple of miles ahead. Deep in the purple shadows beneath it, against the horizon, hung striding sheets of rain.

Of a sudden the high prairie fell away into a little valley, down the center of which sparkled a twisting creek. Gooseberries and a few ash trees grew along the steep banks. Again she thought it a lovely surprise.

Rollo's trail dipped down to the creek and crossed a red gravel ford. Two red rocks straddled the stream like the portals of a gate to a city. The two rocks, once a single rock, had been split down the middle and parted just enough to let the stream through.

She was about to start down the slope, when she spied the purple flowers of wild onions. Beside them grew a tangle of wild roses. She pulled up a dozen of the pencil-slim onions and gathered a handful of rose hips, then sat down on thick grass to eat them. She would save the strips of bacon in the parfleche for supper.

She ate slowly, chewing thoroughly. The wild onions were

gently sweet, while the rose hips had the taste of citron. She wondered if the rose hips wouldn't go good in a fruitcake.

She lay back in the grass a moment. She liked the warm spot in
the lee of the rosebushes. On the slow wind came the smell of
freshly fallen sweet rain. Lightning as swift as fireflies flew through
the high escarpment of clouds.

She fell asleep.

A whispering in her ear awoke her.

She looked up into the blue sky. Again she had dreamed of
Scarlet Plume. This time Scarlet Plume had led her back across the
stepping-stones and up a path toward a white tepee. He whispered
urgently to her in the pure Yankton Sioux tongue and she replied
in kind. Ahead lay a horror of some sort. The dream left her feeling depressed.

Well, it was hardly surprising. She'd often found herself thinking about Scarlet Plume. Too often. And thoughts bred dreams.
What a fool she'd been to let her mind dwell on him at all. He
was red; she was white. He was a Stone Age savage; she was a
civilized American. Yes. Yes. Therefore it was plainly sin to think
of him. He was part of a past she had to forget. Gritting her teeth,
determined to do the right thing from then on, she sprang to her
feet.

She discovered then where the whispering came from. A roll of
boiling brown water was coming down the little valley. It came
on like curling surf. It swept up everything in its path: broken
branches, tumbleweeds, uprooted bushes, buffalo bones, loose dirt,
buffalo chips. Even as she watched, the whispering sound of it
slowly swelled into a low tumbling roar. It was a cloudburst, of all
things.

She looked northeast. The towering cloud bank had moved on
while she'd slept. But it had thinned out to almost nothing, a
dreamlike gauze. She understood then what had happened. The
mountain cloud had opened up and let go.

The first surge of the cloudburst shot between the two split halves of red rock and rolled by in front of her. Too late she realized that her path was blocked. Now not even a good swimmer could make it.

She stared at the driving brown flood. It kept rising and rising, until finally it covered the split rocks, even came a third of the way up the slope. Dear Lord. As if she already hadn't enough troubles.

Well, there was nothing for it now but that she would have to go around the cloudburst. It couldn't have started too far upstream. A dozen miles at most. Soon she would come to where the stream ran shallow again, and then she could cross it and pick up Rollo's trail somewhere to the east.

She had gone about a mile, when on one of her quick, furtive looks around to all sides, she sensed as much as spotted something following her. It was gray, and large, and it kept to the bushes. A wolf had picked up her trail.

Gasping, trembling, yet somehow managing to find it in herself to be resolute, she turned to face it. Her heart began to beat violently, her knees turned to mush.

The gray something stopped dead still at the edge of a clump of wild roses. As she watched, the gray something gradually vanished from sight. It reminded her of gray mist slimming away under a hot sun. Perhaps it wasn't a wolf after all.

She waited to see if it would reappear out of the wild roses. It didn't. She moved her head slowly from side to side to make sure it wasn't spots before her eyes. It wasn't. All the while the roaring flood in Split Rock Creek kept rising.

Her thoughts were like squirrels with their tails tied together and straining to go in all directions at once. If only she hadn't come to Skywater to visit her sister Theodosia. None of this would then have come to pass. And Angela would have been alive. "Good night, Mama." Those little words, how sweet they were. They were sweeter even than the doxology of the Christian Church.

A meadowlark lighted on a little ash. The top of the little ash had been cropped off by passing buffalo. The meadowlark sang, "I am the bird of fidelity and this I know for a certainty. Relief is near!"

She glanced at the wild roses again. Still no sign of anything gray moving in them.

She looked ahead. The little valley in that direction was bare of all growth. She decided that would be the test. If something really was following her it would have to cross that open space.

She had gone about a mile, when sure enough, there it was crossing the open space. The creature was gray, as she'd first thought, with a touch of cream over the shoulders where the wind ruffed the hair. And it was big.

She cried out, and broke into a stumbling run. As she ran she kept looking back over her shoulder.

After a bit it seemed to her that the creature moved oddly for a wolf. It had more the heavy-footed gait of a bear than the easy lope of a wolf. Somewhat clumsy. Crude even, at times.

She hurried on. She had to work to get her breath. She became light-headed.

The little valley changed. Soft feminine knolls gave way to rocky ground, then to towering palisades of red rock. The palisades took on bizarre forms: blockhouses without windows, foundered arks, fallen pulpits. The sudsing flood whirlpooled down swinging turns. The water took on a winy color from the purplish rock and red gravel. It tumbled along with a low, sullen roar.

The meadowlark followed her. It called from a low rock. Its yellow-streaked gray blended perfectly with lichen-covered rock. "I am the bird of fidelity and this I know for a certainty. Relief is near!"

She looked over her shoulder to see if the great wolf still followed her. It did. It seemed to be picking its way, though, with some care across the rough rocks. And it had fallen behind some.

She took hope at that. She was gaining on it. The wolf probably had a sore paw. Maybe she could lose it in the coming darkness.

She ran.

Wild elders appeared on high land. The sun was about to set, and the elders struck dark-purple shadows across the slender valley. The shadows offered refuge.

She glanced back. The gray shape was gone.

She stopped, catching a hand to her throat, suddenly panting. The gray shape had fallen behind or she had outrun it.

When she got her breath back she hurried on.

The valley deepened into a considerable canyon. The riverbanks became red cliffs. Wild cedars grew dark green on the heights and in clumps as thick as little farm groves. She had to pick her way around deep side gulches. The gullies on her side ran mere trickles, while those on the other side ran bank full. It meant the cloud-burst had dropped mostly on the right side of Split Rock Creek.

The sun set in a sky as opaque as a faded robin egg. It cut a hole into the horizon, slipped into it, disappeared. Bland yellow light lingered for a time, then gradually changed to the color of fall grass.

On one of her quick, furtive looks around she saw it. The gray shape was back. It was directly west of her on a rise of land, not more than a hundred yards away.

All of a flutter, suddenly gone almost crazy, she looked wildly around for a place to hide.

The promontory she stood on was part of where the Split Rock canyon made a curving turn to the left. The promontory ended in an abrupt cliff. The cloudburst boiled some hundred feet straight below. No escape that way.

At the foot of one of the wild cedars along the edge, Judith spied a split in the earth. The rock under the mantle of earth had cracked apart, forming an opening. It resembled an irregularly smiling mouth, gums showing. It shot through her mind that this might be an entrance to a cave. If it was, she was safe. Parfleche in hand, she quickly sat down on the edge of the lip, swung her feet into the opening, then let herself down.

Her hands slipped on the wet red edge. Down she dropped. Her head banged against a rock wall. All light vanished.

A tear fell on her cheek. Again. Again.

Gradually she came to. She rose out of darkness, only to find she was still lying in darkness.

Something dropped on her cheek again. It was cold, so it couldn't be tears. It had to be water dripping from somewhere above her. She moved slightly to avoid the drops.

She stared upward, straining, trying to make out where she was. She saw stars, one, two, three, four. She could just vaguely make out a frost-edged patch of black sky. The patch was shaped like a partly opened mouth. Then she knew where she was. Late at dusk she had tried to escape a gray wolf by dropping into a crack in the earth, and had come tumbling down into this place, cracking her head against a rock.

She ran her hands over her body. Nothing seemed broken. Everything felt all right.

She was surprised to find herself lying flat on her back. Nurses in a hospital couldn't have done a better job of putting her to bed. She had been quite lucky after all. It was a miracle she wasn't lying all of a tangle with a broken neck.

She ran a hand under her body and found a matting of cedar twigs, and under that a layer of soft dirt. She could smell the spicy aroma of the twigs. Only in one spot was there a hard lump, under her shoulder. She moved slightly. There. Comfortable again.

The sound of the rushing flood below seemed to have softened some. Most of the cloudburst had probably passed by. In the morning she could cross the creek and then head east to pick up the mail carrier's buggy trail again.

She stared up at the four stars in the mouth of the cave. She could imagine, almost see, the gray wolf lying stretched out on the grass on the edge of the lip, head on its paws, patiently waiting for her to emerge. The wolf would lie as still as a lichen-covered stone. Only its eyes and nostrils would look alive.

She shuddered. "How could I have been such an utter fool as to let myself get into such an awful mess? All because of a silly notion, thinking I had to visit my sister once."

Her buckskin clothes clung warmly to her skin. With both hands she slowly stroked her pear breasts upward. Fleetingly her lips shaped themselves to receive a kiss.

The stars moved.

It occurred to her that for once she had not dreamed of red him. Nor had she dreamed in the Sioux tongue. That was because she had lain unconscious, not asleep.

"I've just got to get him out of my mind. Burn out all memory of him."

In her mind's eye she saw him again as he danced up the buffalo near the Blue Mounds. All man. Magnificent. Shockingly a stud. And plainly a sin.

She slept.

She awoke ravenous. Soft light dreamed down through the mouth of the cave. A clean blue sky blossomed high above.

She remembered there were still a few strips of bacon left in her parfleche. She recalled having the parfleche in hand when she let herself down into the mouth of the cave. Ah, there it was. Of all things. Without knowing it she had been using it as a pillow. No wonder her head had felt comfortable all night. For good luck, she decided to save one strip of bacon for later in the day. "It'll go good with broiled gopher." She smiled wryly to herself.

She jerked off a fringe and tucked it away in the parfleche to mark the passing of another day. She was pleased to find herself calm.

She glanced up every now and then to see if the gray wolf was spying on her over the edge of the crack. Pretty soon the wolf would get tired of waiting for her to come out and then there would be an awful time. He would come down after her.

She decided she had better have some kind of weapon handy.

Yet search around as she might, she found nothing, no stick or branch, not even a loose stone.

She recalled the lump under her shoulder in the night. She scratched into the mat of cedar twigs and after a moment unearthed it. A bone. She held it up. It had the look of a human thighbone. It would make a considerable weapon.

Something drew on her eyes to look into the shadow of a water-honed recess.

"Eii! No wonder that was a human bone!"

A chalk-white skeleton sat looking straight at her. There was a wild grin on its face. Fragments of a buckskin shirt still clung to its shoulders and forearms. A war club lay in its lap and war feathers hung adraggle from the base of its skull. Some tribe long ago had buried a beloved chief in the cave with full tribal honors.

"Yii! Dear Lord!"

She looked quickly into each of the dark recesses around her. Thank God. There weren't any other skeletons quietly staring at her.

The cave wasn't large, about as big as a hall in an ordinary house, with several short cul-de-sacs to the right and left. The walls of the cave were flesh red and as smooth as the ventricles of a heart. She could not for the life of her imagine how the walls of the cave could have been formed to be so snake smooth.

"Unless it was scoured by an ocean of grit. Millenniums of it."

She became aware of another source of light behind her. It came from a curving passage. Perhaps it was a second entrance to the cave. It had to be.

"Because this is no place for a Christian."

Scrambling to her feet, she decided to explore it. The passage was narrow, and low, and she had to go on hands and knees to get through it. Once she almost got stuck, but by some adroit wriggling, and keeping calm, she made it. Another time she had to cross a tiny running spring. She stopped for a cool, refreshing drink.

Presently she came out on a ledge. Far below, at the foot of a sheer red cliff, water boiled in a series of reversing whirlpools. Looking across at the sandbar on the other side of the creek, she saw that the flash flood had subsided considerably at that.

With the wolf still waiting for her to emerge above, she wondered if she couldn't work her way down the sheer cliff, find handholds and toeholds in its face somehow, and after that swim for it and land on the sandbar. The other side of the canyon wasn't very steep and she saw she could easily climb it. With luck she could be across and gone before the big wolf became aware of what had happened.

Another passage loomed up on her right. It resembled a huge artery. It occurred to her the passage might lead to yet another outlet, lower down and nearer the level of the creek bed. She decided to try it.

The new passage was pitch dark for a dozen feet, then opened out on a narrow, deep cut. The cut led steeply down toward the boiling creek. Though the cut was but a yard wide, enough sunlight fell into it to encourage a few chokecherry shrubs. Near the bottom dangled a thick grapevine. Here was her chance.

She descended the thin cut with care. Her toes felt the cold of the damp rock through her moccasins. She grabbed at shrubs, sharp projections, narrow cracks for handholds and toeholds.

About halfway, the cut became so steep she had to back down. She maneuvered carefully. She strapped the parfleche around her belly under her doeskin. She slid over a breast of rock. With her toes, blindly, she reached for a red ledge. But stretch as she might, she couldn't quite make it.

She decided to let herself drop. But the red ledge wasn't quite what she had expected it to be. The flat of her moccasins hit the edge of a sloping wet surface, and slid off. She lost her balance, began to topple backward. A scream rose in her throat. Remembering the wolf above, at the last second, she gulped the scream back.

She was going to go. Knowing she would hit rock below if she fell straight down, she gave herself a backward kick with both

feet, like an expert diver pushing away from a springboard. Her
body arched out. As she began her plunge, she sucked in a deep
breath and held it. She made a complete somersault in free fall
before sudsing water abruptly appeared beneath her nose. She
slipped in splashless, a falling human arrow.

She hit water-honed rock bottom with her hands, lightly. The
driving stream tipped her, began to carry her off. She righted, got
her head up, and opened the surface above. She changed air in one
quick breath. She bobbed along. An underwater rock hit her hip
a glancing blow.

A whirlpool sucked at her. Before she could do anything about
it, the whirlpool began to swing her around in a circle. It reminded
her of a merry-go-round she had once ridden as a kid at a carnival.
A snort broke from her. This was one merry-go-round ride she
didn't want, even if there was no charge for the ride. Furiously she
flailed her arms and kicked her legs. But she couldn't quite work
free of its grip. She made a complete circle a half-dozen times. It
was obscene the way it held onto her, a passionate whirlpool. A
short gray log bobbed around and around exactly across from her.
She wished she could latch onto it so she could rest a moment and
catch her breath. She swam for all she was worth. Still she couldn't
escape the whirlpool's tremendous sucking action. Her furious
paddling only served to keep her from being drawn immediately
into the center of the twisting pit. She thought she could hear,
over the splashing gallop of the waves, a weird whining *ipp*ing
sound. The sound of the centering suction terrified her. The log
across from her slowly began to slide into the depth of the twisting pit. It went around faster and faster. On one of its swifter turns
the gray log shot past her. It took one more turn, upended, held
a moment, *ulp!* went down. Then she truly was terrified. She
flailed and flailed. Her soft doeskins became completely saturated
with water. They dragged on her arms and legs like sheets of syrup.
"Dear Lord, have mercy." It was like being caught in some awful
nightmare. Dark arms from the deeps had grabbed hold of her
and were trying to drag her down. And she was going down. She

flailed and flailed. Eii! now there was no doubt of it. Like the log she too began to go around faster and faster as she inexorably neared the whistling center of the whirlpool. Why, really! It was as if she were drowning in one of her own nightmares. Frantic, she wondered how she was to wake herself if she wasn't already awake. Somehow she had to get herself out of this mesmeric gyrating whirlpool. "God!" She fought, knowing she was doomed. What a terrible thing it was to have a true-to-life whirlpool turn into a desperate nightmare. "Yii!"

She was hit an awful thump from below smack in the belly. *Akk.* She was hit so hard she had to let go the swimming and clutch her stomach. Her hands hit a heavy round object, fastened onto it. It was the gray log. After being sucked to the bottom, it had escaped the whirlpool, shot out from under and come thrusting to the surface. The log pushed her clear of the whirlpool, outside the ring of it. It had hit her so hard it almost knocked her out of breath. She groaned. She worked for breath. She groaned. She went under. She rose to the surface. She flailed her arms and legs. She went under. She rose. She went under. Then her chest hit hardpacked gravel. She got both hands under her, then her feet, and to her surprise found she could stand up. She was in water only up to her hips. She had made it to the other side.

She staggered to shore. She managed to stumble up the slow slope of the bank. She turned behind a big red rock, and, out of sight of the wolf, collapsed.

She lay gasping for breath. Her fingers worked spasmodically, digging eight little grooves in the red gravel.

She vomited. Her innards seemed to want to get out of her all at the same time. The vomiting seemed to have a definite mind of its own and shook her like a wolf might shake a cottontail by the neck. Bits of chewed bacon and blood gushed from her.

"Oh, misery me."

She rolled over to get out of her own scarlet vomit.

She lay a long time. She rested. Slowly the crazy jumping of her heart quieted.

She spoke aloud her mind, in outrage. "Of what earthly good is all this wilderness anyway? God must have had a mad on when he made it. Terrible. Crazy. Some of these little valleys might make a cozy location for a town, all right, like Sioux Falls, like here. But for the rest, it's all too crazy lonesome to be good for anything decent and civilized. No boundaries. No fences. No sheltering little hills. Just open to all sides to anything and everything that wants to come along. Wolves. Bears. Pumas. I wouldn't take it as a gift even if they were to pay me. I say, this wild country belonged to the Indian, it fit the Indian, the Indian liked it, so let the Indian keep it. Amen."

3

She had to tear off four more fringes from the sleeve of her tunic before she found the mail carrier's trail again. She found the trail at the foot of the Blue Mounds, between the base of the red cliffs and the River Of The Rock, buggy ruts and horse tracks cutting across a short stretch of hard gravel.

She fell to the ground and kissed the tracks. Thank God, at last, at last. Ahead lay Fort Ridgely and New Ulm. Then St. Paul.

She had got lost once during those four days. She had to turn south to get around a huge swamp, and when later she swung north again she began to go around in a circle. A morning sun after a cloudy night got her on course once more. Mosquitoes rose from the swamp so thick she breathed them in with every breath. Their stinging was ferocious. To keep from getting all bit up, she made a hood out of her parfleche to cover her head and neck. To see where she was going she had to take a quick peek now and then. She couldn't remember Indians complaining about mosquitoes. She wondered if maybe the Indian way of life, sitting half-smoked all day long in a fumid tepee, accounted for it. There were also terrific dews at night, so heavy that water gushed from her moccasins at every step. The humidity was so heavy she could drink dew by drawing blades of grass through her lips. All she had to eat was that last strip of bacon, and rose hips and grape leaves. She remembered Pa saying his cattle always did well on grape leaves.

She rolled over on her back. Out of the corner of her eye she could see the crest of the Blue Mounds high above her. In what now seemed a long, long time ago she remembered how she had run across the top to help the Yanktons drive buffalo over the Jump. A light south wind ruffled the tan leaves of the oaks at the foot of Buffalo Jump. Scent of drying grass hung sweet and fermentive on the breeze.

Meat. She needed meat. Any kind of meat. She was starved. She was so exhausted she could taste dust. A juicy mouse, raw, would be a treat. A real delight.

She was empty of feelings. What was grief again? Angela, Theodosia—had there actually been such people?

She stirred on the hard gravel. It crunched softly under her.

"No matter how I lay myself my bones still burn."

She rolled over on her belly.

Directly in front of her, on a small stone the size of an egg, stood a grasshopper flexing its big rear legs. It twigged its nose, sideways, twice. A spit of tobacco juice dripped from its green behind.

Her eyes fixed on the flexing legs. She thought she could detect the workings of muscles in them. Meat. In her gaunted mind the muscles of the grasshopper loomed large. Meat's meat.

Cautiously she moved up a hand, got herself set to strike. She would make a snatch at it, strike as swift as the flick of a frog's tongue. She took a slow, soft breath; and snapped at it. Miracle. She caught it between thumb and forefinger. She was careful not to squash it. It struggled. Its straining reminded her of a safety pin trying to unsnap itself. She gave it a hot, intent look, then downed it in a single gulp. She didn't care to taste it. She just wanted the muscles, the meat.

She noticed green flies buzzing around her. Slowly she sat up. The green flies seemed to be interested in her legs. Looking down, she realized for the first time that she was bleeding. The dipping ripgut grass she had walked through that morning had cut her toes and shins to the bone. Both her moccasins and her leggings had long ago worn away. She had patched one worn pair of moccasins with the other worn pair, yet even the combined pair had been threshed to shreds. The leggings hung in tatters from her knees.

"Put an end to it."

Sight of blood gave her an idea. Carefully she selected a rough-edged blade of grass, and sawing it back and forth, managed to open a vein in her arm. She drank a little of her own blood to blunt her hunger. It startled her that blood should taste salty.

When she lay down again she was astonished to see an eagle hovering above her. The eagle lay on the breeze like a pair of brown drapes wavering on a rising column of furnace heat. Its snaky golden-brown head hung down, a brown eye fixed piercingly on her. Her lying down had startled the eagle, causing it to mount the air a few feet. It had been about to strike.

It was the green flies. The eagle thought her carrion. Pa had often remarked that where you find green flies, there you find buzzards.

A snarl gathered in her throat. Her feet and hands came up like a cat's, clawing the air. She showed her teeth, ferocious.

The eagle gave her a startled eye, shook its golden head, then with huge flaps of its paired drapes carried itself off toward the heights of the Blue Mounds. A few moments later it lighted on a red crag. It fluffed its wing feathers, settled down to watch her. It could wait.

She breathed shallow. She waited for the meat of the grasshopper and her own blood to restore her strength.

She napped. She dreamed of a fat, perky gopher. The gopher stood erect beside the entrance of its lair. It whistled at her. Then it spoke to her. "You want me? Guess again." And down the hole it plunged, in.

Something brushed against her. She awoke. Too tired to turn her head, she looked sidewise.

Snakes. Families of them. Hundreds of them. Papa snakes and bigger mama snakes. Baby snakes of all sizes. All had diamond markings and a green-brown hue. Rattlesnakes.

Too spent to be frightened, she watched the wrigglers crawl around and over each other. Some were six feet long; some only two feet. The rattles on their tails were silent. They quivered scarlet tongues at each other as if exchanging lickerish bits of snake gossip. There was an odd air of amiability about them. It took her a while to see this. Her idea had always been that a snake was naturally surly and went around being dangerous most of the time. She watched. Yes, there was no doubt of it, these snakes were having a party, sporting in the sun on warm gravel. They were playing tag with each other. As one family left, another family replaced it. They all seemed to be coming from the river and heading for the stone heights above. Their company was agreeable. She even thought she could understand, a little, why Eve had let herself be beguiled by a snake in the Garden of Eden.

She breathed shallow.

The presence of the snakes explained something to her. With them around, it was hardly a wonder she hadn't seen any gophers or mice the last while. In filmy reverie, smiling bemused to herself, she wondered how all those snakes could have missed that fat gopher in her dream.

She itched at the edges of her hairline. It was time to go on. She staggered to her feet.

Careful of where she walked amongst the snakes, she followed Rollo's trail across the patch of gravel and then through more deep ripgrass.

The eagle saw her go. It fluffed its wings in disgust; then, falling from its perch, it lifted and disappeared into the northern skies.

Her toes and shins bled again. She stopped. She stared at the oozing scarlet. She would have to do something about it.

She emptied her parfleche. To her astonishment she found four strips of dried meat neatly tucked in one corner.

She stared at the dried jerky. How in God's name had it got into her parfleche? She couldn't for the life of her recall having packed the jerky when she escaped the Yanktons. And she certainly hadn't taken it from that cabin in Sioux Falls. She couldn't understand it. Couldn't. Bible times were surely past. Another Elijah miracle was hardly likely. "And the barrel of meal wasted not, neither did the cruse of oil fail."

Well, there the jerky was and she was hungry. She should just simply accept it and eat it without worrying about where it came from.

"So many outlandish things have happened to me lately it really shouldn't surprise me though. Live long enough and a miracle is bound to happen to you sometime."

After a little chewing the jerky became quite savory. The four strips worked down to a little ball of tough tissue. She chewed and chewed the little ball. It retained its savor. It reminded her of one of her childhood dreams, that she could buy a piece of gum that would never lose its sweetness no matter how much she chewed it.

She stumbled down to the edge of the River Of The Rock, between some golden ash, and cupped herself a long drink to wash it down. She washed her face and hands and laved her cut, bleeding feet. The tough, dry jerky and the tepid water restored her.

Up on the riverbank gleamed a flat red rock. It gave her an idea. She spread her parfleche out on it and with a sharp-edged stone pounded and cut the parfleche in half. With a pointed stick she punched holes along the edges. She took the fringes she had saved, one for each day since her escape, and fashioned crude shoes for her raw feet. It was clumsy footwear but it would do. As for the fringes she had saved so far, well, what was the use of counting the passing days? She would get to St. Paul when she got there.

She walked on, light-headed.

She came upon a meadow where the grass had been cropped short by passing buffalo. Patches of sunflowers nodded in the soft

wind. She loved the flowing wash of the sunned petals. Her brain
hazed over with gold. She took one of the riper flowers and ate it.
It was all a dream.

"Cannibal at last."

Her hair itched. She was too tired to scratch the itching.

She could feel sweat gather between her shoulder blades. It
trickled down her spine and then down along the inside of her
legs. Splotches of sweat showed in the armpits of her weathered
tunic.

She walked.

Within the hour the gnawing in her belly was back. It came
with a scalding thirst in the throat. She drank more water from the
warm river. It didn't help. She kneaded the gnawing with her
knuckles. She was so gaunt she could feel the buttony knob of her
navel through her leather tunic. It slid around under her knuckles
like a fifty-cent piece lost in the lining of a coat.

Once, looking down, she was surprised to find herself trudging
along pigeon-toed through the prairie grass. It was the way Smoky
Day walked. And Tinkling. And all the Yankton women. It was
the manner of all women with heavy burdens to bear. She recalled
the days when she used to walk with her toes pointed out a little.
As in a fresh tintype she could see herself stepping briskly along
in black kid button shoes down a boardwalk in St. Paul.

She watched herself walk. Yes. She now definitely walked different. Well, why not. It seemed the sensible way to walk, especially if one was weak. Walking with the toes turned in helped a
body keep one's balance. Also, it enabled one to take full advantage
of the length of the foot. Walking mile after mile, every inch
counted.

She followed the river north. The ridge of the Blue Mounds
fell away behind her. Trees became fewer. Except where beavers
had built dams, the river ran shallow.

She crossed a ford. She gave herself another long drink. She
groomed her hair in the mirroring surface, retightening the rope of
gold braids about her head.

A meadowlark sang from a nodding sunflower. "I am the bird
of fidelity and this I know for a certainty. Relief is near!"

Memory of the gray shape came to her. She hadn't seen it since
Split Rock Creek. Casually she looked around to see if it might not
have returned. It hadn't.

The itching along her hairline became so fiendish she finally
just had to dig into it with her fingernails. A scab, something,
caught under a fingernail. It felt like something caught between
one's teeth. The something scab seemed to move. She held it close
up. Yes, it moved. A louse. Her blue eyes widened. She looked
again to make doubly sure. Yes, all its little legs were waving
madly at her. Lice had awakened in her hair. The Yanktons had
been lousy after all, despite Smoky Day's assurances they were a
clean people. Judith cracked the louse carefully between her
thumbnails.

She found more lice, using her fingernails as a rake. She killed
them too. She recalled having seen Sunflower searching through
her husband, Pounce's, hair for lice. When Sunflower found some
she carefully bit into them, then ate them. A case of where the
eaten turned on the eater.

She trudged on, one big toe after another.

The sun slowly eyed itself down the sky.

A pinkish-brown bird, a ruffed grouse, a hen, fluttered in the
grass ahead of her. It flapped along as though one of its wings
were broken, crying piteously.

It took Judith a moment to understand it was a ruse. The ruffed
grouse was a mother and to protect her chicks she was trying to
draw attention to herself.

Tender fowl. Meat. Judith's tongue worked. Somewhere underfoot sat hidden a half-dozen wild pullets. She loved pullets. Mmm.
A single suck on a well-done pullet leg and the meat just fell off
in one's mouth.

She searched the wind-woven grass very carefully. The pullets
had to be somewhere around.

The mother became desperate. She put on an even more elaborate act of being hurt.

Judith decided the wild pullets were immediately underfoot. She knelt. She lifted first one swatch of gray-green grass, then another.

A fingertip touched a prickly fallen rose. Judith sucked at the fingertip, then nipped out a thorn with her nails.

Ah, there they were. Cleverly hidden under a burdock. All six were sitting in a row, very much like six Sioux children sitting in a Bible class, brown eyes bright, waiting for the magic word. Mmm, they looked good. Broiled over a stick fire out in the open, they would be just wonderful. The second on the right was the fattest.

She set herself. Then she pounced. She caught the one she wanted, the second on the right. The grouse pullet squealed. It struggled desperately. The other five pullets immediately fluttered up, and on a cry from the mother, dove into the grass a dozen feet away, disappearing in perfect camouflage. The mother next flew straight for Judith, bristling, beak foremost. The mother came at her with such fury Judith had to throw up an arm to protect her eyes. The mother with her pecking beak and snapping wingtips and scratching toes seemed to be everywhere at once. Judith finally had to put up both arms, and in so doing involuntarily let go of the chick. On that the attack ceased, and by the time Judith's eyes cleared, mother and chick had also vanished in perfect camouflage.

Judith sighed. "Well, I can't say as I really blame her. Poor creature."

Judith tramped on. Presently the mail carrier's trail left the River Of The Rock and went northeast up a creek valley.

Two days later, Judith came upon fresh moccasin tracks. She spotted them as she knelt for a drink in a sandy place along the creek. The moccasin tracks were clearly fresh and they belonged to a grown man. The man's moccasins had been patched and the mark of the seam was the first to fill with water seeping up from below.

Judith snapped a quick jerking look around, so quick her neck cracked. No one was in sight.

Yet the tracks were fresh. Whoever it was had seen her coming and had quickly hidden himself. It was probably some red brute from Mad Bear's band and playfully biding his time to scalp her.

Well, let him scalp her. She was too tired to care. She was ready for the hereafter, as ready as she ever would be.

She knelt. Nose tip touching running water, she sipped herself a slow drink.

As she rose to her feet, she spotted a plum pit lying off to one side of the moccasin tracks. The pit was fresh, still wet. Someone had spit it out only moments before.

Plums? Again she looked around to all sides, this time slowly. There were no plum trees in the little creek valley that she could see. And wasn't it a bit late in the season for plums? In fact, too late. What was going on?

She looked down at the fresh moccasin prints again. In a vague way, forlornly, she wished she were strong again, as she was in the days when she'd helped her father make hay. Let her have that strength again and she would take a club to the Indian and kill him. Yes. Kill him. And, now that she thought of it, maybe even eat him. It certainly was an idea.

In her mind she could see herself skulking after the Indian. If he were fat, all the better. She would overtake him from the rear and bash his head in. She would have one good hearty meal at last. Broil one of his big muscular arms and slowly gnaw away on it, a hand to either end of the bone. Mmm. Good. People were fools not to eat human flesh when they were starving to death. It had to be the best meat, no? since the human being was the true end of creation. The best for the best. Yes. Her mouth watered. Nothing like a well-broiled human arm. Savor it with some sweet wild onion, sprinkle on a little ground-up rose hips, and it would make quite a delicacy.

She blinked. She caught herself standing crouched, ready to pounce, hand up as though about to strike with a club.

A most unhappy thought came to her. She stood very still, considering it, full of patience for herself. Yes. Yes. It was probably true. She knew now. She was slowly losing her mind.

She wavered on. She hardly realized she moved.

The creek ran quietly through seas of deep bluejoint. Sometimes the effect of the wind streaming through the top of the head-high grass was like a pack of bushy-tailed dogs chasing across a meadow. The sides of the valley gradually deepened. Naturally terraced bluffs and ribboned cliffs appeared. Scars of old Indian villages were visible on some of the hills, ocher spots where the green flesh was worn away. One of the bluffs, on which the sun shone just right, had the look of a freshly baked loaf of bread shiny with melted butter. There were plover everywhere and the calls of the curlew were maddening.

Ahead of her, on a slight rise of ground where a side stream came in from the north, a body lay prone in the air about a dozen feet above ground.

She stopped dead in her tracks. She was at last, truly, seeing things. She had come to the end of her rope. Her brain had snapped.

She fastened all of her attention on it. Her eyes went over the apparition piece by piece. She stood slightly humped over, trying to ride out the blow, the shock, of knowing she had gone insane.

At last, staring hotly, she saw it wasn't an apparition after all, that it was actually an Indian wrapped in a buffalo robe. The Indian lay on some kind of platform. Four posts supported it.

It was an Indian burial out on the plains. An honored chief of some sort lay on a scaffold.

She approached it warily, looking up at it. She wondered if relatives had left food behind to sustain the chief on his long journey down the spirit road. She hoped so. She could use the food better than a dead body could.

Then she began to wonder how fresh the body was. If it was

only a day or so old, she could still have herself that broiled arm after all.

She stood under it. She shook the posts supporting it. A gourd made a soft belling noise. She shook the scaffold again. A piece of buffalo fur slipped open on one side, and out rolled a white skull. The skull fell with a light thump at her feet.

She looked at the weathered skull with regret. No meat there.

A voice suddenly sounded behind her, a familiar voice. "I see that the white woman feels sad. I want to shake hands with her. That is all I have to say."

Judith turned slowly, not wanting to see what she knew she was going to see.

Scarlet Plume. He was holding out a hand to her. There was a warm, grave smile on his wide, dark face. The usual yellow dot inside the blue circle lay on his left cheekbone.

She also saw something else. It made her wild inside. He was wearing a creamy wolfskin over his shoulders, the same wolfskin she had left behind in the brown cabin in Sioux Falls. Numbly she realized he had been following her all along. He was the gray shape that had been haunting her.

4

She was caught.

She flew at him in a fury. She tried to scratch him, hit him, bite him.

Scarlet Plume suffered her.

Soon the little strength she had left was expended, and she fell at his feet in a heap.

He stood looking down at her. A smile wavered on his warm, liberal lips. "I see that the Woman With The Sunned Hair has painted herself for a dance in a special way. There are roses of starvation upon her skin."

She lay quivering.

"Also I see that she has come to honor the grave of stranger dead."

Sioux words burst from her. "Why do you bury your dead in midair? So that anybody can find the body?"

"Let the white man hide his dead in the ground if he is ashamed of them. That is his way. But the red man keeps his dead in sight so that he may remember them. That is his way." The scarlet plume at the back of his head twiggled a little in the soft breeze. "Later, when the flesh has departed, and there is nothing left but the bones, then the red man returns the bones to the earth his mother."

She quivered under his frank regard of her.

"It was not my wish to show myself," he said. "I saw that Sunned Hair wanted to make her way alone to the white man's country. This was a good thing. I watched to see that no enemy stood in her path. I prayed to Wakantanka that he might give her a straight road, smooth waters, and a clear sky. Yet when Sunned Hair wished to"—he paused as if hunting for the right phrase—"wished to cry at the foot of the grave of a dead chief, it had to be told her that there was another way."

She hated him. He had of course known she'd had cannibalism in mind but out of the largeness of his heart he had deliberately cast a favorable light on it. "Was this chief one of you? A Yankton?"

"He was one of Mad Bear's band. Yet he was a brave man. His children loved him. We must honor him now that he has departed."

"Where are we?"

"You have walked to a place where many grapes hang down." He pointed ahead. "Do you see?"

About a mile ahead on the left, a small valley cut back into the line of bald bluffs. In it grew a grove of golden trees.

"Once again it's prairies all around," she whispered, "and then all of a sudden a little valley full of lovely trees. Some lost timber."

She nodded to herself. "That's what gets you about these prairies."

"It will be a good place to hide. I will bring home the game until Sunned Hair has found her flesh and is fat again. Then she can continue her journey to her white cities."

She rolled over on her back. She gazed up at his red face. His exquisitely cut lips welled over in a richly expressive smile. It shot through her half-crazed mind it was too bad the Indians did not kiss. Because his lips were made for kissing.

"Arise. Come," he said.

Hate changed to mad desire. She suddenly yearned with all her belly that he would pick her up and do with her as a man would. Her thoughts became plainly and deliciously shameful. It was sweet to think of kissing his large, warm lips. She wanted a spoonful of his bumblebee honey. Wild fruit was even sweeter than stolen fruit.

He divined her feelings. A sharpness came into his black eyes. The warm smile left his lips. His face went back to being impassive. At last he said, "Come, let us go to this lost timber you speak of. I will make you a shelter where you can rest. Soon you will be as sleek as a pony in the Moon of Making Fat."

She made a show of getting to her feet; deliberately let herself collapse.

"Come, Woman With The Sunned Hair."

She lay craven under his hawk look. She liked his cockarouse dignity. She twisted invitingly on the grass. She was a silly, dizzy hen.

"Come."

Memory of romantic fantasies about him dreamed through her mind. Shameful. Lickerish. He reminded her of puccoons blooming in June, full of ecstatic scent, the blossoms gold, the roots yellow.

"The roses of starvation become thee, but there are better roses. Come."

She saw him again as he'd once danced up the buffalo, dark body a gleaming bronze in the red firelight, a stud rampant. Her limbs parted slightly under her tunic. She willed it. He must possess her. He must. It was pagan. But it would be heavenly.

"Come."

A wan coquettish smile opened her lips. Again she made a show of struggling to her feet. Again she let herself fall to earth.

A grunt of impatience escaped him. Then, face still impassive, he picked her up. He carried her along the creek, easily. She was hardly more than an empty parfleche to him.

He turned up a side stream and entered the golden grove. Steep, grassy hills slanted upward on either side. A wind rustled through the lemon leaves of the ash. The leather leaves of the oak barely stirred. Grape leaves, turning purple, hung in sweeping loops through the lower reaches of the trees. Birds had cleaned off all the hanging spikes. A small trickle of a stream glinted in the deeper shadows.

Scarlet Plume carried her well into the little hidden valley. Then, under a thick bower of grape vines beside an overhanging clay bank, he stooped and put her down on a bed of leaves.

She would not let him go. She threw her thin arms around his neck and held onto him. She gave him her most winning smile, white teeth open, eyelids almost closed on dilated blue eyes. She kissed his bold cheekbone. With her nose she pushed aside his heavy black hair and kissed his ear. She was surprised at how sweet he smelled, reminding her of a fresh buffalo hide scented with the smoke of burning sweet grass. She nuzzled through his long black hair and at last kissed his supple copper lips. She drew back and looked at his lips. She smiled. Next she nipped his lips. She could feel the full outline of his lower lip inside her own parted lips. She kissed and kissed him. A dark being awoke in her, took over all direction of her. She slid around in his arms, a lissome child at play in a tree house, became completely shameless, tunic well up over her hips, wildly scandalous, clasping him about the hips with her limbs, locking herself tight against him, undulating against him with utter abandon, until every part of her body seemed to be in motion at the same time.

Scarlet Plume suffered her. He still leaned stooped over her, unable to be rid of her.

She unclasped the gray wolfskin from his neck. It slipped away and fell on the bed of leaves beside them. She stroked his coppery body. The muscles of him were as the limbs of a young maple. She found the knot to the string supporting his breechclout and undid that too. The breechclout fell to his feet. He was again as she had once seen him dancing up the buffalo.

He endured her witchery in wondering silence.

"Lover," she whispered.

At last he spoke. "What is this? Does Sunned Hair wish to be taken under the robe?"

"Yes, yes."

There was more wondering silence in him as he suffered her her enticements.

"Lover," she whispered again.

His eyes turned black in their sockets. "Why is this?"

"Yes," she hissed in his ear.

"But the man you see before you does not have with him a proper courting robe." There was a vibrant quaver in his voice.

"Yes, yes."

"Sunned Hair is lonesome. She misses her white husband very much. I am sad for her."

She swarmed his face with moist kisses.

"Perhaps when I meet the husband of Sunned Hair he will agree to become my kodah."

"Yes."

"A good Yankton knows a wife may be shared with a kodah without impropriety. But it is not the way of the whites."

Fiercely she drew him down so that he sank to his knees. She took his hand and passed it between her thighs to let him know that the juices of love were ready. She cried huskily in his ear.

A relenting gentleness softened his heavy voice. "My helper is talking to me. He tells me it will be a good thing to do. Thus, if the white woman wishes it, it shall be done." With fine delicacy, as if guardedly indulging a loved and willful child, he settled over her.

He moved too slowly for her. She took hold of his coppery knob and helped him. She saw that he had a wonderful cucumber of love for her. She gasped at the engorged red color of it. She helped him enter her. His proud flesh was already warm when it parted her. She could feel herself widening and deepening, and then surrounding him. She cried aloud. She drummed her pelvic bone up against him.

He loved her rhythmically, with a gentle motion.

Stars rose. Stars fell.

His insistent breathing was sweet in her ear.

A strange new feeling awakened in her womb. Her womb was like an animal inside her belly. She had never in her life felt such sweet burning. It was an urgent suckling, a ravening hunger, yet it was also selfless. It became clutching joy. Her thighs became bathed with sheathing dew. Her face crimsoned over with surprise and shame and wonder. What was it the minister back home said? That lust was a vile expression of one's animal nature? Well, there the minister for once was wrong. Lust was wonderful. It was a radiant passage. Winged. Suddenly.

He loved her rhythmically, with a gentle suction.

She rose, rose. Lightning-like sensations shot through her belly. Fireflies darted through her brain. She began to tremble all over. She rose, rose. "God in heaven."

He loved her rhythmically, with a gentle urgency.

She loved his arrogant flesh. She wished it were even more arrogant. She longed for a king. Let there come a king holding a golden bowl flowing over with cream. She drummed harder against him, swifter. Her eyes rolled bloodstone dark under tight lids. Her lips widened. Her teeth set. Extravagant raptures swelled in her. She was a great plum about to burst.

Abruptly Scarlet Plume changed in her arms. A dark being had also awakened in him. His breathing became a husky catching purr. The gentle lover in him changed into a demanding puma. The dark being made him thrust and thrust into her with abandon. Utterly necessary. It had to be. His purring deepened into a moan of vibrating guttural pleasure. Every part of him seemed to be in motion at once.

He was hers. He was hers. She responded to his imperious hips. "King!" Her velvet leaves slipped marvelous full around him.

A yell, gurgling, rose in his throat. Unfettered. Savage.

Suddenly knotlike spasms worked slowly and irrevocably in her womb. Her womb suddenly became her brain. The spasms ran their own course. A cry also erupted in her, free, from far within her.

"He-han!" he cried.

"O Lord!" she cried.

He wept tears upon her.

The beat of the overriding pulse throbbed in the depths of her quick. There was no stopping it. Never before had this happened to her. All of Vince's wiles and tricks and strange demands in bed had never come close to awakening a blinding revelation like this in her. It was the first time. The first time. At last.

He lowered upon her.

A long sigh let her down, gently, into a lethargy as soft as cat-tail down. She sank away into oblivion.

She slept.
And slept.

When she awoke, slowly, sunlight struck across her face in a wide band of sharp saffron.

She didn't know why but she felt new.

She remembered the claybank and the bower of wild grape vines and the golden grove. Lost Timber.

She found herself lying on an aromatic mat of woven switches. Under it rustled tree leaves. She was covered by the gray wolfskin. She remembered being pursued for many days by the haunt wolf. Scarlet Plume.

Scarlet Plume had been busy while she slept. He had built two walls of interwoven willows into the claybank. New bark shingles made the roof of the bower rain-tight. The east wall he left open, facing the stream.

She sensed his presence. Without turning her head, letting her eyes widen a little, she could make him out to the left of the opening. He was sitting on his heels and cleaning his teeth with a blade of grass. A small stick fire burned at his feet. Smoke from it rose in soft gray tendrils, gradually trailing off and disappearing against the matted roof. Above him, to one side, hung a strip of cured meat.

A crimson blush suffused her as she recalled their moment of love and the new sweet burning in her belly. She could feel the sudden blush heating her body like a warm silk nightgown falling to her feet. Yes. She had at last awakened to love and light. She let her eyes close as she relived again that moment of blinding revelation.

She stirred, languorously.

He instantly turned. A warm, grave smile curved his fleshy lips. "You have slept well."

"Mmm."

"You have slept two suns to bed."

"Two whole days? In a row?"

"You also ate well. The she-wolf does not live that eats as well as Sunned Hair."

She sat up on her elbows. Hair from the wolfskin tickled her chin. "I've been eating for two whole days?"

He threw a look at the strip of hanging meat. "Already you have devoured most of one doe. Much soup and boiled meat. Even the rib ends were well-chewed."

She ran a hand over her stomach and found that her buttony navel was half lost in flesh again. So. Scarlet Plume had fed her then like she might have been a gravely ill one. Two whole days.

Well. For the life of her, she couldn't remember a thing of it.

"Sunned Hair came a great distance on foot with little food. She was not used to this. She was very tired. She needed the sleep and the food."

She found herself desiring him again. She smiled at him in a winning way.

Scarlet Plume understood the look on her face. He turned slowly and gazed down at the little wriggling flames of the stick fire. He picked his teeth some more with the blade of grass. Reverie wavered in his black-glass eyes.

"He-han," she said with a sweet smile. "To that place that far."

He dropped the blade of grass in the fire. He glanced up at the strip of venison. "There is need for more meat. I will go hunt the game while you take the morning bath."

"But—"

"I have made a watering place for you in the little stream. I shall remain within easy call of it."

She saw there was no use talking to him, at least not for the moment.

With a slow hand Scarlet Plume picked up a little stick and stirred up the embers of the fire some and then placed the stick in the fire. Glints of an inward fire jumped in his dark eyes.

It came to her, as she studied him, that something was missing. Of course. He had washed off the face-marking on his left cheekbone, the yellow dot inside the blue circle.

She said, "I wish to ask my scarlet friend a question."

"I wait to hear."

"Why can we not shake hands?"

He gave her a tormented look. Abruptly he stood up, grabbed up a spear, newly made, and as quick as the flip of a beaver tail was gone.

Her eyes opened in surprise. "Why," she said with a gasp, "he's shy."

She lay by herself awhile. She watched the little palpitating flames in the fire. Petulance twitched at the edges of her pink lips.

"It's probably just as well," she said at last. "And it is time I took a bath. Because I stink."

She threw aside the wolfskin. As she was about to get to her feet, she noticed that her toes and shins gleamed as though greased. Wonderingly she touched them, then smelled her fingertips. Her nostrils opened. Scarlet Plume had more than just watched over her and fed her; he had also doctored her as any true medicine man was required to do. He had treated her bleeding skin with some kind of native salve, herbs in a film of venison grease.

She stepped outside. The sun shone glinting just above the steep bluff across the stream. Tilted glades of grass gleamed light-green between the trees. There was a chill in the air as if there might have been frost during the night. Leaves were shivering off some of the ash trees, sifting down the slopes like lavish throws of gold coins. A single wild plum stood like a decanter of dark wine in a far ravine. The buckskin leaves of the scrub oaks hung motionless.

She tripped down a green, mossy path. Silver-tinted black moss grew on the underside of a thick-armed grape vine immediately beside the path. She found Scarlet Plume's watering place, a dam of rocks and twigs thrown across the stream much like a beaver might build it. She could make out individual pebbles on the gravelly bottom of the stream, red and gold and black and green.

She glanced around to make sure she was alone, then shed her tattered tunic. Golden naked, she stepped into the pool. The water had an edge to it as if it had been run through a filter of ice. She shivered. She moved into the water until it touched the backs of her knees. She cupped water over her elbows. "Ieee, it's cold." She waded in until water lapped up under her seat. Then, taking a daring breath, she dropped in. She came up spluttering, flailing her arms. She cried out in pleased shock. She splashed herself some more, took another plunge.

She scrubbed herself with sand. She let her hair down and undid the braids. She lashed her hair back and forth in the water, a flowing gold in a green liquid. She scrubbed her hair, again and again, remembering the lice. She wrung her hair out and spread it over her shoulders to dry.

She next scrubbed her doeskin tunic, inside and out, especially the seams. She put spreader sticks in it to keep it from shrinking too much, then laid it out on the grass in the sun.

Naked she skipped to their bower and draped herself in the wolfskin. She found a sunny place on a fallen tree outside the doorway and settled down to warm herself.

She waited for him to come. "My scarlet lover was sad."

The sun shone on her. There was a wide golden silence. Water twinkled. More ash leaves drifted to earth. Her drying hair fluffed out on her shoulders with little springing leaps.

She waited.

A whimpering sound came to her from downstream. A fawn was hurt. The whimpering was pitiful. It seemed to come from behind some gooseberry bushes.

"Poor thing," she whispered. "Now I suppose some puma will get it."

Out of the shadow on the far side of the stream came a doe. Head up, wary, it advanced a few steps; stopped; listened; advanced some more.

The whimpering became more pronounced. It now definitely came from behind the gooseberry bushes.

The doe slowly advanced to within a few feet of the gooseberries. It listened, ears alert; and stared, soft, dark eyes gleaming.

Then Judith saw Scarlet Plume. What she'd thought a shadow was really brown skin. He was squatted on his heels, new spear in hand and set to throw. He sat very still, unmoving. The whimpering sound came from him. He made the sound by sucking on a leaf folded between his lips.

Before she could cry out in warning, his arm flowed and the spear sprang. The spear caught the deer in the breast, transfixing it. Scarlet Plume followed his spear, leaping, as silent as a puma. Stooping, knife glinting, he cut the doe's throat.

Judith caught a hand to her throat. "That wasn't fair!" she gasped.

Scarlet Plume watched the fallen doe a moment, then turned and flashed Judith a victory smile. He had been aware of her all along.

Judith sat numb.

He kneeled beside the fallen doe and cupped up a handful of its blood and drank it.

Judith stiffened. Her scarlet lover drank blood? For a fleeting second, enormous, she realized what she had let herself in for. She and this man-savage were ice ages apart.

When the deer had bled sufficiently, he came bearing it toward her. The smile on his lips had changed to a look of quiet purpose.

He laid the doe on the ground. He cut slits down the backs of the rear legs and pried out the Achilles tendons. He passed a stout ash stick under the tendons and strung the body up on a tree limb. Starting at the head he skinned the doe skillfully. The pink carcass emerged as if with the motions of birthing. Scarlet Plume spread the skin out on the grass, raw side up. He next butchered the carcass, deftly, not wasting a motion. Everything usable was placed in neat rows on the skin. When he broke out the shinbone from the shank, Judith for the first time realized where the Yanktons got their lovely armor-like bone vests. Each shinbone was hollow and, like a bead, could be strung on a cord.

A drop of blood lay dried on the edge of Scarlet Plume's nether lip. Judith shivered. She feared him. She huddled under her wolf-skin.

He was hanging up the jerky to dry, when she at last found tongue. "I see that a Yankton warrior considers it manly to deceive a poor mother uneasy for the safety of her young."

A patient, gentle look appeared in his black eyes. "While you were taking the morning bath, I prayed to the morning star for a good hunt. This I said: 'We have need. Sunned Hair needs the food and the doeskin. Forgive us for taking this doe. Yet she is needed. She is not a mother at this time. We promise not to kill more than is needed.' "

"Nevertheless you awakened a mother's love in her and preyed on it."

He looked down at the deer head on the green grass where it lay with its dulled-over eyes. "She understands. The Yanktons were once animals before they were people. Her family and my family have been neighbors for many grandfathers. She and I are of one blood. Therefore the Yanktons are cousins to the deer and must apologize to her and thank her for the food and the doeskin. We do not ask her to carry burdens for us as the white man asks of his animals. We only need the blood of one at a time."

"Do not your dogs carry sticks many weary miles across the prairies?"

"The dog is a pet friend of the woman. Sometimes when the puppy has no mother the woman gives him to suck. It is not for a man to say."

"Well, has not the red man made a slave of the spirit dog, the horse, when he rides on his back?"

"It is a sad truth that horses were made to carry burdens. This we learned from the white man." Finished with dismembering the carcass, Scarlet Plume began to scrape the inside of the doeskin.

"Suppose this poor mother needed the blood of a Yankton? Your blood?"

He lifted a shoulder eloquently. "If it were fated to be, it would be for us to understand. A good thing."

"Does the Yankton consider the deer more of a brother than he does the white man?"

Scarlet Plume opened his eyes wide. "In the beginning the red man welcomed the white man into his tepee. He considered him his kodah. He cried tears over him when he first met him. This was a great thing. But soon it could be seen that the white man wanted to cut up his mother into black strips and mutilate her. Our wise men saw that even as the red man gives when he has plenty, the white man takes when he has plenty. Does not the white man know that whatever one steals from his brother in this world he will have to carry it in the next world? Can he carry the world?" Scarlet Plume shook his head gravely. "The white man's thoughts are upside down."

Judith fell silent.

Scarlet Plume looked up from his scraping. "If the red man tried to make the white man live like him, the white man would want to fight him. Well, that is why the red man fights. If the red man were to let the white man feel, 'We are better than you,' the white man would be very bitter. Well, that is why the red man is also very bitter."

Judith grudged him his ancient pride.

A shadow, swift, like a quick basso profundo passage in a fugue, touched his face, darkened his eyes. He spoke quietly. "Yet the power of the whites will prevail. We will be annihilated. This is a terrible thing for a Yankton to think about. Not even Whitebone will survive. It is a fated thing. Just as this mother deer is feeding us, so too the Yankton will be killed up and fed to the white man."

Judith's eyes began to glow from within.

"We are all dead men. Yet we will fight as long as we can."

Judith found herself back on his side of the fence. It was shocking to think that the Yanktons she had known might be destroyed.

"What part of the deer does Sunned Hair wish to eat?"

"What?"

"Does not the white woman know that like parts nourish like parts? There are no special like parts for me as I am a man and this deer was a mother at one time. What special part of the deer does Sunned Hair wish?"

It was with an effort that Judith spoke. "I do not wish for any special part today."

When he finished working the doeskin, he said, "Even the grasses are related to us. They do not hesitate to feed on our fleshes after we die. Someday soon I too shall lie down and fold my arms for a last time and feed the grasses. We are all one. We have a common mother. But the white man considers himself apart from this mother. Can it be that the white man has become overproud because Wakantanka fleshed him"—Scarlet Plume glanced at her white skin—"in wakan white? It is something to think about. The white man has been made part God when he does not deserve it perhaps."

Her soul went out to him. She remembered the thrilling moment of his urgent thrusting. With her hands she slowly stroked her pear breasts upward. She thought, "All of my life I have tried to stamp out my passional nature, yet here I now sit, in this wilderness, perfectly willing to live in sin with this wild man."

Scarlet Plume staked out the doeskin to dry.

Judith took a deep breath and went over to where he sat on his heels. Wetting a finger, she gently rubbed the drop of dried blood off his nether lip. She bent down to kiss him.

Quickly he put on he did not know what she was about and managed to slide out from under her reaching lips and stand up with a slab of venison in hand.

She yearned for him.

He said, gently, "My helper is talking to me again. He warns me that a man who has been with a woman lately is prone to wounds. Arrows and bullets are drawn toward such a man. Mad Bear's band is about."

A weakness swept over her. She staggered against him and clutched him about the hips.

"We must be careful that we do not break some law that will cover the sun with blackness."

"Am I not an agreeable lover in your eyes?"

"You are going toward the day. I am going toward the dark. Your people and my people were born too far apart."

"Then I am now dirt in your eyes?"

"It is our times. Your time is one time and mine is another."

"I wish to teach my scarlet friend how to kiss."

"Kiss? What is kiss?"

"Let us touch lips. When done in the proper manner it gives much pleasure."

Gravely he unclasped her arms.

She sank to the ground.

A cold draft woke her.

It was night. She was lying on her matting of willow switches. Embers in the hearth fell into each other with soft, expiring sounds. There was a good wind out and it wrestled through the trees and sometimes it touched into the bower and brought out a dull orange blush in the graying ashes. She could smell Scarlet Plume's buckskin odor behind her somewhere. She guessed he was sleeping.

She felt forlorn.

Everyone else had their proper place in the world, as if they truly belonged where they did—yes, even those in death like Theodosia and Angela. But she herself was a misfit. Unwanted. God had not really planned on having her around. No wonder the Yanktons had finally set her apart and made of her a goddess. She was better off dead.

She begrudged her belly its delight with the red man.

"I must be out of my mind thinking I can be in love with a Stone Age man. Ma always did say I was over-notional as a child."

For the thousandth time she picked at an old sore in her heart. She had never enjoyed bedding with Vince. It had always been a chore for her. Though truth to tell it had never been much of a delight for Vince either.

The difference between Vince and Scarlet Plume was the difference between a dust rag and a scarf, the one made of old cheesecloth and the other of scarlet silk.

Yet, plainly, by decree, her duty lay in St. Paul. Vince was still her husband under God, and she had better have a cozy home prepared for him when he returned from the wars. And perhaps have more babies with him to make up for the loss of Angela. She had made her bed, now she had better lie in it.

She recalled one night in particular. . . .

She and Vince were in bed together, breathing quietly, preparing themselves for sleep. She was about to drop off, when Vince's hand came itching over under the covers.

Her lips curled in disgust. She hated it when he came at her this way. It was so mouselike. Like some scared errand boy with a harelip. Vince sometimes not only bored her, he sometimes revolted her. She let her tongue play along the edge of her lips, until the tip of her tongue found the four black hairs on the upper lip.

Vince's hand went itching down her leg. Near her ankle it found the hem of her nightgown, then, still itching, it began to work up her leg, taking the nightgown with it, baring her thigh.

"Don't," she said, flatly.

"My precious pet. Mmm."

"Stop it." With a quick motion she pushed her nightgown down.

Presently the itching hand began to pull the nightgown up again.

"I said don't."

Vince lay still for a few seconds, very still, then brusquely, roughly, he grabbed hold of her nightgown and stripped her to her chin in one swift sweep of the hand under the covers.

"Stop it, I said!" She tried to push her nightgown down again.

Before she could stop him, Vince managed to get a lock on her and rolled her over on her belly. "This way, sweet," he said, urgent. "My precious pet."

"No!"

But Vince had her down. There was nothing she could do about it. He laughed a lover's soft laugh in her ear. "You know what Lucretius says."

"I don't care what he or any of those dirty old Latins say. Including even Caesar Augustus. I don't want to and that's final."

"Come, my precious pet."

"And I certainly don't want to that way. Never. Disgusting!" With a sudden lashing of her long legs she tried to break free.

But for all his soft white clerk's hands, Vince was still the stronger, and he held her down. The soft, wallowing featherbed under them didn't help any either. All her squirmings to avoid his thrusting only served to help him. He got both knees between her legs and held them forcibly apart.

"Vince," she hissed, "you crazy jackass you!"

"Wives conceive more readily in the manner of wild beasts."

"But I don't want any more children. One is enough. You agreed to that too."

"After the custom of the four-footed breeds. Because so postured, with the breasts beneath and the buttocks upreared, the seed can take its proper place."

"Angela will hear us."

"Judy, darling. Oh, darling. You're wonderful."

She bucked him off. She was furious. A couple of times before, he had talked her into this manner of lovemaking, but she hated it. It made her sick to her stomach. She would not let herself be mounted like some mare of the field. The other way, face to face, was the human, dignified way.

In addition to being a lecherous devil, Vince was also old-fashioned. He wanted her to lie placid, and on her belly. It was her business, he said, to lie still and be calm about the whole thing. Here he quoted Lucretius again. "The woman hinders her own conception if, with haunches heaving and all her bosom yielding like the billows of the sea, she treats the Venus of the man too joyously. Aye, she throws the plowshare's even course from the furrow and diverts the spurt of seed away from its proper place. Courtesans are wont to move for their own ends to keep from pregnancy, all the while they render the Venus of the man the more pleasure. This our wives have not need of."

"You know you hate having children of your own," Judith hissed, face pressed into her pillow. "You hate Angela. Why do you want more?"

"I didn't say I wanted more," Vince whispered.

"Well, then why this way?"

"It's that I want the pleasure of pretending to want more."

"Get off."

But Vince was not to be denied this night. He seized her just above the hips so that her rearing motion served his end all the better. His breath came hoarse in her ear.

Finally, tiring of the struggle, she let him have his way.

"Oh, Judy, Judy," he gasped, thick with fulfillment. "Judith!"

After a bit, Angela called in the dark from her bed, "Mama, why is Papa puffing so?"

"Oh!" Judith was shocked to learn that Angela had heard them.

Vince, still lying on her back, let go a final groan of pleasure. "My precious pet."

"Why is Papa puffing so?" Angela asked again.

Judith burned. Baring her teeth in the dark, she said, "Oh, it's nothing. Just that your Papa has a bad heart. Go to sleep now, child. . . ."

It was morning when Judith awoke again. The sun was shining through the wide doorway. Scarlet Plume had a spanking fire going. A wonderful smell of meat soup and broiling venison drifted through the bower.

A black spider with a red belly hung from a piece of bark just above her. It seemed to be bouncing in the air, up and down, and up again. She couldn't make out the thread it hung from. It was a good fat spider and she wondered if it was poisonous. Pioneers often talked about seeing deadly black widow spiders in the woods.

Her head itched. On both sides and especially over the temples.

Cautiously she drew a catching fingernail through her long, loose hair, hard across the scalp. She examined the fingernail. Yes, there was one. Infinitely tiny legs wriggling. Lord, they were back. She killed it between her thumbnails. It made a light crack of a sound.

Scarlet Plume spoke directly above her head. He was kneeling behind her. "Sometimes when one is very weak the little creatures awaken out of one's skin like little drops of sweat."

She felt humiliated that she had been caught unclean. "It is because your people are lousy."

"The old and dying ones sometimes have them."

"And not the young and the healthy?"

He said, surprised, "But the Yankton grooms his neighbor's hair after the daily morning bath. How can this be?"

She twitched under her wolfskin cover.

Gently, with warm, firm hands, he lifted her by the shoulders onto his thighs so that sunlight fell on her gold hair, then began to search her scalp.

She liked lying on his taut, vibrant copper thigh.

He searched diligently.

After some moments, she asked, "Well, are there more?"

"There are none. He was the last. Even as the Yankton."

Once more, suddenly, irresistibly, she found herself desiring him. She felt a contraction in her womb and a swelling in her breasts. She wanted to go to that place that far. He-han.

She turned on his copper thigh and reached up and with naked arms embraced him. The faintest of luring smiles gleamed within her half-dropped eyelash.

He sat immobile. Presently large, warm tears fell on her exposed breast. He was crying copious tears upon her in the ancient Sioux manner.

She didn't know what to do. A grown man crying tears on her when her own thoughts were already too dark for tears?

Above her the black spider with the red dot in its belly retreated upward, taking in its own thread as it went. When its hairy black legs touched bark, it turned over and in two quick rowing motions vanished.

The thought flashed through her mind that she should grab Scarlet Plume's knife and cut her own throat. Because she was caught no matter what she did. She couldn't, really, live with his people, nor he with hers. Scarlet Plume had been born to the wrong people at the wrong time. "I'll never again have a single happy moment. Ever."

At the same time memory of that wonderful burning moment when Scarlet Plume's thrusting had brought her to fulfillment also flamed in her mind. Why was devil's work so enticing and God's work so forbidding? Why couldn't it be the other way around? Perhaps Scarlet Plume was right when he said the whites were upside down in their thinking. Truly. Maybe the white man had the wrong names for his gods.

Her eye fell on an odd growth at the end of one of the hackberry branches in the wall of the bower. She had noted such tufted growths before. Her mother called them witchbrooms or hexenbesen. The abnormal growths always reminded her of a woman with a mustache. It was out of place. Like her own four black hairs were on her upper lip. Everyone else might seem proper to the world but not a woman with a mustache. Misfit.

Vince had been wrong for her too. Pa had put his finger on it, exactly, when he said, "Child, marry him, if that's your mind. But don't come whimperin' back to me a year from now when you find he ain't much of a man. I saw him driving a team of horses to town the other day. Give them horses a week and they'll be his boss."

At the same time Vince had represented the finer things of life. Things she thought she couldn't do without. Music. Theater. Books. High talk.

"When I am not in love I am nothing."

She stared wide-eyed at the little jumping fire. Reveries moved in her eye like clouds across a valley.

She had suffered cruelly at the hands of the Indians. Yet the sheen of an idyll lay upon the harrowing times she had had with them. Shimmering images floated across her vision. She saw again with moving, even terrible nostalgia, the night when Whitebone momentarily went berserk in grief over his lost wife, the evening when Scarlet Plume impregnated a wooden effigy with his will power and made it dance on a little mound of sand, the night when Scarlet Plume with risen phallus danced up the buffalo, the day of the gory buffalo jump and the shouting of the little children when the hunting party brought home the game, the day when Smoky Day died, followed by the giveaway dance, the haunting ceremony of the Virgin's Feast, and then the day she swam alone in the pink pool in the Dells. Already she felt more lonesome for those days with the Yanktons in Siouxland than for all her days with the whites in St. Paul.

The Yankton custom of giving she would never forget. Did one family have good luck in the hunt, then it was immediately shared with the neighbors. They lived together as sharing members of one big family and against the world. Yankton life was devoted to the sheer joy of living, not to getting.

The Yanktons had no property, no gold stored in temples. Yet their sense of wealth was profound. They shared freely what they found to hand.

They had no records. Yet their sense of history was profound. They not only loved their own children, if such there were, but all children.

They had no clocks. Yet their sense of time was profound. They lived spontaneous from moment to moment, a wandering across a flowering prairie.

Scarlet Plume's tears continued to fall on her naked breast.

She considered his strange crying. It was not the usual kind of weeping. It was not personal. It was more as if a tribe, a history, were using him to weep.

She thought, "How stupid of the white man. When he came upon this Eden prairie, why did he take by force what he could have had by love?"

In the midst of her thoughts, there was suddenly a strange wild strangled cry outside. It came from the bluff across the stream. It was as if a woman were struggling with all her might to keep from being choked to death.

Scarlet Plume's thigh stiffened under Judith. He grunted, short, then lifted her to one side. With the fluid motion of a puma he moved to the entrance. Head up, eyes glittering, he listened, so intently that his ears seemed to quiver. He reached for his spear and a new war shield he'd just made.

Judith grabbed up her wolfskin and cowered under it.

Again the eerie caterwauling wail floated down to them.

"Ho-uh-kah." He spoke to himself, with a low, guttural sound. "It is intended to be the voice of the terrible cat, the puma. Yet the puma does not prowl while the sun shines."

Judith shivered with fear.

Calmly he set his spear and shield to one side. "It is not the true puma. It is the enemy. Only an outcast Dakota would be so foolish as to make the call of the puma while the sun shines." He turned to Judith. "Woman, we must be swift. They will soon be upon us and find you."

He rolled up the matting on the floor directly in front of the fire, spread out the fresh deerhide to one side, then with clawing hands began to dig a hole in the ground, heaping it onto the deerhide. He dug faster than she had ever seen a dog dig. Dirt flew. The hole deepened rapidly. Yet for all the furious digging not a particle of the flying earth fell anywhere but on the deer-hide.

Huddled in shock, she asked, "Wh-what are you doing?"

A few more handfuls and he was done. He jerked the wolfskin from her, then took hold of her roughly and lifted her naked into the hole. He pressed her down firmly. "Fold thyself," he commanded, urgent. "Make yourself small, woman. I will cover you with branches and this wolfskin, and then sit on thee as though this was my accustomed place before the fire."

She protested, struggling. "But what about all that dirt? Won't they see that?"

"It shall be wrapped up in the deerhide as though it were a huge parfleche of pemmican."

"But—"

"Down, woman, if you would save your life." His eyes glittered blackly down at her. "Scarlet Plume commands. I have sworn to my helper to deliver you safely to your people in the white cities." He grabbed her by the neck and the knees and folded her together, so tight her spine cracked. Her chin became caught between her knees and she couldn't move. Dirt crumbled off the sides of the hole and got into her eyes. Loose dirt also filled in around her nates and in between the slopes of her thighs. Scarlet Plume swiftly crisscrossed some branches over her, covered them with her wolfskin. She was abruptly plunged into black choking darkness. With a thump he settled himself directly above her. He sat heavy on her, crushing her down. Then, after he had tied up the deerhide of dirt, he waited, very still.

"But I shall choke to death," she whimpered under him. "I cannot breathe in here."

"Does Sunned Hair wish to have Mad Bear count a bull's coup on her again, the white man's way?"

Swallowing back a groan, she suffered it. The loose earth was warm and pressed in on her.

She could feel him stir above her. Presently she smelled tobacco smoke. She understood. Should anyone stumble in on him they would find him having a quiet smoke by himself.

Scarlet Plume did not have long to wait. There was a cough outside. Then another. Footfalls sounded almost in her ear, a pair of them. She could sense the two strangers standing inside the door, examining Scarlet Plume. She heard them sit down across the fire.

A heavy voice finally said, "Does Scarlet Plume have a second belly that we do not see? There is overmuch warm food."

She recognized the voice instantly. Mad Bear. As Scarlet Plume had guessed. A prickling charge as of electricity bumped through her.

Scarlet Plume said gravely, "The stranger is always welcome at my fire. Take the food and divide it between you. You have come a long way and are very hungry. It shall make me happy to see you eat it. I have much meat."

Mad Bear grunted.

The other stranger spoke. "Do we not smell a woman about?"

Judith also instantly recognized that voice. Bone Gnawer. The fiendish renegade who had raped Angela. Another prickling, of sudden raging hate, bumped through her. She longed to get her claws on him. Scratch out his eyeballs. Rip off his testicles. She swallowed, swallowed, sure she would strangle to death with her nose so tight between her knees. She knew the click of her swallowing might be heard but she didn't care. She longed to kill that monster Bone Gnawer. Darling Angela lying on her back, golden legs and slim child arms outflung and tied to stakes driven into the ground, silver-blond hair outspread upon the green grass, crude surgery performed on her to accommodate grown men and her body then brutally violated by God only knew how many bullish savages . . . O Lord, how long?

Scarlet Plume said, "I have just killed this doe. Eat it."

A short silence followed. The three warriors studied each other's features.

Finally the two strangers grunted assent. Scarlet Plume passed out the food. He himself did not eat. Both Mad Bear and Bone Gnawer smacked their lips loudly as they broke fast. The meat was good.

When they finished, Scarlet Plume passed the pipe. The three took turns smoking, leisurely.

Mad Bear was the first to speak again. "We are looking for game. The band is hungry. Have you seen many deer in this place?"

"I have seen sufficient for one."

"There are not many?"

"For one brave, yes. For a band, no."

"Where does Whitebone's son go? What does he here?"

"I have stood at the foot of the bier of one of you. Along the stream to the south of here."

"Is it not a strange thing that one of Whitebone's band comes to cry under the grave of one of Mad Bear's band?"

"I have said."

"When do you return?"

"A vision has come to me. This I must do first."

"Wakan?"

Silence.

"It is good." Mad Bear turned to Bone Gnawer. "Come, kodah, we have much traveling to do."

Both Mad Bear and Bone Gnawer got to their feet.

Scarlet Plume stood up with them. "Be careful of the puma. There is a great one skulking in the woods. Did you not hear him?"

Silence.

Abruptly the two visitors turned on grinding heels and were gone. There were no good-byes.

Scarlet Plume waited awhile, then once again sat in his accustomed place, directly upon Judith. He sat heavy. Judith had to labor for breath. More dirt rained down on her, in her ears and eyes.

Just when she thought she was going to smother to death, Scarlet Plume slid to one side, whipped back the wolfskin, and scratched away the crisscrossed branches. He smiled broadly down at her. "Would you have the breath of life?"

She lifted her nose from between her knees. "Help me," she said weakly. "I cannot move. My limbs have fallen asleep."

Gently he lifted her out. He set her before the fire. He covered her solicitously with the wolfskin. "Sit quietly, my kodah, and I will make thee yet another bag of soup to break the fast."

It took her a while before she was breathing naturally again. She trembled all over.

After Scarlet Plume filled the hole in which he had hid her, he cut another serving of marbled venison steaks and spitted them on green sticks along the edge of the red embers. He took the boiling bag, the inverted stomach of a buffalo cow, and refilled it with fresh water and bits of meat and fat. He lowered it into the small cooking hole in the ground on the other side of the fire, carefully staking out the edges so the bag would hold up. Some of his heating stones were still in the fire and with green-twig tongs he picked them out, gray hot, and dropped them into the boiling bag, one by one, until steam rose. He sprinkled in a few sprigs of wild onion and a slice of wild turnip. While the food readied, he washed a handful of prairie sorrel for a green salad.

Judith found the square, lush sorrel leaves delicious, sourish wild. They made her mouth water. As an appetizer she had never tasted better.

The two ate in silent appreciation of the food. The soup was savory with primitive aromas. The broiled venison fell apart in the mouth. Judith believed she could actually feel strength returning to her body. The trembles left her. Her eyes cleared.

Presently both stepped down to the little stream. Scarlet Plume fancied a glassy spot for a mirror next to the dam and with a small pair of pointed stones for tweezers patiently searched his face for hairs to pull. Beards belonged to the white man. He sat with his back to her. Judith meantime slipped into the deeper part of the pool for a quick morning sponge bath. The warm food and the cold water restored her. She too found herself a pair of pointed stones for tweezers and pulled out the pesky four black hairs that grew on her upper lip. She did this stealthily for she did not want him to know of them.

When Scarlet Plume returned at dusk from a scouting trip, she had supper ready for him. With a fine sense of tepee etiquette he stepped around the fire on the right and settled himself in his accustomed place. He set his spear and shield to one side within easy reach.

After he had his fill, he spread the new deerhide, fur side up, on the matting and in a quietly assured manner stretched himself full length upon it, moccasins toward the fire.

Judith, though she was dead tired, removed his moccasins and bathed his feet. Gently she washed in between each toe.

He murmured his satisfaction. He closed his eyes and folded his hands over his lean belly, composing himself for sleep. Light from the orange flames played over his fingers, giving them a burnished coppery shine. His fingers were those of an aristocrat, slim, tapered at the tips, well-shaped. She observed his hairless chin and cheeks. They were as smooth as water-honed quartzite stone. She liked his calm in the tepee. His stance as compared to Vince's was wise and lofty in mien.

It puzzled her that after that one glorious moment together he should have turned shy. He was different from other men. He was a potent male and at the same time a man of discipline.

In the morning, after a dip in the pool, Scarlet Plume told her he had seen antelope the evening before. "The meat of the antelope is very rich. It will chase away Sunned Hair's roses of starvation."

A frown crossed her eyes. "You will not kill another trusting mother?"

"Whichever comes nearest. The antelope cannot forbear to come close for a look when he sees a new thing."

"May I see you catch the antelope?"

"I will hide you where you can see it all."

He prepared himself a medicine to help him as a runner. He took scrapings from the four hoofs of the slain deer, next carefully selected four gray hairs from the tail of the wolfskin, then picked four silk-tailed seeds from a milkweed pod, and chewed them all thoroughly. Finally satisfied he had the right mixture, he smeared the juice on the soles of his moccasins.

Judith was fascinated. "Does Scarlet Plume know how many of each he has put into his charm?"

His brows came up surprised. "Four. Four is the sacred number of the Yankton. It is the number of harmony. Can one think of the great directions as having only three directions? There are always four."

"And what does each of these do for my warrior?"

"The scrapings from the deer hoofs gives the hunter swiftness, the hairs from the wolf give him cunning, the milkweed seeds give him lightness of foot so that he can skim over the ground, and the spit from his mouth gives him reassurance that when he catches the antelope he will have the hunger to eat it."

She watched him as he turned aside and opened a small pouch hanging from the belt of his clout. He took the point of his knife and touched something inside the pouch. What it was she could neither see nor make out. She watched his lips move as if speaking to someone. She guessed it was his helper.

"Come," he said, thrusting his knife in his belt. "The antelope waits."

They walked down the little stream toward the end of the wooded ravine. He secreted her behind some second-growth ash. He pointed quietly across the creek. There, up on a balding bluff, grazed a small herd of antelope. Two prongbucks, one young and one old, stood as sentinels on the near side.

"Watch carefully," he said. "Make no outcry. The wind is in our face and I have taken the steam bath in the purification hut; thus they can not catch scent of us. I shall try to catch the young buck sentinel. Do you see him? His flesh will be tender. He will not yet have the musk smell from having covered a doe. The old father has kept him from it."

Scarlet Plume covered his head and shoulders with his deerskin, then settled on his hands and knees and began to edge out through the tall slough grass. He moved as a grazing deer might.

Both the old buck and the young buck spotted Scarlet Plume immediately. They stared down at him. Presently both prong-bucks left the band and came partway down the ribbed bluff. The old sentinel advanced in a reluctant yet curious mood. The young buck was more daring. He seemed to think Scarlet Plume was a lost she-antelope come to join their band. Here was his chance to form his own family.

Scarlet Plume rustled quietly along through the slough, stopping for a nip of grass here and a nip of wild sorrel there.

The old sentinel stopped. He was suspicious.

The young prongbuck, however, kept coming down the bluff.

Scarlet Plume reached the bank of the creek and stopped as though for a drink.

The young prongbuck approached for a drink too.

Judith watched it all from her covert, motionless.

Just as the young prongbuck reached the opposite bank of the creek, Scarlet Plume, drawing his knife, let his deerskin and clout drop to the ground, and leaped for the young prongbuck. Scarlet Plume's flying torso glinted bright copper in the morning sun.

Scarlet Plume missed. Just barely.

With a startled cry the young prongbuck sprang straight up, then wheeled and was off down the valley. The old prongbuck halfway down the bluff and the rest of the band up on the bald spot all sprang straight up too, then jumped into flight, flashing white tails.

Scarlet Plume gave chase. Scarlet Plume was careful to run precisely in the tracks of the young prongbuck so that his medicine could work on the creature. The prongbuck bounded; Scarlet Plume ran. The prongbuck hit earth with all four hoofs gathered to one point; exploded ahead with all four hoofs thrown out. Scarlet Plume ran on his toes, with a skipping motion, hardly seeming to touch earth. The two of them raced, four and two, four and two, as fast as they could go.

A half mile downstream the young prongbuck tried jumping

across the creek and doubling back. Scarlet Plume followed the prongbuck as if he were its inseparable shadow.

The young prongbuck tried to speed up. He fled like a swiftly bounding ball. Scarlet Plume, smiling, did the same. His sudden spurt of speed gave the illusion he was more than just running one leg after the other—both of his coppery limbs seemed to be running even with each other. His motion was like the pulsing of a hurrying heart.

The two darted past where Judith crouched hidden.

Scarlet Plume taunted the springing buck. "Ha. You are not the only one on this prairie who can run. Your brother is directly behind you. He is a Yankton runner and he has a knife. His kodah needs the meat. Begone. Run very fast. Go!"

Again the young prongbuck dodged, jumping across the creek. Once again Scarlet Plume followed him like a shadow. They came beating back.

They ran and ran. Down the valley and up the valley. Back and forth. They ran a half-dozen miles.

Scarlet Plume began to gain ground on the prongbuck. The prongbuck tired badly. Presently the prongbuck was gasping for breath, mouth wide open, tongue hanging. A few leaps more and Scarlet Plume was running beside the poor buck.

Scarlet Plume, running high and lightly, reached out with his free hand, got hold of the hair in the crotch under the prong-buck's hip. Scarlet Plume's knife gleamed in the sun.

The prongbuck threw Scarlet Plume an agonized look. A muffled cough broke from the prongbuck. He was done, winded.

Yet the prongbuck had in him one last spurt of power. He sought to break away, slanting off to his right. He slipped out of Scarlet Plume's grasp.

Again Scarlet Plume closed the gap. This time Scarlet Plume caught hold of the young buck's pronglike horns.

The prongbuck lunged the other way, almost throwing Scarlet Plume off balance.

Yet Scarlet Plume hung on. Then Scarlet Plume's knife flashed across the young prongbuck's throat. Blood blew over the slough grass.

The prongbuck bounded a short ways, coughed deeply and wetly, fell to earth.

Judith jumped up from her covert. A cheer broke from her. She couldn't help it. What she had seen was a marvel. Her scarlet lover was a matchless hunter.

Scarlet Plume let his pace slacken gradually, and slowly came to a stop. He turned, came back.

Scarlet Plume stood over the slain prongbuck. He spoke down to it. "Brother, we thank you for the meat." He reached down and plucked a few stems of grass and scattered them over the prongbuck. "We needed the meat. We shall not forget. Soon the Yankton bodies will be feeding the grasses and then it will be your turn to eat us. It is all one."

Judith stood looking down at the antelope. "I never thought it possible," she whispered, "that a human being could outrun an antelope. Never."

Scarlet Plume stood quietly, even negligently, beside her. He was stark naked. His limp phallus dangled like an empty slingshot. He hardly puffed. Only his copper skin showed evidence of his tremendous effort. It was slicked over with a sheen of sweat.

"I never thought it possible. Lord, Lord."

"Let us skin him and see," Scarlet Plume said. "He could not run very fast. Perhaps he was a cripple. He may have had a broken limb at one time."

"My scarlet husband!" Judith cried, clutching him by the arm. "You know there is nothing wrong with him. You just outran a perfect specimen."

"My charm was wakan. My helper whispered in my ear as I ran. He told me what to do."

The next day Scarlet Plume came to her with a changed visage.

Startled, she stared up at him from where she sat making a new tunic.

He asked in a gruff voice, "Are you now strong enough to remove to the white cities?"

"Is there something wrong?"

"Are you strong enough to walk as many as four sleeps?"

"Let us remain in this place yet another day, my husband."

At the word "husband," Scarlet Plume's face broke. His eyes glazed over with a film and his rose-brown cheeks took on the color of scratched slate. His large lips worked, thinning out and turning down at the corners.

She sprang to her feet. "What is it? What has happened?"

"You are not ready?"

She placed a slim white hand on his bulging coppery arm. "Please, my husband, what is it?"

At her touch he shivered from head to foot. A moan broke from him. He ground his teeth together with a terrible sound. Then, abruptly whirling, he stalked outside.

She followed him to the door.

He sat down on a stone beside the pool. He set his feet evenly and neatly in front of him. Then, leaning forward, elbows on knees, he let his eyes rest on the glimmering water.

She went halfway down the path. "Husband?"

He sat as one turned to stone.

She saw it was useless to talk to him. Brother-in-law Claude had often said that in certain braves, unaccountably, a lava-like melancholy seemed to erupt in them overnight. Claude spoke of the black melancholies as coming from the devil himself. "The Indian has them so deep, so profound," he said, "there is no touching him. You might as well try to talk a lowering sky out of an impending thunderstorm than think of talking an Indian out of his dumps." Claude said he had learned to let them alone. Either the black funk would take its course or the brave would take care of it in his own way, deliberately expose himself in battle and get himself killed.

Blue eyes milky with sympathy, wonder, Judith went back to her sewing.

She stitched carefully. Occasional sighs broke from her. Her mind kept edging around to what might be troubling Scarlet Plume. She hated to see him in torment.

Scarlet Plume sat stonily alone by the pool all day long.

She thought she could appreciate his mood of black bile a little. She had at first felt terrible herself while living with his people the Yanktons.

When Scarlet Plume didn't come in at dark, she went out to talk to him.

"I have meat on a stick by the fire for a brave man. It sizzles merrily. There is also some soup which has been sprinkled with wild onion and sorrel."

Scarlet Plume's breath came slow and shallow. His eyes were fixed inexorably on the pool. The pool was now hardly more than a black shimmer.

"The meat waits."

Scarlet Plume's breath came slow and shallow.

"It will be as my husband wishes. I await him." She returned to her fire.

Scarlet Plume sat in bondage. A dark being from the underworld possessed him.

The next morning he was still sitting beside the pool. From his frozen attitude it was apparent he hadn't moved all night.

It was gloomy out. Clouds as heavy as pregnant sows slopped across the sky from northwest to southeast. Occasionally a little rain mizzled down.

"My husband, it is not a good thing to sit in a cold rain."

There wasn't the slightest hint he had heard her.

She got her wolfskin and draped it over his shoulders.

He ignored it.

She took up her sewing again. Tunic finished, she began to work on a new pair of leggings. Occasionally she threw a look at him. She worried.

The sun came out at noon. Glaring yellow light struck him directly over the back of the head. It gave his long, loose black hair the shine of a burnished crow.

After an hour of warm sun he stirred. It took him several minutes to get to his feet.

He got a hot coal from the hearth in their bower and started a small fire in front of his little round purification hut. He heated some white stones, carried a leather bag of water into the little leather hut, sprinkled a few handfuls of silver sage on the ground both inside and outside. He prayed. He stripped himself, and placing the heated stones handy, crawled inside. Soon plumes of steam leaked through the cracks of the leather hut. At last, purified, broiled to almost a roast red, he came leaping out and dove into the pool.

He washed his clout, wrung it out, and put it back on.

He went downstream a dozen yards, took his knife and cut himself a slender tough branch of bur oak. He came back and sat down on his stone again. He began to adze the branch down. Despite the hot purification bath, his cheekbones were still an ashen gray.

He was making a bow. Judith began to feel better about him. At least he was moving about. He would no doubt come around in his own good time.

She knew enough not to go near him. The dark spirit of the woman was alien to the hunt. The hunt was one of man's oldest skills and had to be revered accordingly.

He cut the bow a certain length, measuring from his right hip across to his extended left fingertips. With his knife he beveled the bow with a sure touch. He cut grooves down the back of the bow. Carrying a coal from his sweathouse fire, he made a stick fire near his workbench and boiled antelope hoofs and tendons until he had a sticky glue. He spread the glue over the back of the bow in several thin layers and pasted on two sinews with the wide ends together in the middle. He spread on more glue and powdered it with white clay. He repeated the treatment several times. He wrapped a piece of buckskin the width of a hand around the middle of the bow. The bowstring he made from the antelope's rear-leg tendons. Done, he set the bow aside to dry.

Next, searching the floor of the pool, he found a stone the shape and size of a chicken's heart. He built a flint-maker, a tool with a long wooden handle and tipped with a piece of deer antler. The handle fitted exactly under his right arm, from the tip of his middle finger to the point of his elbow. He set the butt of the handle against his chest to form a steady fulcrum, then, pressing the antler point against the edge of the heart-shaped stone held in his left hand, pressed firmly. Presently the stone fractured and a half-moon flake flew off. Flake after flake jumped off around the entire rim of the stone. He worked both sides.

By evening he had a half-dozen arrowheads ready, all of them beautifully executed, all of them needle-sharp.

He selected a half-dozen second-growth chokecherry shoots and cut them a certain length.

It became dark out and he came inside to work by the light of the hearth. His face was still ashen. His eyes sputtered more than glittered. He still would not eat.

Judith remembered having seen such a face before. Pa had looked like that after his two-day headaches.

Scarlet Plume worked until he had six gleaming arrows, perfectly tipped and deftly feathered. All the arrows were properly grooved so that blood could flow from the wound they would make. He set the arrows a certain distance from the fire to let them dry gradually. There was a magical sense of rightness in all he did.

Weapon-making done, he sat quietly a moment.

He rubbed a hand along his jaw. The hand paused. It had found something. With a fingertip he explored his teeth. He winced when he touched a back molar, a wisdom tooth. He selected a splinter from a mound of twigs to one side of the fire. Gingerly he picked at the wisdom tooth. After some careful poking around, he pried out a tiny ball of decayed food.

The removal of the little speck of food let air into the cavity of the tooth. He sat very still for a while. Then, of a sudden, he took the splinter and held it in the fire. The moment it blazed up, he quickly jammed its burning end into the cavity of the tooth. There was a sizzling sound. He held it in the cavity until the splinter turned cold. Not a ripple of pain showed on his face.

Judith sat like a scared rabbit.

He sat immobile some more. Gradually his wide, haunted eyes filled with lava-like torment again. The dark being from the underworld still possessed him.

Judith decided to help him. She would ask him the most horrendous thing she could think of. She would shock him out of it.

"Brave one," she said, "we have now lived together as man and wife for some time. Yet you have not told me your secret name. Do you have secrets from your wife? I wish to know."

He quivered as if struck with a whip.

"What is your secret name? I wish to know."

He shuddered.

"Well, then, at least tell your wife the name of your helper. Who is he?"

"He is wakan. I cannot speak of it."

"Speak to your wife. I would know what your trouble is."

He shuddered some more.

"Husband, there is also another thing I would know. What is the secret name of Wakantanka?"

The effect of the question on him was like a blow on a tense string. He vibrated violently all over. And only gradually did the vibrations die away.

She felt miserable, even ashamed, asking such questions. Yet she felt she had to help him with her white-man kind of medicine. "What is his name? I wish to know. When I reach the home of my white friends I want to tell them about the god of the Yanktons, that he is a very great god."

He spoke. His voice was so cracked, so hollow, it was more the voice of a ghost than that of a man. "Woman, one touches Wakantanka himself when one mentions his true name. If I mention his true name he will surely strike me dead. That is why he is also spoken of as He Who Has A Secret Name."

"I have heard it said by my sister, the Good Book Woman, that Wakantanka is sometimes known by the name of The Great Master Of All Breath."

Terrible awe showed in his eyes. He jerked away from her as if truly expecting her to be struck dead. She had hit on the correct name.

"And now that I know his secret name, can you not tell me your secret name?"

"No!" he cried hoarsely, eyes wild and rolling. "No! No!"

She herself began to shake all over. Yet the devil in her pushed her on. "Tell me, what is your secret name?"

"No!"

"Speak to your wife. I would know what your trouble is."

A massive breath made his chest shudder. He swallowed and swallowed.

"Speak to your wife. I would know what your trouble is."

At last, after swallowing and swallowing, he managed to find tongue. "You are the white goddess. When you command I must speak. Therefore I do. The day before this day I saw a burning in the swamp. It was a ghost and it was dancing on top of the grass. It was on the other side of the bier of Mad Bear's departed warrior. I saw that it was the dead man's spirit. He followed me and told me he was unhappy. He said I had done a great wrong to the Dakota people. He told me it was not permitted a Yankton to make connection with a white goddess. He said that it was a terrible wrong. It was for this that Whitebone lost his old mother, Smoky Day. The swamp ghost said it was against the vision that was given me. He told me to take you to the white cities quickly."

Another shudder shook Scarlet Plume. "When one sees a swamp

ghost it is always a sign that death lies waiting near for someone. I saw him very plainly. He had two great glowing eyes."

Judith fell silent. What could she tell this man?

Scarlet Plume again made a move to fight off the black miseries.

He made himself a drum by staking out a piece of rawhide over the hole in the earth on the other side of the hearth where he boiled the meat. He made himself a drumstick with a piece of ash and a wrapping of leather.

Then he began to beat the earth drum slowly, *tok-t-tok-t-tok*.

Presently he warmed to the task and began to sing. The singing was a barbaric *rhu*ing deep in his throat. The sound of it was as if a lizard were trying to sing a psalm. The words were more than sad, they were guttural. The melody always fell away at the end. The melody had come down a long, long road, out of the savage deeps of time.

The drumming came to her through the earth under the hearth and entered her belly. It entered the seat of all things.

He drummed and sang on into the night, without interruption, beating with first one hand then the other, holding his free hand, palm open, alongside his mouth for resonance.

She lay down on her hide bed. She covered her ears with a parfleche to mute the sound of the drumming. It exhausted her to listen to it.

It was well past midnight before he stopped.

The pause that followed was full of ringing echoes.

He said, "The Yanktons will soon be dead. All of them. Our homeland will soon be plowed and burned away. All of it. We and our land, we are too naked. The great wagon-guns of the white man's war and the hard plows of the white man's peace have put holes in us." His face was so ashen it resembled bleached placenta. "My dreams have deserted me, even those that come only in the night. I have no dreams. When I look forward I look into blackness. When I look backward I look into blackness. I am dead ahead and I am dead behind. I have no more to say."

There was a further slight quiver in his eyelids. Then he lay down and composed himself for sleep.

An hour later there was an awesome scream outside their shelter. Both Judith and Scarlet Plume sat up out of sleep like seeds suddenly popped out of milkweed pods.

"What was that?" Judith whispered. Her scalp puckered up on her skull.

Scarlet Plume reached over and placed a hand on her mouth. The hand was warm with a brother's touch.

A single red ember, no larger than the eye of a squirrel, showed in the hearth. There was just enough light inside the lodge for Judith to make out the silhouette of Scarlet Plume's face. His blacks were gone.

The voice in the night erupted horribly outside the door again. It was as if a hundred crucified Christs were letting go at once.

"It is the puma," Scarlet Plume whispered. "The terrible cat."

"A true puma? Not Mad Bear and his band?"

"It is the true puma."

Judith quick slipped out of her bed and crawled in with Scarlet Plume. She hugged him. Her belly humped up.

The scream of the great cat ripped the night air again. This time it was so close they could hear spit crackling in its throat. In her mind's eye Judith saw an enormous wild beast, lips wide and snarling, teeth as sharp as icicles, throat a *rhu*ing red—all of it an unreasoning ravening hunger.

"Ahh." Scarlet Plume let go a slow breath. "It can now be seen that what I saw two days ago was not the true swamp ghost."

"Swamp ghost?"

He took her head in both of his hands and slowly turned it about. "See? There it is."

Two circling balls of fire glowed in the doorway.

She shrank in his arms.

"I saw instead the eyes of this puma and not the eyes of the swamp ghost."

She hugged him about the waist.

He spoke to the two eyes, clear and resonant. "Big cat, you stand on the threshold of a Yankton lodge. Welcome. Enter. Eat with us. There is much meat in the parfleche. Big cat, you see the hearth of a true Yankton. Step forward. Sleep with us. The ground is dry on this side of the fire."

The paired glowing eyes wavered, then flicked out. There was a sound of paw pads leaving the ground with a heavy push, followed by a thump. Then the glowing eyes came on again, a dozen feet back from the doorway. The puma had leaped in retreat on hearing Scarlet Plume's strong voice.

"Come, great one. We wait."

The puma roared. The sound of its deep wrawling was like a scraping in the bottom of a great barrel.

Scarlet Plume took Judith gently by the arms and lifted her back into her own bed. He threw the wolfskin over her and tucked her in. Then, naked, he padded over on hands and knees and stirred up the embers. He dropped a ball of antelope fat into the red ashes, and instantly a flame shot up, tall, like a small bolt of red lightning leaping out of the earth. The whole interior of the lodge lit up, so bright that for a moment there were no shadows. Scarlet Plume threw a handful of dry twigs onto the flame, then placed a dozen sticks on it, neatly, in the manner of a squaw setting up tepee poles. The single flame gradually spread into a corona of steady flames.

Again Scarlet Plume called out, firmly. "Come, i-nmu-tan-ka. It is warm here. We wait."

More growling. The puma sounded as if he was sitting in the path to the pool, blocking it. His paired eyes burned bluish disks at them.

"Come, my brother, be not afraid. In this lodge there are only Yankton friends."

The paired eyes burned orange, then violet.

Still buck naked, Scarlet Plume settled down before the hearth.

He dug out his red gossip pipe and lit up. He had himself a leisurely smoke.

Goose pimples prickled out all over Judith's skin.

They waited.

An hour later dawn broke over the high bluff. It came swiftly, very clear and very cool. Gold leaves drifted down the grassy slopes of the ravine.

Yellow leaves also fell on the big cat where it lay crouched directly in the path to the pool. The puma faced the door, its big forepaws placed together in front of its chest, its rear legs doubled under its belly and ready to spring. The fur over the body of the cat was the color of fall hay, a honey brown. Its long cylindrical tail curled and snapped and curled. A powdery white glowed over its throat and inside its round ears, and a patch of black quivered on either side of its muzzle. Its white whiskers were long. The puma was in the prime of its life.

Scarlet Plume spoke up from where he sat naked before his fire. His phallus had awakened a little. "Yeh-he-toe. I see that the great cat does not wish us to take the customary morning bath. Perhaps the terrible cat thinks he will break his fast by eating a bad smeller. Well, some big cats are known to fancy strong meat early in the morning."

Judith couldn't help but worship Scarlet Plume. He was once again the serene, handsome brave.

Scarlet Plume put aside his pipe and got to his feet. He cried, "Hoppo! Up!" and stretched to his full naked height. Then he stepped into his clout and thrust his knife in his belt.

Judith sat up. "My husband?"

"Shhh." Scarlet Plume smiled down at her. "It is fated." He went over and stood in the doorway.

Judith, wolfskin tight around her body, scrambled out of bed to watch.

The big cat stared at Scarlet Plume, switching and snapping its tail from side to side.

Scarlet Plume spoke as if consulting aloud with a friend. "Pumas have never been known to attack a grown man. Well, perhaps this puma has been given a special vision."

The cat wrawled at him in a deep, low voice.

"Perhaps i-nmu-tan-ka fancies the meat of a wakan white woman. Houw! It will be a thing to see."

The cat's tail continued to snap back and forth.

Scarlet Plume picked up his bow and arrows. "Hoka-hey! It is time to fight!" He stepped outside and settled into a crouching position. "I see that my arrows already cry for the blood." He nocked an arrow on the bowstring, lifted the bow diagonally across the front of his body, and with a single fluid motion of flexible wrists drew the bow deep and released the arrow, the bow turning over in his hand after the shot.

The arrow flicked the puma's round right ear. The puma came off the ground in hairy outrage. Back humped, hair all bristled, the big cat advanced a few steps, then crouched down again.

Scarlet Plume also advanced a few steps, and once more settled into a crouching position. He reached for a second arrow. "Begone, cat. Run, cat. This arrow will kill thee. The first arrow was only sent in warning that this Yankton has also had a vision. If you will not be his guest, then this Yankton is prepared to defend his lodge. Houw!"

The cat charged. It snapped off the ground. It came at Scarlet Plume so dazzling quick that Scarlet Plume did not have time to nock the second arrow.

Judith screamed.

Scarlet Plume rose to meet the onslaught, powerful big toes heaving him up, bow and arrow dropping away.

Hands outstretched, he caught the cat's forepaws in midair, high over his head. He almost buckled under the shock of the big cat's hit. His knife fell out of his belt. Yet Scarlet Plume held up. With all his force, rippling, he held the cat away to keep it from pulling his head forward and biting him in the back of the neck. He heaved himself hard around in a quick tight swinging circle, taking the puma with him. Before the cat could recover, he whirled it around yet again, and then, with a folding motion, threw it on its back. He came down on the cat's stomach with all his driving weight. His belt broke and his clout fell off. With great effort he pinned the cat's forepaws down on the ground wide apart.

The big cat roared in outrage.

Scarlet Plume screamed defiance.

They wrawled at each other, wild, necks humped, ready to strike and bite. Tooth and claw, it became a battle of emmaddened backbones.

Judith screeched.

Scarlet Plume hunched himself as far back and as far down as he could on the cat's belly. He pushed his buttocks hard against the cat's clawing rear legs, forcing the rear legs back at the hip joints, keeping them from tearing up his back. At the same time Scarlet Plume also had to lean forward as far as he could to keep the cat's front paws pinned to the ground. He pressed his chin hard into the puma's ratching breastbone. Scarlet Plume's eyes glittered like a serpent's, black, implacable.

The muscles of the two bodies battling were like two alien families of snakes intertwined and struggling mad.

Scarlet Plume held hard.

The big cat strained to break free, spitting and snapping and roaring.

Once, in the middle of all the coiling and writhing, the puma managed to get in one good bite. Its mouth caught Scarlet Plume's wrist like a vise. Scarlet Plume gave a tremendous jerk and managed to wrest it free. His wrist bled.

They writhed and wrestled and writhed. The puma was strong. Scarlet Plume was strong.

At last Scarlet Plume saw that the puma would win if he didn't do something to end it immediately.

He whispered to his helper. He listened to hear what his helper had to say.

Then he moved. He let go the cat's left forepaw and with his right hand caught the cat powerfully around the throat. He squeezed with all his might. His shoulder muscles came up in a hump. His thumb dug in, deep, deep, until, of a sudden, *pungg,* his thumbnail punched through the live hide under the fur.

The puma worked him over with its free paw. It clawed his shoulders. It cut deep gashes in his taut cheek.

Scarlet Plume shouted and shouted. "Hoka-hey! Hoka-hey!"

Slowly the puma's hoarse wrawling fell away to a choked gagging sound.

Scarlet Plume gave the puma's throat yet another powerful squeeze. "Today is your die day! Die!"

At last the puma went limp. Its head fell to one side, its big red mouth hung open, its popped eyes twisted up.

Scarlet Plume jumped up and back. He was free. His eyes, bloodshot, rolled wild. The knob of his aroused phallus gleamed with a silken purple sheen. He gave a whoop of joy at his marvelous escape. "Hoka-hey!"

Judith pitched forward from her kneeling position, her face landing in the sandy path.

Scarlet Plume saw that the puma still twitched. He grabbed a club from a pile of firewood near the door of their lodge and beat the puma over the head. He beat it and beat it until its brains poured out of its eyeholes like watery gruel. His phallus bounced with every swing of the club.

Judith rolled over on her back and looked up at him.

Scarlet Plume placed his foot on the chest of the puma and cried the death cry for the puma. It was wild, haunting. The cry hung quavering on the air. He cried large tears.

"Husband."

Scarlet Plume picked up his knife and cut a slit in the chest of the puma and removed the heart. He held the puma's heart up to the skies. "Like parts strengthen like parts!" He sliced up the heart and ate it raw, all of it. "Now the heart of the terrible cat lives within me."

"Husband."

Again Scarlet Plume knelt and quickly, deftly, skinned out the puma. He offered up the skin to the six great directions. He spread the golden-brown skin upon the grass to dry. When he finished he was sheathed in blood. He himself resembled a skinned puma. "I am all blood!" he cried. "Yet the great puma is dead. He-han! To that place that far!"

Judith closed her eyes.

There was a hoarse rutting cry and Scarlet Plume fell upon Judith. Blood touched her everywhere. His big phallus lay between them. He made a motion as if to break her neck with a big bite, as a puma might; instead restrained himself and bit her lightly. He tore the wolfskin from her.

"No!" she cried, gasping at all the blood. "No, no."

He was full of biting. He play-bit her over the cheeks, on the nose, over the brows. He nipped her chocolate teats. He play-snarled in her ears. He pretended to eat her from head to foot. He was so wild his face was luminous.

"Don't."

His eyes closed over. Blood dripped from his neck over her white belly. He bit her lightly over her golden brush.

She jumped under his intimate biting, then bit him back in his torn neck. She bit him so hard she started fresh blood.

He cried aloud. He laughed crazily. He bit her in the belly.

Again she bit him in the neck, deep, drawing more blood.

He placed his hand on her tufted pubes and thrust in a finger, searching, deep. "He-han!"

"No, no," she cried, yet pushing her brush against his strong hand, writhing and wriggling back and forth on the sandy path. "No, no."

He bit her sharply in the neck under the ear.

"Don't hurt me," she cried.

He bit her under the other ear.

She was afraid. Yet she was wild with joy. "I am all blood with thee," she cried. "We have overcome the terrible cat together."

An urgent wrawling entered his crying. He took hold of her ankles with powerful copper hands, threw her legs apart. He knelt between her knees. He thrust in. Rutting grunts shook his hard belly. "He-han!"

"No, no," she cried.

He clutched her about the hips. He bounced her on the ground.

There was no hurt. What he was impelled to give she was willing to receive. "Yes, yes!" she cried. In turn she bounced him in the air. They were all blood. She clasped his slippery body to her. "Yes, yes."

His red belly strained against her white belly.

She loved him with her whole body and soul. A hunger as from protoplast times drew them together. They were joined again. There was no greater delight on earth than the delight of giving him an urgent quick go-up for his equally urgent strong go-down. There was no greater giving on earth than the lovely mutually urgent giving of fleshes, utterly. She had a hot ring of fire for his probing arrogant stalk of flesh. Her hot ring clasped catchingly as his phallus slid up and down into her, again, again, again.

"The Yankton man commands!" he cried.

"The Yankton woman entreats!" she cried.

Once more her womb became like an animal in her belly. Clutching joy returned to her. She rose, rose. Lightning darted through her brain. Then, once again, sudden knotlike spasms worked in her belly. There was no stopping them. They rode through her flesh. A blinding light rose out of her belly and lighted up her eyes on the inside.

The cry of fulfillment sounded from the two of them at the same time. "He-han!" "O Lord! My lord!"

He lay upon her, languid. She supported him, languid. Films of blood glistened on their bodies.

"When I am not in love I am nothing."

They took the morning bath together, naked, in the running water below the pool. The stream ran pink.

She treated his wounds with herbs and scented venison lard.

He smiled in sleepy appreciation.

At last, finished, he picked her up by the neck and ankles and carried her into their lodge.

"We marry?" he said.

"We marry," she said.

He laid her gently on the wolfskin. The morning sun shone through the door. He lay beside her. He nuzzled her. She kissed him.

Presently the knob of his phallus began to swell again and slowly it emerged from the folds of its foreskin. They made love once more, this time gentle. His flesh was firm and probing. Her flesh was delicate and yielding.

The sweet fit came upon them both at the same time.

"It wasn't quite the same," she whispered up into the sunlight. "But in a way it was even better."

They slept the whole day through, skin to skin, red next to white.

She taught him to kiss.

Scarlet Plume thought it an outlandish custom. He preferred crying over one in the old way and stroking the hair. His heavy lips were almost an encumbrance to kissing. He saw how her clear blue eyes melted into milky love when she pressed her partially opened lips over his lips. Yet he felt no melting when he tried it.

"Come, brave husband," she said, sliding her white leg over his red leg, dropping her sunned hair around his red-brown face

in a rain of gold. "Try it the white-man way. This way. Kiss. See?
Kiss, and in a moment you will see a falling star even in broad
daylight."

He laughed a wide laugh. "It makes the end of my nose hot."

She laughed in turn. She gave his high nose a pull. She ran her
fingertips along the edges of his exquisitely carven lips. "Yes,
your nose is warm. Perhaps that is why your lips remain cold."
She took his hand and got him to touch her nose and then her
lips. "Do you not see? My lips are warm and my nose is cold."

"Even as a puppy's nose is cold and its tongue is warm."

"No, no. Come now. If you will think hard on it, your nose
will turn cold and your lips warm, even as mine, and then you
will see the falling star. Come now. Kiss. Kiss."

"Let me cry warm tears on your brow while you k-isss warm
touchings on my lips. Will it not be the same thing?"

"No, no. Come. Close your eyes and think of wonderful things.
Let the warmth that is in your eyes go to your lips. This way."

They murmured together.

She said, "Let it be this way." She shivered. "Let the lips play
with each other as though they were fingertips, full of tender
touching, thy lips as well as my lips."

She kissed him. His breath was sweet. She kissed him. She
delighted in the full firm molding of his fleshen bronze lips. With
the edges of her lips she could feel, clearly, the edges of his lips
where they shaped off into the cheek at the corners. She could
not get enough of them. She also came to love the touch of his
muscled cheeks and his broad jutting chin. They were hairless but
the skin on them was taut and manly. She ran her fingertips
around the curve of his jaw and up under his ear and around over
his temple and then over his cheekbones. The cheekbones also
fascinated her. It was as if he had a hard crab apple under each
cheek. She wanted to bite them.

He smiled huskily in her ear. "If a woman we know by the
name of Sunned Hair k-issses too much she will find that a war-

rior we know by the name of The Plume will have a warm nose in an unexpected place."

"Come," she said, "this way. Let us play at biting with the edges of our lips upon the other's mouth. This way."

"It is a strange place to bite another."

"Can you think of a better place?"

"In the neck perhaps? If we are to bite as our brother the puma?"

"My scarlet lover."

"Not all birds can sing."

"What does my lover mean by that?"

"Every child knows that certain birds do not sing. Thus perhaps the red man's lips were not made to touch the white man's k-isss."

"Let us try it." She covered his mouth with her mouth, delicate pink upon elastic bronze. She kissed him tenderly sensual.

"M-mmm."

"Is it not a good thing?"

"M-mmm."

"When a Dakota speaks of a thing as being very good, what does he say?"

"A Dakota says a thing is scarlet when it is excellent. It is sha, he says."

"Yes. Sha. Is this not sha?"

He held his head to one side as though to consider it as a grave chief might consider an offer of peace from the enemy. A faint smile lurked along the roots of his nose.

"Scarlet Plume is like a stubborn boy who will not eat meat even when it is sha."

This he took seriously. A flick of sadness, even annoyance, twitched the bronze skin under each eye.

"Tell me," she said, recalling something. "Why did you give me a wild swan with a broken neck? At Skywater before the massacre? Why did you not speak to me instead? I wish to know."

"It was forbidden me to speak to the whites."

"By whom? Whitebone?"

"By the soldiers' lodge. Their rule, once made, cannot be broken until a new soldiers' lodge is chosen."

"Suppose my sister, the Good Book Woman, had not known what it meant to give one a white swan with a broken neck?"

He shrugged ever so delicately. "Then it was meant to be."

"Tell me how it is among the Yankton young. What is the young man told to do by the old men when it comes time for him to woo the maiden?" With the tip of her forefinger Judith traced the edges of his thick lower lip. "Is he told to overcome her as the prairie cock does the hen?"

He smiled at her, close up, in a warm, musing manner. "He is told to approach the maiden as one would approach a very shy creature of the earth, gently, slowly, one step and one finger at a time, as one approaches a young antelope trembling in a cactus patch. Are not all shy hearts the same?"

"There," she cried, "there. Kiss me now. Now. Just the way your lips were just then. Your heart was just then in your lips."

"M-mmm."

"Is it not sha? Very sha?"

"M-mmm."

She sighed. "At last I've had my honeymoon."

"Nnnh?"

Her eye caught movement on his body. She looked down. His testes were slowly stirring, first one, then the other, inside his scrotum. Their movement reminded her of moles working under a turf of grass, of a pair of little pigs caught in a sack and snouting quietly around trying to get out.

She slid her white limb up and down on his red limb. She pushed her knee high enough to touch the round wrinkly corms of his manhood. Above the corms, already tottering, stood a newly risen jack-in-the-pulpit. The three of them had a life all their own. She thrilled to the touch of the warm swollen flesh. She swooned to think of the delight of the fleshes they would soon have together again.

"Honey—moon?"

She explained what the white man meant by the word. With a soft, coy hand she took hold of his risen stalk of proud flesh. She delighted in the firm cylindrical supple feel of it. It reminded her of a suspension bridge. It arched across chasms of time. It was a root risen out of flesh and become stalk, and tipped with a glistening anther.

"Honey—moon," he repeated, musing inwardly. "When the moon is sweet."

"Yes. When the moon is very sweet. Also, honey does not spoil. Honey never turns sour."

He gave her a lidded look. "Yet it is known that the moon turns dark each month."

She skipped over this. "Honey never turns sour." She did not want to think of his severe Dakota taboos, of the lonely wretched darkness she'd experienced in the separation hut. With a finger-tip she touched the silken pink eye of his standing anther.

He mused. "The Dakota have a ceremony in which the newly married maiden is requested to think of sexual things. This is done so that the tribe may increase in number. It is held in The Moon When The Strawberries Turn Red."

"In what manner are the maidens to think?"

He smiled a sly smile. "They must think of the squirrel who hides an acorn in the earth against the hungry winter. The squirrel does not know that when he hides the acorn for himself he is also planting for Wakantanka so that an oak may grow."

She placed the flat of her hand on his broad bronze chest and stroked it back and forth. "And what does the warrior say in Dakota when he speaks of love to the maiden?"

"He says, 'I have a fast hold on your heart. You have a fast hold on my heart. Let us run away on my swift pony and set up a tepee with our cousins in another band.'"

"Ah!" she cried. "That is what we call the honeymoon."

Scarlet Plume went on. " 'You are my pretty woman, and a brave man likes to see a pretty woman who is modest and meant for him alone.' "

"This is what he says to her?"

"He also says, 'Do you have the boiling stones ready? I am coming with the game.' "

She nipped his ear. She loved the smell of him after the morning bath. He reminded her of spring grass after a rain. "Tell me, how does the white man smell to the red man?"

He thought a moment. "That he does not bathe overmuch."

"You do not like his smell when he sweats?"

He spoke frankly. "The smell of the white man when he sweats is like the odor of old deerhide after it has lain in a damp place for a long time."

"But when he bathes? As I have done with thee?"

"Then it is sha. Sha."

"Very sha?"

"Sha."

She kissed him. "Tell me, what does my scarlet lover think of the k-isss now?"

"It has become sha. It is difficult to learn. Nevertheless after a time it becomes sha. As scarlet as the flying redbird."

She kissed him. "Has not the time come for the squirrel to plant yet another acorn?"

They loved together.

"It is sha," he whispered at last. "Very sha."

Night came. They slept skin to skin under the wolfskin robe, their feet exposed to the fire. When the fire died out both instinctively drew their feet back in under the robe. The toes of themselves tucked the robe under, warmly.

PART FOUR

Camp Release

Scarlet Plume spoke firmly from the doorway. The sun had just dawned. "Hoppo! Up! I have caught us two tame horses. Are you ready to remove?"

Judith sat up. Lazy gold hair slid across her shoulders. "Horses? Where did you find them?"

Scarlet Plume looked broader and more formidable than usual. He had on a newly made buckskin shirt and a pair of fringed leggings. "I arose while it was still dark and made a cast about our camp. I found the horses at the springs above us. They were white-man horses and in need of a fresh drink. When I called them by their white names, they let me catch them."

Judith hugged herself in the chill air. Her nipples rode like little pig snouts on her crossed forearms. She hoped her nakedness would divert him. "What names were these?"

"A blaze lay on the red horse's nose. Him I called Old Paint. Gray and very fat was the other horse. Him I called Buckskin Belly."

Judith smiled. "How does my husband know they are white-man horses?"

"They would not let me mount in the Yankton way, on the right side. Also, they were cut the white-man way."

"But my husband, I have turned my mind around and do not wish to return to St. Paul."

"It is time to go. The horses wait. Already I carry food in my legging sash."

"But I do not wish to go back to the white cities."

He looked quietly down at her. He crossed his arms slowly over his great chest. "I have already painted the horses in a sacred way. Now the arrows of the enemy cannot touch them."

"I wish instead to go back to your people, the Yanktons. Do they not live in the center of the world? My heart turns black when I think of living again in the white cities."

"Your white husband awaits you. He wishes to be father again. He needs a new baby to take the place of his lost daughter."

Judith fought off weeping. She held up her slender arms to Scarlet Plume. "My husband, do not ask me to return to the whites. My husband, I like raw liver so much I want to live with your people. I want to go where you go. Your people are my people and your gods my God. When I die I want to be buried beside you in a little lost valley somewhere. Let The Great Master Of All Breath punish me, and more, if I let anything but death part us."

Iron control settled over his face. "Woman, I cannot go against the vision. The vision is wakan. Also, Whitebone will surely kill us if you are not now returned to the whites. Come, the horses wait."

She let her arms fall in her lap. She shivered in the chilly air. "Then you must come and live with me among the whites. I cannot live without you. You have made a woman of me. This I can never forget."

"The round toes of the red man will fit poorly in the white man's square dance."

She beseeched him with dazzling blue eyes. "I cannot live without you. There was once a time when I walked ahead of my man. This I now regret. I wish to be your wife the Yankton way."

"It is not a good thing."

Again she held up her arms, imploring him to join her on the hide bed. "We could live at the edge of the white settlement somewhere. When it was needed I could walk into the town. When it was needed you could walk out upon the prairie. We could be free each in our own way."

"Woman, would you laugh and sing all day with people who are takers while I smoked and danced all day with people who are givers, and then expect us to be happy lovers at night?"

She let her arms fall. "But my husband, you have stolen my heart. What am I to do? I shall kill myself if I cannot live with you."

"The white man makes his poor work for him. The poor must give him much gold to live in the houses he owns. That is not the way of the red man. When the red man returns from a raid with many horses, he gives them away and keeps only the poorest for himself. The more he gives away, the greater he becomes."

"Well, has not my white sister, the Good Book Woman, often said to the red man, 'God loveth the cheerful giver'?"

He flashed her a smug, slitted look. "It can be said that the Good Book Woman and her husband learned much from the Dakota gods. It was because of this that a white swan was given to Sunned Hair."

Judith gave him a look of love with all her soul. "Come, my scarlet lover, let us lie yet once again in the arms of rapture."

He gave her a further penetrating look. "My heart does not run with white blood. Nor does your heart run with red blood. The two can never beat as one."

Her eyes flashed a high blue. "Yet when the red man thinks of death, does he not see a white ghost? And when the white man thinks of death, does he not see a dark-skinned spirit? Is this not a like strangeness?"

He looked down at her with grave indulgence. "This Yankton brave has taken the morning bath. Has Sunned Hair?"

"Let us have children together. In their veins will run a blood as pink as the prairie rose."

A look of contempt wrinkled his high nose. "Half-breeds! Ha! Are they not always children who are cut off from both the white man and the red man? Do they not run about in both camps with dropped heads like beaten dogs, neither wolf nor man? Half-breeds! Are they not always hungry? So that if they wish to eat they must devour their own babies?"

"Then let us start a new nation in this place. We will make Lost Timber our village and live here until the whites begin to surround us, and then if we must we will look for yet another Lost Timber somewhere farther west."

"It is not a good thing."

"I want your babies. Come and lie beside me."

"It is a bad thing."

"But, my husband—"

He broke in roughly. "The horses wait. Take the bath!"

"Husband."

He plumped down before the fire. He stirred up the embers and added some fuel. He got out his red gossip pipe and had himself a stoic's smoke.

Finally, sighing, she got up and went down to the pool and took the morning bath.

Naked, cleansed pink, she re-entered their vine lodge. Her hair hung loose about her face in light-gold showers. She made herself appear more modest than usual to draw his eye.

He sat smoking his gossip pipe and did not look up.

She saw that while she had been gone he had quickly packed up their possessions in two big parfleches. Her heart sank. She had lost. He really meant it. They were going. He would never touch her again.

He held up his pipe as if to some invisible person. "Here,

ghost, take a smoke and give us a good day. Let the road be straight, the waters smooth, and the sky clear." Then he clapped out his pipe in the palm of his brown hand, threw the curd of tobacco in the embers, and stood up.

Still naked, she held out her arms to him in a last appeal. "Let us k-isss. Was it not always sha before?"

He stared past her.

She embraced him. She rubbed her belly against him. Her naked skin made a sucking sound on his buckskin shirt. She caressed his hard bronze cheek with her pink cheek, lightly, brushingly.

He stood neither stiff nor melting. "The horses wait. Put on your clothes."

"My husband, let us sit yet for a little time by our fire while you tell me about the old times when the Yanktons were a great people. I wish to know."

"If one tells stories of the old days, snakes will appear in one's bed at night."

"Do you not love your wakan wife?"

He stared straight ahead. "Sometimes when a Yankton speaks of the whites as wakan he also thinks to himself that they are the no-good ones."

"Have I become your enemy?"

"You are a woman from the other side and I have done my people great wrong in lying beside you skin to skin. You stole my heart and I could not stop myself. Also, I have gone against the vision. There is nothing but blackness ahead for my people. There is also nothing but blackness ahead for me. It is now fated. I hasten to that place where the blackness dwells. I have said."

"My husband."

He continued to stare ahead with an iron gravity.

She was afraid he would fall into one of his Indian melancholies again. She cried. She too saw nothing ahead but blackness. Both were doomed.

He saw her tears. Yet he took her by the shoulders, and gently, with infinite consideration, turned her about. He picked up her tunic and gestured for her to put it on. "First we go to visit Sky-water to see if any of the whites are yet alive. If we find them we will return them to the white cities also." He coughed delicately. "Perhaps Sunned Hair may wish to weep at the grave of her daughter."

Cold closed over Judith's heart.

He picked up their parfleches, threw them over his shoulder, and carried them outside.

She dressed. When she stepped outside she found him already mounted on the red horse, Old Paint.

He sat easily, parfleches neatly balanced in front of him across the horse's neck. Besides the natural blaze over his nose, Old Paint also had a series of white circles painted across his belly and over his rump. The horse's black mane and tail had been decked out with small blue feathers.

Scarlet Plume held Buckskin Belly by his rope. The gray horse stood alongside their sitting stone. Buckskin Belly too had been painted with wakan circles, though with red paint, not white, in vivid contrast to his gray hair. Yellow feathers fluttered in his tail and mane.

Sighing, forlorn, Judith lifted her tunic to her hips and climbed aboard the gray. She sat as a man would, legs astride. The stiff hair on the horse's spine tickled her. She thought it a bitter thing that she should be holding a horse between her bare legs instead of the man she loved, and that that horse should be carrying her back to white captivity.

Scarlet Plume turned his horse about and led the way. He did not once glance back at their love lodge in the wild vines. It was done.

They rode up the bed of the ravine. There were green glades under the barren trees, all the way to the top of the hills. The morning sun shone brilliantly through the brown arms of the oaks. Light seemed to concentrate in dancing halos above the springs. Tree leaves rustled underfoot. The horses plodded along sedately. She guessed the horses had once belonged to some out-post pioneer, now killed.

Near the head of the ravine she spotted what at first she took to be a single wind-tortured wild mulberry. But coming closer, she saw that it was two mulberries, the one white and the other red, twined through each other in mortal embrace. It reminded her of two huge bull snakes wrestling. They lay sprawled over and around a granite boulder.

When they reached the plateau above, she looked back a final time at their love lodge in the ravine. She cried. Slowly her eyes swelled red with grief.

Scarlet Plume rode in front, heading into the northeast. His eyes kept working the grass in front of the horse for sign, then the filmy horizon ahead.

Judith was struck by how much Scarlet Plume's flowing hair resembled his horse's trailing tail, black; how his cheeks were exactly the color of his horse's coat, red-bronze. The man and the horse were one.

Her gray hurried to keep up. Her gray was so fat and wide across the middle that sitting astraddle made her thighbones ache in her hips. The stiff hair on the horse's spine continued to tickle the bare insides of her legs.

They rode into a wind. It lifted the black manes and tails of the horses. It lifted Scarlet Plume's loose black hair and her loose sunned hair. They rode on, silent.

A whimsy chased through Judith's mind. Both horses had black manes and black tails. It meant that, though one was a bay and the other a gray, far back they were related. She wished her hair were black. Then she could claim that, though their skins were different, she and Scarlet Plume at least had the same hair and probably far back were also related.

Scarlet Plume pushed the horses. Sometimes he lightly whipped his horse with an ash switch. He rode urgently. He was in a hurry to get it over with. He was a wolf on a horse.

The sun mounted behind them. The day opened. The sky became a coneflower with drooping blue rays and a bronzy head. The green wind from the north brushed their cheeks. The air was so thin it opened the nose and made the brain giddy.

Many rains that fall had given the plains the look of spring. Swollen streams gurgled on all sides. Scarlet Plume steered a route along the higher contours to avoid the soppy swales. Waving grass shaded off imperceptibly into lapping ponds.

A whitewing blackbird lived cheerfully in the midst of a flock of late redwings. One meadow was completely taken over by yellowhead blackbirds. The yellowheads sang short autumn songs, then lifted up and flew south.

As she jogged along, Judith thought to herself, "Well, I've at last had my honeymoon. And in Indian summer too." She held the leather reins lightly in her hand. Her gray horse followed the bay ahead as if tied to its tail. "A honeymoon in Indian summer. A warm spell between the first frost and winter freeze-up."

Late in the day they came upon a stream two jumps wide. It ran northeast. A swatch of willows bristled along a turn. They watered their horses. They got down and had themselves a drink. Then, after a leisurely groaning stretch, they rode on. They crested a light rise. Before them spread the tree-fringed shores of Skywater.

Judith steeled herself against what they might find.

The first pile of ashes marked the Utterback homestead. Bits of fine white down from an Utterback featherbed still lay scattered through the deep grass, reminding Judith of the first traces of winter snow. The burned-off Utterback stubble field had come back some with the glittering green of fall grass.

Next came the ashes of Crydenwise's sod shanty. The skeleton of the wolf that Crydenwise had skinned alive still hung on its crude cross. The Sioux had not touched it for reasons of their own.

Over the next rise lay traces of Theodosia's cabin.

Scarlet Plume halted. He looked sternly around. His black eyes glittered in memory.

Judith forced herself to look down. She saw gray ashes faintly tinged with yellow. They were sodden and compressed from many heavy rains. A piece of curled-up paper hung caught in the silent lilacs. A ripped book lay open in the grass, its hieroglyphic ecstasy leached away by the weather. The ripped book reminded her of a gutted chicken. A single hollyhock, stunted by the fire, also frost-touched, nodded stiffly at the edge of where the cabin had once stood. The climbing sweet peas and the wooden fence on which they had grown were completely gone. The vegetable-and-flower garden could just barely be made out. It was overgrown with new, rough grass. The little paths leading away in various directions were filled with thick crabgrass. Even the black scars of the fire on the ground had already vanished under a new, virulent green. Another summer's growing and the gray ashes of the cabin would also be obliterated with healing rings of grass. In two years there would be no mark or record whatever that this had once been a white man's outpost in virgin wilderness.

It flashed through her mind that there would be many such lost places. With no regular mail route, or neighbors to leave the gossip with, cut off for a time while they dug in, many and many a first settler had no doubt vanished forever from all knowledge of men during the terrible uprising. Kith and kin back east would wonder about them in vain. They had just simply disappeared. A couple hundred years from now, some plow might turn up a rusted bit of iron. The stranger behind the plow would stop the horses and stoop to pick up the bit of iron. He would wonder over it, fumble it around in his hand, make a guess as to what it might have been, part of a flatiron or a hinge, shake his head, toss it up and down a few times, then let it drop in the furrow again, pass on, and on the next round cover it forever.

Judith abruptly turned her horse about and headed for Slaughter Slough. Now that she had come that far she had to know.

Scarlet Plume rode behind her.

She came upon a flattened place in the gray-green slough. In the

middle of it lay a skeleton. She reined in her horse. The spot was
about where her brother-in-law Claude had been murdered. Yes.
It was he, all right. There lay his shot-shredded skull. Judith could
still see her sister Theodosia stroking his bald nose, lightly, tenderly, after the killing, still see her kissing his closed eyes, each in
turn, and his cold, fallen lips.

Looking closer, Judith saw that hundreds of little sticks had
been thrust into the turf next to the skull. Indians who had known
Claude had visited his grave and each had shown his respect by
leaving behind a little marker.

She slid to the ground. She brushed horse hair from between her
legs. She knelt a moment beside the skeleton. She thought, "Dear
Claude, I was not always sympathetic to everything you stood for.
But you were a noble man. Forgive me."

She looked up at where Scarlet Plume still sat dark on his red
horse. "Can we not at least bury his bones?"

"Mad Bear's people took the white man's digging stick with
them."

"Can we not find a fresh badger hole somewhere in which to
place the remains?"

Scarlet Plume slid off his horse. "I have a knife. Perhaps a little
hole can be dug under the thick grass."

The horses, released, slowly grazed off by themselves. They
cropped hungrily, tearing off grass by the mouthful.

Scarlet Plume cut squares in the turf and pried them up. He
placed the webbed squares neatly to one side. Then he dug into the
sour black humus until he had a hole the size of a laundry basket.
He stepped back.

Gray-eyed, Judith picked up the bones in pairs and placed them
in the hole. She set the skull carefully at the head. The bones were
chalk dry. Certain of the softer joints seemed to have been gnawed
down by wolves. A tear ran down one side of her nose. Another
tear let go of her eyelash and dropped dead center through the
grinning mouth of the skull. She stood up and brushed off her
knees and hands. She stood back, a hand to her bosom.

Scarlet Plume threw the dirt back in, then carefully replaced the squares of turf and stomped them down firm and tight.

Evening stole up around them. It seemed to come in on the green wind. The fringes along the hem of Judith's tunic fluttered lightly against her legs.

Scarlet Plume stood very still. He seemed to be waiting for her to find something else.

The knowledge of what it was he wanted her to see next came to her just as her eyes spotted it: a scaffold burial. A woven willow platform supported by four slender posts. On a slight rise in the land.

On the platform lay a slim body wrapped in leather. From the top of one of the posts hung the shreds of what was left of a green silk dress. It was the soft whispering of the green silk in the wind which really told her what it was. Angela.

Judith took several steps toward the scaffold, then stopped short. With a great effort of will she held herself tight together. Her gold brows almost touched over the bridge of her nose. Her blue eyes took on the glint of gun metal. "Who did this thing?"

"Bullhead took her scalp."

Judith almost toppled over. "Yes, yes. I know that. I did not mean that. I meant, who buried her in this manner? Who gave you that right?"

"There was no digging stick." Scarlet Plume spoke with some reluctance. "With a knife one could not dig deep enough to hide the flesh from the wolves."

"So that's what you meant when you told the Good Book Woman that you buried the child in the proper manner."

"Does Sunned Hair scorn the Dakota manner?"

Judith blanched so white she could feel it draw at her face. "I wish to know."

His self-control broke. In the expression around his eyes and at the roots of his nose there was the suggestion that he had willingly let it break. Reverently he stepped across the grass until he stood under the scaffold. He knelt. He lifted his face to the skies and of

a sudden filled the evening air with an awful, eerie Dakota lamentation. Echoing howls returned from the groves along the lake.

Judith stood behind him. His behavior stunned her. Real tears
were streaming down his coppery cheeks. Real grief corrugated his
face. He meant it. Yet there was also in it the beat of an old ritual.

Her hand came to her throat. A cold fury seized her. She resented his wailing. It was her grief, not his. Only that morning he
had told her that his heart did not run with white blood. What did
he mean now by falling to his knees at Angela's bier before she
herself did? He had stolen her grief.

Yet it was not in her to order him off.

She let him cry until her shadow reached him from where she
stood. Then she said, quietly, speech clipped, "Is it not also the
Dakota custom to remove the bones from the scaffold when the
wind and sun have done with them?"

Scarlet Plume cried yet a short time, then abruptly cut it off. He
let his face resolve again into an expression of stoic hauteur. He
got to his feet. "Is it your wish?"

"It is."

"Where does Sunned Hair wish to place the bones?"

She turned to gaze across endless stretches of prairie. She thought
it a bitter thing that the evening breeze should have on it a penetrating smell not unlike boar semen. She turned to look back at the
lake behind them. At last she said, "Let us bury her under the ashes
of the Good Book Woman's cabin. It is my wish. Will you gather
up the bones?"

Gravely, with the courtesy of a mannered prince, he took down
the scaffold post by post. He caught the skeleton wrapped in its
leather shroud before it fell to the ground. He placed the shreds
of what was left of Angela's green dress inside the bundle. He
held Angela's remains deferentially in his arms.

Judith stepped closer. Her manner was crisp. Her wide blue eyes
took in every detail. "Is it all there?"

"Even to the ghost."

Judith steeled herself not to start. Ghost?

"But now that we have wept, her manes will be free to go to the white man's heaven."

Manes? Yes. In a white man's brain the word also had another meaning. She remembered seeing Angela's silver mane smoking in Bullhead's hair, burned, after a lightning bolt had struck near him.

The two geldings continued to graze by themselves, reins trailing in the grass, occasionally stomping a hoof at a fly.

Scarlet Plume led the way to Theodosia's cabin. His decorum was that of a solemn medicine man leading a procession of ghosts. It was almost dusk. With his hands Scarlet Plume scooped aside the ashes of the cabin. He dug a pit. Gently he placed the tangle of bones and skull in the hole. He stepped aside for Judith to say the last words, to cry the last tears.

Belly taut, Judith gestured for him to fill the grave.

Scarlet Plume hesitated a second. His eyes swung from left to right. He spotted the flowerless, stunted hollyhock. He seemed to nod in his black eyes. He stepped over and pulled the hollyhock up by the roots. Carefully he placed it in the fold of the leather shroud. He began to refill the hole.

Beyond him, through an opening in the trees, Judith saw six wild swans swimming irregularly on the blue surface of the lake. The old father swan up front was trumpeting hoarsely. Suddenly his wings slapped hard on the surface of the water, and he rose, water trailing from his long legs like clear syrup, and was off. After a moment the other five white swans broke free of the surface too. They lifted steadily, up, up, then veered off in a wide turn to the south. With their legs trailing after them, they resembled frogs suddenly flying. Faintly there came down to Judith the call of the father swan: *whooo-whooo-whooo*. It reminded her of an Indian lover's flageolet.

Scarlet Plume finished. He covered the grave with the ashes. He patted the ashes down with a spray of oak leaves to hide all trace that a grave had been made on the spot.

Judith turned, walked a few steps toward the grazing horses, pitched forward. She lost consciousness before she hit the ground.

A twirling sound awoke her. There was also the lovely liquid sound of lapping waves.

She opened her eyes. Above her, not a foot away, hung her gray wolfskin. It took her a moment to understand that she was lying on the prairie with the wolfskin serving as a shelter, that the lake Skywater lay below and behind her.

But the twirling? She turned her head.

Scarlet Plume sat on his heels almost beside her. He was making a fire with a primitive fire drill. The female piece he had made out of soft, very dry willow, the male piece out of hard oak. He held the female piece down with his toes while he rotated the male stick between the flat palms of his hands, back and forth, the point set in a small notched hole. He rotated the drill rapidly at the same time that he pressed it down. The sharp friction made the twirling, squeaking sound she had heard.

Wood powder presently began to appear around the edges of the small hole. The wood powder turned brown, then began to smoke, then turned a deep black, then began to smoke in earnest. More wood powder piled up around the rotating point. Of a sudden a tiny spark glowed off to one side of the hole, in the notch. Slowly the spark spread through the powder around the hole. As soon as the spark was glowing well, Scarlet Plume let go of the drill and dropped a pinch of tinder on the spark. The tinder caught. He dropped on some coarser shavings. They caught too. He next dropped on a handful of dry grass. A billow of acrid smoke drifted around his bronze face. He leaned down and blew on it gently. A flame jumped up. Quickly he transferred the little flame to some tinder beside a stick tepee already prepared. In a few seconds the oak sticks were blazing merrily.

Judith had never seen fire making done before. It was a thing to see, an exquisite skill that men were about to discard in favor of the match. Once again, for a fleeting moment, Judith had a vivid glimpse down a long, long road leading all the way back to savage deeps of time. Thought of it helped her hold down the deep fog of grief that lay in her.

Scarlet Plume saw that she was awake. "Hoppo! The morning star is up. Already it hangs in the scarlet sky as bright as the blue egg of the redbreast."

She sat up, and in so doing she bumped her head against one of the supports holding up the wolfskin. The wolfskin fell around her. It scared her and for a second she fought it as though it were alive.

Smiling a little, Scarlet Plume helped her.

She rubbed her eyes. "Have I slept long?"

"From sun to sun."

She got to her feet and stretched. She smoothed out her wrinkled tunic with the flat of her hand.

She saw that he had gathered a few white boiling stones and had dug a boiling hole beside the fire. The thought of more boiled meat momentarily gagged her. But then she saw a neat pile of pinkish-brown potatoes on the other side of the fire. Her eyes opened. "Where were these found?"

"In the Good Book Woman's garden." He pointed to where he had gone rooting through a grass-choked patch of ground.

Her eyes lighted up a high blue. It had been months since she had had a good boiled potato. "Mmmm."

"They will be ready when you return from the morning bath."

Later, just before they left, after she had mounted her gray gelding, Scarlet Plume did something that endeared him more than ever to her. He touched a tree, a wolfberry bush, a sunflower, a cricket sitting on a nodding spear of grass. He also reached out a hand as though to touch the morning sun. The easy dignity of the true fatalist lay over his wide face.

They jogged northeast, loose hair flowing, gold and black. There was no wind except that created by their own going. Mosquitoes rose in clouds as they passed by placid water in low green

sloughs. Thousands upon thousands of ducks and geese flew by
overhead, going south. All morning long the skies were filled with
their vague, haunting cries. Sometimes they dipped through dry
coulees. When an occasional odd hump in the land came along,
Scarlet Plume ascended it for a long searching look around.

The sun had climbed to near noon, when Scarlet Plume abruptly
stopped and got down off his horse. He squatted in front of a large
white boulder, staring intently at something on it.

Judith urged her horse up close to have a look too. "What is it?"

"Sign."

"Where?"

His brown finger traced out faint red markings on the white
surface of the stone. Rain seemed to have washed much of it away.

"What does it say?"

He pointed to two irregular circles, several twiglike human figures, a rough sketch of a cannon, a wide diagonal stripe. "Here are
two lakes. One of them is known as Talking Water, the other
Wood Lake. Here are white soldiers fighting with red warriors.
Here is the River Of The Milky Water." He next pointed to a
series of dots. "This tells that almost a moon ago"—he pointed
straight north—"there was a battle in that direction. Red warriors
were defeated by a great camp of white soldiers. There are many
red prisoners. Many white captives have also been returned by the
red men." He stood up. He nodded to himself. "It is to this place
that we must go."

Judith didn't understand the hieroglyphic markings and she
didn't understand the reasoning. She sat drooping on her horse.
"Whatever you say. I suppose there's no turning you back now."

"A runner from Whitebone's band has been here. He left this
message for whoever might pass. This was six sleeps ago." Scarlet
Plume turned around, looking to all sides. "Perhaps he has done
this for us as it was done for you when you were traveling alone."

Judith nodded. Whitebone had sent out yet another guard to
make sure she arrived safely. She was touched by the thought. The
old chief had meant nothing but good for her after all.

Scarlet Plume saw something else. He leaped up on the white rock, beside her horse. He stared north, head thrust out like a hound that had got hint of game up ahead.

Judith stared north too.

"There are two of them," Scarlet Plume said.

"What? Where?"

"Do you see the cattail? Look the length of a good bow to the left of it."

She stared. She thought it strange that he should have noticed something before the horses did.

"One is carrying the other because the other is hurt," Scarlet Plume said. "It cannot be the enemy."

"Can it be Mad Bear carrying Bone Gnawer?"

Scarlet Plume's black eyes narrowed until they resembled a pair of obsidian arrowheads. His concentration became so deep he exuded a strong male smell. "They are children," he said at last.

"What?"

"The one being carried is a baby and the one carrying him is a boy. The boy is very tired. He walks as does a white boy, with the toes out."

Her skin began to prickle all over. She didn't dare to guess who the children might be. She stared and stared. She knew she had good eyes compared to most people, but she still couldn't make out anything in the tossing ocean of grass. She envied Scarlet Plume his powerful eyes.

"Come," he cried, "we must hurry before they die. We must help them." He bounded onto his horse and quirted it, sharp. "Hoppo! Hurry, Old Paint."

The bay snorted in surprise, responded with an irregularly clodding clumsy gallop.

Judith's gray gelding perked up. He neighed complaint at being left behind so suddenly, then gathered himself into a heavy gallop too.

They had gone about a mile when Judith saw them. Only the upper parts of them could be seen above the waving gray-green grass, and to her it looked more like a boy carrying a ragged bundle than a baby. The little boy was trudging along uncertainly, bent over, the bundle of rags hooked about his neck. A flash of sunlight struck the bundle a certain way. Then she saw that the bundle was a baby as Scarlet Plume had said. Its hands were pulled up around the boy's neck.

Ted and Johnnie. Theodosia's children. Her nephews. The Woods line through the women had not been wiped out after all. Ted and Johnnie had somehow survived the clubbing by the crazy squaw.

When she caught up with them, she hauled in her horse, hard, and slid to the ground. Her loose gold hair cascaded around her face so that for a moment she was blinded. Scarlet Plume already stood in the grass to one side, a sad, withdrawn look on his face.

Ted stopped and turned around. He stared at Judith open-mouthed. His towhead was black with crusted blood. All that was left of his clothes was the belt to his pantaloons. His naked body was tanned to a deep Indian brown. His little peter was so swollen, so pitifully sunburned and scabbed over, it protruded out of its foreskin. His legs from the knees down were terribly cut by ripgut grass and pocked over with sores. He was so dirty and his lips so swollen, she knew him more by his form than by his features.

What a wonderful boy Ted was to have carried his little baby brother all that way. Wonderful boy.

Little Johnnie hung draped unconscious on Ted's back. His little arms and legs were fleshless, his belly so distended it shone.

Judith lifted baby Johnnie from Ted's back and cradled his fragile body in her arms. She tried to say his name, Johnnie, but found her voice gone. Her breath came in flutters of compassion. Tears gathered behind her eyes. She couldn't cry them. The tears swelled until they felt like balloons about to burst. At last a moan broke from her and the sound of it in her throat was like the raw billing of a mother lizard.

With the burden of Johnnie removed, Ted straightened up. He

tried to focus his eyes on Judith. The pupils of his blue eyes were unnaturally large and blood-flecked.

"Mama, is that you?"

Judith opened her mouth to say something white, but found her tongue strangely stuck. She couldn't talk white. Instead her tongue and lips shaped themselves to speak Sioux. Sioux had become her heart language.

"Mama?"

Judith at last found a few American words and broke through. She had to work at it. "Don't you remember your Aunt Judith? I'm your auntie."

"Mama?"

"Don't you remember your Aunt Judith?"

"Mama, give me some bread. Please, Mama."

"Ted."

"Johnnie couldn't walk much, Mama. I had to carry him all the way mostly."

"You are a very brave brother."

"Is Johnnie dead yet, Mama?"

"Johnnie's fine, Ted. Just fine." Her tongue continued to work strangely stiff. "You're a good boy to take care of him so. A true brother."

"Give me some bread, Mama. With some bumblebee honey on."

"Ted."

"Is the fort close by, Mama?"

"Yes, dear boy. We are almost there."

"I'm so hungry, Mama."

Scarlet Plume stood beside her. He spoke Sioux. "I see willows ahead. They grow beside The River Where A Piece Of Wood Is Painted Red. It is a pleasant river. The waters in it are lazy."

Ted jumped at the sound of the heavy Indian voice. He began to shake all over. He tried to focus his eyes on Scarlet Plume. "It's the Indians again, Mama! Is he going to kill us?"

Johnnie stirred too.

Judith hugged Johnnie close and warm. "It's all right, boys. Don't be afraid. This is Scarlet Plume, a friendly. So you don't need to worry. He's bringing us back to the white cities. He wants to help us."

"I'm afraid, Mama."

"Shh, now. It's all right." She looked up at Scarlet Plume. "Just how far is it to the willows?"

"A few running steps for the horses."

Judith decided she would walk and carry Johnnie, while Ted could ride her horse. But Ted screamed when his swollen pudendum touched the horse's hairy spine. Scarlet Plume had to help him down again.

"Ted."

Scarlet Plume then took Ted in his arms and began carrying him toward the river. The horses followed them, neighing wonderingly, not wanting to be left behind.

Scarlet Plume found a dry, sandy beach under red willows. He filled a skin with water and helped Judith wash the children. He dug out an Indian salve from his legging sash, the same herb he had once used to dress Judith's wounds. He rubbed the limbs and bodies of the children gently, working in the salve. His firm ministrations soothed them.

"Mama, give me some bread."

"Soon now, darling. But first we've got to doctor you a little."

"Am I dying, Mama?"

"Course not."

"I can't see very good though."

"Shh, now."

"I feel just like Jesus did when he was dying on the cross. Slowly he couldn't see no more."

"Shh."

"Mama, will there be water to drink in heaven?"

It didn't take Judith long to decide they would never be able to wash the black clots of old blood out of the children's hair. Scarlet

Plume suggested that he hack all the hair off with his sharp knife. When it was done the children's bald heads resembled the rough surface of washed walnuts.

Scarlet Plume next built a fire and quickly made soup from jerky and wild greens.

The drifting aroma of the soup at last reached Johnnie where he lay inert. He stirred. His lips moved. "I want mum-mum."

"Poor darling."

A smile as warm as an indulgent grandmother's wreathed Scarlet Plume's face. "He lives."

Judith echoed him. "Yes, he lives. Thank God."

It was dark by the time they had the children fed and washed. The children slept like bags of grain. They lay on a bed of willow twigs, the wolfskin covering them. In the light of the little twinkling fire the children's faces once again took on a pink color.

Scarlet Plume spoke over his red gossip pipe. "We will rest here one day." He looked up at the stars. "After that we must hurry or we will miss the white soldiers' encampment. They must stay ahead of the snow."

"It will snow?"

"The time for it has come."

They sat in silence awhile, a man and a woman and two children resting around a fire of an evening. Judith wished with all her soul that they truly might be a family together.

Scarlet Plume clapped out his pipe. He stood up and stretched. Then he vanished into the willows. He would stand guard for the night.

Judith gave the children a last look, then, utterly exhausted herself, curled up on the sand beside them.

Her last waking thoughts were of Scarlet Plume. She loved his tender way with children, even enemy white children. She adored his husbandly manner in the lodge, his warm, grave silences as well as his warm, grave laughter. She admired his considerate mien when around old women, as he was around Smoky Day. His stance in life was that of a brave man as well as that of an exceedingly wise one. Smiling, snuggling under a deerhide, she indulged in passionate feminine fantasies.

The next day a late fall blackbird sang in the red willows.

Ted told of how he and his little baby brother managed to exist upon finding themselves alive after the massacre at Skywater. He too had dug up potatoes in Theodosia's patch near the cabin, except that he and Johnnie ate theirs raw. They mostly drank from the lake. They found candy and tobacco on some of the dead bodies. Ted had quite a time keeping Johnnie from crawling back to his father Claude's body. Johnnie kept crying, "Papa, Papa, don't sleep so long." At last Ted decided that everybody at Skywater was dead, that no one was coming for them, not even the mailman Rollo. So Ted started out with Johnnie, heading up the buggy trail toward Fort Ridgely. They walked days. Finally they lost the faint trail in the deep grass. Somehow Ted managed to keep them heading mostly north. They drank water from sloughs and dew from grass in the mornings. They ate grass and sorrel and wild onions and rose hips. Miraculously one day they found a friendly settler cow. She was fresh and apparently very anxious to be milked. They obliged her. They milked in a cupped hand and drank from it. "The milk was so good, Mama. It was better than when Johnnie let me share some of his titty." Sometimes they got down on their hands and knees under the cow and suckled her tits. It was delicious. But then one night wolves spooked the cow and she disappeared. They trudged on. They thirsted. Their lips and tongues became cracked. Sometimes the mosquitoes sat so thick on their cheeks they could grab them by the handful and eat them.

Judith wept. She hugged the two children each in turn, her loose gold hair falling around them.

Scarlet Plume continued to rub their limbs with his Indian salve. He fed them soup. He caught perch in the stream, using a hook cut from a deer hoof.

The following morning Ted awoke with his sight returned to him.

"You're not Mama," he said, looking up at Judith from his bed. "Your hair is different. You're Aunt Judith. I thought your voice sounded kinda funny."

"Ted."

"What happened to Mama?"

Judith decided to tell him the truth. "She went to heaven."

"Did the Indians kill her like they did Papa?"

"I'm afraid so, Ted."

The reflective look of a man already old came over his face. He mused to himself. "So Mama went to live with Jesus. It's where she always wanted to go. She loved Him so much."

Judith's eyes closed over.

"Is Angela in heaven too?"

A cramp grabbed Judith in the belly. "I hope so, Ted. It is my fond hope."

"What's going to happen to us?"

"By tomorrow night we'll all be safe in camp. With our own soldiers."

"Will they be nice to Scarlet Plume?"

"They better."

"I like Scarlet Plume. He's a good Indian, ain't he, Auntie?"

"He's a wonderful great man."

They traveled easy. Johnnie rode with Judith, Ted with Scarlet Plume.

Scarlet Plume taught Ted how to stave off thirst on a long run by chewing on a little stick, creating saliva. He also taught him to put small cuts of jerky in his cheek so that trickling juices would keep his tongue wet.

Brilliant yellow warblers, heading the other way, south, rose out of every wolfberry bush they passed.

The farther they rode, the more the children began to chatter happily. It was almost a joyous homecoming.

They came upon the River Of The Milky Water, the Minnesota, late in the day. Fringed with leafless elm and ash, the river wound slowly, very lazily, through a great wide valley. The valley was so lovely it made Judith wonder if it weren't all a dream, a phantasma. For a few faint fleeting seconds it reminded her more of a painting she had once seen of the Rhine valley in Germany than truth in Minnesota.

They sat a moment, looking down. The heavy leaves of an oak rattled beside them on the bluff. Prevailing winds had strangely contorted the oak. It lay on the curve of the bluff like a loaf of brown bread baked on a boulder.

Scarlet Plume slid to the ground and once again went about gently touching things: a blade of buffalo grass, a gray stone, a gooseberry bush, an acorn. He cried over them all in the ancient way.

Judith understood.

What he did next, however, startled her, scared her. He dug a metal mirror out of his kit bag and set it up on a low limb of the bent oak. He combed his black hair neatly with a dried buffalo tongue, brushing it until it shone like a well-curried pony's tail. He carefully fixed his scarlet plume in the loose, flowing hair at the back of his head. Last he painted his left cheekbone: a yellow dot inside a blue circle. The yellow dot was a sign to let the sun know that all men needed light to sustain life. The blue circle was the blue sky, a symbol of peace.

"Why is this done?" she asked.

He threw her a look that was almost one of contempt. Her ignorance of the ways of men, red or white, was considerable.

"The white general will think you have painted your face for war," she warned.

He climbed back on his horse, sitting in front of Ted. With Ted's arms around his middle, he said, "Come, let us return the children. The time has at last come for me to throw my body away."

"I'll never let them touch you," Judith said fiercely. "Never!"

Scarlet Plume pointed west. "The white chief waits. He lives in a white lodge but a short distance away."

2

Scarlet Plume and Judith and the children rode under elms along the top of the bluff. Flocks of crows rose cawing from barren branches. Far to the west, along the entire horizon from north to south, hung a pall of churning smoke. Here and there distant swords of flame jumped red and menacing. Soon black ashes, riding the northwest wind, began to fall around them like black snow. The defeated Indians in a last desperate act of defiance had fired the prairies.

They rode as if into the outer reaches of hell itself. The velvet wind whipped Scarlet Plume's black pony hair. It tugged at Judith's loose flowing gold hair.

Scarlet Plume began to sing a death song in a high, quavering voice.

A patrol of blue soldiers suddenly blocked their way. The soldiers came springing out from behind a plum thicket. They stood leaning forward, bayonets at the ready, arms tense, lean brown faces taut. Two were but boys, but the others were old men with most of their teeth missing. There was a raggle-taggle look about the patrol: day laborers wearing second-hand soldier suits. Most bizarre of all were the blue-bearded chins of the older men.

It was with a wrench of her mind that Judith recalled all the patriotic furor when Vince and the other boys in blue left St. Paul to put down the rebellion. Even the taste in her mouth was suddenly offish, as if there had been a violent change in the weather around. Scarlet Plume's eerie death song abruptly took on new meaning.

The nearest soldier took dead aim at Scarlet Plume's broad chest. "Will you shut up, you howlin' banshee?"

"Wait!" Judith cried. "Don't shoot. He's a friendly."

A soldier with a corporal's stripe on his arm cried, "Biggs! Wait!" The corporal whacked Biggs's gun down and away. "There'll be no shootin' now. You know the Gen'ral's orders. 'No undue or unnecessary violence toward the Indians.' "

Scarlet Plume quit singing. He seemed to understand what was being said. He raised his left hand in greeting. "Houw!" With his right hand he held up his bow and war shield.

"Hey, there," the corporal cried. "Be careful with that bow now."

Judith said quickly, "Scarlet Plume comes in peace. He wishes to give you his arms. Don't you see? Holding up his left hand like that means peace. It is the hand nearest the heart. It has shed no blood."

"Lady," the corporal said, "we ain't takin' no chances. If the red devil comes in peace, fine and dandy. But we've already lost too many people, not bein' careful." The corporal squared his eyes at Scarlet Plume, going over him point by point. " 'Pears to me he's got a good-sized war bump, men. Like a panther even. And around panthers a man has got to be mighty careful." The corporal gave an order in a low voice. In a flash all six bayonets were trained on Scarlet Plume's belly. "Now, lady, I'm Corporal Deloss. Who be you, and where you from?"

Judith gave her name. "These little boys are my nephews and we're all that's left of Skywater."

"Everybody murdered t' Skywater? So that town's wiped out too."

"Everyone."

"Where you been all this time? That happened way back in August, didn't it?"

"I was taken captive by the Indians."

"You was?"

Biggs said, "Poor woman, aww." Biggs's eyes turned damp like an amorous dog's.

Judith resented Biggs's thoughts. "Most of the terrible reports you may have heard are not true. I was not outraged," she said thinly.

"So you warn't raped then, eh, ma'am?" Corporal Deloss exclaimed. "Beggin' your pardon—I meant outraged."

"No. Not by this friendly Indian, at least. This man risked his life for me helping me get back to the white settlements. If it had not been for him, these two little nephews of mine would have died too. He found us all, wandering alone and near crazed."

"Then this red devil here—"

"No!" Judith's eyes turned hail-white. "What you don't seem to understand is that it is taboo for a member of a soldiers' lodge to molest a woman, whether she be red or black . . . or white."

Corporal Deloss looked Scarlet Plume up and down, and thought he knew better. "Like I say, ma'am, the war bump is much more developed in some critters than in others, and if I don't miss my guess, his is really developed." Corporal Deloss considered again; spat tobacco juice to one side; considered some more. "Well, we'll turn him over to the camp guard. Gen'ral Sibley will decide if he's innocent like you say. Now tell that red devil to get down offa that horse."

"He rides until we meet the General," Judith said. "I'm sorry."

Corporal Deloss' lip curled. "Lady, I hate to say this, but the truth is, we've been between a shit and a sweat for nigh unto two months now and we don't take nonsense from nobody. Including even Queen Victoria if she was here. So I say he gets down. He is now a prisoner of war. Until the military court says different."

"Are they holding military court here?"

"They're right now trying all the red-nigger culprits to see which one gets hung and which one gets whipped."

Judith shivered. She knew the Dakota considered hanging the most horrible of all punishments, with whipping hardly any better.

Both hanging and whipping were to the Indian mind certain sign that the whites were an inferior race. Only an inferior race would think of so degrading the human spirit and the human figure. She remembered the suddenly shut faces of the Yanktons when hanging and whipping were mentioned.

Corporal Deloss lightly pricked Scarlet Plume in the belly with his glittering bayonet. "Get down. I don't trust ye up there."

Before Judith could say anything, Scarlet Plume of his own accord leaped nimbly to the ground. He handed over his bow and arrows, his war shield, and his knife. He spoke in Sioux. "Give these to the chief of the Long Knives."

"That's better," Corporal Deloss growled. "Much better."

Tears bit in the corners of Judith's eyes like stinging medicine. "Promise you'll treat him decent? Like he did us? Really, if it had not been for him, all three of us would have died."

"Lady, we promise nothing. He's a prisoner of war. It's out of our hands now."

Biggs spat to one side. "And I still say, the only good Indian is a dead Indian." Biggs snorted. "Haven't seen one yet that looked much like a man. They all look like they're part woman. Narrer hands. Persnickety way of walkin'. And all of 'em as poor as skim piss. Have to follow the buffalo like a pack of wolves to make a livin'. By God, I wouldn't trade my broken pipe for a live one."

Judith bristled at the rough talk.

"Biggs," Corporal Deloss said. "Biggs, don't get your nose out of joint now. There's a lady present."

Biggs gave Judith an ogling roll of the eye. "Her? Ha. If you don't dare ask her, corporal, if she thinks an Indian buck is as good as a white man, by God, I will. It's pretty clear to me she likes her liver raw."

Ted sat alone on Old Paint, holding the reins loosely. "Auntie, are they going to kill Scarlet Plume?"

"No, my boy."

"The hell we ain't," Biggs bawled, shaking his gun over his head. "The rapin' son of a bitch."

"Hup, march!" Corporal Deloss commanded, pricking Scarlet Plume again with the point of his bayonet, gesturing him forward.

Scarlet Plume stepped along calmly. Four of the six soldiers formed a guard around him. Despite the bayonet pricks, Scarlet Plume kept an iron control of his face. The fringes of his buckskin shirt thrashed at every step. The single scarlet feather at the back of his head quivered.

Judith and Johnnie on Buckskin Belly and Ted on Old Paint rode quietly behind, a soldier on either side of them.

Looking ahead, Judith saw the encampment, some thousand white tents spread out like a city on the wide, high prairie, all doors facing inward, with cattle and horses and wagons in the center.

The trees along the edge of the bluff suddenly came alive, wiggling and snapping. Some of the tough oak leaves came off like apples shaken from a tree. And then a great blast of wind was upon them, almost tearing Judith and the boys from their horses. The blue soldiers had to bend at the hips to stay on their feet. Scarlet Plume scorned escape in the uproar. It was fated. On the veiling wind came the acrid smell of grass burning. Black flakes flew past like shot. The vast prairie fire was now plain to see, a rising tumult of racing flames against the evening sky, with an onrushing throw of yellowish-black smoke already leaning over the flames.

"By the Lord," said one of the men. "I hope the Gen'ral has the sense to backfire. Or we'll be roasted alive."

The General had. Little groups of men with burning fagots could be seen racing along the west and north rim of the camp, starting little fires, while other men ran behind them with wet blankets, slapping out the little fires when the wind threatened to explode them toward the camp. The only flames allowed were those backing into the wind toward the oncoming red terror. Judgment day was at last at hand.

Corporal Deloss and his three guards led Scarlet Plume toward a long white tent in the middle of the encampment, while the other two soldiers led Judith and the children toward the white-refugee camp, a cluster of tents set apart by itself.

Judith watched Scarlet Plume go. Her eyes were dry, but her heart pounded. There was no good-bye. The Indian never said good-bye. As Scarlet Plume walked across the trampled dead grass, he looked more like some foreign prince attended by servile guards than what he really was, a hated prisoner of war. With choking pride she watched him diminish in size. Spumes of yellowish-gray smoke and flying black soot soon hid him from view.

A welcoming committee of three white women in the refugee camp helped Judith and the children down from their horses. The two soldiers led the horses away. The three women had young bodies but old faces.

Two of the three women had been uprooted and outraged so often they were hardly more than sodden drudges. The third woman still had some spunk left, and showed it in her hennish eyes.

"I'm Alva Axtell," the spunky one said. "May we help you?"

"If you wish."

Alva Axtell gave Judith's Indian clothes a wondering look. "We'll have to make you some clothes. The soldiers gave us some needle and thread. And some rough sacking."

"These clothes are all right. I don't mind them."

Alva Axtell looked at Judith's flowing gold hair. "Well! At least they didn't make a decoration out of your hair for some horse's tail."

Judith winced. Poor Whitebone. It had been his hope that she would live forever amongst the Yanktons as their white goddess. "I'm not of a mind to wear sackcloth and ashes yet."

"But those leather clothes smell Indian."

"And what is that smell, pray?"

"You sound as if you don't like being rescued."

"True. I was brought here against my wish."

Alva Axtell shot Judith a venomish look. It was as quick as the peck of a hen. "Then why didn't you stay with your red pets?"

"I had the children to return."

"Well, at least the mother in you is still alive."

"The boys are my nephews. My own child was killed."

"Oh." Alva Axtell couldn't resist giving the sleeve of Judith's tunic a feel between her fingers for its texture. "Have you et? All we have these days is hardtack and fat pork."

"I've had a great plenty, thanks. But the children haven't."

A circle of pale, starved faces surrounded Judith and the two boys as they stood on the beaten gray grass. There were fragments of families. Their eyes all had the wild, blanched look of having lived too long in constant dread and alarm. Not a word, not even a hiccup of compassion, came from them. The eyes of the women were especially haunting. There wasn't a woman there but what she didn't read into Judith, into her flesh as well as into her private thoughts, all the atrocities she herself had suffered. The women stared and stared. The two men in the crowd had the cowed look of just-castrated bulls. Most of the refugees had been given such white clothes as the soldiers had recovered from the Indians. In some cases coarse sacking had been cut into dresses for the women and horse blankets into pants for the men. There wasn't a good fit in the lot. Most were barefoot. All were ill at ease with each other. The little children were the worst off. They reminded Judith of the terror-stilled grouse she had found in the grass below Lost Timber.

The two women drudges who made rough sacking into clothes for Ted and Johnnie crooned over them and stroked them, touching their bristly heads again and again. The two women were like sad cows, who, having lost their own calves, were yet excited that other calves had been found. Ted and Johnnie suffered them.

The raging prairie fire hit their neck of the prairie at last. The storm of smoke was suffocating, and everyone turned his back to it, a hand to the mouth, coughing. But the earlier backfiring did the trick, and presently the fire raced around them rather than over them, and went on down the river, enveloping stands of wolfberry and elm and ash, and exploding through sloughs. The

bur oaks still had most of their leaves, brown, and they sometimes took fire, reddish purple, making them appear to be scarlet
oaks for the moment.

Over in the circle of tepees where the captured Sioux were
under guard, the death song of the braves and the lamentations
of the squaws filled the black evening sky with a wild, raw
cacophony. The little Sioux children skirled around and through
the quarters of the white soldiers, shrilling, "Sibilee! Sibilee!" To
them it was all great fun.

When Ted and Johnnie were fed at last, Judith managed to
nibble down a piece of hardtack. It was like eating a shingle. It
took a tin of river water to get it down.

She made a bed for herself on the bare ground, Ted and
Johnnie on either side of her, a smelly red-and-black horse blanket
over them for covering.

A man spoke in the dark. "We will make them pay the forfeit
with their lives yet, you can bet your sweet life on that."

"Yes," another man said, "but curse them, there are not lives
enough in the whole Sioux nation to pay it."

Toward midnight some friendly Indians brought in yet another lot of captive white women and children. The newly rescued
wretches were shown a place where they could sleep. They cried
and prayed through the night.

The next morning, Judith saw to it that Ted and Johnnie were
fed, that they got acquainted with a couple of other white children for playmates, then was off to see what had been done with
Scarlet Plume.

She first tried to find him on her own. In vain.

Soon she ran into a cluster of little Sioux children. She asked
them if they knew what had happened to Scarlet Plume. They
stared at her, then at her doeskin tunic, with the blank eyes of
caged muskrats. She couldn't get a word out of them.

At last she came upon a newly erected log jail in the middle
of the encampment. It was near where the horses were kept.

Corporal Deloss blocked her way. "Sorry, ma'am, but we're under orders not to let anybody see him. But nobody."

"Ah! Then it's here you're keeping him."

"Mmmm. Perhaps." Corporal Deloss quirked square eyes at her.

"Why isn't he kept with the rest of the Sioux?"

"Gen'ral's orders." A stream of brown tobacco juice erupted out of the side of Corporal Deloss' whiskery mouth. "And as you may know by now, Gen'ral Sibley is boss here in Camp Release."

"Why was this done?"

"I dunno. All I know is, he's sittin' in chains in thar and starin' at the ground. He probably knows by now that his life ain't worth a gooser."

Judith screamed, she was so angry. "But why the chains?"

"Dunno." Corporal Deloss stared at her Indian dress, then at her loose, flowing hair. "Didn't any of the sackin' fit ee?"

"Where's General Sibley's headquarters?"

Corporal Deloss pointed a casual hand. "That way. It's the tent with the Union flag there."

Judith took measured steps across the trampled gray grass. Scarlet Plume in chains?

A boyish sentry blocked her way. "Who did you wish to see, ma'am?"

"General Sibley, please."

"And what mought your business be with him, ma'am?"

"I want to see him on a matter of great urgency."

The boy sentry stared her Indian clothes up and down. "Wait here, miss." The boy sentry ducked inside the tent.

Judith started. Miss? To that . . . that boy?

The wind was rising again and slowly the sky began to darken over with flying black soot off the burned prairies. Tents became more black than white. White men began to resemble actors made up as Negroes in a minstrel show. Horses and cows were being led down to the bottoms for water and for what little grass was left. There was a slow, continuous uproar in the captive Sioux sector, with the squaws howling like wild wolves and the braves barking like bears caught in a trap, and the Sioux children still skirling through the whole camp, free and wild, crying incongruously, "Sibilee! Sibilee!" All the while white captives drifted about like eyeless oxen.

"This way, miss," the boy sentry said at her elbow.

She bowed through a peaked opening. At first she found the interior of the tent quite dim. There was an instant smell of trampled grass and dust. As her eyes adjusted, she made out a folding cot, a soldier's foot locker, a pole rack, and oddly enough a blue carpet on the bare ground.

There were two men, both seated on canvas folding chairs, one beside a small table, the other with a writing board on his knee.

The man at the table, after a glance at her face and hair, stood up in a courtly manner. The other man was a little slower getting to his feet.

"Yes?"

"Are you General Sibley?"

"Yes?"

"My name is Judith Raveling and I've come to inquire—"

"Raveling?" General Sibley broke in.

"Yes. And I would like to know—"

"Hmm."

"What's wrong?"

"Nothing, madam. Nothing. Won't you be seated?" General Sibley picked up another folding chair, broke it open for her, and set it on the raw earth so that it faced him. "Please."

Judith sat down, slowly. She crossed her moccasined feet. Her heels rested on the edge of the blue carpet. It was the first time in months that her feet had touched one of the comforts of civilization. It gave her pause.

General Sibley asked, "Have you had breakfast, Mrs. Raveling?"

"I have."

General Sibley stood over her, slim and handsome in blue

military dress. He was a good six feet tall, muscular and vigorous-looking despite his fifty years. His hair was black, his brown eyes piercing, his small black mustache severely clipped. Mingled in with his military bearing was also the air of the much-traveled man who was weary of it all. "I trust you've been treated well?" He spoke in a drawling, cultivated voice. "I am sorry that our accommodations are not of the best."

"I have not come to complain in my own behalf."

"Good." General Sibley gestured toward the other man. There was gracious dignity in the General's every move. "And this is my friend Isaac Heard. A lawyer from St. Paul. You may have met."

Judith nodded toward Heard. "Sorry, but I've not had the pleasure."

Heard nodded in turn. He was shorter than General Sibley and was a trifle portly. He had beady, glittering eyes. His attention seemed more taken up by her Indian garb than by her person.

"Isaac is my aide in camp as well as my recorder. And, I might add, the one friend I have here in these wilds with whom I can talk books." General Sibley let his eyes rest on the table, where the works of Blackstone, Coke, and Kent, as well as Cooper, Gibbon, and Hume, stood. "Were it not for Isaac, and these books, this chase far into enemy country would indeed be most intolerable."

Judith resented Heard's staring at her Indian clothes. She could guess what his thoughts were.

General Sibley also looked at her doeskin tunic with some interest. "I'm sorry we don't have decent dress for you. We didn't know what to expect, therefore could not prepare for it. But I have given orders to issue blankets to those white captives who were brought in nearly naked. Did you not receive your blanket?"

Judith recalled the snub Mrs. Sibley had once given her in a St. Paul millinery. "I am not nearly naked, thank you, and I prefer this dress." Judith sat primly on her canvas chair. "I came here not for myself, as I said, but for my red benefactor. Why was Scarlet Plume put in chains?"

General Sibley sat down and his brows came up. Heard also seated himself. It was plain that General Sibley was taken aback by her attitude. "But, madam, you are not in sympathy with these red vermin?"

"I was among friends when I lived with the Indians, and as soon as I am certain that my nephews will be properly taken care of, I intend to return to my friends. And I also intend to return with my savior, Scarlet Plume."

"But, madam, the Indians are not prepared to keep you as a white woman expects to be kept."

"Nevertheless, I intend to return. They are now my people."

"But the Indian is a monster. A devil in human shape."

"I did not find him so."

"Then you were not one of those who suffered brutal and fiendish violation of her person?"

"I have come to know this: the old-line Yankton never molested women, red or black or white. It is only the renegade Indian and the backslid Christian Indian who did this."

General Sibley regarded her with faintly amused eyes. "I take it then that you do not wish to be restored to your husband's arms?" His eyes lingered on her trailing gold hair.

"No." Judith's eyes caressed the silken surface of the blue rug.

"Nor see your dear children again?"

"We had but one child. And she suffered, as you say, brutish and fiendish violation of her person . . . by the renegade Indian. As well as by your Christianized Indian."

"Then you do not hunger"—General Sibley's eyes caught the movement of Judith's toes stroking the surface of the blue rug—"then you do not hunger for the sweets of civilization?"

"I miss them, yes. But I shall miss them less than something else."

General Sibley regarded her with twinkling scorn. "I suppose you prefer an enemy husband to a white husband?"

"In this one instance . . ." Judith paused. She saw the trap he had led her into.

General Sibley went on. "I suppose you are going to claim that your man shot up?"

"He never took part at all."

"That is not our report on him."

"General Sibley, tell me, what is he accused of? Why does he sit in chains?"

General Sibley turned to Heard. He said in a tired voice, "Read her the charge, will you, Isaac?"

Heard blinked, then opened a gray ledger. He ran his finger along some lines of writing. " 'The Indian known as Scarlet Plume is accused of belonging to Whitebone's band. Whitebone's band was in the vicinity when Pounce and Mad Bear were massacring the settlers at Skywater.' "

Judith gasped. "Then he is being sentenced to death for merely being present?"

"Accomplice to the fact," Heard said primly.

Judith had to work for breath. "Who accused him of this?"

"A boy named Theodore Codman," Heard said.

"You mean, our Ted?" Judith cried. "When?"

"This morning."

"Where was I?"

"I don't know."

Judith spoke in white outrage. "Sneaks! Spiriting Ted out from under me while my back was turned."

"Not at all," Heard said, "not at all. When we went to get your testimony you were not about."

"But I was out looking for Scarlet Plume. You know this."

"Besides, we have several confessions from members of Pounce's band to confirm the boy's report."

Shivers moved under her skin.

General Sibley spoke in a drawling voice. "You deny then that he was present?"

Bitingly, Judith told of how Scarlet Plume had given her a

wild swan with a broken neck in warning, how he had been gone on an errand when the attack started, how when he returned he had persuaded Whitebone to stop the carnage.

General Sibley's lips curled in an imperial sneer. "I take it then that you do not wish to testify against your dusky paramour, Mrs. Raveling?"

"Never. Even amongst the whites I have not seen a greater man. And I'm afraid this includes you, my fine sir."

General Sibley flushed to his eyeballs.

"Tell me, General Sibley, tell me, what were Scarlet Plume's first words when you met him? Was he not the gentleman?"

General Sibley's shoulders came up with a jerk. He made a heroic try at keeping his temper and aplomb. "Why . . . uh . . . ." General Sibley turned to Heard. "You made record, did you not, Isaac, of what was said?"

Heard paged back through the gray ledger. "Er . . . 'The Indian Scarlet Plume stepped up to General Sibley and held out his hand. He said, "I look at you. My heart is glad to see the friend of Sunned Hair. I wish to shake the hand of this friend. I have brought Sunned Hair and her little children back to her people." He said, "My friend, I have never seen you before. I have heard my people talk about you for many winters. Now I see you and my heart feels good toward you. My heart tells me that you are a true friend to Sunned Hair." With his left hand raised, he said, "Let the war trail grass over. That is all I have to say now." ' "

Judith saw the scene completely. A sob escaped her. In a broken voice she asked, "And what did you say in response, General Sibley?"

"What did I say, Heard?"

"You said, sir, 'Does the red man come in peace? Have you come to bury the hatchet so that we may end this harvest of blood?' "

"Oh, Lord, not that, not that!" Judith hid her face in her hands. "I knew it. I just knew it. You're no better than your mangy soldiers, General Sibley. Begging your pardon. They too were full of such asininities. Japery."

General Sibley held himself very stiff inside his blue military jacket.

Judith stood up. Her golden hair hung to her shoulders. Her eyes flashed glows of blue fire. "General Sibley, I have just this to say. If Scarlet Plume is hung, I'm going to shoot you or anybody else who may be responsible for bringing him to the scaffold. And I shall do this just as sure as the sun rises in the east and sets in the west. And then I shall go back to my people, the Yanktons."

General Sibley stood up too. Heard sat. General Sibley said with pinched asperity, "As you will, madam. But remember, you in turn must expect me to do my duty and my whole duty as leader of this expedition."

"*Good*-bye!"

Two days later, in the evening, the encampment having been removed from Camp Release to the Lower Agency site near Redwood Falls because of impending winter storms, Judith made up her mind to see General Sibley again.

She walked across burned desolate earth. Dust and grass soot in darkening clouds drove across the prairie and poured off into the deep valley of the Minnesota River. The black wind filled the eyes, nose, ears. The faces of soldiers had the look of men having suddenly been resurrected from dirty graves. Even the captive Sioux warriors, linked together in pairs by chains forged at the ankles, had darkened faces. The squaws still wailed in grief for their condemned fathers and husbands and sons.

General Sibley granted Judith immediate audience. With him in his field tent was recorder Heard again. The three sat as before, feet on the edge of the blue rug.

Judith broke the ice. "General Sibley, I have just seen Scarlet Plume. From a distance. Your proper guards will not let me get close."

General Sibley spoke with weary urbanity. He fingered his crisp mustache. "I am sorry. Do not blame them. They keep you away in obedience to my orders."

"Why?"

"And I in turn have my orders from General Pope. You see, madam, this is what General Pope has written." General Sibley picked up a letter from his desk and read from it. " 'It is my purpose to utterly exterminate the Sioux. They are to be treated as maniacs or wild beasts.' " General Sibley put the letter aside. "So, go in chains and isolation they must."

"Then I cannot see Scarlet Plume?"

"Madam, you cannot."

"Then you would rather believe the words of a confused little boy just recovered from terrible starvation than the words of a grown person who saw it all? And a woman who was supposed to have been outraged, at that?"

"Madam, were you not nearly deranged by this same starvation?"

"Then what we both say is flimsy evidence, is it not? And if that is true, on what charge do you hold him?"

General Sibley sighed. "Scarlet Plume has admitted being present in Skywater during the massacre, just as certain captured members of Pounce's band have testified."

"Has he been tried yet?"

"The military commission is sitting now." General Sibley pointed through the open flap of his tent toward one of the few remaining log buildings left after the fire. It was a cabin owned by François La Bathe. "His turn comes shortly."

"What!"

"My dear lady. Listen to me now. White women of good family, whose word can be completely trusted, have told us of seeing their children nailed to trees while young braves practiced their marksmanship on them until they died. They have told us of white women being shot in the back so that the arrow came out by the point through the breast. They have told us of repeated sexual assaults at the hands of filthy bucks. One young white girl was ravished seventeen times within the hour. We have heard this sort of thing over and over again. The gravity of these hell-roaring times . . . Well! What do you wish us to do—excuse all these atrocities?"

Judith allowed herself an unladylike snort. "Within the hour, ha. Are you trying to tell me that that young girl really bothered to count all seventeen attacks? That she made a mark or a notch somewhere for each one? And watched the clock while it was being done to her?"

General Sibley's face hardened. "As I say, when one hears of such dreadful things—yes, monstrous things—one's blood is stirred to madness."

"Hmmf. And I have heard the other side of that story. I have visited the Indian refuge camp here many times. One Indian mother told me with tears in her eyes that to save her children she'd had to go one hundred miles on foot to Fort Ridgely and degrade herself. Because she and her children were starving. She no longer could come up with milk for her baby. Her husband was dead and neither the annuities nor the food had yet arrived. This happened only a month before the uprising."

"Oh, I know, I know, our hands are not altogether clean either. Yet, nevertheless—"

"—Not clean!" Judith sat with stiff, arched back on the edge of her chair. "General Sibley, was it honorable of you to invite the Indian chiefs to a council in a newly built log house and after they were assembled to imprison them? And promptly make a log jail out of the log house?"

"One cannot put trust in their word and it was for that reason that it was done."

"General Sibley, I have also talked to our own white captive women many times. From them I hear that a good share of the atrocities done to them were done by our own soldiers, by some of those scavenger half-breed volunteers you have in camp. Also that it was our own whites who did most of the scalping and not

the Indians. As it was always done. You know, of course, don't
you, that it was from the Dutch in New York that the American
Indian learned scalping in the first place? Of course you do. Some
of the Dutch were human bounty hunters."

"What! Whoa. That I cannot believe."

Judith burned her high-white flashing eyes into the general. "I
can give you the names of the soldiers if you want them. Ha. What
you hear from that scared-stiff nigger Godfrey and from those
poor notional young girls is one thing, but what I hear at night
from the older women and given to me in confidence is another."
Judith licked her lips. "White soldiers scalping the bodies of the
dead. White dead."

General Sibley pulled himself together. "The power of life and
death is an awful thing to exercise. Lodged as it is in my hands for
the moment, it makes me shudder. Still, duty must be performed
and judgment visited on the guilty."

"And I still say Scarlet Plume is not guilty. Not guilty, d'you
hear? General Sibley, if you hang him, you hang an innocent man
as well as a great man." Judith shook her finger at General Sibley
as a man might. "My fine sir, I'll say it again. If he dies, you die.
I will shoot you. Somehow."

General Sibley turned to Heard. "Isaac, tell her what you told
me this morning."

Heard humped forward on his canvas chair. All through the
interview his eyes as before had remained fastened on her doeskin tunic. It seemed to possess Heard that she had not wanted
to change to white garb of some sort. "Yesterday one brave testified that he had seen a certain white killed by a white bullet.
Since we knew for an absolute certainty that the white man had
been killed by an arrow, we had him dead to rights. Your red
lover shall hang."

Judith couldn't believe her ears. "And that is evidence? And
you are a lawyer?"

"Nevertheless—"

Judith broke in. She turned her full fury on General Sibley.

"Sir, you have caught the wrong Indians. The real culprits, if there were any, have long ago skipped the country. They are already in British Canada."

General Sibley's eyes first opened a second, then almost closed entirely. He had spotted something. She had made a slip. "Mrs. Raveling, you do not protest when Scarlet Plume is referred to as your red lover? Then it is a fact, is it not, that you are infatuated with him, eh? Possibly more?"

Judith flushed scarlet.

There was a long pause. In Heard's eyes and in the expression on his lips it was patently obvious that he was envisioning her in lascivious embrace with Scarlet Plume.

General Sibley spoke, almost sadly. "I'm sorry, Mrs. Raveling, but your dusky paramour must be tried along with the rest. We must do this to make absolutely certain that not one of the real culprits goes unpunished. We are bound to have a few culprits amongst all those we've caught. We owe this to the bones of all the slaughtered white settlers."

"General Sibley, let me ask you this. I have heard the story many times that a Sioux chief, in gratitude for a favor you did him, once offered you his virgin daughter for the night. In fact, I think you referred to it in an article you wrote for the magazine *Spirit of the Times,* under the pseudonym 'Hal, a Dakotah.' Did you actually refuse her charms?"

General Sibley blushed.

"Did your pet of a white wife approve of this when you told her?"

Judith was not permitted to testify, on the grounds of prejudice.

She caught General Sibley by the arm as the military commission broke up for the noon meal. Her face was blackened over by all the flying soot from the burned grass. Tear streaks down her face resembled Indian face markings.

"General Sibley?"

"They found him guilty."

Judith almost fell to earth.

General Sibley caught her arm, supported her for a moment.

"But, General, he is innocent!"

"So say you."

"What did he say in his defense?"

"He gave no defense. He freely admits to being at Skywater during the time of the massacre. He told us that he was proud to be able to say that there was no one between himself and the enemy at all times."

"Poor man. Poor man. He just will not try to save himself."

"When he was asked if he would try to help catch some of the other culprits, so that some amelioration of his sentence might be considered, he told us"—General Sibley could not help but smile grimly—"he told us we could skin our own skunk."

"He would say that. He would."

"I realize, Mrs. Raveling, that there is much to be said for the romantic noble savage—"

"Romantic? The Sioux is not romantic at all. He is epic!"

"Mrs. Raveling, I agree with you in one respect at least: that this is the greatest Indian tragedy of the age."

"Did that blue-gum nigger presume to testify against him?"

"He did not. Godfrey the Negro is married into another branch of the Sioux."

"General Sibley." Judith gave him a hard tug on the sleeve. "General Sibley, we stole this land from the Indian. It was their homeland, not ours. And whatever they may have done in retaliation to regain it, even the worst, can be excused on that ground. We would have done the same."

"Then you do not believe that a superior civilization has the duty and the right to make a place for itself?"

"At the expense of the dumb? I do not believe there is such a thing as justifiable conquest."

"What about the civilizing the world has undergone at the hands of the Romans?"

Judith thought again of the snub given her by Mrs. Sibley. "I've read some too, General. So let me ask you this. Do you then condone the repeated raids the civilized Spaniards made on the Indian Mayas, when the Indian Mayas had the greater civilization?"

It was a telling comment, and it was immediately apparent that General Sibley's respect for her went up a hundredfold. A mingled look of part sympathy and part apprehension appeared in his dark eyes. He looked at her soot-darkened flowing gold hair, looked at her Indian tunic, and shook his head. "Madam, you almost persuade me."

"Almost is not enough."

General Sibley took her by the arm. "I'm glad you caught me here though. Because I was about to go look for you myself. Uhh, come with me to my quarters a moment. I have someone there who wants to meet you."

Judith started. Some more survivors from Skywater?

"Come."

When they arrived at General Sibley's field tent, the General bowed her inside and then stepped back.

His ushering her alone into the murky tent surprised her. But then her eyes adjusted and she understood.

Rising out of Heard's chair was her soldier husband, Vince.

"What . . . are . . . you . . . doing . . . here?" Judith asked weakly.

"My precious pet."

Vince's ready use of the old endearment, always so revolting to her because it reminded her of his favorite Lucretius position, almost broke her mind. She sagged into a chair.

He stood proudly before her. He was dressed in the snapping blue uniform of a lieutenant, with belt and saber, the quintessence of everything military and manly. He bowed to her, forager cap to his breast and thinning blond hair neatly slicked back.

Judith closed her eyes. This was not the way she remembered

him when he left for the wars, waving to her from the deck of the steamboat *Blue Earth.* He had been craven then, half-drunk, potbellied, sallow.

"Well, pet?"

She shivered.

"Judith?"

She dared to look up. How radiant he was with health now, slim at the hips, broad-shouldered. Bold-eyed, even. The war of rebellion had made a man of him. At last. Slowly her eyes went over him. She saw that he had been wounded, a deep bullet crease at the edge of his hairline. She could see blood pulsing in the soft white scarred hollow.

"Pet?"

"Too late," she murmured, weak.

"Aren't you glad to see me?"

She shook her head. Vince was now the man she had once wanted him to be. But it was too late.

His smile gave him the look of the eager young lover. "I see that you've been through a lot too."

"Too?" she thought.

"This has been a terrible time for all of us."

"Angela is dead," she whispered.

His face quickly grayed over. For a second his face had the old sallow look. "Yes," he finally said, low. "I know. General Sibley told me." He licked his thin lips.

"She was—"

"Don't mention it! I know. What is done is done." He forced a smile to his lips. "I think we owe it to ourselves to concentrate on what lies ahead, not on what lies behind us." He looked at her Indian tunic. "Native garb becomes you."

She covered her face with her hands. "Please."

He spoke gently. "Soon we'll be in Mankato. We'll buy you a whole new wardrobe there."

"Please."

A long silence followed.

A sentry outside paced slowly back and forth. A bugle sounded. Faintly came the endless wailing of the Sioux death song. A sad Dakota war drum beat steady and slow nearby.

Vince sat down opposite her. Elbows on his knees, he began to talk in a low voice. It was strange to hear the new manly accent in his talk. In the old days it was she who did most of the talking. The new vibrancy in him cut her up inside.

After a bit she managed to fasten her mind on what he was saying. . . .

All went well with Vince in the Minnesota Fifth under Colonel Hubbard. Until the battle of Farmington.

It was in May and the hills were in bloom. Vince was made adjutant to Captain Bowman, a rough old file of a man. In the opening skirmish the captain lost his saber and he ordered Vince to go back and get it. Vince was a coward, and knew it, and demurred. He suggested the lost saber was hardly worth a human life. In a rage Captain Bowman ordered him to get it anyway. Vince was more afraid of the captain than he was of the Rebs. Luckily a lull occurred in the shooting just then and he ran back over the ridge and found the saber. When he turned it in, the captain ordered him back once more.

"What for?"

"Why, the gold cord, of course, that's what for. Can't let the Rebs have that."

The cord was worth about ten cents and this time Vince knew for a fact that going back was not worth a Union life. Vince spoke his mind on the matter.

The captain chewed him out. And chewed him out with such maniacal fury that Vince began to wonder if the captain wasn't a fit subject for the lunacy commission.

Vince went again. He had proceeded about a dozen yards over the ridge, stepping over gutted bellies, when the Rebels let go with a barrage from the far crest. One of the musket balls carried away Vince's right heel. Vince jumped straight up, screamed, and returned to the Union lines at 2:40 gait.

Vince hugged the first tree he came to. "I hugged it so hard that had it been an old maid she would have wiggled in sheer delight."

The captain came up and kicked him in the arse. "What the devil you doing here?"

Vince waved his arms up and down on both sides of the tree. "Why, captain, I'm only feeling for a furlough. One little nick from a musket ball on a fingertip and I can go home."

The captain was outraged. He kicked him with all he had a second time. "I never want to see your detestable carcass again in this regiment. You are not only a coward, you are an outright all-day-Sunday coward. They surely left out the sand when they made you."

"Well, captain, beggin' your pardon, you may make a lot of noise, but you're even worse off. They left out the gizzard itself when they made you."

The captain glared. "I can have you shot for that. But you know, I'm instead going to give you an even worse punishment. Until further notice you're in charge of the burial detail."

Vince reported for his new duties the next day. It was a beautiful June morning out, yet already outside the surgeon's tent bodies lay corded up like firewood ready for a steamboat. His detail dug burial trenches all day long.

Toward evening he saw one of the corded bodies move its feet. He got help and took the body out. An hour later, the body came to and walked away, determined to join the battle again.

For many nights Vince's dreams were of rivers and big running springs, of never having enough to drink. He dreamed of swimming in tubs of blood where he was forced to fight off voracious bladders and slimy livers.

Then came the battle of Corinth in October. They got orders

to move in. Frying pans tied to their guns clinked merrily as they tramped along.

Two days later, bivouacked in town near the depot, they were aroused at dawn by shellfire. The Rebs were on the march.

All too soon the Union line on the right collapsed and suddenly dense crowds of men in butternut brown, bounding and yelling, were pouring into Corinth. They came in like flooding brown waters. Without waiting for orders, Colonel Hubbard changed his front, moving by the right flank by file right, and took up a position at right angles to his former position. The enemy flank was presented to his new line. Colonel Hubbard ordered his men to fire. The fire was devastating. At the same time he called for a man to deliver a message to General Stanley. Vince volunteered, glad to get out of the holocaust. He was given a horse that had once been attached to a battery unit. The horse had galloped only a dozen rods, when in all the sudden gunfire, it reversed and headed straight into the hellish inferno beside the depot. The horse was used to running toward a battle, not away from it. The firing from both sides became deadly. Vince ducked behind the horse's head. The horse advanced as if bucking a hailstorm driven by a furious wind. Then he and the horse were suddenly in the lead. The Federals let go with a great roar when they saw Vince and his horse advancing alone. He had become the soul of their stand. They fixed bayonets and advanced on a run behind him. The butternut Confederates tried to hold. They too let go with a great roar, a massive rising cry that sounded like a cross between the Indian death song and the roar of a black bear. But shoot as they might, the Rebs could not drop either Vince or his horse. Vince saw the butternuts falter. To his surprise he was all of a sudden standing up in his saddle and roaring with the best of them, shouting with the fearless passion of sure triumph. He was enjoying it. It was nothing to be a brave man after all, a hero. You just suddenly were. It was easy. If you didn't get hit you were alive. And if you did get hit you were dead. That was all there was to it. The butternuts faded. The boys in blue closed the gap.

It was when he had finally turned his horse about that he got hit. A stray union bullet caught him at the hairline. He was out like a doused candle. And he didn't know where he was or who he was until he woke up on board a boat headed for St. Paul.

When he had fully recovered in a St. Paul hospital, he was told to join General Sibley on the Sioux Indian front. Sibley had sent a hurry-up call to Governor Ramsey for more troops and all available men were ordered upriver to Fort Ridgely. That was how he happened to be in General Sibley's tent. . . .

Vince placed his hand on Judith's shoulder familiarly.

She shrugged it off. "Don't."

"What's the matter, pet?"

"It's too late." The tip of her tongue sought for the four black hairs on the edge of her upper lip. To her surprise the four hairs were gone. They had not reappeared since she had pulled them out beside the pond in Lost Timber.

"Now, pet—"

"Don't."

They locked eyes, blue eyes and gray eyes.

She was the first to break off, and look to one side.

She held her belly in both her hands. She knew that in another eight months there would be a half-breed child with blood as pink as the prairie rose.

"When I am not in love I am nothing."

3

The blue army moved down the Old Fort Road on the New Ulm side of the river. It swung past lonely kames and brown granite outcroppings. Dry axles screeched. Wheels raised little plumes of black dust. Each wagonload of prisoners was flanked by a detail of bristling mounted men. The long succession of wagons resembled a monster caterpillar being harried along by a small swarm of big black ants.

Judith rode Buckskin Belly. She held Johnnie in front of her. Ted rode Old Paint. To either side of them trailed the other rescued whites, most of them on foot, some in wagons.

Wavering V's of ducks and geese were southing. Far-flung arrows of white swans cut across the highest heavens.

Occasionally the remains of families were found sprawled in the burned grass. The skeletons lay as if just fallen after a hard run. Remaining morsels of flesh on the bones had the stink of ripe steak slightly burned.

The column hit a cloud of late-autumn flies. The horses went crazy and the whole line broke up into sections and snapped upon itself for a time. The column next crossed on a corduroy road, the logs undulating underfoot in spongy black muck as if they were the backs of live hogs.

A couple of times Judith managed to ride close behind the army wagon in which Scarlet Plume rode. He sat near the endgate, shackled to an Indian named His Face Resembles An Antheap. Antheap's smallpox-pitted cheeks were as rough as a rasp. Each wagon contained a driver and five pairs of prisoners. All the prisoners wore red-and-black horse blankets.

Scarlet Plume's iron control of his face reminded Judith of a Christ riding impassively to his fate, enduring chains and humiliation because a higher god expected it of him. It made Judith grimace to think that she could compare her red friend to Christ. She had never taken too kindly to Christian reflections. But she had come to appreciate one thing: why it was that Theodosia could have felt such devotion to her Christ. Scarlet Plume's road to Mankato was similar to Christ's road to Calvary. And Scarlet Plume's manly composure made Judith wonder too if Christ had been such a pallid mama's boy after all.

There was one big difference between Theodosia's loving and her loving. Theodosia Woods loved her ideal across the distance of several thousand years at the same time that she cohabited on occasion with a man named Claude Codman, while she, Judith Woods, both loved her great man and cohabited with him, now— with this twist, that Scarlet Plume belonged many times removed to a past before the time of Christ.

Scarlet Plume's stoic self-control cracked once. It happened when Judith brought him a tin of river water as they rode along. For a brief moment he looked at her, black eyes radiant with love. It set her to blushing, making her look down, and she thought, "Please, do not look at me so, my husband." Trembles chased through her limbs, so that she was afraid she would fall off her horse. It was as if, safely on his way to a white man's scaffold, Scarlet Plume had for one moment at last felt free to let her see how he really felt about her.

Manic moods ravished her. One moment she was in despair when she thought of Scarlet Plume being hanged like a common criminal; the next moment she was in heaven when she remembered the burning thrill of his lovemaking. He was going to die; he had to be saved somehow.

The procession stopped to water the horses. The red friendlies went among the whites and put on begging dances in behalf of the chained wretches. It was cold, the ground was frozen, and the little red children wore jackrabbit skins inside their moccasins. The little red ones continued to skirl happily in and out of the entourage.

The whites paid little attention. The soldiers were looking forward to drinking New Ulm beer. New Ulm beer was reputed to be sweet because it had been made out of spring water running off old green rock.

When the soldiers did remark on the red captives, it was always in scorn. "I hear the Gen'ral gave orders we ain't supposed to shoot 'um down with a shotgun no more."

"No?"

"Says it tears 'um up so bad."

"Hum. That it does."

"Well, the Gen'ral is welcome to his job. I know I wouldn't want to swap saliva with that mangy crowd over a peace pipe."

"What are we going to do with 'um now that we've won and are going to hang the bucks? It seems horrible to think of leaving their wives and kids behind to certain starvation."

"Me, I'm for killin' the whole lot of them. Bucks, squaws, kits. They're like rattlesnakes. The less you have around, the safer it makes the country."

"What about the pretty little red rattler girls, eh? I see our boys don't mind splitting a little red oak nights now and then. 'Specially with the little red virgins so willing to wriggle out of their camp and meet you halfway in a holler somewhere."

"Welll."

"Heard some of the white women talking yestiddy. That Alva Axtell in pa'ticular. She said she would crush out even the little baby brains, if she had her way. Wouldn't let one of them go. Lord, the way that Alva Axtell talked. As bad as any female savage I've ever heard."

"It's an awful fix, all right. I pity those who have to decide the matter."

Judith couldn't resist making a biting remark. "Not all white women think like Alva Axtell. I say the worst Indians I ever met were the white people living on the border."

One of the soldiers gave Judith's Indian dress a look. "Lady, have you ever seen the Sioux go into battle? Like they did a couple of weeks ago at Wood Lake? No?" The soldier shivered at the recollection. "They go in like bees swarming out of a hive. God. They won't show fair fight any way you fix it, the mean varmints. I say they'll never behave themselves until we give 'um a clean out-and-out licking. The only way to treat the Indian is to sculp about half of 'um, then the balance will sorter take to you and behave themselves."

"Yes," Judith said. "When the white man fights for his life

he can take comfort in the sure hope of victory. But when the red man fights for his life he knows for a fact that he's going to die no matter how hard he battles."

The soldier gave her Indian garb another look, then his bearded face closed over.

The procession moved on.

The line of bluffs eventually curved away from the river. Between the bluffs and the bottoms lay a wide shelf of land and on it stood what was left of New Ulm. Brick stores and a few wooden homes had somehow survived a fiery Indian holocaust. Cellars gaped on all sides, gray with tumbles of ashes.

At the first sight of the fire-blackened settlement below them, the friendlies recoiled and hung back, falling behind the line of marchers. The mounted soldiers and the line of wagons bearing the prisoners, however, rolled inevitably onward, going down the bluff. The flag of the Union fluttered high above the lead wagon.

Judith was riding with the friendlies at the time and it scared her to see how they shied away from going through New Ulm. From the friendlies she heard talk of how certain Sioux hostiles, now gone west, had made particularly ferocious attacks on the German settlers, killing and scalping many. The Sioux referred to the Germans as "Those Who Speak The Bad Language" or the "Bad Talkers." Looking down onto the wide shelf of land, Judith saw that the New Ulm survivors had emerged from their huts and their holes and had lined up on a high bank overlooking the road. Someone had alerted them that the army was coming through with red prisoners.

Judith knew it meant trouble. She handed Johnnie over to Ted and trotted up to where Scarlet Plume rode in the last wagon.

It was nearly noon. A cold north wind whistled through a cottonwood grove in the river bottoms. An occasional snowflake drifted down from what otherwise appeared to be a clear blue sky.

The head of the line descended below the bank on which the New Ulm Bad Talkers stood. The New Ulm grownups stood up front, with the children pushed back on higher ground. The men came armed with guns and clubs and pitchforks, the women with glistening butcher knives and aprons full of stones. They wore a crazy-quilt mixture of clothes: brown, gray, black, red. Some had even dug out their wedding clothes from storage. It was all they had left.

General Sibley spotted impending trouble too. He urged the infantry to hurry up and form a wall of protection between the captive Sioux and the Bad Talkers.

But the General saw it too late.

Four of the bolder red children were still racing in and out of the line of march, incongruously crying, "Sibilee! Sibilee!" It happened that two New Ulm boys, more adventurous than the rest, and wanting to get a close-up of the passing entourage, had hidden themselves in a clump of honeysuckles immediately along- side the trail. The four red children, chasing each other with play bows and arrows, flushed them.

The four red children stopped dead in their tracks, staring, their black eyes suddenly gleaming like obsidian arrows. The two white boys also stared, their blue eyes suddenly shining like the eyes of surprised fawns.

There was a long moment of silence. Even the shrieking axles seemed muted. Everybody gaped.

One of the red boys, named Already Bold, said quietly in Sioux to the white boys, "It is a good thing to see the enemy. Let us play war. Do you have the toy guns?" Smiling, Already Bold held up his play bow and quiver of arrows.

The face of the shorter of the two white boys opened and he began to screech.

The cry struck the mother chord in every female breast within earshot. Judith herself felt her bowels constrict within her and for a second was inflamed with a violent hate for the red children.

The Bad Talkers let go with a barking roar. Dough bellies bouncing, the wives came down the slope like a bumping avalanche. Butcher knives flashed. Stones flew. Beer bellies humping, the German men came right behind them, yelling like a mob of Beowulfs. Blue guns glinted. Pitchforks shone.

The six children, two white and four red, stood transfixed yet another second, then dove for safety. They flew through the air like frogs. Grass closed over them.

General Sibley bawled an order. Gold braid gleamed. The thin line of blue mounted men stiffened.

But the rush of the wolf women and their pioneer husbands was too strong. They overwhelmed the guard, and in the flick of an eye the Bad Talkers were up and into the wagons. Shrieking vile abuse, they hauled and pulled at the shackled red wretches, clubbing them, stabbing at them with forks, slashing at them with butcher knives. Flying stones hit captive and captor alike. One woman came running with a bucket of scalding-hot water. Many of the prisoners were knocked senseless. Black heads streamed rivulets of blood. One brave was hit so hard he fell backward out of the wagon, dragging with him his shackled mate. The werewolf women soon exhausted their supply of stones, took to dancing in the grass instead. They hopped about like fat mad witches, faces all a toothy snarl, fingers clawing the air, voices shrill. All mouths squared up in violent vituperation, donnernd.

Scarlet Plume accepted the mayhem at the hands of the New Ulm mothers much as he might have accepted mutilation at the hands of hated Chippewa mothers. It was what savage mothers were expected to do with captives. The rest of the captives also bore it with calm equanimity. A few of those stabbed began to chant the death song, blood frothing on their copper lips.

One tall New Ulm mother, about thirty, with hair almost the same sunned hue as Judith's, became a true scourge. She ripped the air with a continuous piercing ear-splitting tenor falsetto. Wielding the longest butcher knife of all, she managed to clamber into Scarlet Plume's wagon and began to flourish her glittering blade left and right so ferociously that no soldier dared disarm her. Some New Ulm men, still on the ground, spotted her charge and immediately let go with a great guttural cry. *"Schlachtvieh,* Gerda! *Schlachtvieh,* Gerda!"

Gerda struck down three red captives, cutting them across the back and shoulder and upper arm. She cut one so deep across the belly, he burst open and his bowels began to pour out like hominy grits boiling over.

Gerda next went for Antheap, the smallpox-pitted Sioux shackled to Scarlet Plume. Antheap ducked, and Gerda missed. Gerda's momentum carried her up against Scarlet Plume, her head butting into his belly.

Scarlet Plume grunted. His eyes opened in some surprise at the quality of her blond hair. "Hoka-hey," he ejaculated in Dakota, as if it was a thing hard to believe. "The Bad Talkers have also a wakan one with sunned hair."

Gerda drew back at the sound of his savage voice. She glared at him with such hate that her eyes resembled ice crystals. She knew a few Sioux words. "You speak wild man!"

Scarlet Plume permitted himself a smile. To him the greatest barbarity of all was the spectacle of a German trying to talk Dakota. High scorn showed in his eyes. He crossed his arms on his chest. His single scarlet feather snapped, once. "Ha! Is it wonderful that I should speak the language of my mother?"

Gerda's lips foamed. She went into such a rage she was like a wolf with rabies. Shrilling, she slashed at him with her knife. He drew back just in time and her knife flashed past. But she still came near enough to rip his red-and-black blanket and cut the belt to his breechclout.

"Ai-ye!" Scarlet Plume cried. He tried to jump free of her; found himself jerked back by the chain tied to Antheap at the ankles.

Gerda paused. She stared down at Scarlet Plume's exposed thighs. A glittering look of animal malice entered her eyes. Suddenly she snatched hold of the head of Scarlet Plume's dangling copper phallus and sliced it off as neatly as she might the tail from a piece of bratwurst. With a shriek of savage triumph, she held it aloft for all to see. Then she hurled it into the grass below. A thunderous shout from the Bad Talkers rumpled the air.

Judith retched. She had to catch hold of her horse's mane to keep from falling.

General Sibley had difficulty in bringing up the foot soldiers. They were in sympathy with the lynchers. By the time he did get them onto the scene, it was too late, and he had worked himself into such a savage lather that blood could almost be seen boiling in his cheeks. His voice sounded husky, like straw being ruffled, as if his palate had been parched to crusts.

"Fire!" he managed to get out at last.

"But, Gen'ral," Corporal Deloss remonstrated, "we can't shoot down white women!"

"White women? White savages, you mean, don't you? Fire!"

"But, Gen'ral—"

"Fix bayonets and charge!" General Sibley husked.

The blue soldiers moved forward, laggard, slow.

General Sibley then rushed in alone amongst the New Ulm settlers, cutting the air left and right with his glittering saber. When his saber at last drew white blood, he found voice. "Drive the barbarians back," he roared. "Even the white she-devils. Gut them if you must."

The settlers gave ground slowly. A low, sullen mutter, as of heavy gravel being rattled in gourds, rose from them.

"Get back, you white-livered cowards! Attacking helpless prisoners of war . . . Why! Get back, or we'll spill German gizzards all over these river bottoms."

At last even the wild, maniacal Gerda let herself be pushed back up the ridge.

General Sibley surveyed the Bad Talkers from the back of his horse. He still breathed fire. It seemed to emanate from him like whiskey fumes. He pointed to the Union flag at the head of the line. "That is the flag of our country. Your country. Old Glory."

The Germans looked at the red, white, and blue with heavy, sulky miens.

"Well! You have just insulted that flag."

Groans rose from the wounded, mutilated Dakotas in the wagons.

"What do you have to say for yourselves, eh?"

No one spoke.

"All right. Lieutenant Raveling, Corporal Deloss, arrest a dozen of these men. Yes, and while you're at it, take a dozen of these madwomen too. Especially that tall blonde there. We shall take them with us and try them in Mankato. That's an order."

There was a cowed, even sheepish, compliance.

Judith managed to climb into the last wagon with Scarlet Plume. She supported him. Her eyes were ringed with outrage and red weeping. Her retching had turned into hiccups.

Scarlet Plume recognized her. He smiled wanly upon her. He apologized for the German attack. "They rage because they wish to appease the manes of their slain children."

General Sibley came over on his horse. He looked. He shuddered when he saw what had been done to Scarlet Plume. His dark, sensitive eyes filmed over with shock. He sagged a little in his saddle. At last he husked, "Woman, Mrs. Raveling, please go back with the rest. This is now a matter for men."

Ten miles farther downriver, toward evening, a Dakota woman burst out of some brush with much wailing and weeping. She ran straight for where Judith rode drooping on her horse. In one hand the Dakota woman carried a familiar-looking leather-bound book. She latched onto Judith's leg, imploring her to stop.

Judith did. The Dakota woman was Pounce's fat wife, Sunflower. Judith also recognized the book. Sunlight caught the gold lettering across the spine. BIBLE.

Sunflower spoke in Sioux. "Sunned Hair, I have waited many sleeps to find you. Now at last you have appeared and I return the white man's wakan message. It is the Good Book from which your sister divined many true things."

"Sunflower."

"I have kept the Good Book carefully all these—lo!—sad moons." Large lemon tears ran down Sunflower's leathery face. "Always it has lain heavy on my heart that the red man might find the Good Book and destroy it and then there would not be its like on earth again. Your sister said there was only one message from the white man's God. Your sister said it was put by this God between the lids of this book."

There was a catch in Judith's breath. The poor wretch, she thought. Sunflower had misunderstood. Also, she would know nothing of printing and book-manufacture, that there would be more than one copy of the Bible. Judith took the old tome. "Thank you, Sunflower."

Judith opened the Good Book. She saw her sister's graceful handwriting as well as her father's almost undecipherable script. She let her eyes run along the blurry brown ink marks. They now meant little or nothing to her. Even the time of her own birth date meant nothing. What for? For what? That part of her that loved to indulge in passionate daydreams was now dead. The heart had fallen asleep. The rock had at last been worn too smooth to catch dew.

Horses on either side of her kept moving downriver. After an exploratory sniff of the ground underfoot, Judith's horse started up again, joining the stream of the caravan. Slowly Judith rode on, leaving Sunflower standing alone beside the trail.

General Sibley pulled his horse over and asked what went on. Judith told him.

Sunflower's act moved General Sibley into a more conciliatory mood. He ordered the two dozen Bad Talkers released. On one thing, though, did he remain firm. The Bad Talkers, women as well as men, would have to go back on foot to New Ulm, all the way and without escort.

The Bad Talkers were still vengeance bent. They were hardly out of earshot when, led by the mad Gerda, they mobbed Sunflower and killed her.

As Judith jogged on, the thought occurred to her that there in the brain of the dead Sunflower had existed the only other knowledge that Scarlet Plume was guiltless. Sunflower had been there. Too late. Too late.

Harnesses creaked. Horses neighed. Children whimpered. Mothers murmured.

"Hup, there, Phenie, Polly! Get along there," a driver bawled to his horses.

The caravan made camp at dusk. Candle lanterns winked all around, stars fallen in the autumn grass. Soon too other Sioux across the river shot up fire arrows from the hills. The signals spelled lamentation and sorrow.

4

It was the day after Christmas. 1862. It was cold out. Gray.

At dawn, in the stone prison, the thirty-eight condemned red prisoners began to sing their death song. "Hi-yi-yi! Hi-yi-yi! Hi-yi-yi!"

An hour later chains were cut from the prisoners' ankles. A few were allowed to paint their faces. Scarlet Plume put on his usual face marking: a yellow dot inside a blue circle. Then the arms of the prisoners were bound at the wrist.

Scarlet Plume was not permitted to put on his single scarlet feather. The provost marshal ordered that a rolled-up cap of white muslin was to be placed on each Indian's head. The caps were to be rolled down over each face just before the execution.

An Indian named Cut Nose, the fiercest and the ugliest of them all, objected strenuously to the caps. He told Reverend Stephen Riggs, missionary and interpreter, that he considered the forced wearing of the cap the greatest humiliation of all. Whipping a human being, as the whites were accustomed to do, that already was very bad. And hanging—ai-ee!—that was also very bad. But covering the eyes of a brave man so that he could not look upon the peaceful skies just as he was about to die—yun!—that was the bitterest of all and barbar bad.

Scarlet Plume accepted the white cap without comment. He calmly rolled his red feather up into a tight wad and swallowed it. It would go with him down the road to the other side.

At 9:30 A.M. all the prisoners were required to empty their bladders and, if possible, their bowels. As a precaution against publicly befouling themselves, they were given burlap sacks for diapers.

At 10 A.M. the white muslin caps were rolled down over the red faces and the thirty-eight were marched from their stone prison to a huge square scaffold in the center of Mankato. The red men walked in total proud silence. Hundreds of curious whites, roughs as well as tenderhearted women and children, lined the streets. Some of the citizenry leaned out of second-story windows while others climbed onto rooftops for a last glimpse of the red devils. Soldiers formed two blue lines to keep away the weeping squaws.

As the condemned marched past, Judith caught the sleeve of missionary Riggs. "There is no hope then of a final reprieve from the President?" The cast of Judith's face was that of a woman prematurely aged.

"None, madam." Reverend Riggs' head resembled a flat pumpkin with two stems for ears. His hair was gray, his nose was pink in the cold air, his eyes were soft-edged from much responsibility. He viewed her soot-spotted Indian clothes in curious wonder. "According to some, President Lincoln was already far too lenient when he cut the number of the condemned from three hundred three to thirty-nine. And finally at the last moment to thirty-eight."

"Reverend, I have heard that when the President pardoned that thirty-ninth man, it was Scarlet Plume he meant to reprieve and not Red Feather."

"It is possible."

"Many Sioux have the same name. Or almost. Chaska. Chaskay.

Chaskaton. Whites are often confused by the two names Red Feather and Scarlet Plume. Even Little Crow has another name, His Scarlet People, which is often confused with the name of my red benefactor."

Reverend Riggs darted a sidelong glance at her. "Why did not your friend Scarlet Plume protest his innocence when the sentence was read to him? You see, madam, it was I who read the sentence to him, in his own tongue. I was there and he did not protest."

"Scarlet Plume did not protest because he is an old-line Yankton Dakota. He has taken a fatalistic attitude toward it all. He believes it is fated that he should die at this time."

"Then you are convinced he never touched a white woman?"

"Reverend, he touched me. But he touched no one else. He touched me because I persuaded him to touch me. We were lovers together. I seduced him, Reverend. Because I loved him. I consider him my husband. I want to save him because he made a woman of me. He fulfilled me."

Reverend Riggs' face abruptly softened with Christian sympathy. "Madam, all of the three hundred three were given numbers as they were indicted. The order for the executions was given in accordance with those numbers."

"But isn't it true, Reverend, that no one has really been able to determine which number was attached to which prisoner?"

Reverend Riggs was shaken. "It is possible, madam, that a terrible wrong is being done here in some instances."

"Possible?" Judith's eyes opened a shocked blue. "And yet he dies? A possibly innocent man?"

"Madam, I am sorry."

"There are also others who are possibly innocent. There is Rdainyanka, for example, who wrote a letter to his father-in-law, Wabasha, protesting his innocence."

"Yes, I helped him write the letter."

"Yes, and I was asked to read it after Wabasha received it. By Wabasha himself. 'You have deceived me,' Rdainyanka wrote.

'You told me if we gave ourselves up to the whites all would go well. I have not killed or injured a white person, and yet today I am set apart for execution and must die in a few days, while men who are guilty are free to run in the grass, far across the Missouri River and far in Canada. Well, when my children are men, tell them that their father died with no white blood on his hands. When the time comes I will stand on the gallows as a brave Dakota.' "

"I know. I know."

A tremulous quiver moved along the edges of Judith's white lips. "Reverend, does it not pinch your conscience a little that a red man can say to a white man: 'Yes, go build your house and forget the homeless; yes, go lay up food in your storeroom and forget the hungry; yes, go look for a neighbor you can take advantage of and seize all he has'?"

"Madam, I am sorry. Truly. But I can do nothing." Red veins showed in the corners of the missionary's eyes. "It is too late."

"He's as white a savage as I ever saw. Whiter even than a white. And yet it is too late."

As the thirty-eight condemned began to mount the gallows, they again chanted the Dakota tune of terror. Fourteen hundred nineteen soldiers immediately formed solid ranks around the square scaffold. Lieutenant Vincent Raveling stood on the inner line.

Guards guided the condemned to their assigned places under the dangling nooses, facing them inward. The nooses were adjusted around the thirty-eight red necks. Reverend Riggs, standing below, prayed for their red souls.

Army drums began a slow, measured drumbeat. Immediately the chanting Sioux began to sway in a last dance. The wooden platform of the gallows began to rock dangerously. There was a shout from the provost marshal for them to stop the death dance. The condemned men ignored the order. They shouted each other's names. They swung from side to side. Some managed to clasp each other's hands despite being bound at the wrist. The platform rocked so violently that nails began to squeal and boards to crack. The trip rope became so taut it hummed. The provost marshal and the guard, their eyes rolling, scurried down to the safety of the ground.

Scarlet Plume cried aloud inside his muslin head covering, "Ai-ee! Ai-ee! I feel the irons in my heart."

On the second roll of drums, the waiting crowd and all the blue soldiers held their breath as one person. The whole village square seemed to enlarge for a moment.

Scarlet Plume cried aloud again. "It will be good to lie down once more with the people of my father!" Then: "You linger! I go! He-han."

Judith turned her back on the sight. She stared at the yellow stone bluffs across the river. Her blue eyes slowly grayed over. Her pupils settled to the bottoms of her eyes. With her nails she began to scarify her cheeks in the ancient manner of the bereaved. Presently a trickle of blood dripped from the point of her chin.

On the third roll of drums a man named Duley from Lake Shetek, father of two massacred children, himself a miraculous escapee, stepped forward. His eyes whirled from side to side. He trembled and the knife he held almost slipped from his grasp. He had been offered five twenty-dollar gold pieces for the privilege of cutting the trip rope. He had refused the money, saying that a hundred times that amount wouldn't be enough. Money couldn't bring back his two massacred children. No, he just wanted the revenge, is all.

The provost marshal gestured, curt, with a downward stroke of the hand.

Duley got hold of himself. His hand steadied. He took a step forward and with a curse cut the vibrating trip rope. The rope parted with the sound of a snapped bowstring.

The platform dropped. In an instant thirty-eight red warriors dangled in the air. Legs kicked. Arms jerked. Bellies ballooned out, then collapsed to gaunt hollows.

A deep guttural roar, abrupt, rose from the soldiers. A broken cheer, short, floated down from the watchers on the rooftops and in the second-story windows.

One of the nooses broke and a body bumped to earth. The body began to bound around on the ground like a just-beheaded rooster. A gasp of horror broke from the watchers. Quickly the provost marshal ordered the red body hanged again.

A silence and a shuffling of feet followed.

One by one the bodies were cut down. Doctors from Mankato and nearby towns examined the bodies and then pronounced them dead.

One of the doctors had to hold his nose because of the stench of the befouled burlap diapers. "Sure don't smell like cream and peaches."

The bodies were loaded into four army wagons in the manner of cordword and hauled behind a grove of red willows along the Minnesota River. A shallow grave twelve feet wide and thirty-six feet long and only four feet deep had been dug into a sandbar. The sandbar was the only earth around not frozen. The bodies were swung into the grave and laid in two rows, heads out, feet in. Blankets were spread over them. A detail of soldiers with shovels soon had the grave heaped full.

Another of the doctors sighed. "Well, that's it. Now back to prescribing calomel."

"Yes. Salts if you're all bound up. Nutmeg if you have the skitters."

Still another doctor said, with a humorous grimace that wrinkled up his eyes at the corners, "Now if we were women we'd have the perfect antidote for this."

"Oh? How so?"

"There's nothing like good honest motherhood to clean out that feeling of sin."

One of the soldiers in the burial detail still stood looking down at the heaped-up grave. He remarked, "Well, they have all went to hell in a pile."

Reverend Riggs also stood beside the grave. Looking up at the sky, he spoke a single sentence. "May my red friends have a straight road, smooth waters, and a clear sky on their way to eternity—whatever it may hold for them." Reverend Riggs' nose was red.

That night, in the dark of the deepest night, certain doctors raided the grave, digging out several bodies and taking them away for anatomical study. One of the bodies was that of Scarlet Plume.

"The next spring flood will wash them out of that soft sand-bar anyway," one of the licensed ghouls said.

In the morning, when Vincent Raveling went to look for Judith in her quarters, he found the door ajar. A window was open and a strong wind was blowing through the house and a rocker was gently rocking alone.

Judith was never seen again by the whites. And the redskins shook their heads when they were questioned about her.

Later Reverend Riggs in confidence told Vincent that he had overheard Judith mutter to herself that she hoped to "go back home." Reverend Riggs said he was greatly mystified when she added, "To a place where all men were once one flesh, with black hair and dark skin."

A yellow dot inside a blue circle.
A wild white swan with a broken neck.

February 29, 1964
Blue Mound
Luverne, Minnesota

ABOUT THE AUTHOR

FREDERICK FEIKEMA MANFRED was born January 6, 1912, on a Siouxland farm north of Doon, Iowa, in Rock township, just a few miles from the Minnesota and South Dakota borders. Mr. Manfred is the oldest of six brothers. His mother died in 1929; his father now lives in California.

He was educated in northwest Iowa until he attended Calvin College, Grand Rapids, Michigan, from which he graduated in 1934. From then until 1937 he wandered back and forth across America, from New York to Los Angeles, stopping off now and then to fill jobs which ran the entire gamut of temporary employment. In May, 1937, he became a reporter for the *Minneapolis Journal*. In 1939 he did social work and opinion polls. In 1942 he married Maryanna Shorba; they now have three children, Freya, Marya, and Frederick.

In 1943 Mr. Manfred, concluding that it was now or never, devoted full time and energy to writing. Since then he has published fourteen books, including the novels *Lord Grizzly, Riders of Judgment, Conquering Horse, Morning Red,* and the trilogy *Wanderlust.* He has received many grants and writing fellowships, from such sponsors as the American Academy of Arts and Letters and the Huntington Hartford Foundation. Until 1951 he wrote under the pen name Feike Feikema, an old Frisian family name, of which Frederick Manfred is a translation. In Frisian genealogy his full name is Feike Feikes Feikema VII.

Mr. Manfred has lived in the Upper Midlands, mostly in Siouxland, all his life. He likes gardening, fixing fence, and chopping wood; and enjoys taking long rambling walks alone through the countryside.

The Buckskin Man Tales
by Frederick Manfred

Conquering Horse
Lord Grizzly
Scarlet Plume
King of Spades
Riders of Judgment

All available in Gregg Press editions.